Jack High

• • •

The intimate story of a bowls club

Deryck Coleman

Bloomington, IN — authorHOUSE® — Milton Keynes, UK

AuthorHouse™
1663 Liberty Drive, Suite 200
Bloomington, IN 47403
www.authorhouse.com
Phone: 1-800-839-8640

AuthorHouse™ UK Ltd.
500 Avebury Boulevard
Central Milton Keynes, MK9 2BE
www.authorhouse.co.uk
Phone: 08001974150

This book is a work of fiction. People, places, events, and situations are the product of the author's imagination. Any resemblance to actual persons, living or dead, or historical events, is purely coincidental.

© 2007 Deryck Coleman. All rights reserved.

No part of this book may be reproduced, stored in a retrieval system, or transmitted by any means without the written permission of the author.

First published by AuthorHouse 4/16/2007

ISBN: 978-1-4259-9869-1 (sc)

Printed in the United States of America
Bloomington, Indiana

This book is printed on acid-free paper.

My sincere thanks to my wife FREDA for her
patience and understanding,
to my daughter-in-law LYNDA for her hard
work and dedication with the computer
and to my grandson OSCAR WOOLLEY for
the cover.

CONTENTS

Chapter 1	Rosemary	1
Chapter 2	Peggy	17
Chapter 3	Venus	33
Chapter 4	Eva	47
Chapter 5	Stella	61
Chapter 6	Venus (Dis)covered	79
Chapter 7	Molly And Donna	95
Chapter 8	Pippa	111
Chapter 9	The Dove	129
Chapter 10	Missing Underwear	151
Chapter 11	The Midnight Streaker	167
Chapter 12	Ellie	189
Chapter 13	Carnival Week	209
Chapter 14	The Rubber Boat	229
Chapter 15	The Intruder	251
Chapter 16	Revelations	271
Chapter 17	Drugged Wine?	289
Chapter 18	Another Murder?	309
Chapter 19	The Dropped Glove	331

CHAPTER 1

ROSEMARY

• • •

'Her husband used to be the Treasurer here…and they found poor old Will's body at the bottom of the quarry.'

Until that moment I had been enjoying the match on a lovely Green in balmy sunshine. I had quite recently returned to my home town of Woodymouth, joined the Bowls Club, and was about to take over the job of Treasurer, completely ignorant of the reason for the vacancy. No-one had told me my predecessor, Will Fletcher, had finished up dead at the bottom of a big, rocky hole.

I had just heard Mavis, a Club member, imparting the news to a visiting player on the next rink. Mavis was a very plain girl, known to have a vicious tongue. She was discussing Rosemary Fletcher, our Skip for the day.

Naturally, from the name, I had known Rosemary was Will's very attractive young widow, but for the sake of sensitivity the circumstances of his demise had never been discussed. I was only just hearing the details and Mavis's follow-up remark, spoken in almost a whisper, did nothing to alleviate my concerns: 'and there were one or two, here in the Club, not above suspicion for having pushed the poor chap over the edge.'

I was shocked to see how she was slyly nodding towards our Skip when she whispered the words. Usually I play in the Skip position, but I had persuaded Rosemary to take my place, with a promise to give all the help I could as her number three. So it was fortunate she was playing at the other end of the Green and quite unable to hear any of the malicious gossip.

'Just look at her,' said Arthur, our number two. 'After twenty ends in this sunshine I feel like a wet rag, but she still manages to keep cool and look gorgeous.' He too was talking about our Skip, but like me he saw her in a kindlier light.

The match was reaching its end and play had finished on the other rinks. We were the last rink still to bowl on our last end. I knew the overall scores were level, our opponents holding two vital shots, and Rosemary was about to play the last bowl of the match. 'Fire!' shouted Hubert Sinclair as he walked past us on the adjoining rink, going back towards the Pavilion. 'Something's bound to happen!' He was our Club Secretary, always eager to give advice.

But there was a barrier in front of those two shot bowls, so I signalled to Rosemary to walk up and look at the 'head', to offer her different advice. 'You've got a bowl almost jack high sitting there begging for a 'wick'. If you can bounce off that you could trail the 'pot' across to where we have two bowls waiting.'

Rosemary laughed as she made a quick, final study of the 'head', and said something about little piggies flying. But I reassured her: 'you can do it, and with a bit of luck you'll score three!'

As she walked up the Green to rejoin the opposing Skip I watched, fascinated by that special little wiggle of her bottom.

'Just watch her when she kneels to bowl. She wears the shortest skirts and displays the nicest knees in the Club.' It was Arthur again.

'Since when have you been an authority on girls' knees?' Alice, our number one, wanted to know.

'Well, I've studied a few in my time!'

'It's a good job your Audrey can't hear you.'

'Oh! She knows I'm a naughty old man!'

I watched Rosemary sight the shot, begin the swing, and then as she knelt forward I saw that tug on her cream skirt and I knew that Arthur had been right. Then I watched the bowl leave her hand at the end of its swing and travel towards us with perfect 'weight'. It was a faultless delivery, 'wicking off' the jack high bowl with a gentle 'thwack' to hit the 'pot', trail it across to our two waiting bowls and stay within scoring distance.

It was the shot that won us the match, greeted by a roar from the members standing to watch outside the Pavilion. There were eager handshakes on our rink, and further congratulations for Rosemary when we returned to the Pavilion.

I had hoped to have a chat with her before she left, but when I saw her come out of the Changing Room she seemed in a hurry to get away. So I had to be content with a friendly smile and a wave.

Arthur, however, was always ready to talk to someone, so I decided to mention the Fletcher tragedy to him and enquire how it happened. He was a happy, chubby little man, always eager to help and he seemed to know most things about everyone.

'Was it an accident? Did he fall into the quarry?'

'That was more or less the final verdict, although the police, when they questioned one or two of our Club members who worked there, hadn't ruled out suicide – or a theory that he could have been pushed over the edge and into that deep, rocky grave.'

I remembered as a schoolboy being chased away from there, no doubt for my own safety.

'You'll probably know the quarry is just a few miles from here, up river, and of course poor old Will was part owner and has passed all that on to our lovely Rosemary.'

'Part owner, you said?'

'Yes, his partner was Hubert Sinclair and I suspect it was a bitter disappointment to our Secretary when he found he wouldn't be taking over control of the company. He seems to have a rather creepy love-hate relationship with our Rosie.'

'I'll keep an eye open!'

'Yes, and I've noticed you keeping an eye on her. I can only assume you are interested in more than just her bowling arm...and I wouldn't blame you...she's got a lot to get excited about. But if you're going for it, be warned, our Club Captain Tony has a roving eye and he could be looking in the direction of our pretty young widow. Despite his handsome, debonair appearance he has been known to play funny, some might even say dirty, tricks.'

I had certainly been given a lot to think about and when Hubert came to talk, Arthur left me.

'It was an exciting end to the match, Nathan, but I wanted to see you about the Treasurer's job. We need you to take over the financial reins as soon as possible although I'm afraid I have the books out at my quarry office.'

'No problem, I'm on a two day holiday break.' I knew the office would be at the Woody Valley Concrete Company so I agreed with Hubert to call to collect the following morning.

I drove for some miles through beautiful countryside until I saw the Company sign directing me off the main road to a side track which I could see would lead me to a house half way up a hill. But before I reached the house there was a barrier across the track with a man standing behind it holding a large red 'lollipop' which ordered me to stop.

'They're blasting, sir,' was the information shouted from behind the 'lollipop' and the next moment there was the sound of a loud explosion coming from the top of the hill beyond the house, and fragments of dust, dirt, and stone seemed to shower down just a few yards ahead of us. I was glad I had obeyed the order.

When the barrier lifted I drove up the hill and parked on a large gravel square facing the house. For a few moments I sat gazing at the battered brickwork and damaged roof-tiles and felt that the house would have been more at home on the MOD Artillery practice range. But when I entered the building I found the interior to be much more comforting. Immediately it presented an office atmosphere, with a reception desk and waiting room beyond the hall on the left and two doors marked 'Private' which I assumed hid the kitchen and staff room.

There was a bell to press, but Hubert's bellow at the top of the stairs forestalled me.

'Come up, Nathan,' and once more I followed orders. Upstairs there were two small rooms marked 'Private', and what I imagined had once been three large bedrooms had been nicely converted into offices.

I was warmly greeted by our Club Secretary...that being the first time I had met him in his day job...and he took me on a brief tour, starting with the main office where I met his wife Muriel, a shy, modestly-dressed brunette, who I had often heard Arthur refer to as 'Hubert's little mouse'.

Sitting at another desk was a young blonde girl who looked as though she had just left school, and was celebrating her privilege to wear the shortest skirt and lowest-cut top that no headmistress would ever have allowed. Both of them were sorting through piles of worksheets. Hubert explained, 'we have well over a hundred on the workforce at the moment and they have to be paid every week...which keeps Muriel and Tracey very busy.' I noticed that Muriel was putting information into a computer.

Hubert's office was smaller, but more expensively furnished, and before we sat down he drew me over to the window to show me the extensive spread of buildings that comprised the company's Works, nestled in the valley below. There were lorries moving back and forth to the quarry, a constant hum from machinery, and a cloud of cement dust that seemed to hang over everything.

'We're busy at the moment with a contract to supply coloured paving slabs for the Promenade at Rydemouth, and if Rosemary can pull off a similar one at Padquay today, then we will be going full out. Of course contracts are always awarded by tender, but our lady boss can be very persuasive with a Clerk of Works or some of these old buffers on the Councils...especially when she crosses her legs!' And Hubert always laughed at his own jokes.

When Muriel brought in the Club books, the handover was quite a simple matter. She said, 'I think you will find everything in order as I have maintained the records of paid and outstanding subscriptions since poor old Will died.'

When she left, Tracey brought us a tray carrying cups and a thermos jug of coffee which she placed on Hubert's desk and stood at the side of his chair to pour the coffee. Obviously she was proud of her display of firm, young thigh and unmistakably her boss was full of appreciation. Seeing them together like that I wondered if he had ever reached out to...

He thanked her with a big smile and when she had gone he leaned forward to confide in me. 'Naturally, when she dresses like that I would never dream of sending her down to the Works. A pretty young girl can be such a temptation, so Muriel and I keep a watchful eye on her.' I was sure they would both do that but I was wondering if it would be for entirely different reasons.

The tour ended on the edge of the quarry. I was far from happy up there looking down at a huge, deep hole that had been blasted out of the rock, especially when Hubert pointed to the spot where "poor old Will's" life had come to an end.

Back in the house I was obliged to thank Hubert and from the hall shouted farewell to Muriel and Tracey. Then as I drove down the hill I noticed how the grass was discoloured by the powdery dust I had seen shrouding the Works.

Once back into the countryside, driving home, I thought over the past few hours. Tracey had certainly made me wonder...a really provocative young girl. I had not enjoyed seeing the rocky grave where "poor old Will's" life had come to an end, being puzzled a little, because Hubert had not mentioned anything about him falling over the edge.

Then there was Rosemary Fletcher's locked office, which was something that clearly rankled with both Hubert and Muriel, and there were snide remarks like, 'the boss insists on keeping it closed,' and then when I had glanced through the glass door to admire the furnishings, 'yes, the wealthy widow had it completely refurbished after poor old Will died.'

Until my visit to the Woody Valley Concrete Company I had not known a great deal about Hubert Sinclair. He was pompous, but most of the Club members tended to accept or ignore that. In the Club he fawned on Rosemary, but at work when she was not about, his resentment showed.

Putting my thoughts together I realised I was questioning my respect for the man and beginning to wonder if he was perhaps quite a different person..

It was in the middle of the afternoon when I returned home to my harbour-side apartment and decided to sit out on my little balcony with a gin and tonic. Beneath me was a narrow strip of sand, with two or three rowing boats tipped over on their sides, and before me was the harbour with its sandbank in the middle and a view for miles up the river Woody. There were boats moored against the quays, but so many bobbed about at anchor in the harbour waters and I noticed they were just turning about to face the incoming tide.

The action took me back many years to when I was a naïve young schoolboy of perhaps fourteen and venturing to row a young schoolgirl friend up the river. As a local lad I should have known all about the tides, but I miscalculated, or maybe just got 'carried away'. Whatever the reason, we became well and truly stuck on a sandbank for hours.

Thinking back, I seemed to recall that sex and intimacy were things you looked forward to...to the day when you would be courting in a firm, loving relationship...leading to marriage. So we talked quite happily for ages before we even kissed. Then it was by a timid mutual consent that we began to fondle. I still remembered the excitement of sliding my hand into her shirt to feel her young breast, and thinking, as my fingers caressed and explored, it was thrusting out proudly like a half lemon. Not hard like the fruit, but just a similar shape, being firm and deliciously pliable.

I know we both enjoyed that afternoon, but as our emotions rose, so did the waters from the incoming tide, and our boat floated off the sandbank before we found any further temptation.

Our friendship never had time to blossom as her Dad got a job up North and they moved away quite suddenly...we just lost contact. The little girl would now have grown up and I wondered if she still remembered that afternoon on the sandbank.

Of course, I was lonely. I was also dreaming back to that sunny morning almost nine years ago when I was waiting at the altar in that little church in the pretty village of Laxley...waiting for my lovely bride-to-be, Sonja, smiling on Dad's arm and followed by my young sister Peggy who was the only bridesmaid. Dad gave her away because Sonja was an orphan.

Mum, Dad, and Peggy had come up from Woodymouth and we had many friends to share in the celebrations. It was, some would say, a modest ceremony, followed by a lovely honeymoon, and we enjoyed a happy marriage for almost six years. We planned to have a family, but for various reasons decided to wait.

Fate had other plans.

My parents owned a small hotel on the sea front at Woodymouth and we were staying with them for a few days. A trip was planned to see my sister Peggy, who lived with a boyfriend at Upper Woody, but with raging toothache I had to make an emergency appointment to see the dentist. So Mum and Dad said they would take Sonja, and that was the last time I saw them alive. All three were killed almost instantly by a 'joy-rider' in a stolen car.

I was shattered by the tragedy and have spent three long, troubled years trying to get my life back to normality. The guilty driver walked out of hospital after a month to receive a custodial sentence, but due to 'good behaviour', I have been told he was released back into the community.

I have tried to avoid or deny bitterness but it has persisted. I hoped that perhaps in time it would fade.

I picked up my library book and for the rest of the afternoon I escaped to an island in the Caribbean, being distracted just the once by a very attractive young lady on the sands who was walking by with a black Labrador. Then the thunderstorm came, with flashes and bangs from above, and everyone in the harbour area disappeared from view.

I sat in my study (which was the small room the Estate Agents had advertised as the second bedroom) and looked through the books and papers which represented the Club's accounts. I discovered there was just a little sorting out to be done, but decided that before I could arrive at a proper assessment I needed a complete roll of the current membership. I had a list, but it was in my locker at the Pavilion. So I abandoned the books and got myself a meal.

The storm had passed over and the rain had stopped, when I resolved to give myself a little exercise with a brisk walk along the Promenade. There was no sun, although the coloured paving slabs were beginning to dry. It was perhaps the first time I had really noticed them, and studied the intricate patterns produced by the variation of shades. I smiled at my own thoughts...had the Woody Valley Concrete Company supplied these, and had Rosemary used her charms on the local Clerk of Works, just as Hubert had suggested?

When I got as far as the slope leading down to the Bowling Green, I decided to call in at the Pavilion and collect my list. I knew there had been no match that day, and the rain would certainly have driven away all the casual bowlers so that Dominic, the Groundsman, (who was also our part-time coach) would be able to lock up and go home without waiting for the storm to end. No problem, I thought, as I had keys.

However, there was a serious problem. The door had been locked and, as I closed it behind me, I heard low voices. The Pavilion had just the one large Clubroom providing about a dozen tables and the appropriate chairs. On a non-match day these were neatly packed up at one end to facilitate cleaning the floor, so the room had the appearance of being almost empty. On my left was the kitchen/bar from which refreshments were served and ahead of me were two doors, leading, one to the ladies' changing room with toilets, and the other to the gents' changing room with similar facilities.

With the door closed behind me I stood quite still, not daring to make a sound, fearful that I was about to face a couple of burglars. Not clever ones, I thought, as the few trophies we had managed to win were kept in a safer place and there would be no petty cash on the premises. So if they were frustrated burglars then they could be even more nasty minded. Outside the light had been failing and inside it was darker but I could still see an empty milk bottle at the side of the door and I grabbed that as a weapon.

The sounds came from the ladies' changing room, so I crept cautiously towards the half open door. Then I realised it was a man talking to a female and slowly began to recognise that the man's voice belonged to our Groundsman. I realised he must be entertaining a girl in there and I decided to turn around and leave.

But then the voice continued in harsher tones and I was startled. He was scolding the girl and I feared it might be a serious assault. If I was to attack Dominic to save the girl I would certainly need the bottle as he was a fitness fanatic who 'pumped iron', and had biceps (and other muscles) that fascinated most of the lady members. I listened, mesmerised by his words. 'You know how to use the correct bias, because I am always telling you. But you don't pay enough attention and so I shall just have to punish you again. Do you understand?'

There was a weak, timid reply of 'yes' and then came Dominic's voice of command. 'You know what you must do. This is phase one: prepare yourself.'

Then I heard that faint 'rustling' sound that had always got me excited when Sonja was undressing.

'Now it's phase two: come over to the table, lift your skirt up and bend over. Right up, please, I know you are not shy.' Then there was silence for seconds, a murmur from the table, and then Dominic's voice again: 'keep still, I want to make sure you are just right to receive 'the persuader'.

I needed to know if I was present at the abuse of a frightened young girl, so I moved cautiously towards the half open door to peer in, gripping hold of the milk bottle. I suppose I was partly prepared, but nevertheless shocked to see Dominic, with his back to me, bending over the table completely naked. I had seen the top half of him before as he liked to display his bronzed torso. He enjoyed showing his powerful arms with their rather weird collection of tattoos to the ladies, whenever there was a chance. At that moment I was looking at the muscular body of an athlete with a rampant dragon tattooed on his left buttock, and the realisation of my predicament was beginning to frighten me.

Then there was his commanding voice again: 'all is well for phase three, so I will fetch 'the persuader'.' Immediately a horrible thought struck me that he was coming to fetch something from the Clubroom and that we were about to come face-to-face. But then he just moved aside and reached over to a bench. In those moments I was able to see his victim...at least, the rear end of her. I was looking at a large, plump bottom with well-rounded, very mature thighs. Not those of a young girl, but of a more matronly woman, and some realisation began to dawn. This was no shy maiden in need of a knight in shining armour, and no way would either of those two be pleased to see me charging in, without armour, clutching an empty milk bottle.

But I had to wait for the enactment of phase three. I needed some noise from them to cover my departure.

When Dominic returned to his former position at the table he was holding a man's size ten rubber overshoe in his right hand...the sort he issues to bowlers to wear if they turn up with unsuitable shoes. It was a hard, flexible weapon and I could just see that with his other hand he was stroking the target.

'Three times this week you have played the wrong bias. I can remember the last occasion you came to me, we used 'the persuader' on the top of your nice plump thighs, but this time it will be a hard slap on each cheek and then, of course, I will prepare you for 'the rod'.' His words were followed by a kind of moan from the table and she (I sensed) and I, waited breathlessly for the action.

The man, I realised, was an expert in playing on the emotions engendered by suspense, fear, and anticipation and there were long moments before 'the persuader' brought forth muffled screams from the ladies' changing room and I was able to creep back cautiously to the front door.

There were gentle moans as Dominic announced that he was preparing her for phase four and 'the rod' but I did not wait to hear any more and, putting the milk bottle back in its place, let myself quietly out.

As I walked back along the Promenade, I still had visions of that plump, round bottom. Naturally, I didn't recognise it, but there was something about the voice...disguised a little perhaps by soft pleading and suppliance...but there was something about it that made me fairly sure the lady was a Club member.

CHAPTER 2

PEGGY

• • •

It was Saturday and I was sitting on one of the benches on the Promenade looking out over a calm sea. There were one or two dinghies anchored fairly well inshore with the occupants obviously fishing and a couple of small craft, further out, sailing quite swiftly despite the fact that I could feel very little breeze.

Then a young lad came to the top of the steps which led down to the sands, shouted to his Dad and then disappeared. I knew he would run down the steps, across a concrete platform for about six feet and then run up the steps on the other side to appear back on the Promenade, thus ignoring the steps that led down to the beach.

I knew he would do it, because I had done just that when I was his age.

But there was a big difference. My young friends and I used to do it when the seas were rough, playing a daring game to beat the waves as they pounded against the base of the steps and the sea wall. For defence reasons the Promenade was high above the sands and I could still recall the excitement I had felt standing at the top of the steps as a wave broke against the base and then daring to run down and across the wet, slippery platform at the bottom and up the steps on the other side, challenging the next wave to catch me. Our parents never knew the foolhardy risks we took, defying the power of the waves, nor the dangers when we weren't quite fast enough. They would just admonish us for coming home soaked to the skin. To us it was adventure...something we enjoyed at the seaside.

Looking around me, I decided I had made the right decision in coming back to Woodymouth, my home town. After the tragedy Peggy and I had inherited, in equal shares, the small hotel property known as Sea View which had been owned (with a small mortgage) by our parents. It held a prime position on the sea front and would have fetched a good price for the property value and also its potential as a well-established business but we were both very reluctant to sell what had, for our lifetime, been our home. But neither of us fancied becoming hoteliers, so we agreed to let it on a twenty year lease. Happily James and Julie Gosling moved in almost immediately to take over.

I had wondered if coming back home would bring me too close to where I lost Sonja and my parents, but time was beginning to heal and I had so many happy memories of my growing up years that they formed a kind of compensation. Then, of course, I enjoyed the bowls, playing for the Club. For some moments as I sat gazing out to sea, I pondered on that thought... was it just the bowls or was I beginning to acquire other interests? I was certainly looking forward to the afternoon's game.

Jack High

As I stood up to go, I looked to the end of the Pier where I could just make out holiday-makers in their life-jackets going carefully down the wet iron steps to the lower jetty where the speedboat waited. I could see them being handed in and then the boat being set adrift with a steersman at the controls. There was a roar as the engine started, I saw it lift its nose and then speed away into the bay.

It was a short walk to the Bowling Green and I was soon mingling in front of the Pavilion with the members of Woodymouth and the visiting bowlers from Upper Woody. There would be thirty-two players there, all suitably dressed, eager to provide four teams of four to represent each Club on four Rinks. I was delighted to meet Jon there, sister Peggy's partner, who had just recently been invalided out of the Police Force. He had taken part in a 'raid' and had been confronted by two villains with baseball bats who left him in need of hospital attention. I had seen him recently at their home moving about on crutches, but he was obviously pleased he could cast aside the crutches and walk with the aid of a stick. They shared a cottage, up river, so he would have come with the visitors. We had a few words and I praised his handiwork in fitting the stick with a padded end so it would not damage the Green.

I was pleased when Rosemary came and spoke to us both. Apparently she and Jon had met before. I noticed that Arthur and Alice were there, so I looked forward to a pleasant afternoon of bowling. We were chatting happily when the two Team Captains came out with the score cards to call out the names of players and their allocation to the rinks.

Tony began with the words of greeting and a welcome to the visitors.

Tony Fairclough was our Team Captain and he and I had agreed on our selections some days ago. Obviously members are moved about but my feelings were that when you have a winning team on a rink, keep it. So I liked to have Rosemary, Arthur, and Alice with me.

But after allocating the teams to rinks one and two, Tony announced he had made a slight adjustment to the players on rinks three and four for the purpose of 'team balance', and moved a lady called Miranda into my team in place of Rosemary. It would be unusual to question a Captain's decision on such a trivial matter, so the two ladies changed rinks and the match began. I had little knowledge of Miranda's standard of play but, as Skip, I welcomed her into our team and as we played I soon realised that she was a bowler with considerable experience, particularly as a number three. She was playing very well and we were soon taking the lead on our score board.

But she was a woman with a rather dour disposition and made little effort to disguise the fact that she had not been pleased about the exchange. I was well aware of the help she was giving me, but like her, I found it hard to conceal my annoyance...my disappointment that Rosemary had been moved.

It was Arthur who added to my irritation when Miranda walked away up the Green to bowl. 'Changing those two for 'team balance' was a load of poppycock,' he said. 'Just compare them. Rosemary goes in and out in all the right places but this one's as exciting as a bean pole!'

We watched as Miranda made a perfect delivery to the jack and we all clapped, while Arthur continued. 'Tony will miss her on his rink, his score will be down, because she's been propping him up for ages. No, mark my words, his reasons for the switch are personal and devious. He just fancies our Rosie and wants her in his team.'

'Perhaps he's another one who likes her knees,' chipped in Alice.

'Yes, and knowing Tony's reputation, he'll be interested in more than her knees.'

After that I played two awful shots which allowed the visitors to win the end and shorten the gap between the scores. It was usual for us to enjoy an interval break for light refreshments served in the Pavilion and when the bell was rung, the two teams on each rink filed in as they finished playing on that particular end. There would be four tables, each one displaying the rink number, set out to seat the eight players from that rink.

It was an opportunity to talk and socialise and as soon as we were seated one of the lady visitors made us laugh telling us about her very pregnant young daughter who was travelling on the local bus to the pre-natal clinic. She had the usual urine sample with her, but as she had mislaid the proper container, had used a small whisky bottle. Then when she arrived at the clinic she was unable to find it and suspected that the young lad who had been sitting behind her could have leaned forward and stolen it from her shopping basket.

When our laughter had died down, Arthur, of course, had to add his bit.

'After drinking that lot, the lad could be put off whisky forever.'

Miranda apparently did not seem very amused and actually left us, taking her chair, to squeeze herself into the team on rink four. This time it was Alice who noticed my surprise and whispered an explanation. 'She will be missing her friend Mabel,' following the remark with a sly wink.

I had no chance to speak to Rosemary on the way back to the Green as I was sure Tony Fairclough was deliberately keeping her in conversation and steering her away from me. I did, however, talk to Jon. I learned that he was meeting my sister in town so I was able to invite them to spend the evening with me.

The second half of the match was almost uneventful. Miranda continued to play very well and my team widened our lead against the visitors, but then to everyone's surprise Miranda threw a shot away by playing the wrong bias. It is something that happens to every bowler at some time, but rarely to an experienced player and it threw my mind into overdrive and chaos. Memories came flooding back of what I had seen the other evening in the Ladies' Changing Room. I felt sure I had been witness to some kind of kinky charade brought about with feeble protest from the matronly lady involved.

But I was perplexed...Dominic had seemed very pleased with the ample charms that his 'victim' had presented to him, revelling in cellulite, but no way could I imagine him wanting a 'bean pole' bent over the table. Nor, with Alice's insinuations about her friend Mabel, did it seem in character with Miranda's inclinations.

I abandoned my thoughts and concentrated on the game. Thanks, partly, to Miranda's skills we continued to a comfortable win on our rink and at the end of the match, when the scores were tallied, our Club had beaten the Upper Woody team by six shots.

It was then that Arthur drew my attention to the scores on rink four. 'Just as I forecast, without Miranda our scheming Team Captain suffered a humiliating defeat. But judging from the grin on his face, he could have made a conquest elsewhere.' I didn't like that.

I had arranged to spend the evening with Jon and Peggy and in the throng of bowlers in the Pavilion, I waited for a chance to see Rosemary and invite her to join us. Jon waited with me, but when Rosemary stopped to chat, I was disappointed to learn she had accepted an invitation from Tony Fairclough to spend the evening with him. She said he was going to pick her up at home and take her for an evening at 'Flutters', the new local restaurant with its own plush Casino.

Word had reached me that our Team Captain was fond of a regular gamble. When Tony joined us, I lied to say I hoped they would enjoy the evening and I flinched at his remark about being sure it would be an exciting one.

I enjoyed having Jon and sister Peggy in the apartment. With Peggs there it seemed as though the rooms had suddenly become alive...just as our home used to be when Sonja was with me. When we were younger it seemed that Peggy and I were always fighting and quarrelling over some minor disagreement, but after the death of our parents we were drawn together in a united bond of grief. We were there to comfort each other, and with my additional sorrow of losing my wife,

I had Peggy to give me that little extra bit of consolation and strength, making the tie between us stronger.

She bustled about my apartment giving the place a homely atmosphere in no time at all... opened the bag she had brought from the Supermarket...took charge of my fridge and freezer...shooed us out of the kitchen... and immediately set to work to prepare a meal.

Jon and I sat in the lounge/dining room with an apéritif, looking out on the darkening waters of the harbour. The boats anchored off shore were making just a slight movement against the incoming tide and the lights from the bridge which spanned the river were just beginning to come on.

Since being invalided out of the Police Force, I knew Jon had set up as a 'private eye' and I was anxious to know how the business was progressing, with Peggy as his part-time secretary/typist/accountant.

'I have already had three 'domestics'. You know, the kind of cases we wouldn't handle in the Force. One was with a chap cheating on his wife...not the sort of case I enjoyed...creeping around to watch a wayward spouse sneaking into clandestine meetings. The other two are still on-going with two bored wives suspected of deceiving their husbands, although in one case I don't think they are actually married.'

'Do you think you will get used to dealing with those sort of cases?'

'Oh yes, I must, because in this business I think they will form the bread- and-butter cases. But I keep in touch with the lads at the Nick and I think they will get me involved in more interesting jobs, outside their brief. My pal Bert was telling me about one nasty incident that could develop into something in need of my help. I believe we can work together...unofficially, of course... and help each other.

At that moment there was a cry from the kitchen for Jon to go and open a bottle of Chardonnay because 'the poor "sludge-bump" was dying of thirst'.

When he came back I asked if Peggs was all right and he assured me: 'she's enjoying herself...in her element,' and he continued with his story.

'Bert was telling me that some guy has phoned the school here and had a long conversation with the headmistress to tell her he is very interested in some of the young girls in the school. He said he has enjoyed watching them in the play-ground, looking forward to the summer when they wear skirts rather than trousers.'

'Hell, what are the Police going to do about it?' I asked.

Jon tried to explain to me. 'There is really nothing of any significance the Police can do. Naturally they have been to the school to review security arrangements, to check on any possible voyeurs outside the play-ground, and to try and allay the obvious signs of panic among the staff. But as there was no direct threat...at the time...to any specific girl, there is little action they can take.'

'Are they aware of any known paedophiles in the area?'

'Yes, they had the address of one, but now find he has left his lodgings without advising them. He's not really a suspect, though, as he's homosexual and his convictions relate to young boys.'

'But it could develop into a nasty business; with this twisted character giving his own warning of a terrifying scenario.'

'Yes, I'm afraid it could and in anticipation of being involved, I'm making a few discreet enquiries. There is, however, always a faint chance that the guy is a nutter.'

I wondered where on earth Jon would begin to make his enquiries and, with 'tongue in cheek', I was about to ask him if that was the reason for his increased interest in the Bowls Club...but there was an interruption with a command for us to come to the dining-table. We sat down to a meal of smoked mackerel, served with a salad and Jersey Royals, complemented nicely by what remained of the Chardonnay. We chatted about our work and this, that and the other, and I was able to study my two visitors. I liked Jon...he had friendly features... not handsome perhaps, but certainly good-looking... with the physique of an athlete. I regarded him as a strong, dependable guy with his feet still firmly on the ground.

Peggy, of course, I was very fond of and I had seen her grow from a rather lanky teenager into, and I am sure Jon would agree, a very attractive young woman. I used to think she bubbled along with her mind in the clouds, but recently I had been made very aware of the situation after Jon's injuries. She had taken hold of the tiller in firm hands and was steering their ship very well through troubled waters. Looking at them, and listening to the conversation and backchat, I decided they were a very happy couple.

Peggy knew I had been watching and assessing their relationship, so when she had served up Peach Melbas and I saw the familiar smile with the mischievous glint in her eyes, I realised she was going to come out on the attack. 'What's all this I hear about you having the hots for Rosemary Fletcher?'

'I didn't know I had,' I said, trying to avoid the issue. But my sister kept on with her tease, laughing at my discomfort.

'Don't be ridiculous. Jon says you had eyes for nobody else during the afternoon...he is a detective you know...and her name has been the only one you've mentioned all evening.'

So then I had to confess that I was interested and mentioned about my visit to the Concrete Works... being a little disappointed when she was not there... and the silly incident earlier this afternoon when Tony Fairclough transferred her to his rink and then dated her up for an evening visit to the Restaurant and Casino.

The mischievous look disappeared and she became more serious. 'Look Nathan there's no kind way of saying this, but I think you should take stock and think carefully about getting involved with that young lady.'

'The only attempt I have made, so far, to get involved has been thwarted by Tony Fairclough,' I answered with a slightly despondent note creeping in.

'Well, quite honestly, it could be for the best if you let him get on with it.'

'But I don't see that...'

'I know it's got nothing to do with me, but you weren't living here when her husband's body was found at the bottom of that quarry. We were, and Jon was in the Investigation Team. The circumstances were a bit 'iffy' and I know Rosemary, and Fletcher's partner, were under suspicion.'

I could see Jon was showing disapproval at these revelations, but I knew Peggy intended to ignore him.

'Jon's not in the Force now, but I know he will want you to regard this as confidential. As I understand it, the company had financial problems until old man Fletcher's death. Then his young wife was able to step in to take over, and with the help of Life Insurance, all the cash flow problems disappeared.'

Here Jon butted in. 'Sorry Peggs, but you are not presenting all the facts. Yes, they had some financial difficulties, but we unearthed a scam which had been going on, and robbing them, for a long time. The size of the workforce there fluctuated from contract to contract and extra hands would be chosen and engaged by the Foreman, a chap called Harry Wilks, who was also responsible for checking and handing in their worksheets and on payday, collecting their pay packets from the office. Through laxity in the office controls he was able to claim for a number of non-existent casual employees, thus robbing his Company on a regular basis. We nicked him on charges of fraud and he was duly convicted although I understand he is now back in circulation.'

I was puzzled how they could have dealt with tax and national insurance, but Jon continued.

'Before his case went to Court, Wilks claimed the partner, Sinclair, was involved in the scam, but then suddenly he withdrew all accusations so we were not able to pin anything on Sinclair. We understood, however, that the senior partner, Fletcher, was furious with him for the incompetence and was threatening to break up the partnership.'

He took a sip of the brandy I had served and then continued.

'Then about a week later Fletcher's body was found at the bottom of the Company's quarry. It all looked very suspicious at the time with two or three possible suspects in the frame for murder, but we were never able to establish that it was a homicide. Suicide was ruled out, so after exhaustive enquiries, they settled for the conclusion that he had slipped and fallen over the cliff. There was a feeling that the poor guy was accident-prone. During the course of our enquiries we learnt that in the last couple of years of his life he had suffered a number of accidents, some minor, but others quite serious.'

'Were these work related?'

Jon was thinking while he took another sip of his brandy. 'Some were, but there were two or three which happened on the Bowling Green and in your Pavilion.' Naturally I was intrigued by this information, beginning to wonder once more if the misfortunes actually attached to the person of Will Fletcher...or perhaps to his position as Club Treasurer. I had pondered over why I had been inaugurated into the job in such a hurry.

But at that point Peggy came back into the attack. 'I grant you that Rosemary Fletcher survived all the Police questions...but I got the impression that they were all a scheming lot in that firm. Keep away Nathan, I don't want to hear that someone has found your body at the bottom of the Cliff Walk.'

'A gruesome thought,' I chipped in, managing a smile.

'I think it is time you found yourself a nice lady friend...' and the mischievous twinkle crept back in... 'why not go back to the little girl you seduced on the sandbank up river, Molly wasn't it?' She checked Jon's interest in that remark with a wink and a promise to explain later.

'I didn't seduce her and I don't know where she lives now or whether she's still fancy-free.'

'Well it so happens she works at the same bank as me and it was quite by accident about a week ago that I realised she had been the young girl you had had that hanky-panky with, all those years ago.'

'As you say, all those years ago. I expect she's married now with a cluster of kids and may not even remember me.'

'She is not married...has had a broken engagement... and as far as I know has no kids. I made myself known to her and at mention of your name I'll swear she went all dewy-eyed. She did remember...probably wants you to do it again!'

I looked across the table and once more recognised the teasing merriment in her eyes. She knew I hadn't seduced young Molly because when I returned home, from what had been for me a new, exciting experience she had pleaded with me to tell her all about it. Then, day by day, the little minx wheedled all the facts from me...eager to learn all the intimate details. 'Maybe I should find a reason to call in at the bank then?'

'You do that. Of course she has matured from that little girl you had on the sandbank. She's much bigger now in all the right places!'

I knew exactly what she meant and we both laughed.

CHAPTER 3

VENUS

• • •

It was early on Sunday morning and the sun was shining, making the harbour waters sparkle. We were only just into May but it felt as though summer had already arrived. The tide was well out, with all the anchored boats facing up river and the sandbank in the centre of the harbour showing as a prominent feature...large enough to attract a group of cockle or mussel pickers who must have rowed across at early light.

Beneath my patio window the beach was larger... extended well below the tidemarks of seaweed and as I studied the tracks where a dinghy had been dragged down into the water, I saw the girl with the black Labrador. Although it was early, it was the beginning of a warm day and she was neatly dressed in a colourful woollen jacket, shorts and sandals and I decided she had very nice legs. When she saw me standing at the window, she promptly returned my wave with an adorably friendly smile.

The dog ambled along at her side carrying what looked like an old slipper in his mouth and I watched them until they turned and disappeared up the slipway for the Lifeboat. I was realising as my sister had suggested last night that it was time I found myself a girlfriend. Maybe I should take an interest in Labradors or perhaps make some enquiries about investments or something at the bank. I had a shower, got myself a boiled egg, toast and an apple and then walked along the Promenade to the Bowls Pavilion. Our Secretary, Hubert, had called what he described as an Extraordinary Meeting. I was intrigued to know the reasons, but far from enthusiastic about the prospect of spending Sunday morning arguing about some hiccup in the running of the Club. Hubert liked to impress upon us the importance of his job as Secretary.

I saw parents carrying rolled up wind-breaks, fold up chairs, blown up rubber ducks, with their offspring clutching buckets and spades. Then as I approached the Pier I met a group of teenage boys and girls waving towels and bathing gear. They were all heading for the sands and sea and I decided they were too brave for me, so early in the season.

For many years Mum and Dad rented a couple of the Council's beach huts... Number 16 and Number 19. My sister and I kept on the tradition and while Number 16 was taken over by the Goslings, for the benefit of their guests at Sea View, Peggy and I kept on the lease of Number 19. Naturally, upon my return to Woodymouth, I knew I would soon appreciate the facilities of a hut on the beach...somewhere where you could change for a swim, with privacy, and then enjoy an hour or two in a deck-chair with a cup of tea or something stronger. As I watched holidaymakers heading towards the steps and slipways to the beach, I knew that was where I would rather be. But Hubert had summoned his committee to a meeting, so that was where I went.

Looking around the Green, I admired the work done by Dominic and his team. We bowled on short, lush green grass and the flower-beds were a riot of colour from pansies, primroses and primulas. The bank behind me which sloped up towards the Promenade had, weeks ago, been a bright yellow carpet, a brilliant reminder of Wordsworth's host of dancing daffodils. But after their radiant glory, they had drooped and faded and the groundsmen had beheaded them. The bank was left green with their stalks in the long grass waiting for their final fate from the mower.

Dominic had 'opened up' the Green and was already issuing mats and jacks to some holiday visitors and taking the opportunity to display his muscles and tattoos to the ladies. While on one of the Greens, Arthur, his wife Audrey, Alice, and a man I didn't know, were deciding who was going to play who, before they got started on what was obviously just a friendly 'roll-up'.

I was glad that I was very early for the meeting, otherwise I would not have met Harry Wilks and James Gosling. Wilks was the man playing on the Green with Arthur and when introductions were made, I learned he was in fact his brother-in-law and that Arthur had proposed Wilks' name as a prospective member of the Club, explaining that he had an excellent bowling record over previous years.

I shook hands with a pale and rather gaunt-looking man who had what I would regard as shifty eyes. Immediately I recalled having seen his name on the Honours Board in the Clubhouse as having won a number of trophies, but also recalled his name from my conversation with Jon yesterday evening. Obviously

Arthur had omitted to tell me that Harry Wilks had just recently been released from prison.

I was sitting on the bench outside the Pavilion watching Dominic give his coaching advice, in particular to the lady visitors, when James came, carrying a rolled up towel under his arm with hair still wet from a swim in the sea. His greeting was friendly, as usual, but spoken in a hurry.

James was our Club President for that year and Hubert would delight in calling him to the meeting, quite oblivious of the fact that James managed a seasonal business.

I gestured towards the towel and his wet hair: 'you're a braver man than I...was it very cold?'

'Not too bad, but I had to go down to examine the hut. I'm so pleased I caught you Nathan, because I just can't spare the time for Hubert's ruddy meeting and I want you to convey my apologies. I must get back to organise a special lunch and I can't sit around arguing whether or not we should accept the nomination of Harry Wilks.'

He had moderated his voice, although the gentleman mentioned was well out of earshot. There were some shouts from Alice as someone had fired off her shot wood and then he continued.

'When the fraud at the quarry was disclosed they were at each other's throats, but now Hubert seems in favour of the nomination to put him back in the Club and is even talking about giving Wilks his old job back. Seems most odd to me.'

This was giving me new information about the meeting...why it was being called and also about Harry Wilks, and I too had become a little puzzled.

James stood up for a few seconds as if to leave but then sat down again.

'Really I should go but I have been meaning to tell you about the break-in at the Beach Hut...'

'Your Number 16? When was this?'

'On Friday night, and the police forensic lads were there for hours yesterday.'

'You don't usually get that sort of attention for a break-in to a beach hut!'

'Well, it was a lot more than that as it concerned a young, teenage girl...a visitor...not staying at Sea View, thank Heaven...she was from the Caravan Park, holidaying with three other girls...all from London.' I didn't dare interrupt because I knew James wanted to get back to the hotel, and I needed to hear the story.

'The police took me down to the hut as they wanted to know details of anything that had been stolen, and they told me about what had happened. All four girls went for a last night of the holiday fling at the Dungeon Night Club and of course did a bit of binge drinking. Three of the girls had already palled up with three lads from the same Caravan Park and, at about midnight, the six of them walked back together, but the fourth girl had found another young guy who told her he was a naval cadet over from Plymouth. They left the Club at about the same time, planning a stroll along the Promenade, the girl saying she felt a bit dizzy and thought the fresh air would clear her head.'

'As they strolled along she was easily persuaded to walk on the beach and then the lad 'just happened to notice' that one of the beach huts had its lock broken... that was ours...and he went to investigate. Then he called her in, suggesting he should make them a nice, strong cup of coffee, as someone had left all the bits and pieces there. She said she was glad of a sit down and the strong, hot drink. After that, apparently, she felt drowsy and says the lad pulled the chair out to form a sun-bed and gently pushed her down onto it, making her comfortable and being very attentive. That described...'

He was distracted by another shout from Alice as she trailed their jack into the ditch. Then he continued.

'That described our reclining chair which the police took away for examination.'

'Did he assault her?'

'Well, the police were a bit cagey about that and I understand they are puzzled about the girl's story of another man. They are sure she was drugged, but not too sure if they can give credence to all of her story. She says that when she felt drowsy, the lad supported her head with a pillow and then a much older man came and, in a very gentle voice, told her to be calm. She said her mind was 'befuddled' and when she tried to get up the man kept telling her to relax and have a little sleep. She says she tried to stay awake and roused a little when the man said he was a Doctor and needed to examine her. She remembers him putting on latex gloves and was quite helpless when he began to undress her. She says he was unhurried...taking his time to take her clothes off. Vaguely she remembers the gloves feeling over her body, but then her mind became a complete blank until morning.'

'What a dreadful experience for the poor girl.'

'Yes... she woke with a thumping headache, lying naked on the sun-bed and covered by a tarpaulin sheet which had been taken away from the Council deck-chairs stacked about twenty metres away. She told the police she ached all over and they said her body was covered in bruises. They suspect it was not a casual crime but one that was premeditated...carefully planned.'

James was back on his feet, having seen Hubert and Tony walking up the path from the town... 'I must go Nathan...please give my apologies.' Then with a wave to all the members in sight, he hurried up the path, in the opposite direction, towards the Promenade. When Hubert arrived he was blustering. 'Was that James I saw hurrying away? What the hell is he doing? I wanted to have him in the meeting.'

So I had to convey James' apologies and suffer Hubert's ranting. The meeting was, in fact, a farce. Hubert continued to roar on about James leaving: 'not the serious attitude one might expect from the Club's President'. And then he slated Rosemary (his boss) for not turning up.

There, Tony Fairclough was able to supply some very strong excuses: 'she was with me last night at the Casino and it was in the early hours when I took her home. The last thing we wanted this morning was a summons to a ruddy bowls meeting.'

I hated the wink he gave me and the emphasis he put on the word 'we'...suggesting that they might still have been together?

When the meeting was called to order we discussed one or two expenditure items for the Canteen and then

Hubert came around to the main topic...the reinstatement of Harry Wilks...and at that point Fairclough almost reiterated James' remarks.

'When you had all that trouble at the quarry you seemed almost happy that he was going to be locked away, so why the hell are you supporting his application now to be re-elected as a member?'

Hubert huffed and puffed and then mumbled about Wilks serving his time and saying it was now up to us to forget and welcome him back. When it was put to the vote there was one in favour and one against, so the decision rested with me...until Fairclough pointed out that the meeting was actually invalid as we needed four members to constitute a quorum required for a valid meeting.

Hubert's frustrations boiled over and he left the Pavilion shouting that the matter would have to be resolved another time. Tony and I had a good laugh and then we went our separate ways. Although he did remark he thought it very strange Hubert should try to put through Wilks' application. 'As Secretary he would know damn well it was not a valid meeting.'

He stopped to chat to the bowlers, while I walked into town. I needed to pick up my camera from the Photographic Studio. It was a new digital that had developed a fault with the flash after just six months use. I collected it and then went to the ironmongers to get a heavy-duty hasp and staple with padlock for the beach hut. The huts are very vulnerable and after listening to James' story of what happened in number sixteen, I decided to give ours a little extra protection. Then I collected some sandwiches, a can of beer and walked back towards the Promenade. My plan was to relax in one of the comfy folding chairs to read the newspaper I had bought, have my lunch and then see to the locks...I always kept tools in a locker. But we all know the maxim about mice and men and I was ill-prepared for the consternation that was waiting for me, or to finish up being chased like a mouse.

I used the main path leading from town to the Promenade, with 'the Rec' on my right which is used to host the annual Sports Day and similar functions. That afternoon it was being used by a family for a friendly game of cricket, but I noticed there was a very unfriendly dispute going on between a man and a boy... presumably father and son...because father refused to accept the son's cry of 'LBW!'

On my left was the bowling Green and Pavilion and I saw Dominic giving one of his tuition sessions to three or four of our lady members, so I waved, but then realised the ladies were paying too much attention to their Coach to notice me. Perhaps there was one...or maybe two...who knew how forceful he could be with his lady pupils if they kept making mistakes. But I was consoled and cheered immediately by a young girl passing me on her way from the beach, wearing, to suit the warm sunny afternoon, brief T-shirt and shorts. As I appraised the slightly tanned bare legs and midriff she rewarded me with a happy smile.

When I stood at the top of the steps leading down to the sands, I surveyed the scene before me: out on the ocean there were some sailing boats, closer to the shore a few dinghies, some obviously anchored with the occupants fishing. Then closer in there were one or two swimmers and in the shallows young children running and splashing about.

The tide was coming in and on the flat wet sand there were older children frantically trying to defend their sandcastles against the encroaching sea. Here and there I noticed adults trying to fold up deck-chairs to carry them back up the beach, holding towels, wet costumes and other holiday paraphernalia.

Once I was on the sands I turned to my right past the Ice Cream Cabin and then threaded my way around sun seekers lying on towels or loungers or sitting in deck-chairs. I avoided children with buckets and spades building mounds, roadways, or digging deep holes, until I reached the beach huts. These were arranged in a block of twenty at the back of the sands against the sea wall. Then I noticed two young lads playing suspiciously with the lock on number twenty...one holding a very large bunch of keys...I shouted and the boys ran off. Immediately I glanced at our hut, next door, and saw that the small hasp was open from its staple and the padlock was missing. Presumably the lads had been able to get in to remove any items of value.

Then I heard a very slight sound coming from within and decided that one of the young blighters was still inside, so I prepared a shock tactic for him. The sand in front of the huts was soft, so I made a silent approach, holding the camera in my left hand and the two bags in the other...one containing my lunch and the other, the heavy metal ironmongery.

I proposed to take hold of the hasp fastened to one door and the staple fastened to the other and with a sudden wrench, open them wide, knowing that the bolt on the back had been broken. I would step back a pace and raise the camera for repeat flash photos of the interior of the hut. I figured the trespasser would be too shocked to run for it and if he proved to be violent I could cosh him with my lunch bag which contained a large size can of beer.

The plan worked smoothly without any warning to the intruder, but the sudden shock was backlashed to me. As the camera flashed and worked I suddenly realised that I was not filming some petty thief, but a beautiful statue of Venus. From my astonished glance it seemed to have no head, but with raised arms revealing creamy white skin in the hollows. From shock reflex I was slowly lowering the camera and my eyes were doing the same, taking in the firm sculptured breasts, the taut tummy so delightfully moulded, down to the tuft of hair above the parted thighs.

It was a vision that my eyes savoured for just seconds until the statue erupted into life with a shattering scream that must have awakened any sleeping sun seekers within half a mile. I clung on to my two bags and the camera, but turned at the sound of a woman's angry voice to my left.

From the hut next door but one, there was a matronly figure in an over-filled blue costume running towards me brandishing a parasol. I reacted instantly and ran.

Running on soft sand on a busy beach is not easy. I threaded my way through and around the hazards until I almost collided with a 'deckie'. He is the Council employee known officially as 'the Attendant and Conductor in charge of deck-chairs'...the person who collects money and issues tickets for the hire of the chairs. I knew most of them, but this fellow was a stranger.

For vital moments we faced each other and as the matronly lady in the blue costume gained ground she shouted 'stop that man' and the 'deckie' made a grab at me. Unfortunately for him he misjudged the proximity of a large mound that had been lovingly adorned with stones, shells and seaweed and when he stumbled over that, there were more screams and cries from the small boy and girl who had spent the whole morning creating a masterpiece. That brought father out of his chair shouting 'clumsy git,' and chasing the 'deckie'.

The matronly lady continued to stumble on and she began shouting 'stop that pervert,' which quickly created a menacing circle of people around the 'deckie'. Gratefully I was able to reach the steps, run up and then mingle with the folk on the Promenade. When I glanced over the sea wall I saw the group around the harassed 'deckie' was very agitated, the matronly lady threatening them with her parasol... presumably blaming them for my escape.

It was early evening when I returned to the beach. The tide had brought gentle but determined waves halfway up the sands and was then receding. All the castles, cars, speed-boats and animal creations had been trampled underfoot by the departing visitors who had left their usual legacy of litter.

I was surprised to find the yellow doors of Number Nineteen secured by the 'missing' padlock. As well as supplying the numbers, the Council painted the huts... green, yellow, blue, brown...in that order and sequence down the line. A design to try and avoid any naughty confusion. I unlocked the hut and went in and looked around. The tea and coffee making facilities had been used...as a mug had been washed and left to drain. So Venus de Milo had departed, presumably complete with a head, all her arms and I hoped with her clothes on, leaving everything spick and span. I was baffled. I repaired the inside bolts and fixed the extra heavy duty hasp and staple, with the new padlock, on the outside, pondering on who the young lady could have been. Peggs was the only other person to have a key to the hut and whilst it was many, many years since I had seen my young sister in her birthday suit, I felt certain it was not her that I had photographed. She must have lent the key to a friend without telling me...which was just the sort of mischievous thing she would do. We now had two locks on the hut... over-cautious on my part perhaps, but after James' story of what happened in Number Sixteen, also yellow, I felt happier with the extra protection. I would have to contact Peggs and give her one of the extra keys.

After getting myself an evening meal, I sat watching a TV programme about Ancient Egypt. I was interested, but my thoughts kept returning to the events of the afternoon. Who was that girl?

When I got back to the apartment I had at first felt like an excited young teenager about to have a furtive look at that forbidden girly magazine. I had a digital camera with memory viewer and the machine to print. Within a few seconds I could have pictures of her on the table. But I had hesitated. What must she be thinking... wondering who I could be?

How shocked or ashamed would she be knowing that there was some stranger with photos...full frontal...

of her completely naked...apart from what I suspect was a towel over her head whilst she was drying her hair?

I knew that eventually I would weaken and print and study them, but at that moment I was struggling with my conscience and I went to bed remembering how lovely she looked...wondering who she was and if we would ever meet again.

CHAPTER 4

EVA

• • •

It was early evening when I left my office at the Royal Eagle Insurance Group, grabbed a snack at the nearby café and walked up to the Bowling Green. It was the quarter-final of an inter-town singles competition with our Club Captain, Duncan Peters, competing against a bowler from Rydemouth. There was quite a turnout of our Club members and I had noticed a mini-bus in the car park which had obviously brought supporters from Rydemouth. The bowlers were not strangers to each other and stood around in groups talking. Soon they would be using the seats and benches, so when I spotted Eva Sheen already occupying one with a young girl, I was pleased when she waved for me to go and join them.

I had had friendly conversations with Eva once or twice, although at the last Saturday match I thought she had probably been a little embarrassed knowing she hadn't paid her Club subscription. Her name was on my overdue subs list, but I had refrained from putting on any pressure for payment as I knew there had been domestic problems. I had been told that her partner had walked out on her two or three years ago leaving her with a teenage daughter. Naturally, I felt sympathy towards them.

The competition was for twenty-one ends and Duncan had just lost the thirteenth end to give his opponent a two shots lead. Apparently our Captain had started well and on the sixth end was four shots ahead, but the man from Rydemouth had suddenly found his form and came back to take the lead.

I looked around for Amy, Duncan's wife, knowing that she was usually a keen supporter whenever he was in any of the important competitions. Invariably she was on the Green to shout encouragement, but I saw no sign of her.

I walked to the bench and met Eva who always seemed to have a friendly smile. She was a very attractive, fair-haired young woman who I judged to be in her early thirties. She was no longer embarrassed, but opened the conversation: 'I was hoping I would see you Nathan because I have a cheque here for my outstanding sub.'

I was pleased she had included her daughter in the renewal as the Club liked to see the youngsters taking an interest in the game and provided them, of course, with free membership. The girl was as pretty and friendly as her mum and introduced herself as Chloe. Conversation came easy and I soon learned that she was interested in joining our junior Club and that mum had spent the last hour coaching her. Apparently Dominic had not been available for those duties.

There was some strong clapping from the Rydemouth supporters as their man increased his lead by another shot. He looked to be in control of the game and playing with a lot of confidence.

It was at that point that Hubert Sinclair arrived and made straight for our bench, with a nod to me and a most genial greeting for Eva and Chloe.

Then he apologised that he was the bearer of unhappy news: 'Rosemary has been involved in a car accident and has been taken to hospital.'

Naturally we wanted to know the details and learned that Hubert had been told there were no serious injuries, but she was being kept in for tests and observation. I asked about visits and Hubert said she would probably be allowed home in two or three days.

There was more strong clapping from the Rydemouth supporters as their man increased his lead to four shots and Hubert chose that moment to leave us, to join a group nearer the match...no doubt wishing to spread the news about Rosemary.

I was concerned and I sensed that Eva was too, so realising my curiosity she explained: 'I used to work at the quarry, so naturally I know Rosemary quite well.'

'Oh, I didn't know that. How long ago was that?'

'Aah...over four years...I worked for Mr. Fletcher then, the chap everyone refers to as 'poor old Will'. I just hope Rosemary hasn't inherited all his misfortunes.'

Interruption was caused by cheers from the Woodymouth supporters as Duncan managed to trail the jack into the ditch and pick up two shots from his back bowls, thus, no doubt, restoring some of his waning confidence. Chloe was then more interested in the match and ran off to join her friend Abigail, a young girl about her own age who had been operating the score-board at the end of the match rink.

I had been intrigued by Eva's remarks about my predecessor, 'poor old Will' and I wanted to know more.

'Presumably you worked in the main office with Muriel?'

'Yes, but not with Muriel all the time. I started there on my eighteenth birthday and with some guidance from Hubert...I always called him Mr. Sinclair then...I took over the wages and from time to time had help from younger girls straight out of school. I think there were four or five over the years and they seemed to settle in, learn how to be useful and then leave for one reason or another...quite frustrating really. Working under Hubert we dealt with all the wages and problems connected to the quarry and the Concrete Works. Mr. Fletcher saw to all the sales promotion side of the business and he seemed to spend a lot of his time away...mainly on golf courses with clients,' she added with a chuckle. 'Rosemary was typist to Sinclair and secretary to the boss, dealing with all his correspondence and appointments.'

'How long did you work there?'

For the first time, when she turned to face me, I noticed what lovely blue eyes she had and saw a merry twinkle so reminiscent of my mischievous sister.

'I don't usually allow strange men to trap me into disclosing my age, but it was for over ten years.'

Of course, I had already guessed her age. I was only interested in any facts that would enlighten me about Will Fletcher's death. I redeemed myself with a very honest statement that she looked much younger than her years anyway...then I added, again quite honestly, that I hoped we were not going to be strangers. We both laughed.

Eva continued with her story. 'When Chloe was a baby I had Mother's help to let me go back to the office and Muriel was a stalwart friend in the early years, then again when my partner Archie left me she came in part-time, but when the young girl Jessica had to leave, she stayed on full-time.

'Why did Jessica have to leave?' She gave me a knowing expression.

'The usual, although there was a lot of trouble at the time because she was so young and I believe her boyfriend said it wasn't his. Then they seemed to sort things out, set up home together and Jessica had the baby. The last I heard they seemed quite happy.'

Engrossed in our conversation, we had not been watching the competition and missed the end when the Rydemouth man had increased his lead to five, but joined in the clapping as Duncan played a shot with 'weight' to split his opponent's scoring bowls to pick up two shots on the seventeenth end. He was still fighting back.

I was hesitating on a crucial question, but Eva seemed to anticipate me, with a smile.

'You want to know why I left...well that's not too difficult to answer. Rosemary had married the boss and there was friction and resentment in the office. Obviously she was an ambitious young woman, marrying into money, to a much older man, but I have always liked her and I believed she was genuinely fond of Will Fletcher. Unfortunately my feelings were not shared by the Sinclairs.'

There she broke off to wave and make some kind of signal to Chloe, treating me to an outline display of a fine figure beneath her thin white shirt. We watched the game as Duncan moved it forward with another shot to reduce his opponent's lead back to two. Then Eva continued.

'There was another reason. When Archie left me, Tony Fairclough took an interest. His mother, of course, was Muriel's sister and when Tony lost both his parents he went to live with the Sinclairs as a kind of adopted nephew. For a while I thought we were an item. Tony can be very charming and he captivated Chloe. I was wined and dined and taken to all the nice places, but after a time I began to realise it was all a bit of a sham.'

Again she held my gaze with those lovely blue eyes: 'I'm not engaging in a character assassination of Tony Fairclough because I'm sure everyone in the Club knows he has a roving eye. It would be easy for a girl to get fond of him but one day I realised he thought I was opportune...just a love-starved single Mum eager to share her bed with him. So we had to split before that happened. We parted as friends...but as he came to the quarry quite often, things became a little difficult, so I found myself another job...and that's it.'

She turned to me with a smile: 'I seem to have given you my life story...so one day you'll have to give me yours.'

It was almost impossible for me to reply because the Green had erupted into clamour and excitement. Eva and I, with our interest in each other, had been distracted from the game for two ends and our Club Captain had fought back to level the scores on the penultimate end, to tumultuous applause from all the spectators.

Now we watched and there was a hush on the Green as Duncan played a full-length jack and bowled in to finish jack high with a space of about six inches on his forehand side. The Rydemouth man followed and there was clapping and moans as he nudged the shot wood out. But then there were different hands clapping and different voices moaning as Duncan managed to follow and rest out his opponent's bowl. A tit-for-tat shot and it was obvious to all that the two contestants were very evenly matched.

There followed generous applause all round as the Rydemouth man managed to bowl in to about four inches from the jack, thus putting himself in the lead. But the little white ball was clearly visible and I think Duncan fancied his chances at moving it back further. Sadly the bowl fell short and there were more groans from our Club supporters. Realising the danger, the Rydemouth man placed a bowl well behind, about a foot from the ditch but slightly out of line. There was complete silence as Duncan took aim for a firing shot. It was a perfect delivery and he took the jack back to rest on it in the ditch. Pandemonium broke loose as the two men ran up to examine the end. The 'toucher' was touching and although the Rydemouth man still had a bowl to play, he had to concede defeat; Duncan would go through to the semi-finals.

We joined those crowding around our Club Captain to congratulate him and once more I was surprised that Amy was not there to share in her husband's triumph.

Eva and I joined up with Chloe and her friend and I learned that Abigail's Mum was taking the four of them home in her car. So I bade my farewells, but not before I had given Eva a business card, asking her to ring me as I would very much like to take her out one evening. She seemed very pleased to accept and I thought she might even be blushing.

As I went through the gate to make my way home, the deputy Groundsman was standing at the door of his hut and we exchanged 'good-nights'.

'Dominic missed all the excitement,' I added.

'Yes, I think he's doing a bit of gardening at your Club Captain's house.'

I knew all the Groundsmen earned a little extra with some part-time jobs, but as I walked home I began pondering on that last bit of information…thinking that perhaps I may know the owner of the whimpering voice I had heard in the ladies' changing room.

I thought about Eva over the next three days and kept wondering if and when she would ring. I made plans to spend some time with her and asked myself if she would want me to invite her for an evening alone or perhaps at a weekend with Chloe.

But it was Hubert who phoned me at the office to tell me that Rosemary had been sent home from the hospital to recuperate, so I gave her a ring and arranged to call that evening.

Then within just a few minutes I had a strange phone message from Eva's father saying that Eva wanted to speak to me rather urgently. She and Chloe had gone to the Swimming Baths and she had asked if I could call in to see her. A rather odd meeting place, I thought, but then it could be a pleasant opportunity for me to see more of her! It was in the middle of the morning, but as I had no immediate appointments I wanted to go, confiding in my secretary Paula on the way out.

I knew the building, although the babble of voices and children's shrieks would be enough to guide a stranger to the pool. There was a girl in the reception cubicle, but she was busy talking to a woman standing in front, so I just hurried by and pushed open the swing doors, to be assailed by the clamour from within.

The pool was half full of moving heads and bodies and on the sides there were young girls frolicking about generally enjoying themselves. I looked around for Eva and my eyes scanned over some rather plump, matronly figures to finally alight on two that were much more finely moulded. One was Eva and whilst she recognised me, I was surprised that her wave seemed more from amazement than eagerness to speak to me.

It was the other one that came quickly towards me looking gorgeous, but far from friendly, demanding to know what I was doing there. Then I saw Chloe climbing out of the pool and I watched as she hurried towards her Mum. I was hoping to be able to wave, but my ravishing challenger had been joined by one of the matronly figures and the two women propelled me, quite forcibly, into a small room which was empty apart from a table and four chairs. I was told to sit down.

It was the younger one who spoke and, with a glare, made the introductions.

'This lady is a senior teacher at the local school and I am WPC Donna Dove. Will you please tell me, sir, what you were doing entering the pool area during the period which is always reserved for ladies and the young girls from the school. I am not carrying my warrant card at the moment, but I will produce it in a few minutes.'

I had studied the girl from head to toe and would concede that trying to hide a leather warrant pouch anywhere within that rather brief costume would have been a criminal act. But I realised that to express my thoughts with such a flippant remark would not be appreciated.

I was puzzled and beginning to feel real concern about my predicament. I said I was sorry to have bungled into a 'ladies only' session at the pool, of which I was completely unaware and tried to explain that I had come in answer to a phone message from Mr. Sheen.

Another matronly figure appeared with two large council-supplied dressing gowns and WPC Dove quickly disappeared into hers. It obliterated the shape of her and instantly killed off all the interests I had been feeling.

The two ladies listened to my story almost without interruption and then the police officer asked me to remain while she dressed and made some enquiries. I sat and talked, probably making inane remarks, to the elderly teacher.

I didn't get to see WPC Dove's warrant card or to see the young woman dressed. Within little more than a few minutes two plain clothes officers arrived and produced their warrant cards to explain that one was an Inspector and the other a Sergeant. They sat down with me, the teacher left and questions and answers began all over again with me reiterating my apologies.

The Inspector did most of the talking and it was he who asked the first embarrassing question.

'How well do you know Mr. Sheen, sir?'

'We have never met.'

'WPC Dove has spoken to his daughter here at the pool and she said her father doesn't know you.'

'That may be true, but the phone message came from a man claiming to be Eva's father.'

'I see.' He said that in a tone of voice that suggested he didn't see at all. 'The local school has received anonymous telephone calls from a man stating how he likes to watch the young girls in the playground.'

I looked across to express my shock and surprise at the statement. 'Yes, I had heard,' and I saw the two men exchange a glance.

'WPC Dove said you were studying the young girls in their costumes and ogling...I think that was the term she used...some of the more mature figures.'

'I was only studying the young girls because I wanted to try and identify Chloe Sheen. I spotted her and I did watch as she walked towards her mother. If I did any ogling then that would have been directed at your young officer. Her figure, half undressed in that cut-away costume was enough to make any man ogle.'

The inspector tried to hide a slight smile. Then he returned to the attack. 'We need to move on, sir. Would you have any objections if we came home with you...we would like to examine your computer.'

I decided that objections would be futile, so we set off in convoy for my apartment. Immediately on arrival the Sergeant went to my study. I heard him searching among my files and then he apparently settled down with my computer. The Inspector was with me in the conservatory and had spent minutes admiring the harbour view before he turned to flip through some photo albums which I kept on a shelf.

'You seem to be fond of photography and I see you now have a digital.'

'Yes, it's a bit of a hobby and I expect your Sergeant will find some photos on the computer.'

'Are there many in the camera memory now?'

'Well, just a few.' If I had shown concern or alarm then I am sure the Inspector would not have missed it.

'We like to be thorough, sir, so I will take the camera and let the sergeant print out what you have.'

It didn't take long and within minutes we were looking at a collection of prints spread out on the table.

'Some nice views of the harbour and river, sir, and some very clear pictures of a young woman without any clothes on. Who would she be?'

'I don't know.'

There was a long silent pause before the Inspector spoke again.

'Here we have a number of intimate, explicit photos of a naked young woman, taken with your camera, and you say you don't know who she is. I think this calls for some explanation, don't you, sir?'

I had been trying to stay calm, but panic was beginning to take a grip. I felt like someone standing in a black hole and I could foresee that the hole might get deeper and deeper. I realised the explanation would sound fanciful, but decided I must stick to the truth and hope for the best. I told the story exactly as it had happened and was rewarded by the single comment: 'I see,' conveying more than ever that he didn't.

I added nothing…not wishing to dig into my hole… but the Inspector's next question made me feel that I was sinking anyway.

'What colour are the doors of your beach hut, sir?'

'Yellow.'

'Ah…now that's interesting because it was only a few days ago that we were called to a yellow beach hut, near the end of the row, like yours, to investigate an incident. A young girl had been drugged and undressed by a man. Then when she was naked he examined her and took photos of her in various positions, inflicting severe bruising.'

'I had heard of her ordeal…but I can assure you it certainly wasn't me.'

Then I set about telling him how I had heard details of the girl's assault from James Gosling and why the two huts were both painted yellow by the council but numbered sixteen and nineteen.

Watching the Inspector as he listened I felt I had stopped sinking, until his next remark..

'When I was investigating the assault, Mr. Gosling told me that before he took over Sea View, you and your sister used to rent both beach huts…is that correct?'

'Yes, but that was some time ago.' I was trying to avoid panic, guessing the direction of his thoughts.

'So you have probably kept a key to number sixteen?'

'No, all keys were handed over and in any case I expect the locks have been changed by Mr. Gosling two or three times since then.'

'Yes.' It was more of a non-committal grunt than an agreement. At that moment I was saved by the bell, or rather the bleep from the Inspector's mobile. With an 'excuse me', he left to rejoin the Sergeant who was still working on my computer.

When he returned my panic began to subside.

'I don't think we need to trouble you any further, sir. We have established, almost certainly, that you received a hoax call to go to the Baths and I am quite sure the Senior Teacher of the school has already accepted your apology and would not wish any action to be taken. I must thank you for your patience and trust you will understand that when we are investigating assaults and threatened attacks on young girls, we sometimes have to be ruthless in our enquiries. My apologies for any inconvenience caused.'

I was pleased to shake his hand and so grateful to be pulled out of that black hole.

When the Inspector got to the door he turned to make a final remark: 'apart from receiving information regarding your call, we have confirmation from your sister that she lent her beach hut key to a young lady friend…and if I were you, sir, I wouldn't miss out on a chance to follow it up!'

Then, as he left, I felt sure I heard him chuckle.

CHAPTER 5

STELLA

• • •

After the Inspector and Sergeant had left, I grabbed a quick snack and returned to the office...there to try and dampen down the excitement and curiosity that had been created by the visit of WPC Donna Dove who had come asking if anyone knew if I had received a call from a Mr. Sheen. Paula said she was able to tell the police officer that whilst I had a private direct line, that particular call had come through the inter-office system and she had been able to give her the approximate time of the call.

Paula said she thought WPC Dove seemed surprised at the confirmation ...and I would think disappointed... but she said 'thank you' and left. I told Paula that the call had been from some cranky hoaxer and asked her to quell any gossip in the office.

Then I was told I had received a telephone 'summons' from my sister and opted to deal with that on my private line. I waited an age for my call to be handed round at the bank, but when I achieved contact it was typical. 'What the hell's going on, Nathan? We've had a WPC Dove in here asking me questions about the beach hut key…and when I confirmed I'd lent it to a friend she left like a scalded cat.'

I tried to explain about the peculiar hoax call and the police needing to verify it. But Peggs came back into the attack.

'Well, peculiar is the word…that's how it all sounds to me. I lent the key to your old friend Molly and the next day she never said a word about her trip to the beach. I thought I might arrange a surprise meeting…I don't know what happened…but she seems to have gone off you…for ever.' Then we closed the conversation with a promise to meet at the weekend.

I thought over the events of the day. One hoax call and I was thrown under suspicion for being a peeping Tom and girl molester. I hadn't heard a word from Eva and my old school friend Molly had obviously gone off me. Not surprising if she'd guessed I could be the photographer arriving at the beach hut just when she'd taken her costume off ! But as Peggs had asked…what the hell was going on? Hoax calls can be dismissed as schoolboy pranks, but this one had sinister undertones. There was someone in the town who liked abusing young girls. Was that person…or maybe someone else…wanting to throw suspicion onto me? The police had been very quick to move in and show concern.

My mind was preoccupied, going over the Inspector's questions and insinuations…but I had work to do…a problem had cropped up needing my attention before I went home…so it was not until I was locking the papers away that I remembered Rosemary and realised I would be very late for my arranged visit. I should have phoned, but I set off hoping I would still be welcome.

The Fletchers had bought a fine property overlooking the river between Woodymouth and Upper Woody. It was approached by a lane off the main road which led me to tall iron gates. There was a speak-in phone and when I pressed a red button and waited for some time, I heard Rosemary's questioning voice. She expressed surprise that I had come so late and I apologised and said I would return next day. But there followed a slight groaning noise and the gates began to open. I drove in, noting in the half light that the lawns, shrubs and trees were well kept and on one side of me there was a bank of rhododendrons which would be just waiting for the sunshine to present a blaze of colour leading all the way up to the Edwardian house.

I was let in by a housekeeper who scolded me for coming late, reminding me that 'the Mistress' had only recently come out of hospital and needed her rest. I promised not to keep her up too late and was shown into a spacious lounge, with a high ceiling. I noticed an old-fashioned telephone that seemed to set off the period furnishings.

But I ceased to admire the furniture when Rosemary came through the other door wearing a pale green bathrobe. She had been fitted into a neck brace and was walking with the aid of a stick, but still managed to look very attractive. There was more scolding and apologies and then upon her request I poured two drinks and we settled into comfortable chairs.

She said she had been shaken up, battered and bruised, but otherwise intact, without any broken bones. Hubert had arranged for her transport from the hospital, liaising with her housekeeper, while Tony had arrived with a large bunch of flowers and then expressed his sympathy and concern that bad luck seemed to go with her job.

'The silly man meant well, but his words weren't exactly comforting.' I was wondering just how much comfort the 'silly' man was providing. I was not a stranger to temptation…I had admired those legs before and the bath-robe was behaving in a manner alien to modesty.

'Have there been other accidents then?'

'Well, yes, minor ones from time to time and it was Hubert, one day, who said…as a joke…I was getting as accident-prone as poor old Will. It made me worry a bit…because it seemed my misfortunes all began when I took over the firm. But I think their suggestion of a possible connection is ridiculous.'

Naturally I was very concerned about such a connection…but I had also been wondering if she was wearing anything beneath the robe…as she reached over to empty her glass, the question was answered.

It was the housekeeper who cut short my reverie by knocking and then asking if there was anything we needed. Rosemary thanked her and then explained: 'she used to be a nanny and now thinks it's part of her job to fuss over me.'

We embraced in a kiss-on-the-cheek farewell and after driving through the gates I noticed how they closed behind me. It was quite dark as I started down the lane, but even so I noticed the car backed into the field gate. As I passed I thought it would be a couple having a little naughty-naughty but as I reached the main road I suddenly realised it was a Porsche. Not many in the

Woodymouth area…apart from Tony Fairclough's…and Arthur had confided in me he spent quite a few nights playing Internet Poker with a group of guys over in Texas. So if it was his car…what the hell was he doing? Keeping a check on Rosemary's visitors? It didn't make sense, but I certainly wasn't going back to investigate.

On Saturday morning the sun was shining and I felt sure it was the herald of a lovely day. I was in the team for an away match at Upper Woody, with plans to call in to see Rosemary on the way.

Naturally I was sorry she wouldn't be playing, but when Tony and I were making the selections, I had insisted on having Eva in my team in her place. I hadn't received the anticipated phone call but was sure there would be a happy explanation and was looking forward to the outcome.

After breakfast was the usual time, at the weekend, for the black Labrador to appear, so I went into the conservatory to wait for him, looking out as I always did to admire the view. It was an ever-changing scene… with the tide well in…the sandbanks out of sight and the harbour a shimmering expanse of water. The beach had shrunk and the two dinghies were afloat, but there was still room for the dog to amble by and it was not long before I saw him, still carrying the old slipper. I was eager to wave to his pretty companion, being convinced more than ever that she had nice legs. But she never turned to look my way or to wave and when they had gone I felt as though I had been slapped in the face.

Then the phone rang…it was the Upper Woody Team Captain with bad news. Firstly, he couldn't get in touch with Tony, so he picked on me. Secondly, their Green was unfit for play as it had been damaged by foxes during the night. He asked if we could host the match and if so, he would contact their members and make the alternative arrangements. Obviously he wanted an immediate answer. I said I didn't know if our Green would be available, but told him to go ahead and we would hope for the best.

All I got from Tony's flat was his cheerful voice on an answering machine, so I left a message stating I needed urgent contact . Then I phoned Rosemary to explain that I would be unable to call. She seemed genuinely disappointed and I accepted an invitation to visit in the evening.

She said she may know why I couldn't get hold of Tony and her words were of little comfort. 'He often plays Internet Poker on a Friday night and when his chums across the Atlantic begin their evening session Tony has already lost four or five hours…and when the game finishes the good people in Woodymouth are awakening to a new day. He'll be sleeping like a zombie and won't surface until after mid-day.'

I got the car out and raced to the Green to check that the match could be played, but panic gripped. Only one rink was available…left for the benefit of visitors or just casual bowlers and the rest of the Green had been closed for maintenance. Dominic and a couple of the lads were busy with the mowers and garden implements and when I spoke of a takeover for a match there was a stubborn resistance.

But I had seen all the names of the team players… Duncan was down to play, but not his wife Amy…so I decided to test my suspicions and play a devious game of my own. I spoke to Dominic as I turned to leave.

'I realise it's short notice and you chaps have your jobs to do…I'll just phone everyone up and tell them to stay at home and do a bit of gardening!'

It took a few seconds for the implication of my remarks to sink in…and then he called me back.

'We'll get the Green ready for a three o'clock match. These lads don't want to work on a Saturday afternoon anyway.'

I thanked him and hurried back to the car. Once I was back at the apartment I made my phone work overtime trying to advise everyone that it was a home game for three o'clock. Eva was not available but I spoke to her mother and explained the change and asked her to pass on the message that I was looking forward to seeing Eva in the afternoon.

I got myself a well-earned lunch and then set off early for the bowling Green to find to my dismay that the Upper Woody team had already arrived. I had overlooked the fact that the original match had been arranged for two o'clock and soon realised the visitors were getting rather disgruntled having to wait about for an extra hour. Time seemed to drag while I chatted them up, trying to keep them cheerful, until tensions eased when our members began to arrive. Then, just before three o'clock, Tony breezed into the Pavilion in his usual debonair manner with profuse apologies for being detained on business.

I saw Eva and tried to wave but she seemed deep in conversation with friends. Then Tony came onto the Green with the visiting captain and said the usual words of welcome and his apologies for not being available earlier in the day, which effectively put the visitors' waiting time clearly down to me!

Then he read out the names for allocation to the rinks, only to discover there were two missing, so he declared two rinks would have to play one member short. He made a joke that they had obviously not received news of the change and would probably be at the Upper Woody Green having a match with the foxes!

There followed an announcement that took me completely by surprise: he was moving Eva from my rink to change with a lady called Stella...and he hoped we would all have an enjoyable afternoon. Play began but not on my rink, because I walked over to have angry words with him. But his answer set me back: 'keep your shirt on, Nathan, Eva didn't seem to be very pleased with you so I just moved her to try and make her happy.'

I walked away deflated, disappointed and bewildered...back to my rink...to begin a game that could only be described as a disaster. Alice and Arthur were as good as usual but Stella, playing with too much weight, managed to scatter their scoring woods, not once but for two or three ends. Then when she eased up, she bowled short, leaving blockers to stop me getting into the jack...and apart from that I was really off form and being completely out-bowled by the opposing skip. The score was a wash-out and I felt I had let Arthur and Alice down badly...having allowed Stella to take on the number three position.

All through the game I had been trying to attract Eva's attention, but without success. I had thought her a lovely, friendly girl, but I was really getting the cold shoulder. Then as time for the interval approached I realised we had no 'tea makers', so I had a quick word with Tony and we managed to get Stella to 'volunteer' with her husband to join her and the game continued with the Woodymouth team being a player short on each of the four rinks.

When I left my apartment the sun had been shining… beginning to disappear as I reached the Green to greet the unhappy visitors. Then as the game started grey clouds gathered and these, in keeping with my mood, grew darker. When the bell rang for tea there was a flash and a heavenly clap and the rain just poured down. Normally we have an organised file into the Pavilion, but everyone left everything and made a mad dash.

Instead of an orderly queue there was a surge of twenty-eight people crowding into the serving area. Mac and Stella had managed to get the boiler working and seemed to be coping with an array of large teapots on the counter, so it looked as if tempers or disappointments would be soothed with the magic brew.

But all was not well…they were short of teabags… so it was not long before it was discovered the brew had lost its magic and the bowlers began to leave. The match was abandoned and both teams were obliged to return to the Green to collect their bowls and gear in a steady downpour.

Mac and Stella weren't very happy …they had done their best, but obviously it had not been enough…so I went back to the Pavilion to lend a hand clearing away cups half full of a pale, insipid infusion. It had been poor hospitality to the visitors and a dismal end to the match. Tony had gone swanning off, presumably convinced he had delegated all responsibility to me. Two lady members were doing the washing-up…one, I noticed, was Eva…but she seemed too busy to speak to me. We soon had the tables cleared and the cups and saucers packed away and I knew we were pleased to lock up.

In the car park, for a moment, my spirits lifted when Eva came to me…even in the rain, under a hood, looking attractive…yet not the least bit friendly. 'I don't like it,' she said, handing me a large envelope and then running off to a waiting car where I noticed Chloe, Abigail, and her mother. I didn't have chance for an answer but just stood there getting wet as I watched her get in and be driven away.

In the car I tore off the damp envelope to stare at a card…the sort I had seen in racks at the newsagents under the heading of 'humour'. This one looked as though it had been left over from Valentine's Day. On the front was the sketch of a guy waiting by the phone with the words: 'Please Ring – I Beg You – I Urge You'. Inside were the words: 'Then You Can Check on My Urges!!' with a sketch of the guy chasing a partly clad girl into a bedroom. The bottom of the card bore what looked like my signature, 'Nathan'.

Again I stared, looking and reading it over. Eva had said: 'I don't like it,' and then she had run off. I didn't like it and I was furious that someone should have sent it in my name. Copying my signature would be easy as I signed memos pinned to the Notice Board and all membership cards .That had been my first task to issue the cards to paid-up members. I was also a little annoyed and disappointed that Eva should believe that I'd sent it, but after the shenanigans at the Baths I supposed it was only to be expected.

As I drove back to the apartment I was still fuming and puzzled. Being honest with myself I knew that, given half a chance, I would be quite happy to chase Eva, partly clad, into a bedroom. But that wasn't the point at issue, some character was playing sour jokes on me which produced embarrassing and unhappy results. How did that person know I was waiting for a phone call? Casting my mind back to the inter-town singles competition I realised I had spent the whole evening chatting to Eva with a crowd of bowlers as witnesses. Not difficult for someone to make an intelligent guess. But who would bear me such animosity?...and the only person I could think of was Tony Fairclough...but for what possible reason?

I had shown an interest in Rosemary, at the match against Upper Woody, and he had switched her over to his rink...as Arthur had said, for devious reasons. We all knew and accepted he had a roving eye, but then he does it again with Eva...and from our conversation she said she had frustrated him in his iniquitous intentions. Could he be behind the phone call and the joke card? I had accepted him as a debonair playboy...time perhaps to acknowledge a malicious streak in his make-up.

After I had showered and changed I set off in good spirits. Nothing had gone right for me during the day, so my hopes were for a happier evening. At the house I was greeted as before by the housekeeper, but this time there was no scolding and Rosemary was waiting for me in the lounge looking ravishing in a black dress which was a perfect complement to her fair hair. She had discarded the neck brace, but was still using a stick. Once more it was a kiss-on-the-cheek embrace before she dropped into one of the easy chairs and invited me to pour the drinks.

I watched her relax: 'I'll stop worrying about you... it's quite obvious you're making an excellent recovery... looking so lovely.'

She thanked me with a smile: 'I'm pleased you were able to come...I've had a dreadful time here with Hubert, learning about the faults they found with the car. Will always insisted our vehicles were serviced at Upper Woody Garages, but Hubert switched my car over to Crofts Motors – a new firm run by Harry Wilks' half brother. Crofts have agreed to make good all damage...obviously there must have been negligence somewhere...but I'm insisting an independent engineer checks it out before I accept it back.. Hubert reckoned I was being unreasonable but I was adamant.'

'Good for you...we've always found Upper Woody Garages very reliable for satisfying our insured on claims settlements, but I've no knowledge of Crofts... must put my ear to the ground.'

She took a sip of wine and moved the hem of her dress just slightly up her thighs before continuing. 'We had a set-to about our old foreman, Harry Wilks. Hubert runs the production side at the works and I don't normally interfere, but as you probably know Wilks was in prison for fraud and when Hubert said he wanted to give him his old job back, I blew my top.'

Then there was a complete switch as she crossed her legs and smiled: 'but that's enough about my problems...

news has reached me that you've had some excitement yourself just lately...tangling with the law!'

So naturally I had to tell her about the hoax call and my visit to the Baths with the consequent enquiry from the police, which she thought was hilarious. I made no mention of the assault on the girl in beach hut number sixteen nor of my dramatic experience in number nineteen. She was interested to know how I'd got on with the change of plans for the match that afternoon. I told her, with all the sorry details, and mentioned about the card delivered to Eva, revealing my suspicions about Tony Fairclough.

She smiled and held my gaze before speaking: 'well, well...I wonder if you could be right. He certainly fancied Eva a while back and I know it was she who broke off the attachment. You're suggesting a dog in the manger attitude...if he can't have her, he'll make certain you don't! I'm not sure if that would be in character... because to me he has just been charming. Good fun to be with...although when Will was alive I do remember I was puzzled by some of the accidents at the Club, wondering if perhaps Tony had been playing jokes on him. And of course you will know there was nothing funny about the misfortunes that overtook poor Will.'

I wanted to know more, but at that point all serious conversation ended with the housekeeper wheeling in a very appetizing buffet of vol-au-vents, canapés, and tasty bits of this and that. We both relaxed with the wine, and the remainder of the evening floated by until it had to end. I wasn't certain of Rosemary's feelings, but I was acutely aware of mine. I felt sure we would both agree I'd had too much wine to drive home...so I would be offered the sofa. I didn't think I'd be satisfied with that. Then there was Tony Fairclough…Rosemary was expecting him to 'pop in sometime'. The thought of sharing breakfast with Tony was a real turn-off.

So, after a rather fond embrace, I drove home, noticing once more the car pulled into the gateway to the field, and deciding if it wasn't Tony there was someone who must be a wiser and far happier man than me.

Sunday was a dull day, but I was looking forward to lunch with Peggs and Jon, and when I set off the sun was actually trying to brighten the morning.

Like Rosemary they were by the side of the river, further up towards Upper Woody, sharing a 'Fisherman's Cottage'. Peggs said they bought it because it looked and sounded romantic, although there was no evidence that a fisherman had ever lived there.

I received the usual warm welcome from my sister and Jon and an appetising aroma wafting in from the kitchen.

'That's my slow-roast lamb greeting you and I'm hoping to seduce your taste-buds with an experiment of mine for sherry gravy…but that's for later. Let's sit down while Jon pours the aperitifs and you tell us all about the funny business you've got yourself into!'

So once more I had to tell about the call which I believed was from Mr. Sheen, my visit to the Baths, and the consequent police interrogation, this time providing the full story as Jon was well-informed about the assault on the girl in hut number sixteen.

'Do you think the call was just a prank?' Peggs asked.

'I don't know…and the only person I can think of to blame for such a stunt would be our Team Captain,

Tony Fairclough. I have told you how he switched Rosemary out of my team to chat her up for a date...well at yesterday's match he did it again with Eva after she'd been upset by a joke card she'd received with my name on it.'

'You've really got a joker in the Club,' Peggs said, but Jon seemed to think it was more serious.

'He - not to rule out a possible 'she' - could be just a hoaxer but it seems he knew when to pick his moment. Your call to the Baths seemed to trigger off a lot of interest from the lads at the Nick in nasty incidences they were dealing with. My advice would be to watch your back...it seems you have someone trying to finger you...tie you in to unsavoury local crime.'

'I heard Rosemary Fletcher was injured,' Peggs butted in, 'how is she?'

'She said she was battered and bruised, but making a steady recovery...but upset to discover her injuries were due to poor maintenance on the car...Crofts Motors...local firm I believe.'

'Yes, a rather dodgy set-up,' Jon said, 'run by a guy who came down from your old neck of the woods, Nottingham way...believe he's got form for fraud.'

'Sounds a charming man!' Peggs volunteered. 'Hope he wasn't following you, Nathan.'

'I hope not...Rosemary says he's a half brother to Harry Wilks and Jon knows all about him.'

'We always considered Rosemary's husband to be accident-prone...he had one or two car accidents...hope she hasn't taken on his mantle.'

'You're not the first person to wonder about that, and Rosemary's been worried by the suggestion more than once.'

Their dining room had such a pleasant aspect, and as Jon carved the lamb I opened a bottle of rosé and noticed that the river was full with a high tide, the waters tranquil apart from the diving activities of one or two cormorants.

The meal was excellent and the gravy earned our special praises. Peggs was pleased and confessed she didn't know whether to use sweet or dry sherry. 'We had both so I mixed in some from each bottle!'

Peggs mentioned about the hut key being lent to Molly and when I told them about my camera adventure the room echoed with their laughter.

It was then that I noticed the launch passing the window, gliding smoothly up river. The vessel was small, but built with a storm shield cabin in the stern, obviously driven by a powerful inboard engine as it cut smoothly through the water. I saw the man at the helm turn it inshore and cut the power. Then I watched as it glided in and disappeared from sight.

Jon had noticed and smiled. 'Frustrating isn't it… there's a little inlet a few hundred yards up river with a jetty behind those trees. That boat comes and goes and we never see why.'

'Sometimes at night,' my sister chipped in.

'I recognised the man at the helm…it was Harry Wilks.'

'There's a lane leading from the jetty that goes for about half a mile straight into the quarry.'

'Well, well…I wonder what the ex-foreman could be doing visiting on a Sunday afternoon?'

I always enjoyed time spent with my sister and her partner, but I had a lot to think about as I drove home… not least being Jon's advice about watching my back. Who the hell would want to stab me?

CHAPTER 6

VENUS (DIS)COVERED

• • •

The week was spent, fraught perhaps with more than the usual problems...there was nothing I couldn't handle...but they certainly didn't prepare me for the frightening, dramatic events that awaited me at the weekend.

Monday was routine until I returned to the apartment to discover the burglar alarm was malfunctioning. The firm said they would fix it in the morning, but then agreed to come in the evening.

Tuesday, I had confirmation from Head Office that the Managers' Conference would be held at the weekend in London. I had been standing by on that one, because for a number of reasons it had been postponed a couple of times. Paula was consulted to make travel arrangements and to check on my hotel accommodation. I planned to travel up on Saturday, pull in a musical in the evening...the Office usually managed to have a selection of tickets...then socialise with the other managers on Sunday with perhaps a bit of sightseeing. The Conference would be all day on Monday and I would return on Tuesday.

In the evening two men came and fixed the alarm.

On Wednesday I went with our Claims Inspector to see an elderly couple about their claim for storm damage to their garage roof. Our chap had tried and failed to explain that whilst recent storms may have allowed more water through broken felt on the flat roof, the real cause of damage was deterioration and a lack of repair and maintenance over the years...not an easy one.

I was not there to change the facts, but to calm troubled waters. Over a large mug of tea we were able to achieve that with an offer of an *ex gratia* payment towards the cost of repairs. We left the insured quite satisfied. The old boy had warned us the tea was laced with 'a drop of the hard stuff 'which we'd enjoyed .It was not until we were confronted by a frightened cow in a narrow lane that we regretted his generosity.

In the evening I attended a meeting of the Bowls Club Committee. This time there was a quorum: Hubert, Duncan, Tony, James and myself being present. So when Harry Wilks' nomination was again brought forward, I expected Tony to join James and me in opposition. But apparently Hubert had persuaded Duncan and Tony to vote with him, so the nomination was accepted.

There was a number of routine matters to settle and a problem with our match fixture for Saturday. It should have been a home game against Padquay but we received last minute advice they had a village 'get together' on that date and would be unable to muster a team. After discussion it was agreed we would have to advise our members and then invite everyone, via our Notice Board, to a friendly 'round robin' on our Green.

The meeting closed and the members hurried away, except for Tony who stopped to talk to Eva, on one of the rinks, where she had been playing with three lady friends.

As the ladies were just packing up, I was able to speak to Eva as she came into the Pavilion. I stood in the doorway, so she couldn't avoid me! I knew she was still bothered about my visit to the Baths and that stupid card. I tried to explain it had all been a sick hoax, but sensed that our relationship had changed. On the evening of the championship game she had been so friendly, but it seemed I was being denied any fond smiles.

Thursday was routine, except that when I went home I found the alarm was again playing tricks. The firm said they would come early on Friday morning. It was very early, but it was only to tell me an electrical component needed to be replaced and this could not be done until Saturday afternoon. I said I would be away over the weekend, so it was agreed they would make the replacement on Tuesday evening. As a matter of courtesy they said they would advise the local police station that my apartment would be empty and unprotected during the approaching three to four days. I asked the electrician if he thought the police would show any particular interest. He answered with a smile.

'I doubt it, sir, but it's a routine procedure to protect my company's interests as well as yours!'

Friday continued as a day of frustration. When I got to the office I learned that Head Office, with profuse apologies, had once more postponed the Managers'

Conference. So I had to confront Paula with the news and ask her to cancel the arrangements. As she left my office I was surprised to hear her using words I would never have thought she even knew!

In the evening I had arranged to call on Rosemary and I was not too pleased to find a Porsche parked outside her house. I had assumed it would be Tony's night to play poker, but as I was finding, arrangements can be changed and I think it would be fair to say that he blighted my enjoyment for the evening.

I had thought when Saturday came, I would be looking at the Thames, but instead it was the Woody. With the promise of a fine day I decided I would join in the 'round robin' on the Green.

After lunch I had a brisk walk along the Promenade and joined Arthur and his wife Audrey to sit on a bench beside the Pavilion. We were early so able to chat and watch our members arrive for the game. Hubert and Duncan were the organisers. Each player is given a score card and everyone moves around the Green to play with and against different members. Can be good fun.

I saw Eva arrive with one of her friends and noticed Tony come out of the Pavilion to speak to her. I waved but she didn't seem to notice. Jean and Alan Robertson arrived with their friends Phyllis and Howard Blythe. They stood talking together, but it was not long before they had attracted the attention of others and Arthur explained: 'Howard's got himself a real 'shiner' in the left eye...probably broke the rules at one of their meetings.' Which remark brought forth a sharp rebuke from Audrey: 'you shouldn't talk about things like that.'

I was intrigued and told Arthur I didn't know what he was talking about, but as he had started a story he would have to finish it.

'Audrey's quite right, I shouldn't talk about it...but it's common knowledge where we live and I forget others may not know.'

'Well, get on with it,' his wife chipped in, and Arthur continued. 'There is what I think they call a Swingers' Club. The Robertsons and the Blythes belong to it together with three or four more couples. They meet certain weekends in the month for drinks and a game of cards.'

'Sounds quite cosy,' I said.

'Yes, but there is a big difference. The card game is designed to re-arrange the couples so that at the end of the evening they will each go home and to bed with a different partner. It would suit me, but I can't talk Audrey into it!' And for that he was almost pushed off the bench.

'No, seriously, it wouldn't suit me. I understand they play by rigid rules with the cards deciding the partners and preferences being strictly forbidden. You can well imagine jealousy creeping in and someone getting a black eye once in a while!'

At that moment it was Hubert who called us onto the Green and after we had each collected our score card, the game began. Basically it was a social 'get together', although there was a competitive element present as a small prize was offered for the highest scorer and a booby for the lowest.

As we went for the interval tea-break, this time, inside the Pavilion, there was an orderly queue to the counter for the refreshments, but as I went to collect my tea there was disorder and a noisy distraction taking place outside. Apparently there was a strange guy having angry words with Howard...Hubert and Duncan had been called to separate them.

Refreshments completed I singled out Arthur on my way back to the Green, knowing he would be able to relay the facts. He didn't disappoint me.

'That unwelcome visitor was one of the partners from the Swingers' Club. It seems they had a meeting recently and Howard went home with the fella's wife. That was quite acceptable, but Howard must have enjoyed himself particularly well and wanted more. So he went back to the house and stayed too long. That's how he got the black eye, and the fella was here to black the other one. As I said before...strange though it may seem...they have strict rules...when they're broken there's trouble. Howard will probably be drummed out of the Club!'

I found problems before the interval but these just intensified in the second half and when it came to the final count-down I know Tony was delighted to collect the winner's prize of a bottle of plonk. Then even more ecstatic to watch me collect the booby which was a coloured towel used to wipe bowls in inclement weather. It bore the name of the local brewery, presumably the donor at some time, and was very special as it had a tear in the middle!

There was a clap and a cheer for both of us and the afternoon ended in good humour. I think everyone had enjoyed themselves although I wasn't too sure about Howard.

I spent the evening alone watching a TV show and then undressed into my shorts ready for bed, but when I put the lights out I was intrigued as the whole apartment seemed to be bathed in an eerie glow. Above my glass conservatory there was a moon shining from a clear sky. I poured myself a nightcap and sat for a while admiring my view of the harbour in its moonlit splendour.

When I got into bed it was just past midnight and putting my head down usually meant sound sleep until morning. But not that night...I woke with a feeling and then a realisation I had a visitor in the apartment. The lights had not been put on but I knew I had an intruder moving about. He was not the usual stealthy burglar because I could hear him in the study moving files and opening drawers. I was out of bed, able to creep forward silently with bare feet. Questions flashed through my mind: why wasn't he bothered about disturbing me? Could it be someone who thought I would be away and knew the alarm was switched off?

Presumably he must be a bent employee of the alarm company doing a bit of burglary on the side...in which case I didn't think he would be armed with either gun or knife, giving me confidence to creep forward to where I could see him. I had no weapon but evolved a plan: if I startled him he would bolt for the door. He looked quite a small guy dressed in shirt, jeans and trainers, wearing a baseball cap. It was some years since I played rugby, but had faced fifteen stone dynamos, so felt confident

Deryck Coleman

I could bring this fellow down as he passed me on his way out.

Bracing myself, I shouted: 'what the hell are you doing?'

Reaction was as anticipated...an exclamation of startled surprise...a turn...and a run past me to escape. So I threw myself forward to bring off what should have been the easiest of tackles, but I was completely ill-prepared for the counter-attack of someone not playing by the game's rules. I received a nasty hand chop to the throat and stumbled forward clutching at air, with my hands coming to rest on the lapels of his shirt. Instinctively I held on, only to receive a hard punch in the stomach which sent me backwards. I held on, trying to pull him over with me, but he jumped away and I fell flat on my back still clutching half his shirt. I banged my head and it all went dark.

I had no idea how long my blackout lasted but my mind returned to the apartment when I felt fingers pressing on my neck and I realised my assailant must have returned to check that I was still alive! Not many like that these days...or had he fetched a knife from the kitchen to make sure I wouldn't survive?

As my head began to clear I realised I could be in mortal danger and kept my eyes shut and held my breath in case he was checking that. Apparently he was because the next moment I felt his hand over my heart...and wondered. It was not the roughened hand of a worker, but one quite soft and gentle as it caressed over my nipple. Even in my befuddled state I imagined Arthur saying: 'blimey, he's one of those!'

Whilst his interest in my state of health had only taken seconds, I knew I had to move fast and remembered my Territorial Army training for such a predicament: 'using feet and hands to push your body up, roll over and pin the assailant's arms to the floor.'

I acted immediately, using every ounce of strength and every muscle I had, and was amazed to find myself sitting on his tummy with my knees astride, and while he was temporarily winded I found his wrists and held them to the floor.

My action had succeeded only because of the element of surprise, then as I looked down at the torn, open shirt it was my turn to be astonished with an involuntary cry of amazement: 'Hell's bells!'

'Well, they've never been described like that before... and it's the only pair I've got!'

'They're gorgeous...' and I forced my eyes to move up to the lovely but still unfriendly face of WPC Donna Dove.

'Stop gawping and drooling...just tell me what you plan to do.'

'I do have an idea...' and I allowed my eyes to wander back to the torn shirt. 'As you used your hand to check my heart-beat, I would like to do the same to you!'

'Try that and you'll go over my head the instant you touch me, and I'll arrest you for molesting and assaulting a police officer.'

Then the truth of my situation dawned. I was enjoying my position, sitting astride her tummy with a unique view, imagining that I was in charge, calling the shots, but I was sitting on a girl so obviously trained in the art of combat. She could have thrown me, but was probably holding back to prevent me from banging my head on the wall behind her.

My eyes returned to the unfriendly face.

'I propose we both get up from the floor. I can find you a shirt to wear and then we can sit down to talk this over with a suitable drink.'

Once we were on our feet, I suggested we went into the bedroom to get a shirt and that idea was immediately opposed.

'Why can't you just go and fetch one?'

'Because I don't trust you not to run off, even with half a shirt...you've nothing to be scared of...I don't fancy another chop in the throat or a punch in the stomach.'

So we went into the bedroom where I picked out a shirt from the wardrobe: 'try this one on, it should be a good fit and the colour will match your jeans. I will try not to gawp.'

'Is that a promise?'

'No.'

'A good fit you said...it'll be down to my knees.'

'I was thinking more of the chest measurement.'

'Huh!'

I chose a shirt for myself, switched on some lights, and then we sat at the table in my kitchen/dining room discussing what would be suitable drinks, deciding on large whiskies on the rocks.

While we sipped the tipple I suggested she gave me an explanation. The baseball cap had gone and I sat looking across the table at a lovely brunette whose face threatened complete defiance.

'Not a lot to tell really...I learned from our Bulletins and our Shift Briefings that your property would be unoccupied over the weekend so at the end of my shift I thought I should pay it a visit. I found your door unlocked so I came in to check that you hadn't had an intruder...the rest you know.'

'I see.' I must have sounded like the Inspector. 'Without being detailed you came here out of the goodness of your heart to check if I might have been burgled. I can clearly remember locking the door knowing I had no alarm, and I do know that police training often includes a little tuition in opening doors... you were shifting files...looking into drawers...so let's move on and have a true version.'

I suspected the girl had acted stupidly, on impulse perhaps, and was only just realising the possible dire consequences. I had been looking into adorable brown eyes and felt sure they had a green glint when she was angry.

'Well, there is a bit more to it...there's a story going around the Nick that you have some nude photographs of a friend and I thought I might be able to find them.'

'To steal them you mean. What's your friend's name?'

'I'm not prepared to disclose that.'

'You know the photos were taken at a beach hut. You know my sister lent the key to a work-mate, Molly Hales. Is she your friend?'

'I won't say.'

I could see she was embarrassed, blushing profusely and trying bravely not to show concern. But I was being reminded of a sore neck and a throbbing head and couldn't feel too much sympathy.

'I think you are telling me a lot of porkies. I believe you entered my apartment illegally, with intent to steal those photos, knowing the alarm was not working and believing I was away. You say the photos are of a friend, hinting they could be of Molly Hales, but we both know that she has fair hair, so they can't be hers.'

We stared at each other over the table for some time...there was a highly-charged pause.

'But I understood she had a towel over her head.'

'Yes, she did.'

We still stared and I saw how those lovely eyes turned quite green as colour rose to her cheeks. I continued with my attack.

'So, if I take my complaint to the police, my case will be that Molly lent the key to you and the photos are of you and your intention was to steal them.' Some of that was conjecture, but I felt sure it was the truth.

There was no doubt she was angry and I sensed she was frightened, but still fighting.

'It would be your story against mine.'

'True, but could you risk that?'

'Supposing you do make a complaint, you will have no proof that the photos are of me and therefore nothing to substantiate your claim.' She was still fighting.

'But a good lawyer would question you about that fascinating little heart-shaped birth-mark.' That was a trump card and I felt a bit of a creep for playing it.

Apart from the flush in her cheeks, her angry face registered shock and disbelief.

'How on earth could you know...?'

'The photos are of an intimate nature.'

'You bastard...do you sit and drool over them?'

'I've admired the subject, but never drooled, and for your information my parents were happily married.'

'Well I still think you're a bastard because you could be about to end my brief career in the police force.'

'No...I have no wish to end your career and I will not make my complaint provided you comply with my terms of agreement.'

'Terms of agreement! Sounds like ruddy surrender to me and if you think you can blackmail me into going to bed with you...'

'No...no.' I was staring into very green eyes. 'That could be something I might dream about, but there is nothing like that in the agreement.'

'Huh...well what is it and are you going to hand over those photos?'

Hitherto she had refused my attempts to refill her glass by covering it with her hand, but now she allowed me to pour in a generous measure of whisky over fresh ice cubes.

'The agreement is quite simple: I will forget what happened this evening if you promise to spend two hours with me once a week, preferably on Saturday or Sunday, for the next three months, after which time I will hand over the photographs and any other records of them.'

She stared at me in disbelief and then took a good swig of the whisky: 'you must be mad...you're planning to have about a dozen meetings with me...I'm not going to call them dates...we don't know each other...and I'm not sure I even like you.'

'I realise that...and I'm a bit puzzled myself because you haven't exactly charmed your way into my affections...but you fascinate me and I think we both might enjoy the challenge.'

'What's the hidden agenda?'

'None, apart from one small condition...that we end each meeting with a kiss.'

Again she was unbelieving: 'you must be bonkers, it'll be like kissing a cold cod.'

'I've always liked fish.'

'But how do I know you will keep your side of the bargain?'

'You have my word, and if you wish I will repeat the promise in a church of your choice.'

I watched as she drained her glass of its liquid before answering: 'I will think about it.'

'No...we need to settle this tonight, or rather this morning. It is a yes or a no, and the agreement is non-negotiable.'

There was a very long pause and then, with the suspicion of a smile, she said: 'alright, I agree.'

I was amazed there wasn't a spark of green in her eyes, but not surprised when she added, 'I've never been out with an older man before.'

I imagine we were both too tired to argue any more, so when I said she had had too much drink to drive and I wasn't happy about her walking home, suggesting she kipped down on my sofa, she agreed... making me wonder if perhaps she still had plans to try and find those sought-after prints? She declined my offer of pyjamas, but allowed me to cover her with a blanket.

I left her with some friendly advice: 'sleep well, and don't go wandering about looking for photos or a camera...they are safely locked away.'

She was half asleep when she answered. I didn't quite hear the words...but I thought they were very unfriendly.

CHAPTER 7

MOLLY AND DONNA

• • •

When I awoke on the Sunday morning I knew I had overslept. The sun was shining through the curtains and when I turned my head I realised I was not entirely alone...Cindy was lying on what was normally an empty pillow. She was a rather tatty rag doll that had been given to Sonja when she was a toddler and, for reasons long forgotten, had been christened Cinderella, but as that was too much for a little girl, she was always known as Cindy.

Sonja had treasured her over the years and she normally sat on a shelf in my conservatory. Obviously my guest must have crept into my bedroom and put the doll on the pillow. It made me smile, telling me that WPC Donna Dove must only be angry part of the time...and could have a sense of humour with maybe a feel for fun.

As I expected, the apartment was empty. My guest had folded up the blanket and left without leaving a note. But that, of course, would be typical. She had agreed to come here between 3 and 4 o'clock, making this our first meeting under the agreement. Naturally she would want to keep me wondering if she would turn up.

I settled for a light breakfast because I had been invited to the Fisherman's Cottage for lunch. I suspected that apart from nosing into my non-existent sex life, my sister wanted to make sure I had a proper Sunday dinner now and again. Anyway we were always pleased to see each other.

I thought I would be too late to see the girl with the black Labrador, but when I looked out I saw them approaching from the opposite direction, apparently returning from their walk. As I watched I felt sure we knew each other. She had waved...there had been that friendly smile...she knew me...and, of course, if I hadn't been so interested in those nice legs I might have realised the girl was my old school friend Molly Hales. I went down to the beach and with recognition there was an immediate fussy session with the three of us really getting to know each other.

She accepted my offer of coffee while we settled into chairs. Ben the Labrador was very pleased with my gift of a biscuit and was quite happy to settle down on the floor between us. The old slipper had been left on the doormat. Molly apologised for having stopped the friendly waves in the mornings, explaining that she had felt guilty and responsible for problems caused at the beach hut. 'Peggy lent the key to me and I had no right to pass it on to my young cousin Donna.'

I pondered over the last three words.

Obviously they had discussed the rumpus caused at the hut, but maybe she knew nothing about the photos, so they were not mentioned. I also kept silent about what had happened in the early morning hours at the apartment, assuming that the young cousin mentioned would wish to keep that strictly under wraps.

We had much to discuss, reminiscing happily about school days, although we never got around to a mention of our dalliance on the sandbank. Time went so quickly and, too soon, it became my turn to apologise when it was time to keep my lunch date with Peggy and Jon. When Molly left I was happy with the thought this was a friendship rekindled. Over the past few weeks I had begun to think there was a force trying to drive friends away from me.

After Jon had poured the apéritifs, I asked him about the 'private eye' agency and he told me one of his 'domestics' had ended in a mixture of tragedy and happiness. It was a case he had mentioned to me earlier where it was thought a chap was cheating on his wife:

'I think I said it was the sort of case I didn't enjoy... spying on a spouse sneaking into covert meetings with a lover. Well, I found the other woman, only to discover she was dying of cancer and the wayward spouse was frantic with grief and worry about what would happen to a young girl, his daughter. I could see it all ending in death, divorce and tears. But my client had confided she was unable to have children so I confronted the chap and suggested he told all and sought forgiveness. I wouldn't have gambled on his chances. Then the mother died last week and I persuaded my client to see the young girl...there were tears and she was welcomed with open arms. The chap's had a mauling from his wife but I believe they are talking about adopting the girl and I have hopes she will settle into a fairly stable home. The couple are actually members of your Bowls Club.' Then he added with a smile...'but naturally I won't be giving you their names.'

'I can appreciate that. You obviously did a good job and must feel satisfaction closing the case with such a gratifying result.'

'Yes, but I heard something not so good yesterday... a bit more from my pal Bert at the Nick about what they call 'the peeping Tom case'. The guy phoned the school again and said how he enjoyed seeing the girls at the Baths. You can imagine how that had their Inspector wondering about you. But Bert says he's written it off as just coincidence...and there's no evidence that the guy really was in there watching the girls.'

'It's all weird, and I'm beginning...'

Abruptly conversation was ended by a call to the table where we sat down to a fish pie, with the potato topping cooked to a tempting golden brown. I had just enjoyed my first shrimp when Peggs wanted to know 'what I had been up to', which was of course a nosey into my private life.

I told her I had visited Rosemary and then she was very interested in my meeting with Molly, wanting to know if she had forgiven me for taking the pictures at the beach hut. So I had to explain about the guilt complex after lending the key to her cousin, WPC Donna Dove.

My sister stared at me in utter amazement while I enjoyed another shrimp.

'Do tell me,' she asked with deliberation, 'are you saying that those pictures you took at the hut are not of Molly but are of that young police firecracker who came into the bank asking questions?'

'Yes.'

'Then she must have known that at the time.'

'Yes, I think so...' and when they had both stopped laughing I said I didn't think Molly knew anything about the pictures and I would appreciate their silence.

'You, Jon, have friends at the Nick and I'm sure you will agree any leaked information would not only be embarrassing to the WPC, but might damage the girl's career. I've spoken to her and she will expect me to keep quiet...and I would appreciate you both doing the same.'

The meal continued in complete silence for some time until I saw Peggy lift her head with that mischievous twinkle in her eyes: 'come on Nathan, cut out the crap and tell us what's going on!'

'O.K....we have had a long chat and we've a meeting arranged for this afternoon. I said I would take her out for a spin.'

Again there was a look of sheer disbelief: 'you've got a date with that little fireball?'

'It's not been described as a date, just a meeting.'

'Well, well...there's nothing like having a satisfying look at the goods before you get to unwrap them!'

I turned to Jon: 'I think your wife's got a naughty mind...'and the meal continued, ending with a lot of laughter and teasing, mainly at my expense.

As I drove down the ramp to the car park I was thinking about the ribbing I had endured over my 'meeting', a word which my sister had repeated with cynical emphasis. Peggy had calculated Donna would be about a year younger than her and at least five or six years younger than me. Perhaps that was adding to my anxiety as I sat in the car waiting for her to arrive.

The car park was beneath the block of apartments, with a lift to service four floors. I had the first floor suite which had the front door on street level with a conservatory and a balcony at the rear, providing steps leading down to the beach.

All day I had been looking forward to the meeting... more perhaps than I could explain sensibly. When I began my wait it was exactly three o' clock and time just dragged. Thinking about it I decided I was stupid, wondering if she was going to turn up. After all, she had said we didn't know each other and she wasn't sure if she even liked me. Cars came and went, and as four o' clock approached my spirits dropped...I was an idiot.

Then I saw a young girl walking towards me, although I had difficulty in recognising her as Donna Dove. She wore pigtails sticking out on either side, no make-up, blue jeans, white trainers, a pink baggy jumper which smothered her figure, and a yellow baseball cap. The colour combination was ghastly, making her look like a rebellious teenager of about fifteen or sixteen. She was keeping to the agreement, but on her terms!

I probably looked astonished, but managed to smother a laugh as we exchanged 'hellos' and I collected my small 'chilly-bin' from the car. It was not until I had guided her through the back door onto the sands that she registered surprise: 'I thought you said we would be going for a spin'.

'Yes, we are...we'll walk up to the boatyard where I've ordered a little speedboat...not frightened of the sea are you?'

'No.' But it didn't sound completely convincing.

We were soon kitted out and when I had the engines throbbing I took the boat out of the harbour into the open sea. Donna sat beside me grim-faced. I sensed it was not fear but frustration that was upsetting her. She had gone to a lot of trouble to emphasise the gap in our ages ...perhaps to embarrass me...but now she wore a life-jacket and was covered in an oilskin and a sou'wester...her efforts thwarted.

But her expression soon changed when I moved the throttle back and the little boat lifted her nose and sped through the water, 'dancing' over some of the sea horses, throwing spray over us. I knew she was sharing the thrill and excitement as we circled to starboard then to port.

Perhaps she was a little apprehensive when I dropped anchor off one of the tiny beaches along the coast and shed my gear. 'You can take your oilskin and life-jacket off while we're here...the sun's still quite warm and I have a small bottle of wine, nicely cooled, which we can enjoy while we admire the scenery.'

And that we did while I told her about 'The Dead Smuggler's Cove': 'the story is that a long time ago a fisherman was being chased by Customs and Excise officers and escaped to the cove, knowing there was no access from the cliff top. Unfortunately for him there was a very high tide which smashed his boat against the rocks and he was stranded. He tried to climb the cliff face but fell back onto the rocks, where his body was eventually found.'

'Do you think these coves are still being used by smugglers? I have heard quite a lot of talk about it recently. Colleagues seemed convinced it's going on around here.'

'Well, I don't imagine history changes...it's just the commodity...once it was brandy...now it could be drugs, or even people.'

I wanted to tell her what a pretty girl she was, but instead I said: 'now it's time to drink up, put our kit back on and up anchor.'

'Can I drive back?'

'Firstly, that's not exactly nautical language and secondly, looking at you, you don't give the appearance of being old enough.'

'Oh dear, I asked for that didn't I?' And we both laughed.

But of course it was those lovely eyes that turned the tables on me and she got her way, with a strict promise that she wouldn't go too fast, turn too sharply, or fail to hand over before we reached the harbour entrance.

I felt sure we had both enjoyed that afternoon and as she prepared to go I got a nice warm kiss on the cheek.

'That was much better than a cold cod.'

'Only because you let me drive back...' and with that begrudging remark she left me.

For the first part of the week I spent most of my time with the owner of a nearby Country Estate, surveying his property to assess his needs for the insurance of his house, its contents, farm buildings and machinery, plus cattle, crops, and a number of vehicles. It was a very extensive inventory and I was pleased on the Thursday to have his acceptance of our terms when I treated him to lunch at his local Golf Club. He was happy with the business transacted but, when we finished off the afternoon with a round, he was very disappointed with my handicap and rather surprised and cynical when I mentioned I was better at bowls. There were documents to be drawn up and details to be finalised, but all that would be dealt with in the office, so I took the evening off to visit the Club Green where I was able to join Rosemary.

She was sitting on one of the benches where she had been watching Eva and Chloe having a practice game with Abigail and her mother Ruth...two attractive young mothers and their pretty daughters who used to greet me with friendly smiles. They had just finished their game when I joined Rosemary and, as they trooped by to go to the Pavilion changing room, it seemed to be an effort to manage a casual wave.

Rosemary said she had recovered from her injuries, and had plenty to chat about, telling me how Croft Motors had made good all damage to her car and how she enjoyed being back in the driving seat...after having it checked out by an independent engineer. I was busy talking her into joining us on Saturday for an away match when Eva, her friend, and the girls reappeared. I was pleased when Eva approached...and then dismayed when she handed me another envelope.

'I like that one even less,' she said and then flounced off.

I was surprised and speechless...pulling out a card which must have come from the same shop as the other one...virtually a sequel.

On the front was just the one word: URGES? Inside was another sketch of the guy chasing the partly clad girl into the bedroom, and then a second sketch when he was about to push her down onto the bed. Underneath were the words: 'WHEN WILL I GET THE CHANCE TO SHOW MINE?' And it was signed: 'NATHAN'.

When I handed the card to Rosemary she examined it and gave a chuckle: 'it's not really offensive, but I can understand Eva being a little upset. After fending off Tony I imagine she would be expecting you to make a more subtle and kindly approach.'

'Yes, but I've tried to tell her that I didn't send the other damn card!'

'Well, maybe the funny business that followed your trip to the Baths had her wondering if you are some kind of pervert.'

She was teasing me, in fun...but it gave me something to think about: 'gee, thanks, that's all I need!'

'You still think this is Tony's work, but I don't believe that card would be his style...I'm seeing him later so I'll test the water and make a few discreet enquiries.'

Then, in the usual friendly manner, we parted and went our separate ways.

It rained on Friday, but there was promise of a cloudy but dry day for Saturday. We had an afternoon away match arranged against Padquay, a seaside town on the north coast of the county. I was looking forward to a relaxed coach journey with the team, across the moors to their Green, situated almost on top of the cliffs, overlooking the sea. It was an exhilarating position, although I have known the wind strong enough to affect delivery of the bowls.

I had talked Rosemary into joining us and I expected her to be back in my team. In the coach she was sitting up front with our Team Captain, Tony. Arthur's wife Audrey was with Alice, a few seats back, so I went to sit with Arthur. We had been travelling for a while, admiring the scenery, when we heard mention of Roy Sinclair. Naturally, as Treasurer, I knew him...Hubert's brother...and the owner of a cabin cruiser which he used to take paying passengers across the Channel. I was aware he had applied to join us on this trip to Padquay, but knowing the demands of a seasonal business I was not unduly surprised when he hadn't turned up at the coach park. Arthur, of course, knew why.

'You're probably aware he uses his boat to take parties across to France or Holland...certainly not the shortest route but he makes it into a kind of 'booze cruise'. The boat can sleep three or four couples, so the trips are often organised for a number of days and nights.'

'Is business good?'

'Yes, he even has bookings through the big travel agents.' There was a pause while he looked out of the window.

'But you are going to tell me more.'

'Well...yes...I heard the Customs and Excise officers were down at the Marina to meet the boat when she returned from Holland...I believe they impounded her... for a short period anyway.'

'Not just a routine check then?'

'No, far from it. They took along sniffer dogs... obviously looking for drugs.'

'Did they find anything?'

'Only the usual. I think the passengers had bought bits of jewellery, cameras, wooden clog souvenirs, and of course 'duty frees', cigarettes and wine...Roy would have more than his share of fags and liquor, and a few bulbs I expect. Both the Sinclair gardens have a wonderful display of daffs and tulips every year.'

'So did the Customs and Excise chaps leave happy or disappointed?'

'Well, I think they collected some fines for the excess of fags and booze. They, like everyone else, know some of it finds its way into the local pubs and restaurants, so that would make them happy. But otherwise I would say they went away disappointed. This looked like a specific raid...with the dogs...as if they were working on a tip-off...and they didn't find what they were looking for.'

We arrived at the Padquay Pavilion in good time and, after a visit to the changing rooms, we were soon on the Green and play began. We were up against a friendly team although each side was competing keenly for three points on the league fixture table. I was delighted to have Rosemary back in my team, with Arthur and Alice, and very happy that Tony had no plans to make any last minute switches.

At times I thought Rosemary was having a struggle against a strong wind, but when that dropped she seemed to recover, as did our score. At the end of the match we were four shots ahead. Tony won on his rink with defeat on the other two. But we were very satisfied with an overall win of three shots, to take home the vital league points.

Travelling back over the moors, we stopped at the "Highwayman's Retreat" for a snack and liquid refreshment. It made a nice social break, and the quality of the food and beer was good. But when we were settling up before leaving some wit remarked that the highwayman must have left one of his offspring to take over as landlord!

I slept soundly through the night and awoke with a strange feeling of excitement...and I didn't know why. It was Sunday and I had a sense of guilt, knowing that Sonja would have got me into church. I had some office work to do and that was a real turn-off...yet the feeling still persisted. Admittedly there was a meeting arranged with Donna for the evening, but I could hardly consider that as the reason.

In the morning I took a walk along the sands, got myself some lunch, and then worked through the afternoon without interruption, apart from the odd moments when I wondered what Donna might be doing, with a sense of panic creeping in that maybe she wouldn't turn up.

When early evening came I was ready and waiting. She had my spare plastic card to operate the garage boom, so she could park and then use the stairs or the lift to the apartment. I had wondered how she would look but was still a little shocked and surprised when she stood in the doorway and then came towards me. Her appearance was difficult to describe but I supposed it would be somewhere between a nineteen-twenties 'flapper' and a modern day tart. Her hair was attractive, with a fringe, and her face, normally pretty, had received an extravagant application of rouge and lipstick. The dress folded over to give eye-catching cleavage, and ended just below the hips...only just. Beneath were the loveliest legs a chap could wish to see and I was admiring them from top to toe.

'Is it alright?' she asked, stretching her arms out wide.

'Yes, that's a nice dress...and I like your sandals...it just seems there's quite a distance between them.'

'Do you have a problem with that?'

'No, not at all...and she knew I was lying...she would have read my reactions of shock and admiration. But she was still playing a game, fighting me for trapping her into the agreement. She was being as provocative as she dared and I intended to play along and enjoy it.

I planned to take her out of Woodymouth, along the coastal cliff road to a country pub I knew which boasted a fine restaurant. Half way there was a pull-in for cars and we sat on the cliff top, talking. Donna, sitting next to me, dressed as she was, proved most disturbing. She knew it and was enjoying my discomfort. But I was beginning to find her a lovely companion. She said she was a 'townie' and was eager to learn about the county and the countryside, in particular the seaside way of life. She was appreciating the view of the open sea and, to keep my eyes away from the cleavage and the bare legs, I enthused with her.

I learned she had a Mum and Dad and brother in Birmingham, and after passing through Police College had been sent to Woodymouth. She was sharing a flat with another WPC, and when I asked her about men friends she said she was keeping them at arm's length... a remark which had me speculating

As we approached the pub I just hoped we wouldn't meet my secretary, Paula, or anyone else from the office. Our arrival created some confusion as the maître d' didn't quite know what to make of us, then politely ushered us into a quiet alcove. I thought that would frustrate Donna, but when the waiter came she immediately set about flirting with him, all the time watching my reactions. For starters we had iced melon balls and she taunted me: 'if I drop one of these down the front of my dress I hope that waiter will come quickly when I scream!'

But after he had brought us both some delicious lobster thermidor, and we had sampled the wine, her play acting dropped away and the real Donna Dove began to appear. She was chatting away to me quite happily, making it a most enjoyable evening.

We resisted the rich display of sweets and finished the meal with coffees. Then, when the waiter brought the bill on the usual silver plate and I paid, I was surprised that Donna had hidden her face behind the large menu.

'Don't tell me, you've decided you want a knickerbocker glory with extra cream!'

'No, it's our Inspector, just come in with his wife, two tables away, and he's facing this way.'

'Oh, well, we have met, so I'll ask him to come over and meet you!'

Then came the soft, pleading voice: 'I know you wouldn't do that to me...please think of something.'

'OK. I'll go and talk to him to block his view and then you can nip into the loo...if he catches sight of your legs, as you pass, he'll never notice your face.'

The plan worked and we met in the car park. As she stood close to me I realised that the rouge and the extra lipstick had disappeared. As she put a warm kiss on my cheek I noticed the faint scent of gardenias, making me want to take her in my arms...but she stepped back to allow me to open the door: 'that was for being an angel and saving me from the Inspector.'

For a few moments, as we travelled, she was silent, but then began to ask me questions about Sonja. With Peggy working in the bank with her cousin Molly she knew all about the tragedy, but she was interested to hear about our marriage. I told her how happy it had been and then she confided in me.

'I've known love...heartache...and two Christmas's ago, deceit...when I found a boyfriend was playing away, with a lovely wife at home. That put me off men... I've been keeping them at arm's length ever since.'

'Oh, really. I would never have guessed.!' But she ignored my sarcasm.

'Of course, you probably know, Molly was cheated, but she's forgiven her fella and taken him back on a kind of trial basis. I could never do that...any affection I had for my scab of a friend is gone... dead in the water.'

When we reached the apartment block I drove down the ramp, operated the boom and parked...then we walked across to her car and I received another warm kiss on the cheek: 'that's for giving me a lovely evening.'

She got into her car and with a wave drove off.

CHAPTER 8

PIPPA

• • •

It was at the beginning of the week that I met Eva. I was just finishing a snack meal, sitting at the window table of my usual café, when she passed by and recognised me. I waved for her to come in, and she joined me for a coffee. The greeting was affable, but lacked the warm friendliness that she used to show towards me. I asked if she was still upset about the cards and with obvious embarrassment she admitted she had been, but emphasised it had not been just about the cards.

So naturally I asked her to explain.

'Well, it all seems to go back to the evening when Duncan won that competition. We had a nice chat on the Green, and you asked me to give you a ring, for us to see each other again. But I never contacted you because of your telephone messages to Mother and the school. And then you...'

'Just a minute, I must interrupt because I don't know anything about these messages...what were they?'

'Well, you phoned up when I was at work and spoke to Mother. You introduced yourself as Nathan Squires... I had mentioned you to her...and explained you were a new friend, hoping soon to become an intimate one, or something to that effect, which Mother thought was offensive. Then you phoned the school and said you were a close acquaintance of mine and, as you would be passing the school in the afternoon, would call to take Chloe home. They have strict rules about messages like that, so her teacher contacted Mother, then me, and I denied all knowledge of such an arrangement. The school was intent on advising the police, but I asked them to leave it as I would be speaking to you.

This information was coming as a dreadful shock to me, but I chose not to interrupt as I could see she wanted to continue.

'As it happened, of course, I saw you when you came to the Baths, on that 'ladies only' session, but we didn't speak because the police girl ushered you away …coming back to me with a strange story that my father had asked you to come to the Baths to see me. Later I learned that two plain clothes policemen had taken you home…it was all very upsetting and confusing…and next day I received the first of the two cards. On its own I would have accepted it as a joke, but it came as the last straw.'

'This is all a very serious revelation, Eva. I can assure you I did not make those phone calls to your mother or the school and, as I've already said, I did not send the cards. Somewhere there is a sick hoaxer trying to hurt me, trying to turn friends against me, and I am sorry for any trouble this has caused you. Please let me know of anything peculiar happening in future and if necessary we will refer it to the police.'

She seemed reassured and sympathetic, and wondered who the culprit might be.

'I have only been able to think of one person and that is Tony Fairclough.'

I could see that was a surprise and after a while she shook her head, saying she didn't believe it could be him: 'he might be fond of a joke, but there was something nasty about those phone calls and I don't think Tony is like that.'

'I wondered if he was trying to keep us apart.'

'It's true he wasn't happy when we broke up, but he wouldn't be vindictive about it...we are still good friends...and since you have managed to clear the air I really do hope we can be Nathan.'

I was looking across the table at a very attractive young woman with appealing blue eyes. After that evening of the competition I had been looking forward to a date with her, but some sinister hoaxer had kept us apart. I sensed the opportunity was back, waiting perhaps with gentle, open arms. But events had overtaken me, and someone else suddenly entered my mind. She was keeping me at arm's length...but she was very much there.

Standing outside the café I clasped Eva's hand in mine: 'I too want us to be friends, Eva, and when I've sorted this nasty business out we'll have a little celebration.'

As I walked back to the office I felt sure we would both be feeling disappointment and maybe wondering if an opportunity had, at that moment, been turned away and perhaps lost for ever.

The next morning I saw Rosemary. She said she had been to the bank, so called into the office while passing. Paula showed her into my sanctum and followed up

Deryck Coleman

with the coffee tray. Rosemary was looking very smart, as usual, and after crossing her legs a couple of times, quickly got around to discussing the real reason for her visit.

'There have been some startling developments over the weekend, and I want to put you in the picture before you hear some twisted rumours. You will know Roy Sinclair has a Cabin Cruiser which he uses to take parties across to the Continent, and I expect you picked up some of the tittle-tattle that was going around when we were at the Padquay game...about the boat being impounded and a search being made by the Customs and Excise officers?'

'Yes, I did hear something about that, and I understand they took sniffer dogs with them...presumably looking for drugs.'

'Well, no drugs were found, thank Heaven...but they didn't give up. On Sunday, armed with warrants, a Customs man and two police officers arrived at the two Sinclair homes, at exactly the same time, and made a search.'

'Roy's house and Hubert's...but why Hubert's?'

'I think that's because he has a share or financial interest in the boat.'

'Did they find anything?'

'Again no, but they still didn't give up. On the Monday morning I was in my office when a police sergeant presented me with a warrant to search the Quarry.'

'What happened?'

'Well, the Customs men were using their launch, bringing a dog and a policewoman to join the sergeant. They landed at our jetty and walked up the lane to where

Hubert and the sergeant met them at the entrance to the Quarry. They made a thorough search, and got our explosives man to open the store in the cave. The dog apparently got very excited but there was no discovery of what they were looking for.'

'You must feel relieved.'

'Not really, because this has left me wondering why they were suspicious. Naturally I've had an angry session with Hubert, who claims to be innocent, denying all knowledge of any kind of smuggling, but I'm not entirely convinced. This has opened up an old can of worms. Before Will died he had a dreadful row with Hubert and it has made me think back. Had he found out something? And did it bring about his death?'

'That must be worrying for you.'

'Yes, very, and I'm starting to worry for my own safety, remembering one or two accidents with the car. I believe I told you I had an engineer to check it, but unfortunately that was after Croft Motors had put the faults right. He said it was his belief, from his inspection, that the faults could only have happened through gross negligence or malicious intent.'

'Are you going to take action against Crofts?'

'Regrettably, no...he says he expressed his belief or opinion in good faith as a kindly warning to me, but feels certain it would never be accepted as evidence in a Court of Law.'

As she stood up to leave she embraced me, with thanks for listening.

'I'm still seeing Tony quite often, but I felt he's too close to the Sinclairs for me to talk over my problems with him.'

'That's OK...any time. I'll be happy to lend an ear, but meanwhile I suggest you think about having a chat with a solicitor.'

She left saying she would probably do that.

After she had gone I had a client to see. When I'd sorted out his problems I handed the papers over to Paula to deal with and then sat back to think about the information received from Rosemary. It was startling news that the Customs and Excise should have suspicions that the Sinclairs might be smuggling some commodity from the Continent ... setting her off whittling whether her husband Will had discovered something that might have precipitated his death. Not a happy thought for the poor young woman when she was worrying about car accidents happening to her after she took over the firm.

Tony had suggested that misfortune seemed to go with her job. Surely not just by coincidence? Then, of course, Will had another job, Treasurer of the Bowls Club. And there had been a number of strange things happening to me, like weird phone calls, since I stepped into the dead man's shoes. Could that be more coincidence?

Further contemplation was prevented by a business call, and the day continued in its usual pattern. Next morning, however, there was a very agitated call from Arthur asking if I could come to the Pavilion. When I asked why he said he thought there may have been a break-in and he had called the police. It was not yet nine o' clock and my staff were only just arriving, but when Paula came I explained my intentions and set off for the Green which is just a few minutes walk away.

I expected to find hushed concern about burglars having entered our property, but instead there was a heated argument between Arthur and his wife, Dominic, and an embarrassed matronly lady, Nina Holstead. Dominic kept shouting that he was in charge of the Pavilion and should be allowed to get on with his job, while Arthur was yelling that he had called the police and nothing should be done until they arrived.

I was amazed to see that our Groundsman had a black eye, and thought it quite incredible that Arthur would have dared to do that. There was further surprise when a constable arrived with WPC Donna Dove. When introductions were made I couldn't resist remarking to the WPC: 'oh, it's nice to see you again, now that you've got your uniform back on,' which was answered by a puzzled stare from the constable and a scowl from the WPC.

After the constable had been taken to inspect the broken window he had a few words with the WPC and then we all went into the ladies' changing room. When Arthur exclaimed: 'bloody hell!' I think he was speaking for all of us.

The room looked as though it had been trashed by a team of expert vandals. One of the locker units had been dislodged from the wall to fall and crush the table, and in the process had burst open many of its lockers to disgorge their contents of shoes, socks, shirts, and other more personal items of underwear. The broken window had sprayed glass fragments everywhere, and a milk bottle was lodged in the cracked toilet bowl which was dribbling water over the floor.

I was not surprised when the WPC took charge of the situation, and asked why the police had been called to what was clearly a Club matter, there being no evidence of a break-in and much testimony to some kind of 'domestic' quarrel. Arthur offered his apologies for calling them, and Dominic said he could explain what had happened.

So we left the scene of the wreckage and moved into the main hall where the floor was dry. Dominic said he and Mrs. Holstead had a late evening coaching lesson (whereupon the lady's cheeks showed bright pink) and they were discussing certain items in the changing room when Amy Peters burst into the room brandishing a milk bottle. He said she probably mistook him for an intruder and threw the milk bottle, which grazed his cheek on its way to the window, where it broke the glass and then dropped into the toilet bowl. He explained that, recoiling from the shock, he and Mrs. Holstead fell against the table, damaging the locker unit and making it fall and empty its contents.

It was the constable who spoke: 'what happened then? Why did you leave everything?'

'Mrs. Holstead was very upset...being a widow living on her own...I had to see her home. I came early this morning to sort things out...and she must have thought the same and came too. If Mr. Russell and his wife hadn't arrived so early we would have set about putting things right.' Arthur kept quiet.

Everyone had listened in silent amazement to Dominic's story. It sounded a likely one, yet I felt sure each one of us would have doubts about its authenticity, thinking of our own version. I recalled what I had seen, some weeks ago, and in my mind I put Amy Peters in my place, hearing voices, clutching the milk bottle, then peering into the ladies' changing room...and hell hath no fury...

The WPC suggested to Arthur that in future he should think twice before wasting police time, and then turned to me: 'I will leave you Mr. Squires, as Treasurer, to pick up the pieces. It seems there's more excitement going on with Bowls Club members than meets the eye!'

As the WPC had decreed, I was left to pick up the pieces and conferred with Dominic for a local firm to come in and get on with immediate repairs. I contacted Duncan, our Captain, and he agreed to meet me in the evening at the Green, saying that Amy was too distressed to join us. When he inspected the damage the toilet bowl was no longer dripping, the broken window had been boarded up, and all items of ladies' clothing and underwear were neatly stacked on a bench. Some order had been restored to the room, yet I sensed Duncan was unduly disturbed about what had happened. He said he had been to a Masonic Lodge meeting and when Amy realised she had left her watch in her locker she had decided to borrow his Pavilion key and come to collect it. 'She must have been very frightened to find someone in here and, of course, it was very unfortunate for Dominic to be injured as a result of her panic.'

'Yes, I can understand her being scared, but I wouldn't worry about Dominic's injury...he's a tough nut...he won't make a fuss.' I knew he had reasons not to.

From his silence I gathered Duncan was not at all happy about things and I wondered what his interpretation was. I felt sure Amy was not acting out of fear, but of sheer, jealous anger towards Dominic and Nina. I hoped his thoughts were not the same as mine.

Saturday morning gave the promise of a nice day, rather cloudy but with the sun trying to break through. We had an afternoon away match arranged at the Upper Woody Green. Although coach transport had been laid on I intended to use the car as I would be calling in at the Fisherman's Cottage on the way home.

I was pleased to receive a call from Donna saying she would be off duty on Sunday and available for our meeting as usual in the afternoon. I asked her if she would like to go sailing and she sounded delighted with the idea, stating however that the only sales she knew about had been in department stores. Then came a surprising question: 'what shall I wear?' which made us both laugh. After advice on that question I explained it would mean collecting the boat from the Cottage and meeting Peggy and Jon. She said she was quite amenable to that, and from then on the day really brightened up.

I spoke to Jon at the Upper Woody Green and was pleased to see he was recovering well from his injuries. He was still walking with a stick but looking much fitter. My team for the day was Alice, Arthur and Eva, and it was Arthur who decided to liven up the proceedings with a whispered comment to me: 'our Eva's looking especially attractive today, Nathan...I think she could be setting her stall out for you and I reckon the fruit would be very tasty.' Which remark put me off my game for the next two ends. But we soon found our form and by half time we were four shots ahead. Eva was back to her old friendliness and I hoped we would just keep it that way.

At the interval I chatted with Jon and received an invite to spend the evening with them. It was while we were talking that I looked across their hall and received a shock. I had looked into the face of a man who, some years ago, I wished I would never see again. He was wearing oily overalls, obviously still doing his old job of garage mechanic. It was just a split second recognition, before he turned away and left, but it was long enough for me to recognise the same look of hate that he had given me in the Court Room in Nottingham a long time ago. He had just been sentenced and as they led him away he shouted the words: 'you're dead, Nathan Squires!' At that time I was a free man and he was about to start a prison sentence, so after a while I forgot the threat...until that moment in the Upper Woody hall.

Although our team was away from home the main conversation and tittle-tattle was about the events of Tuesday evening back in our Pavilion. Members were asking why Dominic and Nina were in the ladies' changing room so late in the evening. What were they doing there and, of course, rumour was rife, particularly regarding Amy and the milk bottle.

Back on the Green the game continued in a very friendly though competitive atmosphere, and my team managed to preserve the lead to finish four shots ahead of our opponents. Overall the Woodymouth team scraped through for a win and there were handshakes and happy 'cheerios' all round.

Everyone had enjoyed the afternoon and as I went to meet Jon in the car park and watched our delighted team filing towards the coach, none of us had any inclination of the appalling incident that would take place just a few hundred yards from there, putting a nasty shroud of suspicion over so many of us.

The welcome mat was out for me at the Cottage and I suspected that my sister might be especially pleased to see me, having the opportunity to pump me about my 'meetings' with Donna. There were brief questions about the match and we had a laugh when I mentioned that I had left my bowls towel on the Green and someone must have 'walked off' with it during the interval...my booby prize with the big rip down the middle! They were both eager to learn what Rosemary had told me about the Customs and Excise men visiting the Quarry. Then, when we had settled into comfy chairs and Jon had poured some drinks, the inquisition began. Peggs was disappointed with the brief details that I was prepared to give, but brightened up immediately when she knew Jon had agreed to lend us their boat the next day which would, of course, give her the chance to meet Donna.

Then it was Jon who questioned me about Billy Edwards, the chap I had recognised back in their Club Room.

'You reacted as though you had seen a ghost.'

'Well, for a dreadful moment, it felt like it,' and they both listened while I explained how it all began; with a road accident and an insured car which was 'written off' and taken to the scrap yard. Then two years later there was a fatality, with a mother and child being killed, where once again my company covered the insurance. But there was something about the vehicle that bothered me so I submitted my suspicions to the police. Through their engineers it was established that it was the scrap yard vehicle which had been repaired, sold, and put on the road as a death trap. It was the C.P.S. that put Billy Edwards in prison, but he found out I was the one who had instigated the enquiries...I was the one he blamed and threatened with vengeance.

Talking with Jon I soon realised Billy had, in fact, followed me down from the Midlands, not intentionally I hoped, and he had become a partner in Croft Motors, which from details supplied by Rosemary could be a very dodgy outfit.

I stayed for the evening meal and enjoyed my sister's seafood pie baked with a cheese and potato mash. I tasted haddock, missed the shrimps, but was quite happy to find prawns instead.

Sunday had the promise of a lovely day...the sun was shining, and I was going to take Donna sailing. Mornings can drag, so I set off for a brisk walk along the Promenade, then up onto the cliff coastal path. I got back in time to snatch a quick lunch and had tidied the kitchen when Donna arrived.

Once more she stood in the doorway with outstretched arms and asked: 'will I do?' She wore a white T-shirt with pale blue stripes at the neck, with pale blue capri pants reaching just below the knees...I only knew the name because she had mentioned it when asking what to wear. Her feet were in strong sandals and she had remembered to bring a windcheater. She looked beautiful in an outfit that was practical for an afternoon's sailing, but of course it was the shape of the girl wearing the clothes that excited me.

Naturally I couldn't appear to be too appreciative: 'yes, you'll do, and those pants will be much less of a distraction than the dress you nearly wore last Sunday!'

'Huh...don't strain yourself with your compliments!'

On the way to the Cottage I asked Donna if she had been the WPC taken by Customs to the Quarry.

'Yes, they took me in their launch with Pippa, their dog. She was lovely, but quite useless, apparently. When they walked her up the lane they thought she might sniff narcotics, but she'd been trained for terrorist activities, to sniff out firearms or bombs at airports. So you can imagine how excited she got when they took her to the Cave at the Quarry where they keep the explosives.' We both laughed and I told her to tell Peggy about it.

I mentioned we would be sailing in a small sloop, if Jon had managed to get her ready for us, which was a vessel with a fore-and-aft rig and one mast on which is set a mainsail, and a single foresail or jib. I had a most attentive pupil, so continued to explain words like bow and stern, port and starboard, tiller and boom...and she made Peggs laugh when we arrived because she was still muttering the words to herself as we got out of the car.

After introductions were made Jon and I left the girls to chat while we went down the garden path to the mooring. The boat had been rigged and was almost ready for sailing. As we completed the tasks the girls were walking down the path with Peggs shrieking with laughter. The Pippa story was funny, but I knew she had just been told something which she thought far more hilarious...I wondered...

As Jon helped Donna into the boat my sister whispered: 'she's lovely, but you'll have your hands full there!'

'Well, you know my inclinations.'

'I wasn't referring to those, you idiot!'

Once aboard we moved our seating to balance weight. Then, after a push from Jon and waves and shouts, we sailed smoothly down towards the harbour mouth on the outgoing tide. Donna's immediate comment was: 'your sister's nice...I think we could become friends.'

As I negotiated a few anchored boats I was mulling over the remark: 'aren't you forgetting something... something relevant and important...like our friendship, our relationship?'

'Ah, well, there might be some hope for that,' and I was sure I heard her chuckle.

Once out of the harbour our canvas picked up an off-the-sea breeze and we were soon running on the starboard gybe along the coastline in the direction of Dead Smugglers Cove. Donna was excited by our speed, proving an apt pupil, and thrilled to handle tiller or ropes to maintain our progress even with the change of wind direction as we sailed closer to the cliffs. We had a little altercation when I said we were running on the port gybe and she had let the boom out to the starboard side. But we soon sorted that out until I told her that ropes were usually referred to as sheets!

When we reached the cove we were certainly not alone. There were two vessels anchored off shore, and the little beach was thronged with naked bodies. I guessed the boats had brought the members of a nearby Naturist Camp for a swim and a frolic on the sands. Seen from a distance, there were big tums and slim tums, big bums and smaller bums, plus all the appendages. Some jumped about playing volleyball, others stretched out in the sun. Many, including the children, were paddling or swimming. The visitors were clearly enjoying themselves but the residents were swooping down from the cliff face shrieking fiendish protest.

When we sailed fully into view the naturists waved in greeting, and before I realised it Donna had slipped off her life-jacket and windcheater and was about to peel off her T-shirt with the words: 'let's join them!' But I quickly grabbed her forearms and shouted: 'no, you are part of a team here and you just can't abandon a boat in full sail to go for a swim.' For a second those lovely brown eyes had the green glint back, then it was gone: 'I'm sorry, I didn't stop to think about it.' She put her kit back on, then helped me come about and make sail for the harbour, once again enjoying the excitement of the run.

The tide had brought us down river and most obligingly it had turned to take us back, quite swiftly, to the mooring. Jon and Peggs were waiting, and while I helped Jon to take down the canvas and put the boat back in its little house, the girls went off to prepare tea and a snack. We heard them laughing and I was so pleased that they were getting on well together. Donna told them how she had enjoyed the afternoon, and when we had said our thanks for the use of their boat we set off for Woodymouth.

Donna was quiet for the first mile, pondering I imagined on a thought, so I waited until she spoke: 'you remember when we were at the cove and I took my kit off?'

'Yes!'

'Well, I know I was out of order and you had to do your Sea Captain act.'

'Yes,' and I couldn't hide a smile.

'But because I was going to strip my T-shirt off you looked frightened or cross. I'm puzzled because you have pictures of me without any clothes on, and there was a dozen or more naked females on the beach. Why were you so bothered?'

We were just approaching a lay-by, so I pulled in. Such a vital question needed a careful answer: 'seeing you in pictures naked is one thing...but being near you without your clothes on would be something much more disturbing. We meet and spend time together under an agreement...which maybe I forced on you...and you keep me, in a way of speaking, at arm's length. That's OK, but if you break your own rules then I will want to move in close and will need more.'

Neither of us spoke for some time, then Donna broke the silence. 'Are you saying, then, that if we had a closer friendship and we happened to go to the Cove again, with no-one else there, you wouldn't object if I decided to take my clothes off?'

'If we had a closer friendship I would be delighted... provided, of course, you would be prepared for me to try and make it a more intimate one.'

'I see.'

'And that sounds a bit like your ruddy Inspector!' Which remark made us both laugh, and I drove back to the apartment car park.

She turned down my invitation to go up to the flat for a drink, or to stay for a meal, with the excuse: 'sorry, but I have to get back.' I walked with her to her car and received a warm kiss on either cheek: 'one is for that fierce Captain Bligh and the other is for the more friendly Nathan, to say thanks for giving me a lovely afternoon.'

I saw the merry twinkle in her eyes and if she had lingered I would have pulled her into my arms. But, anticipating the move, she slipped into the car seat and was soon gone.

It was still early evening and I was restive, switching back and forth from a book to the TV. I wondered why she had to get back...none of my business really, but I had to face the sorry truth, I was in love with the girl. Back at the Cottage, when we had been putting the boat to bed, Jon had been chatting and told me Donna's arrival at the Nick had turned a few heads. Most of the young coppers had tried to date her, but according to his friend Bert she was keeping them at arm's length. I had nearly added: 'she's good at that,' but kept quiet, happy with the news.

He also mentioned 'The Beach Hut Case', where the girl had been undressed and assaulted. The police had a suspect taken in for questioning, but due to an alibi, or insufficient evidence against him, he had been released. So whoever he might be he must still be about the town, waiting I supposed for another opportunity.

I went to bed and after tossing and turning for some time, had a nasty dream about Donna having to fight someone in a beach hut.

CHAPTER 9

THE DOVE

• • •

The week began full of excitement. One of our brokers phoned to say he had secured all the business for West Country Tours and would be placing it with us. The company had buses and coaches operating all over the Western Counties, and their accident and claims experience over the past five years had been excellent. We knew Head Office would approve and be delighted to accept the business.

Then my friend from the boatyard phoned to say that the little speedboat I had ordered was receiving its finishing touches and would be ready for me to collect in the morning. I was owed holiday, so immediately arranged with Paula to take the time off. Then we sailed through the rest of the day on a happy breeze.

Late afternoon when Paula brought in the letters for my signature and waited, I noticed she was grinning cheerfully and asked: 'you look happy, any special reason?'

'I suppose it's infectious. We've all noticed you've been smiling more these past few weeks and there is conjecture in the office. Is it due to these nice contracts we've been getting...perhaps because you were buying a new boat...or could it...and this is my bet...be something to do with those regular phone calls from a certain WPC?!'

I carried on signing, handed over the letters, adopted a stern face and pointed to the door crying 'out!'

Paula left with a chuckle and a parting shot: 'I knew I was right!'

In the morning I awoke early...not prepared to admit to myself that it was because I was going to collect my little speedboat. Exerting discipline, I got myself a good breakfast and then phoned Jon to tell him the news and ask if he would like to go for a spin. He said he would be delighted, so I locked up and walked along the sands to the boatyard...and there she was already afloat beneath their slipway and waiting for me. The hull was all white and the prow very low towards the water, and then there was an elegant, sweeping curve up to the wind and spray shield, which gave her the appearance of a sea nymph. There were two bright red leather seats set in a little cockpit of pale dove grey. I felt as though she was begging me to get in and drive her away.

I was thrilled, but disappointed she had no name, and my friend explained: 'you take her out for a test run, then if you're happy, bring her back and we'll have the name on ready for the weekend. We know the anchorage you're renting so we'll put her there and then deliver the inflatable. It'll be just big enough to carry two careful paddlers.' So with that advice I got into my little boat, started her up, and went smoothly out into the harbour.

The tide was flowing against me, but I cruised comfortably up to Jon's jetty, observing the strict speed limits. Jon wasn't waiting so I tied up and walked up their path, then following a shout from an open window I went straight into his office. After a brief greeting he said: 'you look like the cat that's just had a saucer of cream.'

'Yes, I suppose I feel like that, but you on the other hand look as though you've lost the cat. Is everything alright?'

'Well, yes and no. We're alright, but I've just been hearing about a nasty incident that happened at the weekend. But I won't spoil your fun...I'll tell you about it later...let's go and see this boat of yours.'

We cruised smoothly down river with the tide, then once outside the harbour I opened up the throttle and put her through her paces. Jon took over the helm and between us we checked the boat out for acceleration, speed, and stability on the turns. If I'd been giving medals she would have had a gold. So we cruised back to Jon's little jetty.

We settled into easy chairs for coffee and biscuits and then I was told about the disturbing incident at the weekend. 'You will know there is a caravan park not far from our Bowling Green. Every week they hold the Welcome Dance on Saturday night. It's a big 'splash' which is open to locals, subject to an admission fee, and a young girl called Tracey Lamb was one of those who went last Saturday with two or three other girls.

The name Tracey rang a bell, but I didn't want to interrupt Jon's story.

'Well, it was the usual thing, the girls had a lot to drink and Tracey wandered off with a young man.. She said she had a 'thick head' and accepted his offer to go into a caravan for a nice black coffee. From then on her experiences compare with remarkable similarity to what happened some weeks ago to the girl in the beach hut. The lads at the Nick reckon she was drugged and then there is a befuddled story of an older man coming to undress her. The dances at the caravan park are noisy events...ask the neighbours...so any cries of protest from the girl would go unheard.'

'What a terrible experience for her. I guess a lot of the girls drink too much and some people might claim they ask for trouble, but they certainly don't deserve to be raped.'

'Ah, now that's a weird thing about each of these cases. Bert tells me there was no trace of semen on either of the girls. They were abused undoubtedly but not raped in the sense that we understand.'

'How odd...still a horrible experience for the girls... and this makes the culprit sound like a real weirdo.'

'Well, I don't know about that, but I can tell you in strict confidence that the lads have been questioning your friend Hubert Sinclair. At the moment there's a gag on the media because Tracey's parents are away, but as soon as they return the press will be told and then everyone will be talking about it.'

'Ah, I thought the name was familiar. Is she the girl who works in the Quarry office?'

'Yes, that's right, and they've been giving Sinclair the third degree because there was once a spot of trouble with another young girl who worked with him.'

'Who found young Tracey?'

'The family which had been renting the caravan for two weeks. They were called home for a couple of days in the middle of their holiday and returned to find the lock on the van door had been forced. They went in and found the girl lying stark naked on one of the bunks.'

'A shock for them.'

'Yes, and from a forensic point of view Bert tells me the beach hut and the caravan, at the end of a busy season, were literally smothered in different finger prints.'

'What a nasty business.'

'I'm told the girl's quite traumatised although she can't recall much about what happened.'

Jon had a phone call so I left, cruising back to the yard where I was sorry to hand over my little boat, but my friend assured me he would take good care of her... and there was the small task of writing a rather large cheque!

With release of the story to the press it was soon on the streets and when I went to the Green on Wednesday evening it was the main topic of conversation. I was playing in a friendly game against Rydemouth, with my usual team of Alice, Arthur, and Eva. Arthur, on his usual form, had to draw my attention, with a whisper, to Eva looking very charming: 'she's still setting her stall out for you Nathan and you must be mad not to sample that juicy fruit!' Which remark I tried to ignore and with deference to Eva, with a pretty young daughter sitting on one of the benches with her friend Abigail, no mention was made of the girl in the Caravan Park.

When we were in the Pavilion for the interval, however, things were different and there was a hubbub of gossip about it. Everyone knew that Hubert had been questioned and that was accepted as a natural consequence of the girl working at the Quarry office, but an elderly matron had remembered about a certain Jessica working there some years ago: 'she was a flighty young thing and there was a lot of bother with her.' The lady felt free to speak as Hubert had not appeared for the game. Her comments spread, raising eyebrows and bringing forth further observations and conjectures.

In the second half of the game Eva was very quiet and off form and we realised she must be frightened by the details she had learned of those two assaults, and worrying as all mothers must be for the safety of her daughter.

We lost by ten shots to the visitors and at the end I felt I should offer some sort of comfort to Eva, but I saw her meet the girls and Abigail's mother, Ruth, and hurry towards her car. I felt distress for two frightened Mums, but I realised there was so little I could do.

On Thursday evening I had a call from Hubert asking me to meet him at the Green. Normally rinks would be available for the use of members and visitors but the gates were shut and Dominic's hut was locked up. Hubert came straight to the point: 'I expect you've heard all about the dreadful assault on young Tracey, and the fact that the police questioned me...a normal, routine procedure as the poor girl works at the Quarry office...but now they are questioning Dominic.'

'Blimey, why the hell should they suspect him?'

'Well, I don't know, but it's my personal opinion that it's linked to that rumpus the other evening in the ladies' changing room. I am told a woman has given his name to the police. They won't tell me who it is or why but I'm wondering if it was Amy Peters, acting for some reason out of sheer spite. That seemed a funny business to me, throwing a milk bottle at Dominic, thinking he was a burglar. I've had a word with Duncan but, naturally I suppose, he's very cagey about his wife's activities... must think I was brought up in a monastery. You were here when Arthur Russell called the police, what do you think?'

That was the big question. I was thinking a lot. I felt sure Amy would have been the one to 'squeal' on Dominic, but I wasn't sure about the reason any more. I had thought it was just spite but I'd been casting my mind back to the evening when I heard our Groundsman warning his 'victim' that he was preparing her for phase four, 'the rod'. Having seen him in his naked splendour I had drawn my own conclusions, believing him to be a virile young man. But my assumptions could be wrong. Jon had said there were strange facts about the assaults on the girls. Could Dominic's behaviour have a similarity? Could there be a link? I was certain Amy was the 'victim' I had seen, and almost certain she had 'shopped' him, but there was no chance she would be likely to talk to Hubert or me about it.

'You're asking me what I think...my deliberations tend to go round in a circle, so I reckon the best thing we can do is leave it to the police.' I was really dodging the question, simply because I had no wish to get involved.

I didn't know at that time that I was already horribly caught up in the whole affair.

Friday started as a normal working day and there was nothing to suggest that it would turn into a nightmare until I received the phone call. Even then I wasn't unduly worried as the Inspector seemed quite friendly, asking me to call at the police station to assist them with their enquiries. I cleared it with Paula, saying it was a Bowls Club matter. The Inspector thanked me for coming so promptly and explained that he had avoided calling at the office to save me embarrassment. It was a friendly, kindly thought, but any efforts to afford me privacy or secrecy were immediately blown apart when I almost collided with Harry Wilks in the corridor. He had just come out of one Interview Room with a Constable, and I was being led into another. Our 'minders' tried to push us apart, but not before Wilks had had his say: 'well, well, Nathan Squires...are you the one? Our Billy will be pleased when I tell him I've seen you here!'

There were more apologies for the confrontation and then I settled into a chair facing two familiar faces... the Inspector and his Sergeant. I had been asked if I wanted a solicitor present but brushed the idea aside. Then the questions began.

'Will you please tell us briefly where you were and what you did last Saturday.'

So I related my activities for the day, with some details of the bowls match at Upper Woody, and then of my visit to the Fisherman's Cottage in the evening.

'And at what time did you leave?'

'Ah...somewhere between nine-thirty and ten.'

'I see.' It was the familiar tone of voice giving me cause to think, and begin to panic, as the questions continued.

'I believe you know Mr. Hubert Sinclair.'

'Yes, of course, he's Secretary of our Bowls Club.'

'I understand you visited him in his office at the Quarry some weeks ago.'

'Yes.'

'And who did you meet?'

'Hubert, his wife Muriel, and a young girl called Tracey.'

'So you know Tracey Lamb.'

'No, I don't know her, I have only met her the once when I visited the Quarry office.'

'What was your opinion of her?'

'From just the one brief meeting...recalling my reactions...I think I would say she was rather precocious.'

'What should I understand from your description, that she was displaying her assets for you?'

'Not for me particularly, but she obviously enjoyed putting them on display.'

'Did that excite you?'

'No, and I don't like the direction of your enquiries.'

'Did you know that the girl was assaulted late on Saturday evening at the Caravan Park in Upper Woody... just a short distance from your sister's cottage...which you left between nine-thirty and ten pm?'

'Yes, I did know, but I can assure you I had nothing to do with it.'

'Then perhaps you can explain this?' He produced and placed on the table a see-through bag which contained something partly wrapped up in a bowls towel. As perception of what the thing was dawned on me, I stared at it in horror and disbelief. At that moment the interview turned into a nightmare.

'That towel has your initials on it and was, I am told, presented to you as a booby prize in a competition. It is now wrapped around what is politely called a sex toy, and we have certain evidence which suggests it was used in the assault on Tracey Lamb. Do you recognise it, Mr. Squires?'

'No, I certainly don't. I lost the towel at the match on Saturday, but I have never seen the other thing. Where did you find it?'

'Hidden in a ventilation duct in the roof of the caravan. Not very cleverly concealed.'

'This is some sort of horrible frame-up, and I must now ask for Rupert Bier, my solicitor.'

When I arrived at the police station it had been quite early in the morning and the ordeal continued throughout the day. I was locked up to await Rupert's arrival and provided with coffee and sandwiches. Then I was interviewed again, with more questions and cross-examinations. I was locked up with more refreshments and then taken for finger-printing and to give a DNA sample. Then back to a cell for more waiting. It was a long agony of not knowing, and then the relief late in the evening when Rupert came with good news. He didn't say: 'you are free to go,' but just that I would be allowed to go home, so it seemed obvious I was still well framed as a suspect.

I drove home and drank much more whisky than I should have done.

In the morning I was suffering and spent the first half-hour of semi-consciousness sitting in the conservatory drinking black coffee and feeling sorry for myself. That was the usual time for Molly and Ben to walk by but presumably, on that particular Saturday morning, they had other plans. Normally I looked forward to a call from Donna, to say when she would be free for our meeting, but as I thought about it realisation dawned that she would not come. I was not familiar with police procedures but stark reality was staring me in the face; it would not be acceptable for a WPC to associate with a man under suspicion for a horrible sex crime. Our 'agreement' would be null and void and I felt a terrible emptiness.

There was a blue sky but it did nothing to lift my spirits and when I looked out over the harbour waters I saw my little boat secured to its yellow buoy, facing the flow of the incoming tide, proudly displaying her name...The Dove. Seeing her should have filled me with happy expectations, but instead there was a hungry hollowness. On the bow of the boat I could clearly see the life size motif of a dove painted in a lovely warm grey with a tinge of pink. The bird was flying forward with an olive branch in its beak...a messenger of peace and deliverance. As I looked, I thought what a bloody laugh that was. For some time, just above it, a live seagull had been perched on the prow and I noticed that even that gave a plaintive cry as it flew off.

When the phone rang it was bad news. The caller was my Area Manager expressing concern that I had been questioned by the police 'over some unsavoury crime in a caravan park'. I was shattered that he should know and dismayed to learn that some unfriendly person had passed on the information to Head Office on the previous day, which had then been relayed to him. Until that moment I believed we shared a happy business relationship. I was disturbed and annoyed that such knowledge had been fed in to my Company where it could do much damage to my career prospects. The informant was also aware that it had, in fact, been the second interrogation!

At first my boss suggested he should come down to Woodymouth to discuss the matter, but when I assured him it had all been an unhappy misunderstanding he seemed pacified and prepared to leave me 'to get the matter cleared up'. So far, so good I thought, but with a horrible feeling of dread that there could be more bad news waiting around the corner.

My second call was from Hubert, at his most pompous: he had noticed my name was down to play in the friendly match against visitors from Rodset and, if I wished to miss the game, Tony would provide a substitute. Naturally I was annoyed and told him I had no intention of dropping out but, as he was still in grandiose mood, I agreed to meet him half an hour before play for a discussion.

I was sufficiently recovered to face lunch and then walked along the Promenade to the Green. Hubert and Tony were both in the Pavilion waiting for me and our imperious Secretary immediately began to express his concern about the unseemly rumours that seemed to be spreading about my 'detention' at the police station the day before. I knew I was an innocent man, and was aware that both he and Dominic had been questioned, so in my mind they were possible suspects. But apparently, in the current story, he had only been interrogated because the girl Tracey worked in his office, and Dominic had been quizzed about the broken window incident, which clearly left me in the proverbial. I was not sure of Tony's reaction to that, but I had a sneaky feeling he was enjoying my discomfort.

Once more I claimed it was all an unfortunate misunderstanding and was adamant about my intention to play in the arranged game. Reluctantly they agreed and I joined my usual team of Alice, Arthur, and Eva. The visitors were very friendly...good players...so we were soon engaged in what should have been a very competitive and enjoyable match. But whilst I found it hard to believe, it was not difficult to recognise, as the game progressed, that the 'unseemly rumours' Hubert had mentioned must have been spread, and were still mushrooming around the Green.

Eva played well, but had once more drawn away from me. It would seem we had a strange kind of 'hot and cold' friendship. Arthur noticed and whispered: 'you've missed your chance there, Nathan...all that nice fruit gone...I think she's shut up the stall!' Alice seemed unusually reserved, but that was understandable as I knew she was a close friend of Arthur's brother-in-law, Harry Wilks, the chap I had met in the police station corridor, and in my book the one responsible for any nasty rumours.

At the tea-break conversation generally seemed normal, but from a few members I sensed hostility which I found hurtful. Back on the Green our play was keenly matched and on our rink we clawed back a deficit of six shots to turn defeat into an exciting finish with a draw. Overall our Club lost by three shots and the visitors' coach took them away waving happily. I was disappointed, but not surprised, to see Eva and her friend Ruth dashing off to the car park, obviously eager to avoid me. But I did speak to Rosemary who had driven in to pick up Tony to take him off somewhere.

As I stood in the car park watching everyone leave, I wondered what I was doing there. But I supposed it was symbolic...my spirits had been draining away over the past two days and I was being left alone...quite alone, as Peggs and Jon were away for a few days.

I set off to walk to the village of Merton, to a little pub which is usually used by one or two of my friends. But there was no sign of them, so I had a meal and one or two drinks, and walked back to the apartment. I was trying to chase away the blues, but recent events kept pervading my thoughts. When I started on a nightcap I began a mental list of the things that had happened, or that some nasty minded person had made to happen, to invade my happy lifestyle.

My problems seemed to date back to when I was showing an interest in Rosemary and hoping for a date with Eva. Tony Fairclough had been pleased to 'switch' them away from me at the beginning of the matches. But was he behind the hoax phone call I received leading me to the Swimming Baths...which brought in the police with questions about my watching the schoolgirls and my possible involvement in the assault on the young girl in the beach hut? If so, why did he want to incriminate me?

The vital question coming to my mind, who was the pervert assaulting that young girl? Of course, I had been witness to a rather kinky charade involving Dominic and a female friend.

Later came what Eva's mother described as an offensive call to her, and another hoax message to the school suggesting that I would be calling to collect Chloe. Tony has the reputation of being a Joker, but those calls had a nasty ring to them. Somebody really meant to cause trouble. At about that time the cards were sent which offended Eva, and any plans I may have had to form a close relationship with her were killed off, stone dead.

But WPC Dove burgled her way into my affections and for the second time in my life I was in love. Then came the shocking assault on the young girl, Tracey, in the Upper Woody Caravan Park. Hubert had been questioned over that, but who hid the sex toy wrapped up in my bowls towel so that the police would find it? Then came interrogations...information to Head Office... unsavoury rumours spreading to my Area Manager and at the Bowls Club.

Obviously some bastard was trying to destroy me and I was very angry because I didn't know who it was, man or woman...and because he or she was going to rob me of someone who had become very dear to me. I couldn't allow her to be dragged down with me.

When I looked at the whisky bottle I realised that once more I had drunk far too much. I almost fell over taking my trousers off, but after a slight struggle managed to tumble into bed.

I slept soundly but when I awoke there were demons banging away in my head. I had not expected to hear from Donna, hence my surprise when she came and we stood staring at each other. Me, unshaven, unkempt, with tousled hair, still in my shorts...she, looking beautiful in a summer dress.

After the gawp came her exclamation: 'bloody hell, you look dreadful!'

'Thank you, I feel dreadful, and I want you to know this is your opportunity to turn around and go.'

'I couldn't leave a dog looking as sick as you do. Go and sit down and I'll mix you something to try and bring you back to life.'

I saw her break an egg into a glass, add sauces from my food cupboard, and then whip it up into a foul-tasting brew...standing over me while I knocked it back.

'That was horrible.'

'Well, I enjoyed it...now you go and have a shave and a shower and get dressed. When you come back I'll have some strong black coffee waiting.'

When I returned to the table the demons had stopped banging and I received praise for my efforts.

'That's better, you look almost human again.'

Then we sat facing each other across the table as we had done some weeks ago, but this time the mood had changed. We were drinking coffee and instead of planning further meetings I was preparing to end them: 'I've been thinking about our "agreement" and I'm telling you it is over...null and void.'

'I see...why?'

'Well, as you said a few weeks ago at this table, you didn't know if you even liked me. I've been thinking along the same lines for myself, with doubts about my feelings for you. After careful reflection I've decided we're not suited or compatible, so I think it would be better if we stopped seeing each other.' The words were painful to me and I almost betrayed my true feelings with a slight catch in my voice, but hopefully she hadn't noticed.

There was a long silence before she spoke: 'well, they were harsh, cruel words, which came as a shock... I was getting the impression you felt otherwise, but if that's what you want, so be it.'

It was my turn to be shocked and as I looked into moist eyes I could see no sign of a green glint. I had expected her to be angry, but apparently she was quite content to terminate our relationship. Presumably I was the idiot thinking that ending it would matter.

She stood up and spoke quite calmly: 'I understand how you might feel, but we've had some happy times together, so I would like to stay with you for an hour or two and then we can end that silly agreement this afternoon...OK?'

'Yes, alright I suppose. Do you have plans?'

'Yes, we'll clear up here and then I'm going to take you to Church.'

'To Church!?'

'Yes, my mother always told me: 'if you have big problems don't sit around feeling sorry for yourself but get down on your knees and pray, preferably in a church. You have big problems, so that's where we're going.'

'Did your mother ever say you were a bully?'

'No, but my brother did, lots of times...let's go.'

She took me in her car to the quaint little church in the village of Merton.

We walked through a lichgate covered in roses, then up a short path to be greeted by Handel's Largo played quite well on the organ. Donna explained that the lady vicar was a friend of hers. She gave a welcoming and encouraging sermon, and I did pray for help and guidance. Then Donna persuaded me to join her in Holy Communion. We knelt side by side to receive the sacrament and I remembered guiltily that the last time had been too long ago...with Sonja.

Sitting in the pew after the final prayer, when the congregation began filing out into the churchyard, Donna held me back until we were alone and then she spoke, just above a whisper: 'look at me, Nathan, and tell me here in this church what your feelings are for me.'

When I looked into her eyes I knew I had been trapped: 'you were quite right about your impressions. I have grown very fond of you...I love you and want to take you in my arms and hold you there, but it is because of those feelings that I believe we should stop seeing each other. Someone is trying to destroy me, and before I can stop him or her, I feel sure there will be more trouble. I could be dragged right down, and I don't want to pull you down with me.'

Her eyes were moist, and for moments she looked away towards the altar. Then, when she stood up, she spoke with a slight tremor: 'I know when you've made up your mind it would be difficult for me to try and change it...so let's go...I'm hungry.'

When we got back into the sunshine the vicar was still waiting to have friendly words with us, but I think she recognised that we were emotionally uptight and settled for a handshake and her good wishes: 'hope to see you again soon.'

As we went through the little gate I suggested we could go to the pub I visited the previous evening, but

Donna insisted on driving me home and showing off some culinary skills by producing a delicious cheese, bacon and apple omelette. When I praised her for her efforts I had to ask, perhaps unkindly, if she was trying to demonstrate some of the delights that I was turning my back on.

'No...I needed to get you back to the apartment because if this is our last day together I want a trip in that little boat that you've got out there in the harbour, tied to that yellow buoy.'

'Ah...so you've seen her...when was that?'

'Well, Molly noticed it when she walked by with Ben yesterday morning.

She called me and we came down together as I was eager to have a look. You would be at your bowls match. 'Please...please...can we go for a spin?'

She knew, of course, I wouldn't be able to deny the pleading in her voice and the hint of tears in her eyes: 'yes, I suppose so.'

All the signs of tears vanished and she became excited: 'good...we'll make it a trip to remember.'

So we launched the inflatable and paddled carefully out to The Dove where Donna insisted on admiring her 'close up'. I unzipped the waterproof sheet over the cockpit and when we had clambered aboard I swapped the ropes over to free The Dove and leave the inflatable secured to the buoy. There were oilskins and life-jackets stowed away under the seats and when we were ready I noticed Donna tucking away a towel she had borrowed from my bathroom.

'Hope you don't mind but I brought it along just in case.'

I didn't ask 'in case of what?' but I had my suspicions.

Once the engine was throbbing we were soon out of the harbour and both enjoyed the excitement of the wind and spray on our faces as I moved the throttle and The Dove lifted her nose and sped over the open seas. We were going in the opposite direction from The Dead Smuggler's Cove but when I allowed Donna to take over she turned about and, with easy curves to starboard and port, continued on course to the cove. She was thrilled to be in control of direction and speed, and cut the engine so that The Dove seemed to glide to a quiet rest just about a hundred yards off shore.

'I wouldn't dare to take her in,' she said, 'those rocks scattered about look nasty.'

'Quite right,' I agreed, 'they could make it dangerous for swimming too.'

On a normal afternoon we would have been chatting away quite happily, but as this was to be our last meeting there was a long silence until Donna stripped off her oilskin and life-jacket and, ignoring my warning, announced she was going to have a swim.

'Have you got a costume beneath that dress?'

'No...will that bother you?'

'No...I won't look.' But of course I did.

When you share a two-seater boat with a lovely girl and she stands up and makes her dress drop to the deck, you must look. A beautifully sculptured package was being unwrapped before me and when she stood, naked, with two smoothly rounded buttocks within kissing distance, asking: 'will you join me?' I was forced to look, stare, and study her vibrant body.

My answer was meant to be defiant: 'no...but you go...and do be careful of those rocks.'

It was agonising for me to just let her slip over the side and swim around the boat, then watch as she swam between the sharp rocks to the shore. Then as she walked up the beach she turned and waved, and a gull swooped down and screeched its protest.

I dropped anchor, and when I looked back to the beach Donna was sitting on a rock with her feet dangling in the sea which kept ebbing away then frothing and flowing around them. Instantly I recalled seeing Renoir's masterpiece of the 'Blonde Bather', where he had painted his young wife in a similar pose, capturing the full beauty of her voluptuous body in a softly blended colour frame of the sea breaking against the rocks. Donna was not blonde, but she was just as naked and just as beautiful, and as I gazed all my resolves crumbled. It was simply a case of body over mind.

I was stripped, over the side, and swimming through rock channels within seconds, and as I splashed out of the water Donna was on the sands walking down towards me.

'For a terrible moment I thought you wouldn't come.' And then she was in my arms and our pent-up emotions just seemed to explode.

We were still clinging together as I carried her up the beach and we dropped down onto the soft sand. The gulls were screeching their protests at our invasion, but I was oblivious because Donna was eagerly welcoming mine.

CHAPTER 10

MISSING UNDERWEAR

• • •

I drove into work with the Monday morning blues. My spirits should have been on high, but instead they were down in the dumps. Last week they went on a roller coaster ride...up with the excitement of taking delivery of The Dove...down with the news of the assault on Tracey...Then up, up, up when Donna came and we went to the cove...and the beautiful excitement that followed.

When I took her in my arms there was a kind of emotional eruption, followed when we ignored the screeching of the gulls by tranquillity with our naked bodies absorbing the afternoon sun. With my lips and tongue I made a very pleasurable exploration, starting with proud breasts and nipples, and working my way down until I found that little heart-shaped birth-mark, almost hidden away. Donna lifted me up to float on cloud nine and apart from the gulls we spent a heavenly afternoon, alone in a world of our own.

I had ignored my ideas of not seeing her again, thinking we had both found a new love and happiness that would surpass all that. But when we got back to the apartment Donna's words acted like a blowtorch on that heavenly cloud. It evaporated and I came down to earth with a bump.

'It has been a wonderful day and I will treasure the memory, but as you said the agreement is now null and void. It will be better if we stop seeing each other.'

At first I was speechless, but then I managed to find my voice: 'taking me to church, what was all that about?'

'I thought you needed to come off the whisky bottle and get down on your knees...and there was something special I needed to know.'

'Those wonderful moments on the sands, I can't forget them, didn't they mean anything to you?'

'Yes, they meant everything. I want you to know there has really only been one other man in my life and he left me something to treasure for all days, and in a similar way you will leave me very happy memories.'

I thought there was a revelation there that seemed to conflict with everything she had told me about herself, but I was given no time to challenge her remarks before she continued.

'Anyway, it was your suggestion in the first place that we should stop seeing each other. I am only agreeing and complying with your wishes.' With those remarks she left the apartment, and a few minutes later I heard the faint sounds from below of a car going through the parking barrier.

I was shattered, but as she had said that had, in the first place, been my idea, my intention. So, I would just have to accept it, and I continued on my way to the office. Yesterday with Donna, the roller-coaster had climbed to the very top facing the Heavens, but it had hurled downwards...to stand empty at the bottom.

I was late. Everyone had settled into their desks and when I walked through I sensed that something was wrong. I got the usual 'good morning's' but I felt there was a strange quietness. At the start of the day there is usually a bit of chatter about yesterday, how it affected them and what the boy- or girl-friend said, but as I walked through any discussion seemed to turn to a hush. So I called Paula, and when she entered my office and closed the door I knew she was embarrassed about something.

I made a gentle approach: 'when I came through the office I sensed there was something wrong...have you any idea what it could be?'

'Well...yes...I think it is to do with a phone call we had this morning from a woman asking if we were expecting you in.'

'Oh...is that so unusual?'

'No, but she said she knew you had been held by the police on Friday and thought you were being interrogated about the assault on the girl at the Upper Woody Caravan Park. She wanted to know if you were still being held by the police or if you would be back in the office today. Naturally everyone found the news rather upsetting.'

It was obvious this was another attack...hitting at my office staff. So I had to put up some defence. I arranged with Paula to gather the staff together at the rear of the office for me to have a talk with them. They were all unusually quiet when I told them that the phone call was one of a series that had been made to tarnish my character, my good name. I said, yes, I had been questioned by the police, not once but twice, in connection with the assaults on the young girls, the one at the beach hut and, more recently, the one at Upper Woody Caravan Park.

But, I tried to stress, I had nothing to do with either crime and I was the victim of a malicious hoaxer. 'There is someone, somewhere, man or woman,' I said, 'trying to destroy me,' and I appealed to them for their support and faith in my innocence. After that the meeting broke up and I went back to my office hoping they might believe me, but I knew seeds of evil had been sown.

I questioned Paula about the woman caller, asking her about her voice, if she spoke with a local or an out-of-county accent. But Paula apologised that it was one of the junior members of staff who took the call, and she was too surprised and alarmed by what the woman said to notice any particular details of that nature. Paula was also very upset she had not been able to stop the news spreading around the office.

I settled down in the hope that the rest of the afternoon would be spent on normal, routine office matters, but it was a forlorn hope. I sensed a strange atmosphere in the outer office whenever I was obliged to leave my desk to speak to someone. I was also apprehensive whenever my phone rang, fearful that it might be Head Office or my Area Manager in receipt of some further scurrilous information.

It was actually about four o' clock when my boss did ring, and I was slightly relieved when he said: 'I'm only checking that you are sorting out your personal problems, and if you would like me to come down and have a chat about things I shall be quite happy to do so.'

That was the last thing I wanted, knowing how upset he would be if told about the latest call to the office. I shrank from the thought of him questioning one or two of my younger, more impressionable members of staff. But once more I was able to pacify him that I had matters 'well in hand'. It was an ambiguous statement as I had no wish to frighten him with the knowledge that things were getting worse by the day, and had become so serious, in fact, that I deemed it necessary to seek help from the local 'private eye'.

I had discussed my problems with Jon on a number of occasions and I was hopeful that, given time, he would be able to dig up some answers. He and Peggs had returned from a short holiday in Scotland, so before I left the office I phoned to invite myself to an evening meal at the Fisherman's Cottage.

I was relaxing with Jon and Peggs in one of their comfy chairs, looking out onto a fast-moving incoming tide, watching once more some cormorants diving to catch their supper as it swam in from the sea. I was sipping an apéritif, anticipating with pleasure the meal to come later. Across the water was the little hamlet of Woodycoombe, nestling beneath the cliffs, which boasted a café famous for its cockle and cream teas... both local products...to be eaten quite separately of course, the cream with home-grown, seasonal fruits such as strawberries or raspberries. I had planned to take Donna, but I couldn't imagine going on my own.

It was Peggs' voice that brought me back to reality. 'Nathan, let's hear about your tangle with the law, and I don't mean what you've been getting up to with Donna. We'll get the gen on that later. We know all about the horrible assault on the girl at the Caravan Park, but we're anxious to learn how you became involved.'

So I told them about being questioned by the police, and how my bowls towel had ended up linking me to the crime. They were both shocked, and wanted to know more about what was happening to me. They already knew about the early events, the hoax call that took me to the Baths on 'ladies day' and the consequent involvement with the police, so I gave them details of all the other calls, including the latest one to the office. I mentioned meeting Harry Wilks at the police station, and how this had led to some nasty rumours spreading at the Bowls Club.

I turned to face them. 'As I have said before, it all seemed to start as a hoax, a bit of a joke, but it has become more serious and sinister each time something has happened. I have begun to fear what the next prank will be. My character and reputation are slowly being torn to shreds.'

Then it was Jon who took over the conversation. 'It is quite obvious that all these hoaxes and phone calls have taken this well beyond a joke. You said in the first place that your suspect was your team captain, Tony Fairclough. Well, I have been doing a little research into his lifestyle, but don't feel I have found anything to put him firmly in the frame. You'll already know he is a womaniser, an addicted gambler, and very fond of a joke or prank. A lot of this information was available to us when we were investigating the death of old man Fletcher. Fairclough had been responsible for some minor 'accidents' to the poor chap, but there were never any charges brought, and they were all dismissed as pranks. Then he milked his firm's business and gambled some of their money away, but again there were never any charges brought because his aunt, Muriel Sinclair, moved in and paid off all his debts.'

'Blimey, it seems 'the mouse' has quite a roar... sorry, I couldn't help butting in with a private thought... please carry on.'

'Well, while it would seem your bowls colleague is a bit of a lad, I can't see why he would want to destroy your character. It is true we weren't too happy about some of the tricks he carried out on old man Fletcher, but unless he is some kind of obsessive joker and prankster he doesn't seem to have a motive to put him in the frame as your culprit.'

'Well, I just thought he went on the offensive when I began to show an interest in Eva Sheen, his ex-girlfriend.'

'But didn't you say he had switched his affections to Rosemary Fletcher?'

'Yes, and Eva doesn't think he's a really nasty one.'

'Well, we won't give up on Tony Fairclough, but I've been concentrating on two other characters. Firstly, Harry Wilks, now one of your Club members and, of course, I had dealings with him when Fletcher's body was found in the quarry. He definitely has form, and from what you said he was eager to spread it around that you were in for questioning at the police station.'

'Yes, and in view of his record I have always been surprised at Sinclair being so eager to get him re-elected into the Club.'

'Maybe the reason, once more, dates back to Fletcher's death.'

'What are you suggesting, some kind of blackmail?'

'Could be, but we shouldn't delve back into that now...let's continue. My second interest has been in the half brother, Billy Edwards, one of our Club members. I find it intriguing that whilst Wilks was tied in with the quarry death Billy, according to what that engineer chap said, might have been trying to cause a fatal accident to Fletcher's widow...could have...or was it just dodgy maintenance work on the car?'

'According to what Rosemary said the faults may have been made with malicious intent, although it was then too late to prove it.'

At that moment it was my sister who butted into the conversation. I was surprised she had kept quiet for so long.

'This is all interesting stuff, showing how these two chaps may be connected to the death in the quarry of poor old Will, with a suggestion now they may be trying to kill off his widow, but how relevant is it to Nathan's present problems?'

'Well, I was getting around to that,' Jon said with a grin, knowing as I did that his wife couldn't stay silent for long. 'I have received some very useful information about the two of them. It has come from my pal Bert at the Nick, but he says there is someone there on the force working like a beaver to help him dig up the dirt for us. We know both these chaps did time, and he tells me that at one stage Harry Wilks and Billy Edwards were together in the same cell block and they both got beaten up in the showers by a prison gang.'

Peggs was listening and kept silent, allowing Jon to continue.

'According to Bert's colleague the gang boss used to live with the woman, and was father to the girl, killed in that accident with the dodgy car. They would know how Billy was responsible for their deaths, and by association his half brother would be equally unpopular. Prison records are not always readily available, but Bert has been told that Billy and Harry were very badly beaten and spent quite a while in the hospital wing. The exact nature of the injuries isn't known but Bert says they are hoping to get details.'

Peggs just had to burst in: 'so what do you think?'

'We feel...I have discussed this with Bert...they had a lot of time to brood and could have come out of prison with an overdose of hate in their twisted minds. As Nathan has said, it was the C.P.S. that put Billy away but he knows it was Nathan who started them on their investigations. And it could be Nathan he blames for his suffering.'

I think Peggy and I thought Jon had made excellent progress with his enquiries, but we were both a little shocked by the revelations. I desperately wanted to know who it could be, man or woman, who was trying to destroy me and Jon, with the help of colleagues, was pointing a very strong finger at a likely suspect, possibly assisted by his half brother. Proving it, and bringing them to justice, would be a problem.

The police were trying to solve the crimes of assault on two young girls and I had been questioned as a suspect ...not just once, but twice. So could I turn to them? Would they be interested in any story I presented, of someone making hoax calls etcetera, in an attempt to damage my character? We discussed all these points and Jon suggested we should wait awhile to allow him to come up with some sort of plan. Peggs stopped further discussion with a call to the supper table.

We sat down to cold chicken which I was told had been crock roasted. It was served with salad and new potatoes, and a stuffing that had a really distinctive flavour of almonds. I was just savouring that when my sister began her usual inquisition.

'Now big brother I want to hear all about Donna and what you two have been getting up to.'

So I confessed how I had got depressed, hit the bottle, and decided in Donna's interests it would be best if we stopped seeing each other...and I had told her so... when she came to the apartment.

'But she insisted we spent the afternoon together. It was wonderful and I felt Donna had given me hopes for the future. But when we got back, much to my surprise, while I had given up on the idea of a break she had accepted it, and she just left.'

After that they seemed to be stunned and we completed the meal in silence. Then Peggy spoke: 'I'm surprised, as you say, she just left you. When she was here I liked the girl, and I thought we were going to have a mutual friendship. She told me you had started with a very strange relationship, but over the weeks she had fallen for you. She told me not to tell because there were complications at home making her want, for the moment, to keep you dangling. I felt sure of her sincerity for the first part, but more than puzzled by the rest of it.'

Then she looked at me with a saucy, challenging grin: 'did she keep you...?'

'I am going to ignore your misinterpretation of her words, but to satisfy your insatiable curiosity I will confess. We made love on the sands at the Cove and I thought we had found happiness together...something to overcome all my problems, but she still left me. Seeing that you're squeezing out confessions, I'm in love with the girl, and I'm going to miss her like hell.'

It was Jon who came back into the conversation. 'Try to realise, Nathan, as you have been questioned about assaults on the girls, both serious sex crimes, Donna's friendship with you would compromise her job in the Force.'

'So she is really breaking off our relationship to save her job.'

'No, that's not precisely what I meant...remember Bert told me there was someone there who had been assisting him to help me with my enquiries, and he said they will be working together.'

'And there's another thing,' my sister added, 'taking you to the church service seemed to me, at first, very odd. But I believe it had serious implications. Think about them. I am sure that afternoon on the sands was not just casual sex. Keep faith Nathan.'

After some sponge pudding and a coffee I went back to the apartment.

My life had changed, or rather someone had changed it for me. At the office Paula was fully supportive, but the rest of the staff seemed much more formal and reserved. When I went to the Green there was a similar kind of atmosphere. I had gone to meet members who were normally friendly and eager to have me join in for a 'roll up' with the usual six or eight players but I was finding myself left as the odd one who would, of course, drop out to find another group to join. I was getting brassed off with that, and thinking about leaving, when Rosemary arrived. She said she had only come to wait for Tony to finish his game, so we sat on one of the benches and chatted happily for half an hour. Most of the lady members seemed to be shrinking away from me, but she was proving the exception and maintaining a friendship. She had fully recovered from her injuries and said she was hoping and praying there wouldn't be any more nasty accidents.

When Rosemary left with Tony I saw that all the members present seemed to have teamed up. So I decided to leave, and call at Donna's flat. I was desperate to see her. At lunchtime I had plucked up courage to visit the police station, asking the duty officer if she was available. He had mumbled something into a telephone and then suggested I call back in about half an hour. I did that, and received a more final answer: 'sorry, sir, WPC Dove will not be available to see you.'

I had not been to the flat before but understood it was shared with another WPC and I assumed it was she who answered to my ring...quite an attractive girl, perhaps a few years older than Donna. When I mentioned my name it was obvious she knew I was a friend of her flatmate and she quickly apologised that Donna wasn't in. When I asked how soon she might be expected I was surprised when told Donna had not been living there for the past two weeks, but was commuting on a regular basis into Rydemouth where her parents were living. I asked for the address but she was sorry she couldn't give me that. She was a very friendly girl and I wondered why she hadn't invited me in, but I heard the sound of movement from within so guessed she was probably entertaining a friend.

I thanked her for the information and went home to finish some work I had started on the computer, remembering to phone Jon to see if he could track down the address of a Mr. and Mrs. Dove who had quite recently moved from Birmingham to Rydemouth.

When Saturday came I was annoyed to receive a call from Tony asking if I still wanted to play in the away match with Padquay, and if I still wished to travel in the coach laid on for the trip. I told him I was looking forward to the game and had every intention of going, adding that I thought his question was impertinent and unfriendly, becoming more angry when he said he was just trying to protect me from the unsavoury rumours that had been spreading. I didn't need to be reminded.

After a light lunch I walked to the car park behind our Green and met the rest of the team. Tony was there, ticking our names off on his list, and when the coach arrived I queued up with the others to put my bowls bag into the luggage compartment at the rear.

Then, when we set off on the very picturesque journey across the moors, I was with Arthur again. Rosemary was sitting up front with Tony, and I noticed Alice on the back seat with Harry Wilks. There was no sign of Eva or her friend Ruth, but I learned they had decided to go by car.

Arthur did most of the talking with snippets of gossip about their local Swingers Club. Leaving the coach at the Padquay car park we walked to the Green where we dumped our bowls and then went on to the changing room. We were already dressed for the game so we just had to change shoes and then go out to listen to the usual speeches of welcome. I remembered to collect my measure and chalk gun from my bag, and a new towel I had acquired.

We had played against the Padquay team on a number of occasions and I was finding them more sociable than my own team members. Eva had arrived and joined me with Arthur and Alice on our allocated rink. She managed to speak a few words of greeting before play began, but as we progressed Alice and Eva confined their conversation to the game. There was no amusing, irrelevant chatter and it was painfully noticeable. But, with the Green being situated on top of the cliffs overlooking the sea, I began to enjoy its atmosphere with opponents who were most genial hosts. On our rink the teams were well matched and the lead on the score went up and down in ding dong fashion until the tea break when the points were level.

In customary manner the teams from each of the rinks sat at separate tables, enjoying their tea and cakes. Conversation continued with some amiable criticism of the game, and a discussion of some local news, until quite suddenly it was brought to a close by Tony Fairclough. He stood up and banged on his table, asking for our attention. He began speaking, and within seconds there was perceptible silence in the hall.

'Most of my Club members will know that some nights ago there was an incident in the ladies' changing room of our Pavilion that caused the locker unit to collapse and throw out its contents of personal items. Subsequently those items...mainly underwear of an intimate nature...were left neatly stacked on a bench, to be identified and collected by the owners. Unhappily I was advised by Eva and Ruth that certain articles belonging to them had gone missing...apparently stolen.'

Interruption came in the form of giggles, some laughter, and murmurs of disbelief, until Tony continued.

'Well, I can tell you the items have been found,' and to everyone's amazement he was waving panties in the air. 'I am not pleased to be able to tell you this because I have just discovered the garments poking out of the bowls bag of our Treasurer, Nathan Squires.'

For seconds there was a hushed silence following his announcement. Then it was broken by an uproar.

CHAPTER 11

THE MIDNIGHT STREAKER

• • •

I awoke to a lovely sunny morning and decided I would try and keep my thoughts and feelings away from the black clouds of yesterday. So, after a refreshing shower, I put on my bathing trunks, shorts and T-shirt, had a leisurely breakfast while reading the Sunday paper, and packed myself a picnic lunch.

Then I walked down the sands with the inflatable and was soon clambering aboard The Dove and stowing away my lunch with a towel and a bottle of wine which I had remembered to collect on my way out. I had refuelled during the week and was confident I could cruise for hours to find solace and consolation on the calm sea eastwards along the beautiful coastline.

But the events of the Padquay match kept pervading my thoughts...I could see Tony Fairclough, the centre of attention, waving those panties above his head for all to see. Our hosts and opponents in the match had a good laugh, treating it all as an hilarious bit of fun. But I noticed a completely different reaction from the Woodymouth Club members, with snide whispers spreading from certain groups.

I thought our return to the Green might provide some relief but Eva and Ruth, to hide their discomfort, had gone straight to their changing room without collecting their panties, and were last seen hurrying towards the car park. Our hosts were in genial mood so I was determined to continue play with a team member short.

Ruth had been playing with Hubert on the next rink, so he too was obliged to continue the game with a member short. Apart from the fuss he made, the absence of the two players reminded everyone of the disturbance that had caused them to leave.

At the end of the match I had a war of words with Tony. I accused him of carrying out a lousy prank... which he denied. I said if he didn't put the items in my bag then he should have realised that someone else did, and he had no right to make such a public announcement of their recovery, causing embarrassment not only to me, but to Eva and Ruth. He just made me furious by mentioning how the Padquay team had treated it as an hilarious joke, and suggested that I should do the same!

The scoreboard at the end of the match had disclosed an easy win for the home team and on the way to our coach I overheard some rather unfriendly grumbles, making me realise that our return journey could prove a little unpleasant. When someone mentioned the word 'pervert' I pretended not to hear. Someone else asked Tony if he'd given the panties back to me, and one of his cronies asked: 'I wonder what he's wearing now?!'

On our last return trip from Padquay we had stopped at the Highwayman's Retreat for liquid refreshment, but

Hubert had decided it would be better if we went straight back. So that upset some of the thirstier members and did nothing to foster general good humour. There was no one more pleased than me when the coach pulled into our Club's car park and I was able to get out and walk home.

But those unhappy thoughts belonged to yesterday... the sun was shining, it was still a lovely day, and I left Woodymouth harbour to cruise past pretty coves, while watching happy holiday-makers enjoying the sands and the sea. The cliffs were picturesque and when I cut the engine The Dove just drifted. I sat enjoying the beauty of my surroundings, observing some windsurfers managing to pick up the slight breeze and sail along quite swiftly.

I had a swim, thought about lunch, but then on impulse went about, passed by the Woodymouth harbour entrance, and headed for Dead Smugglers Cove at full throttle. I didn't expect to see Donna there, but I knew the cove could always draw me back with its very special memories.

As The Dove came to rest about forty yards from the sands I realised I was not alone, seeing a launch riding at anchor about the same distance from the shore. It looked to be deserted but I distinctly heard the giggles of a girl. On the beach there were two couples...a guy and a girl were running to hide behind some rocks and the other two seemed to be having an argument with the beginnings of a struggle.

Then the young woman suddenly broke away and ran for the sea, and kept running and splashing until it was deep enough for her to start swimming. At first she was making for the launch, but then changed direction and made towards The Dove. The guy stood on the sands shouting: 'Rosemary, come back you idiot,' but the swimmer kept coming towards me until she lifted her head above water and cried out: 'Nathan, thank God it's you…help me up…and get me out of here.'

Meanwhile the guy had waded into the sea, still shouting, starting an angry pursuit. I helped Rosemary to clamber aboard and then we heard him bellow as he must have grazed a leg against one of the rocks. As I started the motor we could hear his oaths and curses well above the sound of The Dove's engine and the screeching protests of the gulls.

I was still in my trunks and Rosemary a bikini, so when I opened up the throttle and The Dove lifted her nose towards Woodymouth we both enjoyed the exhilaration of wind and spray on our bodies. Then about half way, and well out from the shore, I brought her to rest and fetched out my picnic lunch and the bottle of wine which I had stowed away in a plastic bag with an ice pack.

Rosemary was impressed. 'Here I am, rescued in the nick of time, and now being wined and dined.'

'Well, it's rather a humble picnic, but I'm eager to hear what this so-called rescue is all about.' Rosemary's legs had been noticed by quite a few gentlemen in the Club, but it was bonus time for me, as I was able to admire all of her very trim figure.

'Once more I have been the victim of one of Tony's pranks, but as far as I'm concerned this will be the last.'

'Oh dear, this seems to have a ring of familiarity!'

'Yes, I know how you were the butt of his joke at Padquay, but my recent predicament reveals a nasty streak in his character that I've only just recognised... I'll tell you...some days ago he asked me to join him and a few of his friends for a trip out on Theo Richmond's launch. I've never liked Theo much but Tony said there would be ten of us altogether, swimming and having some fun, so I agreed.'

'So what went wrong?'

'Well, Theo picked me up in the launch and I was with two guys and two girls I had met before at a party. I was upset to find Tony wasn't there, and very bothered when Theo said he had just received an apology for me on his mobile saying Tony had been shanghai'd into joining Roy Sinclair on one of his business trips to Amsterdam. Of course I was mad with him as there was no excuse for not letting me know before I set off. Then they pacified me a bit on the way down to the Marina, telling me we would pick up another couple and Theo's partner. I wasn't too concerned about being, perhaps, the odd female in the party.'

Rosemary broke off to bite and munch one of my sandwiches and savour my chilled wine served in a plastic beaker!

'When we got to the Marina, things got worse. There was nobody waiting there and Theo said he wasn't going to wait around, and we just cruised on out into the open seas. There was no excuse for that...we had all the day to wait. I was starting to panic, but when we anchored off the cove we all changed into bathing gear and swam around as a party, having fun with a ball.'

She finished the sandwich and emptied the beaker. 'Then on the beach things turned nasty. A couple swam back to the launch, the other two were chasing each other around the rocks and I was left with that beast Theo. He told me he fancied me and thought Tony had really been generous, inviting me along to make up the party numbers. That was a glimpse of the truth that frightened me. Then he said he wanted to see me without the bikini. He was on the boil while I was wearing it, so I was terrified knowing how he would behave if he managed to pull it off. That's what you saw...the start of a struggle...and Nathan Squires came to the rescue!'

We had drifted a long way out to sea and we both noticed the launch passing us closer in shore. We could recognise Theo at the helm, but our little boat was apparently unnoticed. He would no doubt still be moaning about his injuries and feeling frustrated about the outcome of his 'beach party'.

Rosemary and I finished off the sandwiches and the wine and then I put The Dove on course for a leisurely return to the harbour. My companion was obviously feeling anger towards Theo and Tony and had informed me the fellas had been school chums, which made me want to pursue an avenue of thought.

'Do you think if Tony was called away unexpectedly he could perhaps have had no idea or expectancy of how the events of the afternoon would work out?'

'He will expect me to think that...but I don't for one moment. I am convinced I was set up...he knows what a beast Theo can be and I believe they planned it together...with me as the victim of a sick joke.'

'So what can we do about it?'

'As I've always found with Tony's jokes and pranks, there's rarely anything you can do about them.'

On that bitter note we entered the harbour and I delivered Rosemary back to her home jetty, minus her clothes, but she didn't seem too concerned about them. She invited me in to stay for a while, but I gave some excuses with thanks. She had put up a fight with Theo to keep her bikini on but with me I had a feeling she might, just might, be happy to take it off.

Monday was a Bank Holiday...a day when I should have been spared any office problems...but that didn't deter my Area Manager from phoning me at home to let me know he would be calling in at the office within the next two or three days for a nice, friendly chat. Presumably he would never consider himself as an office problem, but I knew he could be. He would have to be told all the facts, and being anxious to protect the good name of the company we both worked for, having one of his local managers questioned in connection with a couple of serious sex crimes would not be something he would dismiss with a shrug of the shoulders and a laugh. I was the innocent victim of a cruel hoaxer. Would I be able to convince him of that?

But it was still a lovely day and my sister had said they would probably be going for a swim and she would be stocking up the beach hut for a snack at tea-time. So I ordered some of my favourite bourbon biscuits and told her to cater for an extra as I had thrown out an invitation for Rosemary to drop in if she felt in need of company.

After a light lunch I walked to the hut, threading my way around deck-chairs and sandcastles to find

Peggy and Molly both stretched out on sun loungers, looking very attractive in their costumes. There was a welcome from both and Molly began telling me why she hadn't seen me on her usual walk by in the mornings. At the moment Ben was a bit unwilling to go for walks because she had taken him to visit friends at a local farm and he had wandered off and caught his foot in a pre-set mousetrap. If we could see the funny side of that, obviously Ben hadn't and was still licking his wounds.

As I studied Molly I realised how nicely she had matured from that young schoolgirl who had been stranded with me on the sand bank...it would certainly be far more exciting if I were ever given the chance to repeat the experience.

I went into the hut to change and then brought out another sun lounger to join the girls who were talking bank business. They were talking about a gang of six men recently arrested for fixing false fronts to their hole-in-the-wall cash machines to obtain sensitive credit card information . This they had used to withdraw thousands of pounds from various accounts. Peggy was saying it had all been done before but what amazed and annoyed her was the disclosure that the gang members were all described as asylum seekers, with London addresses. She was saying she found it hard to believe they could be in possession of such sophisticated equipment and able to carry on their crooked business so far from their home addresses. I was inclined to agree. Molly thought they would probably be granted asylum as the authorities would no doubt consider them to be the sort of visitors we needed...men who showed initiative!

The girls had already been in the sea and when Peggs suggested going again Molly apologised saying she would have to get dressed and leave us. So we said our farewells and Peggs and I ran for the briny. Donna tended to monopolise my thoughts, but it was strange that neither Molly nor I had mentioned her name.

After an invigorating swim we returned to find Jon sitting in one of our fold-up chairs talking to Rosemary who was relaxing on one of the loungers. As usual she looked very appealing in a rather short summer dress. As Peggy and I were rubbing down with our towels Rosemary was just finishing her story of yesterday... briefly I was sure, omitting the intimate details.

It was Jon who replied. 'So your friend Tony Fairclough has been up to his old tricks, has he? Playing pranks on his friends. Well, I should watch him very carefully...I'm sure you will remember how we were bothered about some of his jokes in the weeks before your husband's death. We were amazed what a charmed life he seemed to have.'

Rosemary looked at each one of us before picking up the implication of his words. 'Yes, of course, he's had a guardian angel. He's been in many scrapes, but he's always had his aunt Muriel to bail him out.'

I was intrigued by that. 'I've met Muriel at the Club and at your office and she's always seemed a timid sort of person. In fact she has been described as Hubert's 'little mouse'.'

Rosemary laughed. 'Oh, how appearances can be deceptive, but believe me she runs our office most efficiently. She's a hidden force behind Hubert and still worships him.'

It was Peggs who butted in: 'but how can she manage to keep bailing out the errant Tony?'

'Ah...she is a woman of private means. She inherited a prosperous jewellery business, in the City somewhere, from her father. And 'the mouse', as you call her, has personal jewellery, inherited from her mother, worth thousands. Her collection includes diamond and emerald pieces which are quite unique and a tarzanite and diamond pendant which is priceless. Never worn, of course, but kept at the bank.'

I was interested, 'does she still have the business?'

'Oh yes, and I'm sure she'll be very much in control. She has a regular two day break from our office and takes a trip to London. Very occasionally Tony has gone in her place.'

Then it was Jon who butted in. 'Fairclough's a partner in the Estate Agency business, what the devil does he know about jewellery?'

'I asked him that and the answer's...'nothing'. He said he was just a kind of courier. He dresses up like a City gent, travels first class, delivers Muriel's locked briefcase to the firm's office and then has 'a night on the town'. He stays overnight at a star rated hotel, collects the briefcase in the morning and then returns home.'

I thought my sister was bothered that Rosemary was being embarrassed by persistent questions. So she promptly switched the conversation, asking me if I knew James' mother had been taken ill and he had gone dashing off to Bath to see her, leaving Julie to run the hotel. That was something we needed to discuss at length as it could cause problems at the peak of the season. Our real interests were only as landlords, but the Goslings were friends, so naturally their well-being and the success of the business would be our concern.

We were wondering if we should get in touch to ask if Julie was in need of our help and I agreed for Peggs to phone her with a reminder that I lived just a few hundred yards away and to call me if she had any problems.

Jon told us the police had been questioning a number of local lads who had been at the dance on the night of the assault. They were hoping if they found the lad who had taken Tracey to the caravan it would lead them to the man. But while some of the lads said they fancied her because 'she was putting it on show'...and I could recall the generous display of bare thighs at the Quarry Office...not one of them had taken her out of the hall. Tracey was adamant she had left with 'a visitor', a handsome young man who said he was an army cadet from Aldershot.

I got dressed before tea was brewed and the cakes and biscuits appeared. It was while I was enjoying a Bakewell Tart that Rosemary said she had two reserved tickets for the evening Vaudeville show on the Pier, and would like me to join her in appreciation of my rescue efforts of yesterday. I was surprised, but accepted saying I would call for her early in the evening. There were mutual thanks all round and she left.

It was when we were packing up to leave that I sensed Peggs was unhappy about something, so I challenged her.

'Well, I'm worried about you Nathan. You've been in all this trouble from hoax calls and pranks, and now you're back dating Rosemary Fletcher. You know how

I've always felt about her...I've never been sure she didn't push poor old Will into the Quarry.'

'If he was pushed, I don't think she was the one who did it, but to reassure you I'll be extra careful if I go to look over the edge of the Pier tonight.'

It was a delightful evening...first class entertainment and the only worry I had was after I had taken Rosemary home and accepted her offer of a coffee and brandy. Once more I had the feeling there was a welcome for me to stay, but I made the feeble excuse that I had to prepare some work for my Area Manager's visit in the morning.

That, in fact, was tempting fate because bright and early the next day he arrived at the office. He spent the whole day with me, being very concerned after I had given him a hoax-by-hoax account of events that had befallen me over the past few weeks. His suggestion for a solution was to bring in a locum manager for a couple of weeks while I took a holiday. Whilst I agreed that a break away to some foreign land might cheer me up, I didn't think that would actually solve anything. So he left with the understanding, as before, that 'I sorted things out'.

After he had gone I realised, painfully, I really hadn't got a clue what I should do to 'sort things out'. I was annoyed that my problems had spread to the office. Paula hadn't changed, but I felt a kind of alien reserve when I spoke to the other members of staff. I had always been happy in my job but that contentment had been diminished.

When I needed a break I had always had the Bowls Club...a place where I could relax with friends. But there, things had changed...friends were few and far between. Arthur was still a loyal member of my team and Alice was still there but only, I suspected, as a kind of spy to relay any useful information regarding my problems or activities to her friend Harry Wilks.

At the match on Saturday Hubert told me Eva had refused to play in my team and as he was acting as Team Captain in Tony's absence he was obliged to find a substitute. He asked Miranda to take her place, the dour 'bean-pole'. She played an excellent game, but hardly spoke a word, which was so noticeable that one of the visitors asked if someone had said something to offend her. I said I thought there may be lots of things that could offend her, but nothing for them to worry about.

On our rink we took the lead at the beginning, and managed to widen the gap until the end of the game. We were thus able to help our Club to an overall win to pick up vital points in the League Table. As our members drifted away happy I noticed Hubert was not sharing in their good humour and he signalled that he wanted 'a word' with me.

I recognised he was in pompous mood and was not too surprised by his opening words. 'Look here, Nathan, all this trouble you're in is causing problems all round.'

'Well, I'm the victim there and the problems are not of my making.'

'But it can't be good for the general image of the Club, and I'm just wondering if the time has come for you to think of stepping aside.'

I was not prepared for that and felt very angry. 'If you are suggesting I should resign as Treasurer, the answer is an emphatic 'no'.'

Then he huffed and puffed. 'It wouldn't be something I would like to put to one of our meetings, although I am sure Tony Fairclough would feel the same way as I do.'

'And that would be as far as you could go...if you do try to push me out, you won't have my vote and I don't think you could count on those of James or Rosemary...so you'd better forget any ideas like that Hubert.'

With more huffs and puffs we parted. I had won that argument but I was far from happy with the way things were developing. I felt in need of company and, knowing Rosemary was playing in a tennis match, decided to go along to the courts and watch. Then I changed my mind and walked to Sea View to check how Julie was coping without James.

I met her in their private sitting-room-cum-office and she soon welcomed me with a pot of tea and cakes. Their tariff provided for Bed, Breakfast and Evening Meal, so I accepted her hospitality, promising not to stay, knowing she and the staff would soon be preparing for dinner.

Julie was middle-aged, small in stature, with a mature figure and a personality that seemed to radiate friendship. The sort of woman everyone might want to take their troubles to. But that wasn't my mission. I was there to see if she had any.

She said she was coping alright, although naturally missing James. They were fully booked and very busy she said, but she was glad of an excuse to sit down and have a cuppa and a chat. The hotel was quiet as most of the guests were out for the day, but would soon be returning for drinks and the evening meal. Glancing around the desk I asked if there was any accounting work I could do, and before I left she was happy to hand over a couple of files and a pile of accounts and papers that needed sorting.

So I spent the evening screening and filing letters and accounts that had lacked orderly attention over the past few weeks. Then I had a read and went to bed. I was in a sound sleep having an argument with Donna when the phone brought me back to reality. It was Julie, apologising for disturbing me, saying she was having trouble with a couple of the guests and didn't know what to do.

I knew she was not one prone to panic over minor incidents, so concluded she must be facing a serious situation. I said I would get dressed and come round immediately, the hotel being just a ten minute walk away.

The front door was open, there were lights on in the hall, and I was greeted by the grandfather clock chiming the half hour after midnight. I found Julie still fully dressed in the sitting room, talking to a young woman in a dressing gown worn over a nightdress. She was obviously very upset, and when she wasn't listening to Julie she was talking in a distressed manner into a mobile phone.

Julie immediately took me by the arm and ushered me across the hall into the dining room. With the door open there was no need for a light and, while I noticed

Deryck Coleman

the tables were laid for breakfast, I realised the reason for my being there was just to be out of earshot of the young woman in the sitting room.

'What's going on?' I asked.

I could see she was very concerned, but trying hard not to giggle. Then it just burst out: 'I've got one of our guests running along the Promenade in his birthday suit, being chased by that young woman's husband, and I don't know if I should call the police.'

We both had a muffled chuckle and then I suggested she told me what it was all about. She had stopped giggling and gave me the story in a lowered voice.

'It all began with a booking for a room with two singles for Mrs. Lucy Tansley and her friend Mrs. Lewis, which we later managed to change to two single rooms facing each other across the hall on the second floor. Then three days ago Mrs. Tansley arrived with her friend, Mr. Lewis, claiming there had been some kind of clerical error…it being 'Mr.' and not 'Mrs.' Lewis.'

'So you booked them in knowing Mr. Lewis would just have to sneak across the landing in his pyjamas!'

'Yes…and Mrs. Tarbuck, who makes the beds, reckons that's exactly what he's been doing each night. But late this evening a very angry Mr. Tansley arrived telling me he had been quite happy when his wife arranged a holiday break with her friend Joan Lewis, but furious when he met the lady in the local supermarket and she informed him that her husband was away on business.'

'A carefully laid plan, no doubt, that came unstuck.'

'I couldn't stop Tansley going to her room, banging on the door, threatening to break it down if she didn't let him in. Apparently our Lothario jumped out of bed, couldn't find his pyjamas, climbed out of the window and down the fire escape without them, but grabbed his lady love's pink woolly jumper to wear as a kind of loin cloth.'

Julie was trying hard not to giggle.

'Who's Mrs. Tansley talking to on the mobile?'

'Ah...apparently when lover boy went out the window she thrust her phone into his hand and then opened the door to her husband, trying to pretend she was on her own. But Tansley went to the window and saw her naked lover at the bottom of the fire escape. He assumed lover boy would try to sneak back into the hotel so he went downstairs to wait for him, arming himself with a walking stick from the stand in the hall. But his wife nipped across the landing into Lewis's room...he always left his door unlocked for his midnight trysts...and she warned him from his mobile. She's been talking to him ever since.'

'Where is he now then?'

'The last I heard he was running along the Promenade in sheer panic. Tansley left the hotel to chase after him.'

I thought we should advise the police, and Julie made the call from her office. The duty officer thanked her for the information and said he was glad to hear the naked man had a woolly loin cloth as there was a bit of a nip in the air on the sea front!

Then we went into the room to join the young woman sitting in an armchair, listening, then talking into the mobile.

'Where is he now?' Julie asked.

'Poor Eddy's run all the way along the Promenade, but says there's a gang of young people near the Pier entrance, and one lad has been swimming and is dancing about just in his trunks. Eddy's hoping that will deceive my husband so he's gone down onto the beach. He says it's darker there and he's hoping to double back. Guy's still shouting and running towards the Pier.'

There was silence for quite some time and then we actually heard a woman scream...more silence...then in a breathless voice Eddy Lewis was telling his lover that when climbing over one of the groynes he had lost her woolly then stumbled over a couple on the sands. The girl had screamed in terror and the man had shouted in anger. Fortunately for Eddy the man was not able to give chase, but he feared Guy might have heard the commotion.

For a long while the young woman was calling her lover, but without response. Then there was a very breathless voice telling her that he had run right to the end of the beach and round into the harbour. Guy was some way behind but following on the sands. Eddy said he had found a clean newspaper to wrap around himself, but kept losing sheets, and realised he was laying a sort of paper trail that would help his pursuer. He was going to drop the rest of the paper on the slipway in the hope that Guy would think he had gone back onto the Promenade.

There followed minutes that seemed like hours while Lucy Tansley was seeking further contact, and then the very breathless voice telling her he had reached the Marina. Apparently a breeze had scattered his false paper trail in all directions and her angry husband was still in pursuit.

More long minutes of waiting and then we heard from Eddy that he had seen a cabin light on one of the cruisers, and was approaching the vessel along the walkway. There was an oath as he trod on something sharp, then he said he was on the deck peering into the cabin where he could see two men who seemed to be sorting out packets of cigarettes, bottles of wine, and bulbs...tulip or daffodil bulbs he thought, all different sizes.

Then he became very agitated, saying Guy had seen him and was shouting, brandishing the stick. He said he was going down into the cabin, hoping to receive protection. There was a loud noise as if the phone had been dropped, bringing once more silence, and we decided it was time the police were advised.

Julie spoke to the same duty officer, telling him of Eddy Lewis's present location, and was surprised to learn they had two officers tracking them in the harbour area. He said 'The Streaker' had been an easy one to follow, even in the semi-darkness of the sands, despite the fact that he had kept running to keep warm. The officer confirmed he had the hotel number and would advise her of any developments.

We waited...conversation waned...more waiting, dozing...then we fell asleep. Dawn was breaking when the phone rang, and it was a different officer asking for Mrs. Gosling to tell her they had one of her guests, a

Mr. Eddy Lewis, in custody. He was asking if the hotel could send some of his clothes later in the day. Julie said she would comply, and asked what had happened and if he was alright.

The officer said Mr. Lewis had entered a cabin cruiser, berthed at the Marina, in the early hours of the morning. The owner and an associate were present having just cleaned and 'tidied up' after a pleasure trip over to Amsterdam. Startled by his appearance...as he wore no clothes...they chased him back onto the deck where he was immediately assaulted by another man. The two men fought, tripped over a coiled rope, and fell into the harbour. The owner and his associate were hauling them out of the water when two of their officers arrived on the scene and immediately took them into custody. The two men sustained only minor injuries but were both being held to face charges.

Julie thanked the officer for his precise account of the proceedings and relayed the information to us. Lucy burst into tears and ran back to bed. Julie and I had a laugh and a hug and I went home.

In the morning I called in at Sea View to enquire how things were. Guests were leaving their breakfast tables to go upstairs. Some were already going out for the day. Two or three were talking to Julie at the Reception Desk and I realised that business was back to normal.

I waited a while, then Julie told me Lucy Tansley had checked out early, paying the accounts for her room and that of her friend Eddy Lewis. She had ordered a taxi to the station, leaving Lewis and her husband still in custody. Mrs. Tarbuck had packed Lewis's clothes and belongings in his case which was delivered to the police station.

Sometime later a man's pyjamas, believed to be his, were recovered from the bottom of Lucy Tansley's bed, but it was decided not to post them on to Lewis's home address.

CHAPTER 12

ELLIE

• • •

I awoke to the sound of rain...it was not just raining, but pouring. When I looked out I could see it was trying to bounce back from the harbour waters, and visibility up river was limited. The Dove looked very forlorn, riding at anchor in the thick of it, and I hoped the tarpaulin covers over the cockpit would live up to their waterproof promise.

I turned the radio on and listened to the local news while I had my breakfast. The announcer said he had a follow-up to last week's story of the fisherman from Woodymouth sighting a blue shark. I recalled the story because, whilst we were informed they roamed the Atlantic Ocean, capable of travelling thousands of miles at incredible speeds, I had read that during the Second World War they had hunted with the German U-Boats. When the U-Boats torpedoed our ships to send vital supplies down to Davy Jones' Locker, the sharks were there to attack any survivors left swimming in the sea.

The follow-up story was that local fishermen, while trawling in deeper waters, had caught a ruthless Blue that had become entangled in their nets. When landing

Deryck Coleman

the monster one of the crew had been injured, not by its jaws but by its tail. The injured seaman had been airlifted to hospital.

When I got to the office everyone was crowding around Megan, our junior typist, and I soon learned the injured fisherman was her father. I was eager to know how serious his injuries were and if she needed time off. But she assured me that apart from bruises and broken ribs he was fine. He was still in hospital, but she and her mother had spent a lot of time with him over the weekend and he was expected home before evening. She said she didn't want any time off. I felt sure she was concerned for her father but suspected she might enjoy being the centre of attention.

When the trawler returned to Woodymouth we could expect their catch, the big blue shark, to be transported through the town and outlying districts, it being traditional to display the prize and collect donations for their broken nets. The rain was still lashing down, so I was hoping it wouldn't continue for too long, to spoil their parade. They would need all the support available from locals and visitors flocking around with generous help.

In the middle of the morning Jon phoned and said he would like a chat, private if possible, about lunch time, so I arranged with Paula to bring in some sandwiches and my thermos of coffee. When Jon arrived he approved of her choice of eats and after the usual exchange of pleasantries handed over the address of Mr. and Mrs. Dove in Rydemouth where Donna, presumably, was living.

He had come to tell me something so I waited.

'The Inspector at the Nick, quite unofficially, has asked me to do a spot of checking. He is, of course, working on the assaults on the two girls and the second victim, as you know, works at the Quarry. He's asked me to do a spot of digging on the track record of young girls working in the Quarry office with your Club Secretary Hubert Sinclair. As you've been dragged into the case I thought you ought to be informed, knowing you will be discreet.'

'Thank you, I appreciate that, but don't let me interrupt.'

'I've been making enquiries and found that over the past twelve years, before Tracey Lamb started, there have been four or five young girls employed...each one to replace the other, which I consider to be rather a high turnover. It was a bit difficult to track down the early ones, but I found two or three left 'after a bit of trouble'.'

Jon broke off to tuck into a sandwich and have a drink of coffee before continuing.

'One girl...well, she's quite a young woman now... said she started work at the Quarry office straight from school, and left because one of the bosses became too familiar with his hands. No need to ask her to name him. The last girl before Tracey was called Jessica and she threatened to 'kick up a fuss'. Then someone stepped in and put down the deposit for a house, and after that she settled down quite happily with a boyfriend. I had a lucky break and managed to track down the benefactors...the Sinclairs!'

I recalled Eva hinting at the same story some weeks ago.

'So it appears your friend Hubert likes to have young girls around him, and seems to have a problem keeping them for any length of time...which suggests once again there is someone in the Quarry office with perverse inclinations. My findings will not get the Inspector too excited, but might help him towards a character assessment. Maybe the lads will pay Sinclair another visit...I'm told he doesn't have any sort of alibi for the Saturday night when Tracey Lamb was assaulted.'

We finished the sandwiches and the coffee, then Jon left.

The next morning was dull, the rain had stopped but there was no sign of any sun. When I got to the office Megan was once more the centre of attention, with everyone wanting to know about her father. We learned he had been discharged from hospital and was recovering from his injuries at home. The trawler had returned to home waters and Megan thought the crew would parade their catch through the streets later in the day. Apparently there had been 'a bit of a row' at home because Dad wanted to take part, but Mum was quoting doctor's orders and wouldn't let him.

At lunchtime we heard the clang of handbells and joined the throng of people in the street to see the pointed nosed monster cushioned on a pile of the broken net. The shark was on a large four-wheel handcart being pushed by two men and pulled with ropes by two more members of the crew, all in their sou'-westers. Other crew men rang the bells and rattled clean buckets to collect our donations.

The shark was about six to seven feet long, not nearly fully grown, but still an awesome sight...beautiful in design, capable of high speeds over long distances, yet a ruthless adversary. The clanging and rattling went on down the street, drawing out people to see the magnificent creature and to throw their offerings into the buckets.

Following the excitement the office settled down to routine work for the afternoon. Then, in the evening, I walked up to the Green as Tony and I were due to select the team for the Saturday match. I wasn't looking forward to it as our relationship was a little strained to say the least.

After the rain Dominic had decided the Green was fit to play on and as I went through the gate I noticed a number of the rinks were being used. On one of them Arthur and his wife Audrey were playing a game with a couple of visitors. As I stood watching, Arthur soon seized the opportunity to come and talk: 'I must tell you, Nathan, about the excitement at the Marina over the weekend.'

I could see he would be disappointed if I told him I already knew the story, so I let him carry on.

'Harry told Alice after they got back from Amsterdam, they'd almost finished packing up when he nearly had a heart attack as a naked man suddenly appeared in the cabin. He said they chased him back onto the deck where there was another fella threatening to kill him. They had a fight, fell overboard he said, and he and Roy had to fish them out of the harbour. Then within minutes two cops turned up and took them away. Alice thinks the sight of the boys in blue could have frightened Harry and Roy more than the naked man because they hadn't finished sorting out all the 'duty frees'.'

'What was Harry Wilks doing on the boat?' I asked.

'Oh, he often goes as a crew member, and they took Tony Fairclough on this last trip.' There Audrey called him back to his game.

The meeting with our Team Captain was worse than expected. Apart from his belligerent attitude I found he had already made the selections for the Saturday match without my help, and when I read the list I was angry. I was still down to play but he had dropped Rosemary and not even put her as a reserve. It is true players may need to be rotated when the application card is full, but in her case I thought she should have been selected as she missed a lot of games following the accident. In my mind it had been done out of pure spite...and I told him so. I knew after the incident at the Cove, Rosemary had read the Riot Act to him and I felt sure it was his seditious reaction to that.

'Rosemary and I may have had our differences lately, but I would never allow my private life to affect Club business.'

'Rubbish!' He obviously resented my speaking to him in that manner and the debonair cloak slipped off and I saw the man in a new light.

'As Team Captain I shall insist that the selection list stays as it is. I felt fully justified in choosing the team without your help as Hubert had mentioned that in view of the damage you seem to be doing to the good name of the Club, he had suggested you should think about stepping aside.'

I was furious. 'And did he tell you I had no intention of giving up my job on the Committee, or my membership?'

'I can't remember...but he did say he had been talking to Duncan Peters and naturally our Club Captain is also gravely concerned about the damage you are doing to the Club's image and good name. Therefore, Nathan, you should think seriously about Hubert's advice.'

'I will do no such thing as the suggestion is preposterous.'

After that the conversation descended to a verbal slanging match and Fairclough just walked out of the Pavilion leaving me with the feeling that once more I had been wrong-footed...and again I was the victim.

When I went back to the Green I must have looked a bit flushed with anger because Arthur broke away from his game again to have a word with me.

'By the look on Tony's face and yours, I would hazard a guess you've had some harsh words.'

'That could be an understatement!'

'Well, Audrey's received a bit of gossip that he and Rosemary have had a mammoth row. I don't think he ever made it with her. Audrey was told...' (and I felt sure that must be from the housekeeper), 'that our Rosie wouldn't let him into her bed, which would hurt Tony's pride. Rumour has it he's very much back with Eva... working on the principle, I suppose, "if at first you don't succeed..." sorry, must go!'

The abrupt end to his conversation was brought about by his wife shouting for him to return to their game. So I wandered off and went home.

In the morning I had another visitor...Duncan Peters. Paula told me he was in the office dealing with some personal insurance business and had asked to see me. I agreed, telling her I would signal if we needed coffee.

I had always liked Duncan, despite the fact that he usually dressed and behaved as if he were the local Landowner. But at that moment I thought he might be coming to continue the attack on me where Fairclough had left off. My fears, however, were unfounded. Whilst he wanted to talk Club business and was obviously concerned about its image he wasn't blaming me for any of its latest misfortunes. So graciously he joined me at my coffee table. Paula had been quick to answer my signal.

'I'm very concerned, Nathan, with the way things are going. Hubert's been questioned by the police again... to do with that horrible assault on the young girl at the Upper Woody Caravan Park...saying it's only natural they should talk to him as the girl works in his office.'

'Yes, I imagine so.' I was thinking of what Jon had told me, but wasn't prepared to pass on any of that to Duncan.

'Then yesterday they questioned the Groundsman, Dominic, again. He says it's all to do with that evening in the Ladies' Changing Room when Amy threw a milk bottle at him. It all seems very strange to me that the police should be so bothered about that little incident.'

Duncan drank some coffee, munched a biscuit, and then continued.

'I met Arthur Russell and he says the police are working hard on those assault cases and have been questioning quite a few men in the town. That chubby little fellow always seems to know everything about everybody. If that Groundsman is suspected of assaulting young girls, Nathan, we will have to watch him and do something about the teaching classes. He seems to favour the ladies.'

'Well, he's only been questioned and, as Arthur suggests, one of a number. Whilst he's a Club member he is primarily a Council employee in charge of our Green. We would be ill-advised to act too quickly on such a matter.'

'Yes, I guess you're right, and I suppose we can count on the police to let us know if there's any sort of threat or danger.'

We finished off the coffee and Duncan left.

On Friday it rained all day and through the night, so on Saturday the Green was water-logged and the match was cancelled. I had a little laugh to myself thinking of Fairclough's spiteful decision to drop Rosemary out of the team. It had come to nought.

I was yearning to see Donna and phoned the police station asking to speak to WPC Dove, only to be informed she was not available. I hoped that meant she would be at home, so decided to go over to Rydemouth. I took the coast road which gave me some breathtaking views as I travelled along. I pulled into a lay-by and sat for a few minutes to appreciate the open panorama. I was just a few yards from the cliff edge where there was almost a sheer drop to the rocks and the English Channel below. The rain had stopped and visibility was fair as I watched large vessels moving in both directions; the incessant traffic.

Rydemouth was a very progressive seaside town about the size of Brighton and as I drove along the Promenade I saw it had its share of visitors. But when Jon gave me the address he also included some directions, so I was soon able to locate the house on the outskirts of the town. It was a small detached property with an in-and-out driveway. I decided not to use that and parked on the opposite side of the road, walking to the front door.

When I rang the bell it was answered by a loud bark and then in a few minutes the door was opened by a pretty young girl of about six or seven dressed in blue jeans and a blue top. By her side was the largest Alsatian I had ever seen, which she was holding by its collar. The girl gave me a big smile but I wasn't very sure about the dog's greeting.

'Hello, I'm Ellie and this is Rajah, although I always call him Raj.'

Following such information the dog managed a wag of his tail... 'who are you?'

I was quite taken aback by the pretty face, the lovely dark hair and the gorgeous brown eyes...and that direct manner...all seeming so familiar.

'I'm Nathan Squires and I've come to see Donna Dove...I'm a friend...is she in please?'

'No, I'm sorry, she's at work...do you have a boat? Does it go very fast?'

'Yes.' Again I was taken completely by surprise at the question and her forthright manner. 'It's a little speedboat.'

'What's its name?'

'The Dove.'

'That's alright then. I've heard about it, so if you want to come in you can,' and with that invitation she opened the door for me to go through.

Perhaps I hesitated, so the invitation was repeated.

'It will be OK now I know who you are...and I have Raj with me.' When I looked at the dog he seemed to convey his message: 'you touch her and I'll have you!'

So I followed Ellie into a very homely sitting room where the mantel piece was bedecked with birthday cards and just one photo in a frame. I glanced at the cards, but it was the photo that held my attention. There was a couple with arms around each other standing behind a little girl of perhaps two or three, and as I stared I knew there was no mistaking the girls, three or four years younger, but undoubtedly Donna and Ellie.

'That's Mummy and Daddy and me. Of course I'm a lot smaller there but Mummy says that photo's her favourite.'

Seeing Ellie and talking to her had made me guess who she was, but I still found her words shattering. I had difficulty in remaining composed.

'May I look at the cards...obviously yours, for your seventh birthday? When is that?'

'Tomorrow.'

I read each one in turn. 'You've got a lot from your friends and Grandad and Grandma, but not from your Mummy and Daddy.'

'Well, I will get their cards with their presents in the morning.'

'Oh, yes, of course.'

'She was a lovely girl and I enjoyed talking to her, imagining that perhaps Sonja and I might have had such a daughter...apart from the hair and eyes, as Sonja had been blonde. She was so eager to learn all about The Dove, as it was their name. She asked lots of questions, like how fast did it go, and did it bounce up and down in the water...and would she ever be able to have a trip in it. Most of the questions I could answer.

Emotionally I was twisted up inside. I wanted to share more time with the girl, but there was bitterness in my heart for the way her mother had deceived me. I loved Donna. I could love them both. But apparently it was just not meant to be.

So I made excuses that it was time I left. I wished her a happy birthday, promising that if we should meet in the future I would be very happy to take her for a spin in The Dove.

Our farewell at the door amazed me. She shook my hand, in grown-up fashion, and said: 'thank you, I will remember you as a new friend.' I would have hugged the girl if Raj hadn't given a muted growl.

Ellie and her dog stood in the open doorway watching me cross the road and get into the car. Then she waved and at that moment a van drove up to the front door and a man got out. He didn't look towards me but I guessed he would be about my age. The dog gave a friendly greeting and I saw Ellie open her arms to him and he picked her up in a hug. All three went into the house and the door slammed behind them.

For moments I just sat in the car, brooding. I felt absolutely gutted, empty.

I daren't analyse my feelings towards Donna, but knew there could never be any sense of anger towards her daughter, so I drove along until I found a florist. I ordered seven red roses, picked out a birthday card and signed it: 'from your new friend'. Then, after some financial bribery, they promised to deliver the bouquet that afternoon.

I drove down to the Promenade and had lunch at a café that overlooked the sands and the sea. After a struggle the sun had managed to reappear and, as I was served with a fresh crab salad, I was able to watch holiday-makers enjoying themselves. Nearby there was a group playing volleyball. They were of varying ages, but everyone's attention seemed to be focused on a buxom girl who was obviously having severe problems with the top of her costume every time she leaped into the air. Like me, I think they were waiting for her to burst over the top. But when it happened I was tucking into the crab and missed the excitement!

I spent the afternoon on the Promenade, trying to pick up the happy atmosphere, but failed. I kept brooding about Donna's deceit. But, of course, more importantly on the fact that I had lost her. That was the real blow. She had a daughter and a husband, so I realised she had never really been mine to lose. That heavenly afternoon at the Cove had been just an adventure for her. Through my stupid agreement I had made myself 'the bit on the side'.

I went back to the car feeling angry and dejected, deciding to go home. Then I changed my mind and headed over the moors to the remote Highwayman's Retreat. I journeyed through miles of beautiful heather and gorse, avoiding one or two wild ponies that had strayed onto the road, and finally arrived as daylight was beginning to wane. Despite the Inn's remoteness, there was a number of vehicles in the car park.

I planned to book in for a meal and then hopefully stop the night. I was not surprised when the landlord claimed he had only the one room available and apologised that it was really an attic with basic accommodation. I accepted and, after climbing the stairs to inspect the room, explained I had no luggage and then followed him down to the bar which was throbbing with life in the midst of cigarette and cigar smoke.

The bar counter was actually quite small and almost fully occupied by a bevy of young girls trying to flirt with the barman. He was not much older and I remembered, when our Bowls Club had first called at the Inn on our way back from a Padquay match, how the ladies had all been talking about the very handsome young barman. That was the occasion, when our bill was being paid, when someone suggested the landlord must have been a descendent of the highwayman and everyone had laughed except Harry Wilks. Arthur had explained that Harry was a distant cousin of the present landlord.

As I studied the man I couldn't see any resemblance, but when I thought of his half brother, Billy Edwards (a painful reflection), I could recognise the connection. Not a happy situation for me I decided, after some deliberation. Jon had suggested that Billy might be the one trying to destroy me. So I was wondering if the remote Highwayman's Retreat was the ideal safe place for me to spend the night.

But fears and doubts were quite suddenly cast aside when I was confronted by a very attractive fair-haired girl in a low-cut black evening dress. In mutual surprise we each cried out the other's name... 'Nathan!'...'Molly!'... followed by perhaps the natural question: 'what are you doing here?'

I was the first to answer. 'I've just been to Rydemouth and met Ellie.'

'Oh...as you didn't know, I can guess how you must feel. I'm at an engagement party and my fiancé hasn't turned up!'

'Oh... I can guess how you must feel!'

Then we both laughed and Molly asked me to wait as she was just on her way to the loo. The black evening dress seemed as if it had been moulded to her figure, with a split down each side to give a nice show of leg as she walked. When her venture was completed she insisted I join her friends in a private little room leading off from the lounge bar, where wall lights gave a welcoming glow from the heavily embossed décor, and two or three pictures depicted scenes of highway robbery.

There were three couples there seated around the table, all of a similar age, and all in a happy, celebratory mood. The newly engaged pair sat at the head with two friends on either side. Introductions were immediately made. When Molly said she had just found me at the bar, and mentioned we used to be friends at school, there were a lot of 'ooh's and 'aah's. Obviously the seats at the other end of the table had been intended for Molly and her missing fiancé, Nigel, whose place I was invited to take, and was quickly accepted into the gathering. Nigel and Donna were in the dog-house, so it was agreed that neither of their names should be mentioned during the evening.

The table had been expertly laid and in the centre was a bunch of mixed flowers spreading out from the roof of a small stage-coach. Individual orders had been taken for the starters, and Molly hoped a prawn salad cocktail would be satisfactory for me. I said it could well have been my choice and whispered a question about who was paying. She put a finger to her lips and whispered that it was all taken care of. When I asked about the wine I was told there was a 'kitty' and, after I made a generous contribution to that, it flowed very freely.

The engaged couple, Ethan and Mia, both worked with Molly at the bank, but otherwise the jobs were varied, so the conversation moved from one topic to another and it was quite obvious I was within a group of close friends.

The serving wenches were in period dresses and the main course (which Molly explained to me) was slowly roasted duck, served in a rich red wine gravy, with a variety of vegetables and pumpkin slices. The meal was very appetising and the wine and conversation continued to flow freely until we had to decide on a sweet. Orders were taken and Molly and I chose trifle.

While we waited the guy on our left, an artist, asked the pretty girl opposite if she would pose for him. The girl's partner asked: 'not in the nude, I hope?' giving a little hollow laugh.

'But of course,' came the reply, 'she has the figure for it.' Which brought silence to the room. Presumably they needed time to think about it, so everyone made a start on their sweet.

Molly sat on my left and she was left-handed, so we each had a neighbouring hand free, and as I disturbed some cream on my trifle her hand rested gently on mine and then lifted it first up and then down to go beneath the table to push it into the split in her dress and leave it resting on her knee. I was certainly surprised, knowing her as a shy girl, making the action seem so out of character. But the wine and the frivolous atmosphere was affecting us all.

I had admired her legs from a distance and realised my hand wasn't there to judge the quality of her nylons, but rather to feel what was within. As my spoon explored the contents of the sweet dish, so my hand moved up to find excitement on the warm flesh of her bare thigh. When she moved her leg against mine to give me more room to explore, I knew we were both enjoying that trifle and would be sorry when our dishes were empty and hands returned to the table in readiness for the serving wenches to come and clear away.

Coffee was served with brandy and liqueurs, and I soon realised I wouldn't need two hands to deal with mine. The artist was still talking about having the girl posing for a nude portrait. When his wife offered consolation to the girl's partner by suggesting maybe they could find something to do together to amuse themselves, all attention focused once more in their direction.

So, when I felt Molly's leg pressing against mine, my hand found its own way back to that excitingly warm, bare thigh. The artist was saying how he would discover and reveal the girl's beauty, while I sipped my brandy very slowly, not wishing to rush my own journey of discovery.

But all good things, it seems, must come to an end and when Ethan announced that Mia was falling asleep the party began to break up and they went upstairs with all our good wishes. Molly said she felt the same, so we said our goodnights to the remaining two couples and I supported her towards the door, receiving comments like: 'good night, take care of her, Nathan,' and, 'tuck her in gently Nathan!'

Molly was at the giggling stage as we staggered to the lift and I asked for her room number. She wrapped her arms around me and we kissed until the lift stopped. Without my support she would have fallen over.

Once we were in her room, not spacious but with the comfort of a double bed, she kicked off her shoes and then managed to wriggle and wiggle out of dress and slip, while I pulled down the sheet, before she collapsed onto the bed.

'Oh, dear,' she said, 'things are spinning around, you'll have to help me to undress Nathan.'

The prospect was as sensually exciting as any man could wish...a lovely girl lying across the bed dressed only in bra and panties, with her stocking-clad legs stretched out onto the floor.

'Bra first,' she said and between us we released two well-shaped hemispheres from captivity. I marvelled at how nicely they had developed from the little half lemons I had fondled as a schoolboy. Taking off the stockings was not easy, but delightful as my hands caressed down from thigh to toe. Then with eager anticipation I studied the naked body and reached for the panties. My hands held the elastic top and began to pull them down under her bottom until I revealed a little tuft of fair hair above the crotch.

When I looked up to her face I was surprised to see it calm, without a trace of any excitement, and realised she was either asleep or had just passed out from the alcohol intake. Not much of a boost to my male ego... and her naked body was thrilling me.

Then I saw the rose....a single red rose in a tall glass on the bedside cabinet and for some strange reason I remembered Ellie, my 'new friend', realising I was about to go to bed with Donna's cousin. I knew if I didn't I would look back to the occasion and consider myself a stupid idiot.

But the rose had a strange influence over me...put there as a welcoming gift from the management...for whom? Not me. Molly was mad with Nigel and, with alcohol reducing her inhibitions, was more than willing to have me join her in bed. But how would we both feel in the morning? I was being urged to just live for the night, but something was telling me we would regret it for a long time to come.

So I pulled the panties back up and rolled Molly gently into bed. She never roused, and as I studied her before pulling up the sheets, I knew I was a prize nitwit. I made sure her door was locked behind me and then climbed the stairs to my room.

The attic was small. The bed was short and the mattress bumpy, but as I stared through the skylight above my head I was grateful for the stars as I could see where it leaked in bad weather. I thought once more what a blockhead I was and then fell asleep. Twice during the early hours I was aware of someone at the door. It had one of the old type locks, worked with a key, but as that was missing some protective person had kindly fitted a stout bolt. It was that I had heard rattling and I wondered if maybe Billy Edwards was trying to pay me a visit, but I was too sleepy to worry about it.

In the morning, when I went to the dining room, I found a table laid for eight and sat and had breakfast on my own. As I was finishing the two couples arrived and we had a few words before I left. With knowing gestures they told me Ethan and Mia were having a 'lie in'. They seemed surprised to see me there on my own as apparently Nigel had arrived during the early hours. They were wondering how I had escaped! I had a memory flashback to Sea View, remembering Eddy Lewis's naked break-out down the fire escape. I wouldn't have been so lucky as I had noted it on my way down to breakfast...away from Molly's room at the end of the corridor!

I paid my bill and walked to the car park where I saw the handsome young barman hurrying towards a waiting friend. I noticed them embrace and kiss and I watched as the two young men drove off in a northerly direction. I headed south over the moorlands to Woodymouth.

CHAPTER 13

CARNIVAL WEEK

• • •

It was Sunday morning and as I drove over the moors the rain clouds had been driven away by sunshine, giving me once more a chance to appreciate the colourful landscape of gorse and heather. My thoughts were going back over the day before...my meeting with the captivating Ellie and my hurt after learning of her mother's deceit...but in the aftermath I was facing up to the fact that I loved Donna and without her my heart was empty.

Then there had been the chance meeting with Molly, when we had both been wishing for a night of consolation. I had fought against it and was having to come to terms with my stupidity...although with Nigel's arrival my escape could have been fortuitous. I wondered what sort of meeting they had in the early hours. Had she invited him into her bed with one of those 'all is forgiven' scenes? I was hoping they had managed to sort out their differences.

The wild, bleak beauty of the moorlands lifted my spirits...I had no way of telling or anticipating the horrors that waited to engulf me.

Deliberately I had left my mobile in the car and after travelling a few miles I heard its bleep and pulled in off the road. Immediately I had my sister's typically friendly greeting: 'where the hell have you been? We've been trying to contact you all weekend.'

'Nothing serious, I hope. I'm just returning from a night out at the Highwayman's Retreat.'

'Relax, there's no cause for panic...are you back with Donna then?'

'No, but I did join Molly at a party there.'

'Blimey, I can't wait to learn details. Join us at the hut...I'll have a snack lunch ready for you.'

After that invitation I managed to find a parking spot on the Promenade and then wended my way along the busy beach to the hut. Peggs and Jon were in swimming gear, relaxed on loungers and after the normal greetings I sat down on a spare one and prepared for my sister's inquisition. I said nothing about my journey to Rydemouth, but began with the impulse trip to the Highwayman's Retreat and how I met Molly and had been invited to the party, leaving out, naturally, the intimate details.

I believed, for the time being, she accepted my story, knowing it was only half a tale. I managed to switch the conversation over to Jon, asking him how the Inspector had reacted to his investigation into the office activities of Hubert Sinclair.

'Oh, he was quite interested in my findings, although I don't think he was surprised. I got the impression I was confirming his character assessment.'

'I've always said that lot at the Quarry need watching,' Peggs butted in.

'But I did pick up an interesting bit of information about the assault on the girls from friend Bert,' Jon advised. 'Their investigations have shown that although the two crimes appeared to be very similar, there are what they consider important differences. Bert ran through a lot of detail with me which will be of interest to you, as I know how you have been caught up in both cases.'

'Naturally as I've still got the feeling I could be a suspect, any further information would be welcome.'

'Yes, we know the similarities: how the girls were lured away from a dance by a young man, one to the beach-hut and the other to the caravan. How both crime scenes were used by a host of visitors to provide headaches for Forensics. But while the girls had been binge-drinking and their account of events was not particularly coherent, it seems fairly certain there were two different young men involved.'

'Oh, now that is interesting.'

'We know both girls were drugged and then while in a dozy state were undressed by an older man. Once again there was a blurred description of the men, but apparently a fairly good idea of the sound of their voices, with the first one being quite 'smooth' and articulate while the second was 'rougher' and a bit uncouth.'

'So what do your pals at The Nick think of all that?'

'Well, opinions are divided. Some think that neither of the girls was in a fit state to give reliable evidence, so little credence should be given to what they said. Others think there were two separate copy-cat crimes carried out by different villains. David, the Inspector, believes

Deryck Coleman

there could have been two older men at each scene, with one taking the photographs. He is fearful, if there are any further attacks, the men will be more demanding of their victim.'

I was left with a lot to think about while Jon and Peggy went into the hut to get dressed and fetch out our snack lunch. The sandwiches had been cut small but were nicely filled with prawns, lettuce, and mayonnaise and I was enjoying my second when I noticed and recognised the matronly lady in the over-filled blue costume approaching from the hut next-door-but-one. The last time I had seen her she was brandishing a parasol, but she advanced holding a cup like a begging bowl which she presented to Peggy with a plea to borrow some sugar. She stared at me and spoke: 'I seem to know you, but I can't remember the occasion.'

Peggs knew the story, so quickly introduced me as her brother. We exchanged greetings and the woman thanked us for the sugar and left, looking however most suspiciously at me. We had a chuckle about it because obviously the old dear was trying to identify me to the 'pervert' she had chased along the beach.

It was the first day of Carnival Week and, as Peggs wanted to go to the Parade and election of the young Queen, we packed up, locked up, and hurried to the Promenade and down to the 'Rec' where deckchairs had been arranged in a semi-circle around the Bandstand. As we found three empty chairs (four actually as there was an empty one beside me) the Band was just leaving and there was a queue of about a dozen young girls, in their pretty summer dresses, preparing to take their places.

They filed onto the Stand and sat down while the dignitaries sorted themselves out. Three judges, looking very official, sat at a table a few yards in front of the Stand and the Lady Mayor, displaying her chain of office, took up her position on the podium. Then with the aid of a mike she wished us all welcome and, after a brief explanation of the proceedings, began by calling each girl to come forward and do a little bow or curtsy to the judges and the watching and applauding spectators. I noticed Chloe and Abigail looking particularly attractive and gave a little wave to their parents who were sitting at the end of our row. But they both wished to ignore me, presumably still fretting about their stolen panties.

For the second half of the proceedings the girls were again called forward one by one and asked to speak their names into the mike and say briefly why they wanted to be elected Queen and travel on a float through the town. Most of the girls were nervous, giving strange reasons, but Chloe spoke well, saying how she wanted to be able to wave to the people and try and make them smile and be happy and give lots of money to Cancer Research, which earned her a special round of applause.

It was at that moment I felt a hand on my thigh and realised Molly had slipped into the seat at my side. She looked very fetching in a short summer dress which displayed a lot of bare leg, tempting me to copy her approach, but I was taken by surprise. I had imagined that such intimacy belonged to a night that had passed, when wine had flowed freely, and we were seeking mutual consolation...a night I thought Molly might want to forget...having found solace in Nigel's arms. But I presumed events had not worked out like that and her very friendly greeting almost suggested she wanted to carry on where we had left off, which sent my thoughts into overdrive!

Peggy nodded a greeting to Molly and I could see she had noticed our friendly meeting and, like me, seemed surprised. Then a round of applause recaptured our attention and I realised Chloe and her friend Abigail were still in the last elimination round and were awaiting the judges' final decision.

Then the announcement was made amid cheers and more clapping. Chloe was elected and crowned Carnival Queen, and Abigail and another friend to be ladies-in-waiting. All the girls seemed pleased as they would all take part in the festivities during the week and I could see Eva and Ruth were delighted; still choosing, however, to ignore me.

I imagined they would be thinking back a couple of decades to when they were two young girls sharing that glory, but not realising I could remember the furore that surrounded it…how their two rivals, favourites for the event, had mysteriously lost their dresses just moments before getting ready for the parade…how the two girls had been too distraught to continue and Eva had easily won the Crown with Ruth as one of her ladies–in-waiting.

Neither the dresses nor the culprit were ever found, but amid the bitterness and rancour, a firm finger of suspicion had been pointed at Ruth's elder brother.

The event was brought to a close by a little 'thank you' speech from the Lady Mayor and as everyone began to leave we four strolled back to the Promenade.

We walked to Jon's car and when he said they had to return to their cottage Molly and I waved them off. Then we walked along the Promenade, hand in hand, just like we had in our school days. At that time we had been close friends, in different grades but seeing each other every day. The years had separated us, and apart from the intimacy of the night before we were almost strangers. So we walked and talked, wanting to be friends again...and names like Nigel and Donna were never mentioned.

The Carnival festivities had begun. In the evening the lights were switched on...fairy lights all along the Promenade and the Pier...floodlights shining on the trees and rocks of the Cliff Walk, and in the gardens the paths would be lit by a large size Mickey Mouse, Donald Duck, or one of their friends. With the evenings still being warm the lights drew even more people out for an evening stroll, including Molly and me.

On the Monday morning the Royal Navy frigate arrived to drop anchor in the deep waters off shore and within minutes the local passenger boat owners were offering 'Trips to View the Warship'. All day there would be a flotilla of small craft buzzing around the big ship, each one packed with eager visitors wanting to get a close view. Later in the week there would be excursions to go aboard and be shown around the ship.

All the week there was the Aquatic Carnival...sailing boat races, rowing boat races and, of course, the wind surfers would add a blaze of colour from the multi hues of their sails. A naval team would be competing in many of the races...serious...but not without the occasional clown. Then each afternoon there would be a water polo match between local lads and a team from the frigate. With sailors strolling through the town and along the Promenade there would certainly be more young girls about.

The Bowls Club had tournaments and competitions organised for members and visitors...for the 'fours', 'pairs', and 'singles'. I entered on the Monday evening for the pairs and drew my partner from a lucky dip... it was Eva! She was far more embarrassed than I and hardly spoke in the first round. But we managed to win and after that she seemed to thaw out and settled down in the next round to play really well. I sensed our friendship had been restored and with it came success; by the Friday evening we were competing in the final against Tony and Ruth. It was a tough game, but we sneaked a win by one shot and Eva was so pleased she gave me a hug...much to Tony's obvious disgust! Eva and I received a bottle of wine each, and as Molly was in the group applauding, I naturally invited her home to share my prize.

Saturday was really Carnival Day and everyone was delighted with the fine weather. Over the years it had been a fun day...with happy memories...but this one would be remembered for a very long time with horror.

The procession of the decorated floats began in the morning. First was the butcher with his (plastic) carcasses hanging alongside chickens, turkeys, and rabbits. The butcher was there himself, with his wife, waving strings of sausages at the cheering spectators lining the streets. Then came the baker, his assistants going through the motions of kneading dough and removing baked loaves from an oven, while the baker and his wife were throwing wrapped cakes to children in the crowds. The town had no candlestick-maker, so next came the fishmonger. His wife was reclining on a slab dressed as a mermaid, while fishermen in sou'westers were waving fish as they drove by.

And so the procession went on, displaying fruit and flowers and every other commodity, seeking laughter and fun from those lining the pavements, making them smile and wave back. The Scouts, Cubs, and Brownies were well represented, and finally came the Queen on her throne, surrounded by her ladies-in-waiting and her courtiers, all waving, smiling, and looking very pretty in their very splendid costumes.

After a tour of the town their destination was the 'Rec' where the Queen declared the Sports Day open. The whole field was encircled by deckchairs and these were rapidly being occupied by the crowd wanting to watch the various events. I had arranged to meet Molly by the Band Stand and we just managed to find two empty chairs.

After the speech of welcome the contests and competitions began. The frigate was still at anchor so there was a tug-of-war between a local team and the Navy, followed by various tests and challenges of strength. There were long and short metre races for adults and children, and plenty to provide fun like the egg-and-spoon and sack races. I was laughing at Arthur taking a tumble with his feet tangled up in his sack when I noticed the young Queen and her ladies-in-waiting walking along the line of spectators, calling people out. Chloe seemed to make straight for Molly and me, and we were soon bandaging our legs together for the 'three-legged' race. We didn't run very far before we were both sitting on the grass laughing.

There was a Punch and Judy Show, a bouncy castle, and many items for the children. The finale was a 'live' game of chess with the 'pieces', in mediaeval costume, lined up ready for combat on squares marked out on the grass. Taking part were the members of the Woodymouth and Upper Woody Chess Clubs with adults in the roles of kings, queens and bishops, younger ones for knights and castles, and children in the role of the pawns. Movement of the 'pieces' was rapid, controlled by loudspeakers, and mock combats took place between the attacking and defending pieces with the vanquished having to stagger off the field of battle. Losses were heavy on both sides and then, with a lightning attack, the Woodymouth forces laid a trap for the opposing king; within a couple of moves he was captured...checkmate...with cheers, of course, from the local spectators.

Perhaps for many the climax of the week was the evening dance held at the Royal Hotel where the proceeds have always been donated to Cancer Research or some other deserving charity, and where the patrons would all be dressed to suit the auspicious occasion. I took Molly, looking very glamorous in a long, tightly-moulded green dress which I was pleased to note, when I helped her from the car, had slits at the sides to give a nice display of her shapely legs... and a promise perhaps of excitement to come.

The hall was decorated with garlands, giving it a festive appearance. It was flanked on either side by tables and chairs, while at one end an extra bar had been set up. I noticed it was being run by the two young men I had seen kissing in the car park of the Highwayman's Retreat. Presumably their services had been 'lent' by the inn.

Earlier in the week Hubert had phoned asking if I was going to the dance and if I was taking a partner. When I said yes, Molly and I were immediately invited to join his table. He said we would make the number up to ten, which I naturally assumed would be Bowls Club members, although I knew Rosemary was away on holiday. When we arrived Hubert and his wife were already there...Muriel not quite 'the mouse' as she was wearing some of her valuable jewellery.

Then Duncan and Amy Peters arrived, and finally Tony escorted in two very attractive young mums, Eva and Ruth. With Molly working in the bank few introductions were necessary, and when three or four bottles were placed on the table conversation seemed to begin as the wine was poured into our glasses. Much to the delight of the ladies the handsome young barman from the inn was doing waiter service. As we chatted I felt that the ill-will and acrimony of the past weeks had been forgotten...or swept under the carpet for the night.

There was still an empty chair at the table and Tony explained he had invited a friend along as a companion for Ruth, but unfortunately he had been delayed. And that seemed to confirm the general impression that Tony was trying to re-establish his attachment to Eva.

So when we took to the floor for the first dance we each had our own partner, leaving Ruth alone. I liked having Molly in my arms...she was a good dancer...but I was annoyed with myself wondering how Donna would compare, refusing to admit to myself that I wanted it to be her. Molly and I had rekindled our friendship, and we had enjoyed some affectionate moments. Given time perhaps we would find more. But then, it was not important as we were both enjoying the evening.

We joined in the Paul Jones and I met and danced with Paula, and girls I knew, and some I had never seen before. Within our group we changed partners and after a waltz with Ruth I was escorting her back to our table when I noticed Tony's friend had arrived...someone he obviously thought would be a joker in the pack...it was Nigel! But, of course, I knew who the joker really was. No matter what the occasion you could always count on Tony Fairclough to organise something to cause mischief, and this prank did just that. But no-one was really hurt. Whether or not it formed part of a diabolical plot to put me under suspicion for horrors that were being planned I will never know.

Ruth soon realised Nigel's interest was more towards Molly than to her, and with a bit of an apology to me Nigel whisked Molly off for a slow foxtrot. Tony was obliged to comfort Ruth so I danced with Eva. The Sinclairs and the Peters' were happier sitting and watching, and that developed into a kind of pattern for the later part of the evening. Molly had told me she had made Nigel sleep in his car last Saturday at the inn, but it was obvious they wanted to be 'back together' again!

Tony was paying a lot of attention to Ruth and I was enjoying dancing with Eva. She was friendly (once more) and talkative, telling me her mother was away staying with her sister, and Chloe was keeping Abigail company and intended making it a sleep-over. Back at the table she joked about how she would be all on her own but I picked up a suspicion she was hoping Tony would take advantage and do the same as Chloe.

I danced with Molly and sensed immediately she had that guilt complex again...not wanting to hurt my feelings but wanting to let Nigel take her home. I told her not to worry but just to follow the heart. So before the dance was ended they wished us good-night and left. The ladies in our party expressed their surprise and sympathy towards me, but I reassured them saying things had worked out for the best with their engagement back on track. I noticed Tony was actually smirking.

I did a polka with Ruth, and then towards the end of the evening I was dancing with Eva when she suddenly stood still and exclaimed: 'that two-timer's kissing Ruth!' Then with a brief apology to me she stormed off the floor, collected her handbag from the table, and almost ran to the cloakroom. Quite oblivious, but standing slightly in shadow, Tony was embracing Ruth.

Naturally I was concerned about Eva and went to see if there was anything I could do. She was very distressed, but being comforted by the barman from the inn who was kindly ordering a taxi to take her home. He appeared to be very sympathetic, saying he had noticed the incident.

I waited with her for only a few minutes as presumably, late in the evening, taxis were on stand-by. I offered to see her home but she said she was too upset for company and just allowed the young barman to take her to the taxi. He waved as she was driven away.

As I returned to the hall I met Paula and her husband just leaving and when I got to our table the Sinclairs and the Peters' were preparing to do the same. When the M.C. made the customary request, 'take your partners for the last waltz,' I realised mine had deserted me, so I went home. I saw no sign of Tony or Ruth.

I lay awake for a while with my mind going over the evening and wondering about the friends and acquaintances I had shared it with...not knowing that some of them, like me, would come under suspicion for taking part in a shocking crime being planned that would terrify a young woman before another day dawned.

My first thoughts were of Hubert Sinclair, our pompous Secretary, who had completely changed his attitude towards me. He turned on the charm, particularly towards the young ladies. And Jon, of course, had done more than hint of a weakness there. His wife, Muriel, had been quiet...like a mouse...but in her jewellery she had been a regal rodent. I had formed the impression that while she may not always be in control she would be the one to take final command.

Next there was Duncan Peters, our Club Captain, a quiet, unassuming man I have always admired. He would be mortified if he knew how much of his wife's posterior I had seen while she was bending over the table in the ladies' changing room. During the evening Amy had spent a lot of time watching Dominic with her rival Nina, no doubt wishing she could cast an evil spell on one or the other.

Then there was Tony Fairclough, the Joker, who had arrived as escort to Ruth and Eva, having us believe he was trying to re-establish his attachment to Eva. His prank to split up Molly and me had worked, but then he flirted with Ruth and sent Eva home on her own in a taxi, with final words of comfort to me and the young barman: 'don't worry, I'll take a couple of pills and sleep like a log.' I fell asleep wondering how Tony's mind worked....was he just a joker or a devious planner?

I awoke in the early hours with the need for a drink of water, and having quenched my thirst went back to sleep. Later in the day I would learn that, at that moment, a very drowsy Eva was being awakened by two frightening figures dressed in black boiler suits and hideous Halloween masks. They had pulled the sheets down to the bottom of her bed and were holding her arms outstretched to either side, with one of them pressing a big pair of scissors to her throat, making her too terrified to speak or scream.

'Just relax,' he said, 'or I could hurt you with these,' and then one by one he cut off the buttons of her pyjama top. His voice was muffled by the mask, but she understood his words only too well. 'We want to have a good look at you, and my friend will have a feel around and take some pictures.'

Sunday was a very sombre time once we knew about the break-in at Eva's house during the early hours. Peggs rang me asking if I would like to spend the day with them. So I drove to The Fisherman's Cottage where conversation was soon directed towards Eva's ordeal. Jon had received some information but was expecting more. He was always in contact with his friend Bert, whose life he had once saved. Bert would willingly put his job on the line to provide any help to his former partner. He would be a friend to Peggy knowing I was her brother being framed in connection with the assault cases on the two girls. He believed in my innocence but I was never sure about the Inspector.

After lunch news started to come through...I had never asked how...and we learned that Eva had been taken to hospital, not really suffering from any physical injuries but from shock. WPC Dove was with the victim, in the early morning, providing comfort and seeking as much information from the troubled young woman as she was willing and able to give.

The first report was verbatim in Eva's own words: 'they took off my pyjama top and both of them touched and fondled me, wearing surgical gloves. For the whole of the time only one man spoke and sometimes he called the other one Nathan. I couldn't tell if it was the Nathan Squires I know, as I never heard his voice. The other one terrified me when he touched my nipples with the cold scissors, telling me he would cut them off if I didn't behave and do exactly as I was told.'

There was a footnote regarding the one referred to as Nathan: 'no actual confirmation as to gender'.

We heard from Bert that the Inspector had given instructions to call in five people for questioning: Hubert and Muriel Sinclair, Tony Fairclough, the Bowls Club Groundsman, Dominic, and Nathan Squires. I was not surprised to be included. If one of the villains had been referred to as Nathan then naturally I would expect the Inspector to question me. I just hoped he would realise it was another attempt to frame me. But I was still no nearer to finding the culprit.

Jon agreed with the Inspector's choice of Hubert but said he was puzzled about Muriel, while Peggy pointed out that if the other one never spoke it could be to disguise the fact she had a woman's voice. She also thought that if a husband had a weakness for young girls or younger women a devoted wife might wish to help him in his digressions. They seemed to agree that the assailants could be Hubert and Muriel.

The second report came in, again in Eva's own words: 'I was too frightened to move when the one called Nathan began pulling my pyjama bottoms down and the other one slid his hand down with them. I closed my eyes when I knew I was naked, and felt them touching me all over. I heard the click of the camera and couldn't stop them moving my legs about. They weren't hurting me, but the touching and stroking was horrible.'

Jon said such information had obviously been leaked by Donna after she had interviewed the victim in the morning. 'She's risking her whole career for you Nathan, knowing you're going to be pulled in again... and clearly doesn't think you could be involved.'

'Well, she's had personal experience,' my sister butted in. 'We know those two assaults on the young girls were very kinky and this one, to my mind, has similarities. After spending that afternoon on the beach with Nathan at the Cove, in her birthday suit, I'm sure Donna will know he's just a normal, full-blooded beast!'

'Gee, thanks for that!' I said.

'And what about Tony Fairclough?' she asked. 'Could he have been one of the perpetrators?'

'Quite possible, I suppose...he's got a really twisted mind...he could have planned it, with one of them using my name to get me involved. Ruth had girls at home on a sleep-over so I don't suppose he would be invited to stay the night when he took her home.'

Then Jon had a question for me: 'when we talked about the Inspector's suspects we never mentioned Dominic. How do you think he might fit into this latest horror?'

'Well, I've seen him engaged in some very queer activities in the ladies' changing room in our Pavilion.'

'But there were two of them,' Peggy challenged.

'Yes, but as our Groundsman he is naturally very friendly with Hubert and Tony, so it's possible he could team up with either one. All three will have seen Eva as a very lovely young woman and might be harbouring erotic desires for her. She knows them, but their voices would be muffled by the masks.'

'So it could have been any two of the Inspector's suspects, apart from you, working together,' Peggs added. 'Let's hope he can sort them out.'

We received no further information and Jon thought it would be because of a change in shifts, with Donna being relieved of her duties at the hospital. But while we had our evening meal our thoughts and remarks were still with poor Eva and I wondered what further horrors and humiliations she had endured before the two assailants left.

'Do we know who found her?' I asked.

'Yes, when Bert first told me what had happened he said the villains left by the front door, probably before dawn, leaving it unlocked. When her friend Ruth brought her daughter home, early morning, they found her tied naked to the bed.'

'What a terrible shock for them...especially for the young daughter,'

Peggy said. 'It's abominable.' I agreed, with a mental picture of Eva's terrible torment making me feel very guilty as I sampled a peach tart smothered in crème fraiche..

Then before I left I had their warning. I had, of course, received privileged information...horrible details that an innocent man wouldn't know. So when they called me in for questioning I would need to be very careful of what I said. A careless word and the Inspector would believe I really was the same Nathan that had terrified Eva.

CHAPTER 14

THE RUBBER BOAT

• • •

As my mind cleared through its early morning haze I realised it was Monday and the beginning of another week. Normally I slept well, apart from dreams when Donna usually appeared, and when we weren't having an argument we would be spending the time very pleasantly. But through the night my thoughts had been troubled, reflecting on poor Eva. While I had been brought into the assaults on the two girls, which bore similarities, Eva's anguish seemed much more painful to me...because I knew her, and because only a few hours before her horrible experience I had held her in my arms on the dance floor and she had been happy.

Most mornings I was in a rush over shower, shave and breakfast, but I sat with time to ponder and my thoughts drifted over some of the girls in my life. Going back to school days there was Molly. She was a pretty girl and we were great friends, sharing the experiences and problems of school, and apart from a little hanky-panky when we were stranded on a sandbank up the river, that was it. We wanted to be, and just enjoyed being, friends.

With Sonja it was different. She was such a lovely girl and I fell in love. She filled my every wish and desire, and I was enriched by her love in return. Losing her was a terrible blow, leaving me drained and empty for a very long time.

More recently, after my return to Woodymouth, I met Rosemary and was attracted to her, but immediately thwarted by Tony Fairclough. Then I met Eva, the very charming young mother of Chloe. Plans started to move towards a liaison, but someone decided to intervene with hoax calls and pranks and our relationship went on a joy-ride of ups and downs, peaks and troughs, mainly in the troughs. After her recent terrors would she be thinking I was the one helping to undress her and then take photos? Hard to imagine what she must be thinking of Nathan Squires.

I saw the lovely Venus at the Beach Hut and WPC Dove at the Baths in a bikini...and ogled! She burgled her way into my life and I was fascinated. She brought back feelings that I thought had died, and I managed to entrap her with our agreement. For some weeks she kept me at arms length and I was falling in love. In the first place she said she didn't know if she even liked me, but then I could feel with each meeting she was coming closer...and closer. Then I came under suspicion for the second assault and decided to play the hero and end it all for fear of damaging her career. But she decided otherwise, to sit naked on the rocks at Dead Smuggler's Cove, knowing temptation would be too much for me. What happened on the beach, I felt, was not just an afternoon of sex, but consummation of our love for each other. I was gutted when she went ahead and ended the relationship, although I had suggested it.

Then I went to Rydemouth and met Ellie and, of course, I understood. She was a married mother and I had been her bit of excitement with no-one to know and hurt but me. I never quite understood why we had gone to the little church and taken Holy Communion together. I believed she had wanted to hear me confess my love for her, and as she had plans to seduce me the Communion was to bond us closer together. But presumably I was wrong, she was asking forgiveness for the adultery she was about to commit. Obviously she had discarded our relationship into the memory bin, which I've found difficult to copy. With me being a suspect for sex crimes, finishing our association protects her job...something I will have to learn to live with. Yet according to Jon she is risking her career to leak information about Eva's nightmare, to help me. Why would she do that? I can love her but I don't suppose I will ever understand her.

I had lots of time to spend over breakfast, but still managed to be late getting to work and found everyone in the office discussing the Carnival Dance...what the girls had been wearing, or not wearing...what new partners they had...and the shocking news about the break-in at Eva Sheen's house. One of the girls lived nearby and had seen police cars and a number of officers coming and going at the house when she passed on her way to church. She had managed to coax a little information from a young constable. There had been no press release so few facts were known about Eva's ordeal. But one or two of the staff had seen me sharing the table with her, in fact seen her leave me in a big huff, in the middle of a dance, and go storming off to the cloakroom.

So when Paula and I went through the morning's mail I realised they were hoping I would provide them with more details. But I explained to Paula I had not been Eva's escort on Saturday evening and I had not spoken to her since she left me on the dance floor. She would probably refuse to speak to me, but I didn't mention that.

I explained that the police would be questioning a number of people who attended the dance, and in particular the Sinclairs, Tony Fairclough and myself who shared the table with her. We both knew what repercussions could follow that. When I was called in for questioning after the assault on the young girl in the caravan some mischievous person had informed Head Office. If it should happen again I could foresee problems with my Area Manager.

But it was not all doom and gloom. During the afternoon I had a call from Rosemary saying she would like to see me and asking if I would care to join her one evening for a meal. I said I would be delighted and we agreed on the next evening, Tuesday.

The day dawned full of promise and early in the morning I was motoring over Padmoor, then through wooded valleys, seeking a hidden away farm. I had been walking the fields, in my wellies, with the farmer making a random assessment of the value of his crops and cattle. We discussed my findings in the farmhouse kitchen where his wife offered me a mug of tea while he persuaded me to sample his 'scrumpy'..brewed last year from his own home grown apples. Driving back to the office I realised I should have accepted his wife's offer, but I managed to park the car without hitting anything.

In the evening I set out to see Rosemary. I drove down the lane to the gates, and after a few words on the intercom I was admitted to the drive. There was a friendly greeting from the housekeeper and I was ushered into the lounge to meet my charming hostess. I had always found her attractive and that evening she excelled. When I had been put under suspicion for assault on the two girls, many of the ladies in the Club had withdrawn from me, but Rosemary never had. As tittle-tattle and some vicious rumours had spread she had always ignored them, remaining a loyal friend.

We had a lot to talk about. She had just returned from a holiday in Interlaken, where Sonja and I had spent our honeymoon. So we were soon swapping stories about the breath-taking views at Grindelwald and the never-to-be-forgotten trip through, and to the top of, the snow-capped Jungfrau mountain.

She was eager to hear our local news about the Carnival, the dance, and of course, inevitably, the break-in at Eva's house, although it had become common knowledge that the two villains, assumed to be men, had carried out an assault on her.

I told her how I had enjoyed the evening with the little group at the Sinclairs' table, despite Tony's trick of inviting Nigel to break up my attachment to Molly. She smiled at that: 'it was quite typical of him.'

'Yes, and to follow it he spoilt Eva's evening. When they arrived we all thought they were an item, together again. But towards the end of the evening she saw him kissing Ruth, which sent her home in a big huff...and later came the break-in.'

'Have the police any leads?'

'I've heard they've questioned a number of people who attended the dance and I expect they'll soon be drawing in all of us who sat at the table sharing the evening with Eva.'

'But surely it could be anybody.'

'True, but I think they feel it is more likely to be someone from the dance who knew she was going to be alone. She lives with her mother and daughter, but on Saturday she told us they would both be away for the night.'

'That sounds like careless talk!'

'Well I got the impression she was angling for Tony to copy Chloe and do a sleep-over!'

'I'm surprised he missed out on that...and if the police pull him in they'll know he has a bit of a record concerning a girl who worked in his Estate Agency office. She brought charges for assault, but then it was all hushed up. I suspect Muriel may have bought her off.'

'And what about Hubert?'

'A similar story there, some years ago, regarding a girl who worked in the Quarry office.'

'So it looks as though the police will be doing some probing.'

Further discussion was halted by the housekeeper wheeling in a trolley which bore what she described as Vietnamese chicken salad. Apart from the roast chicken breasts I found the lime flavoured dressing on the lettuce and mixed vegetables very appetising on that warm evening. The strawberry sorbet finished the meal off nicely and over coffee Rosemary told me the strange story of her finding a dead squirrel in the garden.

'Did you bury it?'

'No, I thought its death looked rather suspicious, as if it had been poisoned, and as we have a cat I panicked. I called the vet. He used to be a golfing chum of Will and he kindly agreed to come over and have a look. After making some tests he decided it had died from an overdose of crack/cocaine, and then within hours all hell was let loose.'

'What happened?'

'Customs and Excise men appeared with a sniffer dog and found traces of the drug near where the squirrel had died. They then embarked on a full search of my garden, digging and poking in all the borders.'

'Did they find any more?'

'Fortunately no, but I had a very interesting chat with one of the officers. Apparently crack addiction among squirrels is not a completely unknown phenomenon, but it is usually confined to park areas which are frequented by drug addicts.'

'I have heard of this, although it's difficult to imagine the local squirrels being high on crack! I believe it has been reported in some countries abroad; when the animals are desperate for a fix they have attacked people.'

'He didn't mention that, but he was emphasising the fact that if squirrels smell something they like they will dig it up, and they also like to bury things. Similarly it is often the habit of dealers or pushers to hide parcels of dope in different places, and if there is a danger of a police crackdown they will frequently use gardens or parks.'

'I can see where their thoughts were going, and their dilemma. Had the little creature found a big stash of the drug in your garden, or was he digging out a little packet he had buried? Or again, was he burying one and when it burst he got too greedy? Unfortunately, whatever the answer, it killed him.'

'Well, I don't know if they found any packets, but after digging up half my borders they widened the search with the dog, presumably in the belief that the squirrel had found the stuff in this area and was hiding it. I was told they would again be searching the lane that leads from the river to our Quarry. They never came back so I have no idea if they found more of the stuff. That poor little fellow caused quite a furore...the vet said it was a he...and they took him away when they left.'

But the meal and brandies had put us both in friendly mood and I recalled Hubert's remarks that when Rosemary crossed her legs she could be very persuasive. The rest of the evening was spent very pleasantly. I thought her goodnight kiss as I prepared to leave could hold promises of more intimate moments to come.

But those happy thoughts faded overnight and Wednesday was a dull day providing nothing in the office to lift my spirits. News was spreading about the attack on Eva Sheen and was a topic for conversation. Paula and those members of staff who had been to the Carnival Dance would have seen us enjoying time together. Knowing I had been questioned over the assaults on the girls would provide more food for thought and conjecture. Last time I had spoken to them about hoax calls, but on this occasion decided to carry on and make no excuses.

So routine office work continued for the day.

In the evening I walked up to the Green and joined in a roll-up with Hubert and Muriel, Arthur and wife Audrey, and Alice – they were all members who still spoke to me! Clouds threatened but we enjoyed a few ends of play before the rain started, forcing us back into the Pavilion. Someone had had the foresight to put the urn on, and tea and coffee were being made available.

Hubert was quick to tell me that both he and Muriel had been questioned about the evening at the dance.

'Just routine stuff, of course, and I expect they'll be having a word with you...but I found that Inspector a real cheeky sod, and when he started asking me questions about the young girls we'd employed over the years in the Quarry office I soon put him in his place!'

I could well imagine the pompous attitude. Whilst most men might be satisfied with a high horse, Hubert would climb on a mammoth. But I don't suppose for one moment it would intimidate the Inspector.

When Hubert wandered off, Arthur came and joined me at one of the tables and, of course, after a while conversation came around to a discussion of the dance and Eva's traumatic experience. I expressed surprise because I hadn't seen him there and he explained that Audrey had twisted her ankle slightly and they had spent the evening in the lounge bar adjoining the dance hall.

'So you missed all the dancing then?'

'Yes, but I looked in once or twice and saw you dancing with Ruth, then later it was Eva...you seemed to be enjoying yourself. We weren't alone in the lounge as there were quite a few from the Club. Harry Wilks was there propping up the bar for the later part of the evening with his half brother Billy Edwards.'

'Did they get pie-eyed?'

'Now it's funny you should ask that because Audrey noticed they only had a couple of whiskies and kept quite sober. Was Hubert in a huff about being called in for questioning?'

'Yes, after some routine matters he says the Inspector got nosey about a young girl employed in the Quarry office.'

'Well, if stories are true about the young girls employed up there, I'm sure the Inspector will have ruffled quite a few of his feathers. Did he say anything about Tony being called in?'

'Yes, I believe he was first.'

'Not surprised, of course, because he's been in trouble over girls once or twice and the chaps at the Nick will have kept a file on him.'

I was thinking I could be in the same boat, with my criminal record growing by the week. Arthur obviously thought Tony's was well deserved, but mine on the other hand was fake, due to hoaxes. Unhappily I didn't know if the police would continue to believe that.

'What time did you leave?' I asked.

'Oh, just before midnight, and I was surprised to see those two young bar-lads come over and talk to Harry and Billy. They'd packed up their bar, and when we left they were all four deep in conversation. I was curious because I know the lads don't bowl in the same game, if you get my meaning.'

I knew his meaning as I had seen them locked in fond embrace. It was still raining, and when Audrey came and told Arthur she wanted to go home, I thought I would do the same.

Since Sunday I had been waiting for the call...steeling myself for a dreaded ordeal...then on Friday morning the Inspector and his Sergeant walked into the office. Their car was a plain 'under cover' vehicle, they wore plain clothes, but it was still clear to the staff why they had come. I was obliged to confide in Paula, and she would respect that confidence, but as I walked out with the two men I knew that within two minutes everyone would know I had been taken in for questioning over the assault on Eva Sheen.

It was an unfortunate choice of days because I learned that my solicitor friend, Rupert, had been called away. I was told they could wait until he was available, but with a false sense of bravado I told them it didn't matter. I wasn't supposed to know anything about the assault and as an innocent bystander I shouldn't have any fears anyway.

The surroundings were familiar. A small room with dismal, green décor, and again I sat opposite the Inspector and his Sergeant. I was put at ease by the Inspector thanking me for helping them with their enquiries and we had a friendly chat about the dance and the events of the evening. He was aware I had taken Molly and how she had left with Nigel.

'Were you upset about that?'

'No, they are, after all, an engaged couple.'

'Yes, I see,' his familiar phrase suggesting once more that he didn't. 'So then you transferred your attentions to Mrs. Sheen?'

'Not particularly. I danced with her and her friend Ruth.'

'But you were dancing with her when she became upset and left the hall?'

'Yes, but I did not cause the upset, it was someone else.'

'Quite so, but when she left you would be aware her mother and daughter were both spending the night away from home and she would be at home alone.'

'I will ignore any inference there. Yes, I was aware, just like everyone else on our table, and probably one or two more people in the hall.'

'When we came to your apartment after the assault on the young girl in the beach hut we found you had taken pictures of a young woman without any clothes on.'

'Yes, and I believe I told you the circumstances.'

'Do you enjoy taking photos of naked young women, Mr. Squires?'

I stared into eyes that seemed quite devoid of any feeling or emotion.

'That was the only occasion.'

'Strange you should say that because Mrs. Sheen told us a person referred to as Nathan helped to undress her in the early hours of Sunday morning and then took a number of photos of her when she was moved into various positions.'

When I stared back into the Inspector's eyes I saw they were a cold steel grey. 'Well, it certainly wasn't me.'

'Do you recall being questioned about the assault on the young girl at the Caravan Park?'

Before I could protest in anger the Sergeant joined in the attack. 'We believe you had a frustrating evening, losing your first partner Molly Hales, then Eva Sheen became cross and left you in the middle of a dance. She is a very attractive woman, so you sought the help of a colleague to break into her house, knowing she would be alone. Then you terrorised her to provide both of you with sexual excitement.'

Again my instinct was to shout an angry denial, but I realised if they really believed what they were saying I could be in serious trouble, so I decided caution must prevail. 'I left the dance hall before the end of the last waltz, drove straight home, and I was there until I went to my sister's cottage on Sunday morning.'

'But have you anyone to confirm that?'

I could have strangled him for his smirk. 'No, and if you have any further questions then I must ask for my solicitor to be present.'

I was now frightened. I was innocent but the Inspector and his Sergeant gave the impression of believing I was the Nathan taking photos of the naked Eva. I was taken to a cell to be held for further questioning. I was given a meal and then just sat on the hard bunk waiting and waiting...until Rupert came and we discussed the questions and answers of the morning. Then he left me and there was more waiting until he returned to the cell with the duty officer, and I was allowed to walk out.

We had a couple of whiskies in the New Quay Arms and he told me I had been put in a very tricky situation, but at the end of the day the coppers had no real evidence to hold me.

'But I'm worried, Nathan. You've got to find this character who keeps trying to frame you or next time could be a time too many. He's nasty, and very persistent, and unless you nail him he'll put you behind bars.'

It was a very worrying truth for me to think about as I drove back to the apartment, but I resolved to keep away from the whisky bottle.

Saturday dawned with promise of a fine, sunny day. I didn't actually see it, but when I sat down to breakfast at about nine o' clock, I knew it had. I was down to play in a home match with Rosemary in my team, so spirits rose. Before then I had time for odd jobs and decided to take a close look at The Dove...she appeared all forlorn and neglected.

I swam out with a cloth in my hand and gave her a wash over. A little while ago she had meant excitement and, as I wiped the painting of the dove carrying the olive branch, I thought how it had symbolised hope. But I realised it had turned into a reminder of a dream that had an unhappy ending. But as I clambered aboard to carry on with my chores I knew I couldn't part with the boat...maybe I should just wait a bit, then change the name.

After lunch, when I got to the Green, I met chaos. The visitors had arrived early by coach, and our members were strolling in from the town or the car park making up a gathering of about forty would-be players. But we were learning foxes had got onto the

Green during the night rendering it unfit for play. Some bright spark suggested they could be the same ones that had damaged the Upper Woody Green awhile ago and the Club had sent them down river to us, under cover of darkness, because we were threatening them in the League Table!

I spotted Rosemary in the throng and asked her to wait for me in the car park while I went to help Hubert and Duncan who were trying to pacify some disgruntled visitors.

They were with the deputy groundsman and he too was upset, but from him I was able to learn the cause of the problem. Normally Dominic would have found the damage caused by the foxes, advised our Club Captain or Secretary that the green was unfit for play, and the match would have been cancelled and everyone informed. But unfortunately, upon arrival at the Green early in the morning, before he had seen the damage, Dominic found two police officers waiting to take him in for questioning. He would have thought he would only be gone for a short while, then naturally, if questions had turned nasty he would have ceased to worry about a mere forty people wanting to play in a bowls match.

Explanations were provided and the visitors decided to put their kit back in the coach and spend the afternoon on the Promenade. Our members wandered off while Duncan looked worried and was asking for my advice. 'The police questioned Dominic after that poor girl was assaulted in the Caravan Park. You don't think he could have anything to do with this horrible business of Eva Sheen do you? Do you think he's that sort of man?'

Once more my mind went back to the scene in the ladies' changing room and I wondered. Again I avoided the question. 'I'm sure the police will sort it out, Duncan.' I could have told him his wife, Amy, would be the person best able to answer his question, but of course I didn't. I made an excuse to leave him, explaining I had a charming young woman waiting for me in the car park.

She was indeed a charming companion, sitting beside me as I drove over miles of open moorland, through wooded valleys and farmlands, seeking a nice village Inn. When we found it we ordered an evening meal and then, leaving the car, set off on a circular route to walk the moors. It was warm, but still invigorating, and we hiked for miles enjoying the delightful scenery.

After about four hours Rosemary was convinced we were lost, but my map reading was almost correct and after a slight detour we came within sight of the Inn. It was a real country tavern and we were ready to devour roast pheasant followed by a roly-poly pudding. I had a suspicion we might have been eating the bird 'out of season', but when you are ravenous you don't quibble about things like that.

During the return journey I went onto the coastal road. It was still light, so I pulled into a lay-by to look down and admire one of the beautiful estuaries. What I really wanted was a kiss and a cuddle and I was soon enjoying both. Light was failing when I drove back into the Bowling Green car park where Rosemary had left her sporty tourer. Then with a goodnight kiss and a wave she was on her way home. I knew we were both tired and all we wanted was a relaxed soak in a bath and then bed!

The morning was herald to another warm, sunny day which was comforting as I had arranged to meet Jon and Peggs at the Beach Hut. After a light breakfast I decided to go by boat...The Dove was looking more cared for, quite spick and span with tanks refuelled all ready to go.

It was reassuring to be back at the helm as I cruised out of the harbour, and exhilarating to feel the wind and spray once more as I opened the throttle again and circled the bay. There were quite a few boats about, mostly sailing but some fishing, and the occupants gave me a friendly wave as I deliberately gave them a wide berth.

When I'd had enough amusement I cruised inshore to drop anchor. The sands looked small suggesting the tide was turning to go out, so I anchored well off shore, covered up the cabin and swam to the beach.

Jon and Peggs had apparently just changed into swim gear and when my sister saw me approach dripping wet she said: 'good, you've had your swim, so we'll have ours and leave you to carry out the loungers and put the kettle on for a cuppa!'

'Thanks for the friendly greeting!' I shouted as they ran down to the sea.

But I carried out the orders and fetched out three sun-loungers, and by the time they returned I was relaxed on one of them and the kettle had boiled.

Conversation quickly switched to Eva Sheen and they both wanted to know about my interview at the

Nick. I told them, mentioning how Rupert had secured my release, and I repeated his words of warning.

Naturally Jon agreed with him: 'he's absolutely right, but I've been having words with Donna recently and between us I think we can come up with a few answers to help us find and expose the culprit.'

'That's wonderful, but what the hell's Donna...'

Distraction had come in the form of an attractive young woman in a bikini running towards us and shouting: 'the girls have gone...they've disappeared!' She was quite distraught and we jumped up to learn more.

'They were playing with that silly rubber boat and they promised not to go far, but I can't see them anywhere.' Gently we managed to pacify her and get all the unhappy details. She was Ruth...I hadn't recognised her in the bikini. Eva was at home and Ruth was looking after Chloe and Abigail. She had left them in the sea while she came back to their hut to sit and have a read of the paper. She had only left them for a few minutes, she said, and they had just disappeared. Then she became distressed again and Peggs had to comfort her, telling her Jon would phone and alert the Coastguard, and I chipped in that I had a boat anchored off shore and would go immediately to make a search.

Our words calmed her. But then when she recognised my voice I saw fresh alarm in her eyes and knew Eva must have told her about her assailant being called Nathan. She asked Jon to go with me, but he told her bluntly I would need room for the girls.

We checked that the unhappy drifters had a paddle each and then I listened to Jon's advice as we walked down the sands, he being a better sailor than me. 'The tide will take them seawards, but the river flowing out moves everything to the west.'

'Towards Dead Smuggler's Cove and those rocks?'

'Yes, I think Ruth's few minutes could be an understatement and when the girls panicked and started to paddle for the shore, the tide will have taken them quite a long way along the coast and they could end up in serious trouble. I should sweep, looking outwards, but go in the direction of the Cove...watch those rocks. The Coastguard will come from that direction but will probably be making a more off shore search.'

I swam out to The Dove and was soon beginning my quest. I was thinking of two young girls having fun and then becoming very frightened when they realised they were floating quite swiftly out to sea. In their panic I imagined they would paddle furiously for the shore as Jon had suggested. The cross current would carry them relentlessly towards the cruel rocks. I said a little prayer that they might be safe. I had rescued Rosemary at that Cove, from the clutches of Theo Braithwaite. I was hoping I might be lucky enough to rescue two young girls from the cruel strength of the tides. If they hadn't paddled for the shore then there was a faint hope the Coastguards would see them drifting out to sea.

The Dove held her nose up proudly and was slicing through the water as if she realised speed was of the essence and two young lives could depend on her performance. I took a wide sweep, keeping watch, looking inshore and outwards, but saw nothing to resemble a small rubber boat. Then when I reached the Cove I turned inshore and cut the engine to cruise towards the angry looking rocks.

The gulls were screeching and my heart missed a beat when I saw what looked like a body spread-eagled across a rock. I dropped anchor, jumped overboard, and swam in to find Chloe Sheen weak from exhaustion but otherwise unhurt. There was no sign of her friend or the rubber boat so I waded in to the beach and found Abigail flaked out behind a rock on the sands. She was in a similar state of exhaustion, but thankfully unhurt.

Chloe found the strength to come and join us and we sat together and talked to overcome the trauma of their experience. Through sheer determination they had paddled inshore, but as Jon had predicted the tidal currents had carried them into what must have been a terrifying ordeal. The boat had capsized but they still had the willpower to save themselves, while the boat presumably had returned to the sea.

Knowing they were safe was a powerful tonic and when they were ready to go I swam with them, guiding them through the hazards to The Dove, and helped them to clamber aboard. I lifted anchor and with the two girls huddled together on the one seat I turned towards Woodymouth and began the return journey.

Before the Pier was even in sight I saw the Coastguard boat turn from its search and head towards us. I heard the coxswain call 'ahoy there' through his loud hailer and I cut the engine and allowed him to come alongside. 'Congratulations,' he said, 'but we'll take the girls as we have a nurse on board.'

So the transfer was made and their boat sped off with the two girls being examined and wrapped in blankets. I followed and saw the Coastguard boat being beached and the girls being carried, amid cheers, to the large group of people gathered along the shore. I saw numerous camera flashes and assumed the Press must be there.

It had been wonderful finding the girls alive and uninjured, apart from their fatigue and weariness and a few bruises. But they had left me with a feeling of emptiness. A picture of Sonja had flashed through my mind, with a girl we might have had...and then there was Donna with Ellie...a love I had lost.

Looking to the shore I could see Ruth hugging Chloe and Abigail and I remembered the look in Ruth's eyes when I said I would go and search for them. Last week she was happy to be dancing in my arms, but a few hours ago she had seen me as an evil sexual pervert and voyeur. The hoaxer had done his job well and as my friends have said, unless he's caught, I will be destroyed.

I turned The Dove's nose towards the sea and opened the throttle, determined to let the wind and the spray blow away my blues.

CHAPTER 15

THE INTRUDER

• • •

Another week had begun and when I walked into the office I could feel the tension, knowing they were still talking about the horrors that had been committed against Eva Sheen. There had been a lurid press release and while no-one had been named, my staff seemed to think it was significant that I had been called in, once more, for questioning in connection with another sex crime. Paula was my secretary and I could count on her loyalty, but that did not spread to include the more junior members of staff who were not averse to a little tittle-tattle or fanciful conjecture. When I was transferred to take over the branch, earning their respect was something I valued, but invidiously that had been undermined. My 'friend' the hoaxer continued to do his job well.

But there was a new line of conversation. The local radio had announced the Coastguard had rescued two young girls from drifting out to sea in a rubber boat. The coxswain announced how pleased he was to be able to return the two girls to one of the mothers, but he was most distressed they had been allowed to use an inflatable boat which events had proved could be very dangerous. He was appealing to shopkeepers and stallholders not to sell them and to parents not to allow their children to use them.

It was known that one of the girls was Chloe Sheen and I overheard a young typist saying how fortunate it was she was away from home at the weekend 'otherwise those beasts would have abused her'. It was not an ideal atmosphere for my Area Manager to walk into, but by mid-morning he was there, chatting to one or two of the staff, trying to pick up any concerns or sensitivities. That was before he came to my sanctum to tell me Head Office were very disturbed to be advised their local manager was once more being questioned by the police in connection with a sex crime committed against a lady friend of his.

We sat and talked for most of the morning. I mentioned the Carnival Dance and my friendly and quite innocent involvement in the events which led up to the attack on Eva, and how I was merely one of a number of people to be questioned.

Afterwards he seemed quite affable so I suggested a drive over the moors for a pub lunch. Then I could deliver some figures to the hidden away farm where I was hoping to conclude some business. He said he was very agreeable to all that and we had a pleasant journey and a very enjoyable meal. Then I was able to conclude our business while my boss was happy to accept a large glass of scrumpy and was extremely relaxed for the return journey.

But when we got back to the office things changed. There was news that the West Country Tours coach had crashed with injuries to many of its passengers.

Three of them had been taken to hospital in a critical condition. Names of the injured had not been disclosed, so naturally there was extra concern all round in case they could be family members. The accident had reminded me it was not so long ago that I had submitted the business to Head Office with my glowing report on the company's excellent track record for accidents and claims.

I discussed details of our insurance cover with my boss and after taking into account reinsurances we concluded that final claims could still be enormous. Whilst little personal blame could attach to me, it was not the happiest of news that an Area Manager would want to take back to his Head Office.

So inevitably conversation came back to the telephone calls advising them I was tangled up with the police over various sex crimes that were being committed. 'They are extremely concerned, Nathan, and unless you can get to the bottom of this sordid business they will want to take action. You know the branch was a revolutionary step...a throw back to the past. With offices all over the country getting smaller, following centralisation of business, this was a brave step to buck the trend and create a larger company presence in the South West.'

'I'm well aware of that and our business figures surely show the venture is paying off. I'm not involved in any type of crime but the unhappy victim of a cruel hoaxer.'

'That I fully accept Nathan, but our bosses are saying enough is enough and I have to warn you. If there is any more talk of you being questioned by the police then I know they will move you out. I can tell you the G M has a whiz-kid in the wings, straight out of university with all the degrees they want, just waiting to take over. In strict confidence I can tell you it's his grandson. I'm sorry to be so blunt Nathan, but if they get one more phone call telling them you're mixed up in another sex crime they'll have you packing your bags.'

We shook hands and he left, and I was grateful for the friendlier voice of Paula asking if I would like tea or coffee.

I sat at my desk a long time after everyone had gone, thinking and brooding about my situation. I liked my job and I had proved myself to be good at it. Woodymouth was my home town and I liked it, having no wish to be moved to London or the Outer Hebrides. Since the first phone call from the hoaxer to Head Office I had believed they would accept and understand that I was an innocent victim, but bluntly it had been explained to me, for Area and General Managers, that may not be enough. One more involvement and I could be on my way somewhere. I would have liked to think it was just an idle threat, but I was damn sure it wasn't.

Jon had said there was hope he might be able to name and expose this hoaxer character. I had phoned the cottage and was advised by machine that Jon was not available, which would probably mean they were both out.

Of course, I was lonely and should ring Rosemary, but the one person I really needed and wanted was not available. I was trying hard to forget Donna but she was still in my thoughts and desires.

So I decided to seek solace on the sands at the Adventure Park. A drive over the moors was always bracing. Then when I got to the Park and sat in a flimsy kite-buggy facing hard, flat sands I could feel the adrenalin beginning to flow in anticipation. As the traction kite billowed and tugged on the buggy I knew excitement as a powerful off-sea wind pulled me along at break-neck speed. It was something I needed to experience more than once and then I was happy to go home, ready to take on the hoaxer and any of his cohorts at Head Office.

Tuesday was another worrying day at the office. I learned that Paula's mother had been one of the passengers travelling in the coach at the time of the crash. She hadn't been seriously injured but was apparently suffering from shock. I sent Paula home, and with the help of the senior typist I managed to get all the post away more or less at going home time. In the morning I had phoned Peggs at the bank and after meeting her for lunch in town I invited myself to an evening meal at the Fisherman's Cottage. She was home before I arrived and was busy in the kitchen, so after exchanging a greeting I sought out the man of the house in his study.

'Our last conversation, Jon, was at the beach hut, and you were going to tell me something important about what you and Donna had found out about my friend the hoaxer...when we were suddenly interrupted by Ruth screaming about the missing girls.'

'Ah, yes, I remember...well, Donna has been working with me. I have been doing a little more research into the life and activities of your team colleague Tony Fairclough, while Donna has been digging into the police and prison records of Billy Edwards and Harry Wilks. She has told me the beatings they received while doing their time were vicious and quite serious.'

'So they weren't exactly popular!'

'Far from it. The leader of the gang which carried out the beatings knew Billy had sold the dodgy motor that caused his daughter's death. Donna says she has been to the prison to pick up any stories or gossip and word was around the guy told Billy they would fix it so he would never have a daughter of his own.'

'Nice fellas...and I suppose Harry copped it by association?'

'Yes. They shared a cell and because they were half brothers he was unlucky enough to receive similar treatment. We believe hate and malice has built up against you because it was your testimony that put Billy away. We think, together, they are intent on destroying you. Tony is a practical joker, but these two are evil and we are pretty sure they are your would-be assassins.'

'You pointed and put the finger on these two characters some weeks ago, but we don't seem to be any nearer stopping them!'

'I can assure you we are, and Donna believes if she can see or obtain their hospital records we will be able to stop them carrying out any further hoax attacks.'

At that moment we were called for my sister's 'quick on the table' evening meal. It was a cheese and spring onion pie which she had served in slices with a salad. I was just enjoying the taste of the gorgonzola with a hint of garlic when she broke the news about the problems at Sea View.

'We knew James' mother has been having health problems and he's been popping back and forth to Bath, and now Julie's to go into hospital for tests. At the moment we don't know why, but obviously it is very worrying for them. I've been calling in one or two evenings and offering what little help I can give. If poor Julie needs hospital admission it will give them a real problem.'

'Yes, I'll call in and see if there's anything I can do.' Turning to Jon I thanked him for his efforts with Donna. 'Do you have any cases more lucrative than mine to deal with?'

Peggs served us with coffee and a gateau topped with succulent mixed berries. We both approved before tucking in, then Jon answered my question.

'A domestic, I'm sure you will agree, has developed an amusing twist. A young woman approached me to check on her partner. Usual story, after they had been together for a couple of years she thought he could be having an affair. As she admitted, he was married but still had an affair with her.'

'Suspicious, I suppose, stemming from her own guilt.'

'Maybe...but he and his wife separated and they have each set up home with another partner. I have found my client's suspicions were well founded and the man in her life is having an affair...at every available opportunity he is back in bed with his wife!'

'What do they say, absence makes something grow fonder?!'

After another coffee I left for home.

In the morning I was pleased to see Paula back in the office…glad to hear her mother had recovered from shock following the accident, so work quickly settled back into its normal routine.

In the evening we had a home match against a Club from Rixham, a pretty little village on the way to Rydemouth. I met up with Arthur and Alice and was pleased to have Rosemary joining us in my team. Our visitors provided very friendly competition and we were soon enjoying the game.

We were all playing well and, of course, Arthur had to get in his remarks when Rosemary walked up the green to play her shot as our number three: 'she's a cracker isn't she, and there are whispers she's putting a twinkle in your eye.'

Alice overheard and added her comment: 'talking of eyes, you can keep yours off her knees and just concentrate on the game,' which naturally drew everyone's attention to Rosemary's habit of pulling up her skirt before she bent down to bowl.

We managed another win (of just two shots) and added more vital points to our fixture rating. As we were moving towards the end of the season tensions were rising because we shared top position on the league table with our close neighbours Upper Woody.

Spirits were high in the Club and our visitors were invited to stay for a drink and a game of cards. We didn't actually have a licensed bar, but someone always seemed to find cans of beer and bottles 'left over' in their locker.

Whenever I tried to socialise with some of our Club members I was beginning to get the impression that my character and good name had been flushed down the toilet, so I was delighted when Rosemary suggested a stroll on the Promenade. I ignored Arthur's raised eyebrows and a murmured 'oooh!'.

It was still warm and very pleasant as we stood together looking over the darkening waters. When I put my arm around her she turned to me.

'Tell me about her Nathan...is it the police girl? Ever since you saved me from that cad Theo Richmond I've been trying to draw you in closer. I've felt it's what you want, but there is always hesitation, as if there's someone coming between us.'

So I told her the story...or at least some of it...how I had fallen in love with Donna and then found out about her family entanglements. When we got back to the Club car park it was dark. The visitors' coach had left and our members were drifting out of the Pavilion to their cars. I kissed Rosemary goodnight and she left with a parting whisper: 'don't worry, Nathan, I can wait until your torch for young Donna burns out.'

I thought about that as I was getting into the car, but I didn't slam the door, wanting to keep quiet as I was eavesdropping on a conversation between two of our lady members. I couldn't see them, they couldn't see me. I just listened.

'...she told Ruth they did terrible things to her and one of them took photos. Heaven knows where they'll end up...she's scared it could be the Internet. One of the beasts frightened her to death with a pair of scissors...and they cut her hair off and shaved her...down there...'

'Poor Eva must have been terrified.'

'Yes, and the one that did the shaving was called Nathan.'

'Never...what, our Nathan here?'

'Well, she's not sure about that.'

'But the police have had him in two or three times, haven't they?'

'Yes, and there was all that fuss over those missing knickers.'

'But I hear he did find those two girls.'

'Yes, and Ruth says he helped them into his boat with their costumes all torn.'

'If you ask me it was a mercy the Coastguard took them.'

'I suppose we'll never know where he was going with them.'

I couldn't listen to any more and slammed the car door and drove off feeling very angry. Back in the apartment I fetched out the whisky bottle but drank very cautiously, while brooding over what I had heard. I had been regarded by the police as a sexual pervert and those women were thinking of me as a paedophile! Jon has made suggestions as to who is doing all this evil harm to me...says he can stop it...but I must wait...while I'm haunted by premonitions of worse to come.

With my love life a mess and my job threatened, ideas were beginning to creep in about moving on. But what about Rosemary? Would I be happy just walking out on her?

I took all those troubled thoughts to bed with me and slept very badly.

The next day began with normal office routine until James phoned, asking if I could go over to Sea View to discuss and check on their insurances. I was glad of the excuse to call but a little surprised he should be bothering me in the middle of a busy season...guessing he was probably worrying about his mother's and his wife's health and needed a friend to talk to.

And that, I soon realised, was the case. He sat me down in their little office, withdrew their policies from the safe for me to peruse with the documentation I had brought with me. Then he kept walking in and out, interrupting...to tell me about his mother's stroke...how he had suggested bringing her down to Sea View...how the doctor thought she wasn't fit to travel...how she had managed to convey an adamant refusal to leave her home and her circle of friends. Then he spoke about Julie having to go into hospital for tests. Obviously he was very worried about her and I suspected with fears for their future business capabilities should it turn out to be serious. I think my being there, to listen and comment, helped.

Minutes later when he burst into the little office shouting: 'this is the last bloody straw!' I was able to calm him and get an explanation.

'We're a girl short in the kitchen, and this morning our dishwasher packed up, and now the electrician tells me he can't fix it until tomorrow!'

I actually made him laugh when I volunteered to come back after their evening meal and wash up.

'That would be a wonderful help, but to have you washing the dishes of thirty-four dinner guests would be something I would have to see to believe!' But when he left me (once more) he was chuckling and looking much more cheerful.

I returned in the evening, walked through the hall with the hubbub of voices coming from the dining room, and met Julie. She looked paler but as cheerful as ever and together we went down to join Cook, and her assistant Hannah, in the basement kitchen. Immediately Julie went to help them prepare the hot plates for the main course with the vegetable tureens and gravy boats to be loaded into the service lift for transport up to the dining room. There I knew James and a smart young waitress called Lucy would serve the tables.

The used dishes from the first course were piled high so I rolled up my sleeves and set to work, but not before Cook had given me instructions about making sure all 'waste' was first removed and binned and then all dishes or plates were well 'sluiced' in warm water before being put into the washing up liquid. The kitchen surroundings, with the heat, were very familiar to me and I could remember my mother giving me similar advice when I used to help out sometimes in the school holidays. We didn't have a dishwasher in those days.

The sweets were being prepared and Hannah was giving us her rendering of the number one hit tune until Cook warned her she could curdle the cream! I had just finished washing the first course dishes when I heard the lift trundling down with the dirty plates from the main course, and the washing up went on...and on. But when coffees had been served the ladies joined me to 'dry' and stack away.

When the tables upstairs had been cleared James and Lucy would be busy changing cloths and laying up for breakfast. But they both came down to the kitchen and James saw me with my hands still in the sink, washing the last of the coffee cups and saucers. Hearing him laugh was reward enough.

Later we relaxed together in their little private sitting room and Julie told me about a bit of a domestic problem they had.

'The Taylors in No. 3 have a teenage son and the Goff's in No. 5 have a teenage daughter. They arrived as strangers but have been going out on trips together and seem to have built up a friendship. The youngsters have singles on the floor above and Mrs. Tarbuck tells me the lad has not been sleeping in his bed. Oh, he ruffles it up each morning but Mrs. T has made up too many beds for anyone to be able to deceive her.'

'So what are you going to do, tell the girl's mum?'

It was James who answered. 'Julie was thinking of that, but I don't consider it's our responsibility. All bedroom doors have secure locks and if the guests don't wish to use them that shouldn't be our concern.'

'But it does concern me,' Julie said.

'Well, I'm afraid that's one problem I'm not even going to try to help you with,' I added with a smile. I finished my brandy, kissed her goodnight and walked home.

On Friday morning I had a visit from the Chief Executive of West Country Tours and over coffee and biscuits we discussed his concern and distress over the recent coach accident. He confirmed that three passengers were taken to hospital and whilst one had been released, two remained in a stable but critical condition...one being a friend of his wife. The driver had escaped more or less unhurt but a number of passengers had been treated for minor injuries. He said he was worried because he had already received indication of possible claims.

I advised him they would be inevitable, but we would deal with all letters and correspondence and protect his firm in every way possible. Having regard to his wife's friend I suggested they should try and keep matters on a strictly business basis, avoiding displays of sorrow or sadness that could in any way be misconstrued as suggesting feelings of guilt by the company. Hospital visits with flowers may be a kindly gesture, but can be used as evidence to back up a legal claim. He accepted my points and left, I hoped, reassured.

In the evening I went to a Bowls Club meeting, joining Duncan, Hubert and Tony. Whilst we four would constitute a valid quorum our Club Secretary still moaned about James and Rosemary being absent. We discussed a number of minor items and then the question was raised about decoration expenditure. Whilst the Green and the Pavilion were Council owned, each member paid, through me, an amount to cover our use of those facilities. We had a duty, however, to keep the Pavilion in 'good order', which normally meant a team working with paint and emulsion each Spring. I was able to assure the other committee members I had once more secured a grant towards the costs. Furthermore, thanks to a more prudent organisation of the Canteen and my suggestion of the occasional 'round robin' with a raffle organised, our Club accounts would be showing a profit rather than a loss, as in the past few years. It was duly noted, without any hand-claps.

Keeping my feelings of two nights ago when I was in a defeatist mood, I said I might consider moving away from Woodymouth, in which case I would be handing in my notice for the Treasurer's job at the AGM in November. That created a murmur of surprise.

Tony and Hubert had threatened to push me out of the Club, so I realised I was capitulating to their earlier wishes. But my spirits were very low. While I hadn't expected anyone to plead for me to stay on, I was hurt and a little angry they should all accept it as welcome news. Hubert jumped in to repeat his previous remarks about all the troubles I had been in, saying my going would help to preserve the good name of the Club. Duncan kept silent and Tony appeared to be delighted. As I was an innocent victim of all the troubles I left the meeting feeling very angry.

My temper didn't improve when I got home and found my apartment door unlocked. I pushed it open slowly and entered quietly and cautiously. The light was on and I came face to face with my intruder. She was standing in my bathrobe, looking very beautiful, and I fought hard to stay angry.

'What the hell are you doing here?'

'Well...I knew you would be surprised, but I expected a slightly better welcome!'

'How did you get in?'

'You gave me a card to the car-park boom, and a key, and the alarm number...remember?'

'But why are you here?'

'Apart from expecting a friendlier welcome, I did have one or two other reasons.'

'Please...let's hear them.' I was staring into those lovely brown eyes, but recognised the green glints. I was standing quite close and my emotions were in utter turmoil as I tried to stay angry, waiting for her to answer.

'I've heard you've been seeing too much of Molly, with some naughty- naughty at the Highwayman's.'

'Call me stupid, there was no naughty-naughty. But what the hell's that got to do with you?'

As she stared back at me the glints were flashing. 'I felt we had something good and strong between us. When we agreed not to see each other, I thought that was just until we've tracked down these villains who are trying to ruin you.'

'But you deceived me.....'

'It's not a crime these days, lots of people do it. You have your lady friends at the Bowls Club and Molly tells me you put her to bed...how do I know you're not deceiving me?'

'Because I can tell you nothing happened.'

'Molly's a bit hazy about that, but she can remember you helping her to get undressed. She's a very attractive young woman. Why should I believe you're not telling big porkies?'

'You'll just have to accept my word that I'm not.'

'Well, I'll accept it if you'll stop wingeing about me not telling you I had a young daughter.'

'Coming from you that's typical blackmail and it's only half your deceit... you conveniently forgot to tell me you were living with her father.'

Her mouth almost fell open in surprise. 'No I'm not...I'll tell you...quite some time after you groped a very young Molly,when you were conveniently stranded on a sandbank... back in the top grade at school, I had a terrible crush on a class-mate and on Saturday afternoons when Dad and brother Luke were at the football match, we were tempted to make love...and the outcome was Ellie. There were problems, of course, but my parents were wonderful and we had happy times together. Gerald got himself a job...and a motorbike... and was killed before Ellie's third birthday.'

That shattered me. 'I'm sorry...obviously you also have known tragedy and grief...but when I asked Ellie about birthday cards she said she would get cards and a present from mum and dad in the morning.'

'Yes.' The glints had gone, to be replaced by moisture. 'Her friends at school get presents from their mothers and fathers, and so does Ellie. She knows her dad was killed but he lives on as a kind of Father Christmas figure. I'm sure even you must have believed in him!'

'And the chap I saw arriving in a van, lifting Ellie up?'

'That'd be my brother, and the little minx has him wrapped around her finger!'

I felt all the anger had been drained out of me, but decided I should try to keep up appearances.

'But why did you keep Ellie a secret? Couldn't you trust me to know about her?'

'Oh, I'm sorry about that...but ours wasn't a normal relationship, was it? I didn't seek your friendship, you forced it on me. In the beginning I didn't think I was under any obligation to tell you I had a young daughter... then when I grew fond of you, I just kept putting it off. There have been one or two boyfriends and when I found one perhaps willing to take on a step-daughter, Ellie didn't like him. She can be difficult.'

'Why am I not surprised? Where do I stand with her?'

'You're her "new friend"...she's besotted with you... seduced by seven red roses and your promise to take her out in The Dove! Ever since her birthday she's been pestering me, asking if I've been to see Nathan...when am I going to see Nathan...why haven't I been to see him? That was one of the reasons why I came.'

'Why are you dressed in my bathrobe? Were you planning to seduce me?'

'Of course not...you know I wouldn't do anything like that! I've been chasing a young tearaway and needed to freshen up.'

Either by accident or design, as she was moving her arms about, I noticed the wrap-over belt had become undone and the bathrobe was hanging loose...tempting me.

'Did you have any other reason for coming?'

'Yes...to present to you "my proposition".'

It was my turn to register astonishment because she made it sound so serious, making me lift my eyes away from the opening robe.

'Please tell me.'

'It is your choice: either you sulk and stay angry because I didn't tell you about Ellie, in which case I'll get dressed and leave...or you can.....'

She never finished the sentence because I recognised the mischief in her eyes and made a grab for the robe... too late...she ran for the bedroom. I was not far behind and when she jumped onto the bed, laughing, the robe was lying somewhere on the floor.

After a while we got into bed and when Donna moved her warm naked body into my arms, with that familiar faint fragrance of gardenias, her lips were soft as velvet. I felt the firm thrust of her breasts...vibrant and responsive sculptures...and knew it would be a night to remember.

CHAPTER 16

REVELATIONS

• • •

When I awoke my arm was around her warm, taut tummy and I knew it was going to be a marvellous day as happiness had come back into my life. I always enjoyed the morning shower, but sharing it with Donna provided excitement, and I liked having her padding about the kitchen in a bathrobe helping me with the breakfast.

There were serious matters to discuss and resolve, but at that moment we just wanted to share new-found delights and plan some time together. It was Saturday morning and we both had two 'free' days.

Donna had arrived in uniform straight from the Nick but told me she had a small case in her car with a change of clothes. So while I went to collect that, she phoned home and spoke to Ellie and her mother.

'What did they have to say?'

'Well, they are all reconciled to me working odd shifts, day or night, but when I told Ellie I wouldn't be home until this evening she started whingeing. Then I told her I was going to see Nathan and her mood changed completely...more or less giving me a free pass for the day!'

'Mum was more discerning...she said I sounded particularly happy and she was curious. So I told her I was with you...not with all the details, of course, but she's heard a lot about you, so she would probably guess we spent last night together. She said Dad and Luke would be taking Ellie to the local gymkhana where she would have some pony rides...so I was not to worry, but just enjoy my day.'

That was what we set out to do, and it was wonderful having Donna by my side as I drove along the coastal road in a Lands End direction. She looked lovely in a short summer dress which displayed her legs to perfection.

'Where are you taking me kind sir?'

I knew she was happy, and last night she had said she needed to be with me even if it was just for a day - despite police protocol that might demand she should stay away.

'I'll treat you to some awesome panoramic views and then eventually, when I've stopped once or twice and had my way with you, I'll take you to a beautiful picture postcard village where the cobbled streets are lined with thatched cottages. There the landlady of the little local pub will satisfy your other appetite with her succulent home cooked victuals.'

''tis shameful, sir, that you make demands of me as a price I must pay for my sustenance.'

'You don't look too frightened, so I will carry on with my wicked plan,' and we continued on our way very happily, stopping at times to appreciate the picturesque landscapes, then moving on. When I drove down the lane to the village Donna saw the cottages clustered around a tiny cove and cried out in delight.

We parked the car at the top of the cobbled street and walked down onto the tiny quay which was stacked high with fishing nets and lobster pots. We watched a small group of fishermen guiding their boat out of the harbour waters onto the slipway, to be winched up on greased timbers.

'They have probably been out for two or three days and nights and you can see and smell the rewards for their efforts...possibly a mixed catch with some mullet and monkfish...maybe a few mackerel, but the best time for them is when there are storms at sea to drive the shoals more inshore.'

Most of the noise, apart from the men shouting, came from the sky where the gulls were weaving and diving, screeching and squawking. They had most likely been following the boat as it sailed the Channel, and were in loud protest at being robbed of a meal. But they were ever watchful, waiting for the chance to dive and steal a fish that may have jumped 'free'.

We climbed the steps up to the cliffs and walked along the scenic path to enjoy the views. When we were both feeling hungry we strolled back to the pub where we felt we had stepped back in time...into an 'olde worlde' atmosphere where the landlady made us welcome. She owned the pub, she said, and her mother and grandmother before her, while the menfolk had always been fishermen.

There were three elderly gentlemen supping ale and playing dominoes in an alcove, giving the impression it could be their second home, but otherwise the bar was quiet. In the evenings, we were told, the farmers and fishermen would call in to discuss anything that had happened or was likely to happen in the area. It was the centre of village life and gossip. The meal was excellent and our hostess was a very attentive waitress.

Donna was intrigued by the 'feel' of the place with the landlady telling her about the pilchard industry which once thrived there but in her opinion had been killed off by 'them from Brussels'. She was explaining to us about some of the faded prints and photographs hanging on the walls which related to the ancestors who had been caught smuggling (brandy, she believed) and how Customs and Excise men had, down through the generations, always been barred from the pub.

We were reluctant to leave – it would have been a heavenly place to spend the night – but I knew Donna was anxious to get back to Ellie and her family. So we set off for home and on the way we talked. Donna told me her father and brother were Master Carpenters and had sold up their business in Birmingham and bought into a firm of ship builders in Rydemouth as they both wanted to build boats rather than make furniture. Her brother was engaged and he and his fiancée planned to set up home there.

She spoke about Ellie, telling me how she wanted to be with her more, to have her living in Woodymouth and to start school there. 'Once she starts school in Rydemouth, and begins to make friends over there, that will become her home town, and mine too. We both love my parents, but my commuting can be a pain in the backside. Sometimes the journeys are about an hour, but when the tourists are coming and going it can be nearer three. So I've been trying to find a suitable flat.'

'Well, you know I haven't enough room to ask you to move in with me, but I might be able to fix you both into some hotel accommodation.'

'Woooh mister, hold your horses. I can't afford hotel prices and I'm not having you setting me up as some sort of mistress!'

'Heaven forbid...you've given me some exciting thoughts...but that's not the intention.' Then I told her about Sea View, how it used to be our home (although I omitted to mention that Peggy and I, with a bank mortgage, were still the owners) and about our good friends the Goslings. How they had health problems and as the season was 'running down' how they might welcome a 'resident guest' who would be willing at times to lend a hand with some of the lighter duties in return for a lower weekly rental.

'Don't get me wrong, I'm not trying to push you in as cheap labour, but the Goslings are fine, family people who lost a daughter about your age, a few years back and I have a feeling that you would fit in nicely... Ellie might enjoy it and Julie would spoil her to death. You would probably be offered attic bedrooms to begin with, but when the bookings drop off in the winter, maybe move down to better accommodation. That's how Peggs and I used to live. Why not come with me to meet them...then if they can take you in, you could give it a try for a week or two while you are looking round for a flat.'

Donna was taken aback by my suggestion and said nothing in reply. I don't think she was at all keen and was keeping quiet to avoid offending me. When we reached Woodymouth and I drove down into the car park I could see she was undecided whether to walk with me to the Goslings' or to cut and run to Ellie and her home.

'Just come and meet them...any decisions will be entirely yours.'

A few minutes later, when we walked into the entrance hall of Sea View, Julie was there and when she noticed we were holding hands her welcome couldn't have been more pleasing. Introductions and brief explanations were made and within a few minutes she was ordering me to go and find James while she was taking Donna to the lift with the explanation to me: 'I'm taking her to see your old bedroom up in the sky!' I knew the lift served three floors and then there was a narrow stair-case to the two attic bedrooms.

James and I were standing in the hall chatting when the lift descended and I saw Donna's attitude had completely changed and she was immediately introduced to James as their new 'resident guest'.

Walking back to the apartment she was telling me about the two lovely attic rooms and surprised me by saying she had arranged with Julie to move in next morning. 'We don't have a lot of things to shift so Luke will be able to bring it all in the van while I'll come with Ellie.'

When we said farewell I knew she was happy and excited, and her kiss was passionate. 'I'll be bringing my daughter to meet her 'new friend'...but I must warn him, she can be an artful little monkey,' and with a laugh she drove off.

I thought about the warning and walked down to the Marine Shop and managed to make a purchase before they closed for the day...just in case.

I was awakened early by a phone call from an excited Donna telling me Luke and the van were available, they were already packed and would be arriving at Sea View about ten thirty. Apparently Julie had suggested that as a good time to move in, when the guests had finished breakfast and most of them would have gone out for the day.

I was on the forecourt waiting and watching the visitors' cars leaving when Donna pulled in and I saw Ellie waving excitedly from the passenger seat with their car being followed by Luke in the van. Donna jumped out to kiss me and then Ellie held out her hand as she had done at their home in Rydemouth. 'I'm very glad to meet you again Nathan and I expect I shall want to kiss you when I know you better.'

'Well, I will look forward to that,' and I noticed Donna and Luke grinning.

There was a strong likeness between brother and sister and when Luke and I shook hands I realised his trade had built up his physique, giving him a grip of steel. He was very friendly, but unlike his sister, seemed more of an introvert.

As Donna had said, they hadn't a lot to move, just one case from her car and two larger ones and a couple of boxes from the van. We split up to avoid an overload in the lift, but soon had everything carried up the narrow staircase to the two bedrooms. Ellie held 'her girls' in her left arm and I was introduced to them as Mandie, Emma and Polly. In her right hand she had a tiny case which I was told she had packed that morning with their change of clothes.

I could remember, as a schoolboy, coming up to the attic and finding it a dark, creepy place that seemed to hide all sorts of strange things. Then one winter father called in a builder to put in a large fanlight, almost touching the floor at the front and back of the house, bringing in lots of daylight. Helped by a joiner and an electrician he transformed the gloomy attic into two fine rooms. By the spring each had been decorated, fitted out with a single bed, as they couldn't get a double up the stairs, and the usual comforts of lights, lamps and heaters. I remember mother insisting on her choice and selection for the décor, the curtains and the carpets.

Changes had been made over the years but the rooms were very comfortably furnished and whilst Donna had already seen them and chosen my old room at the back with its outlook over the harbour, Ellie was delighted with hers, being able to look over the Promenade, the pier and the sea. When I called in she was showing the view to Mandie, Emma and Polly. She seemed happily settled and was comforting and reassuring her girls that they would be alright in their new home.

Not wishing to intrude into such an intimate domestic scene, I crept out and found Donna admiring her harbour and river view. 'It's lovely, Nathan...thank you,' and I got an extra kiss as a demonstration of her appreciation. Then Luke arrived with a picture that had apparently been left in his van and told Donna if there was nothing further he could do, he would like to get back home.

That was the signal for us to leave as she said she just wanted to be on her own to unpack and settle in. I left, leaving Luke to say his farewells but not before the girls had promised to come over to the apartment for a snack lunch. As I walked through the hotel hall Julie was on the phone at the reception desk, so I waved and waited outside by the van to say thanks and cheerio to Luke.

When Ellie arrived at the apartment I knew what her first wish would be, so while Donna watched us from the conservatory, I took her daughter down onto the beach to have a good look at The Dove bobbing at anchor, and she was thrilled. Then when she started asking questions about how many seats and how often I took her out I knew she was angling for me to keep my promise.

'How about,' I asked 'if your mummy agrees, me taking you out for a spin next Saturday?'

'Oooh...yes please...lovely,' and she pulled me down for my first kiss. Then with an impish grin, suggested we keep it a secret for a little while.

When we got back Donna was smiling and asked: 'what plot have you two been hatching?' So I just shrugged and said: 'I'm afraid it's a secret,' and Ellie giggled.

It was marvellous having the girls in the apartment, then sitting down to a meal with Donna, Ellie, Mandie, Emma and Polly. Once more I realised the sun was shining, they had brought joy and contentment back into my life and I hoped and prayed that it was there to stay. But, of course, I had no way of looking around the corner.

After the meal Donna asked Ellie to take her girls into the conservatory. 'Just while I talk to Nathan about some police business, darling.' We sat and talked. She wanted to know all about Billy Edwards and Harry Wilks and why they may have bad feelings towards me. So I gave her the story and she said she and her partner would probably be detailed, tomorrow afternoon, to return to the prison hospital wing. 'I'm hoping to persuade the doctors there to break through patient confidentiality and tell us the exact nature of the injuries they sustained. I'm sure it could be vital to our investigations into these assault cases.'

While we were talking we could hear Ellie telling her girls about The Dove. 'It's a boat that goes ever so fast and when mummy's said OK, Nathan's going to take me out in it on Saturday.'

Donna was grinning: 'I guessed that was your secret...I warned you she's crafty...she's got me saying yes before I've even been asked! But I'm afraid there's a disappointment for next week...I'm on 'lates', starting in the afternoons and not finishing until about midnight. I'm sorry it will stop me seeing you, but I can be with Ellie in the mornings...give us a chance to be together and sort out her school and clothes that have to be bought.'

'I guess that's something I can get used to...having you both at Sea View is wonderful and you can pop into the office one morning. Paula will be delighted to get you a coffee and we can plan something for the weekend.'

Julie had booked us in for dinner, and a nice meal was the beginning of a very pleasant evening. Then when Ellie took her girls up to bed Donna and I went for a stroll on the Promenade and we kissed our goodnights with the sound of the waves gently lapping the sands.

I went to work 'bubbling over', knowing Donna and her daughter were living just a few minutes walk away from the apartment and when I went through the morning's post with Paula she, of course, noticed and I had to share my glad tidings.

'I guessed as much the moment you walked through the door, and it will be welcome news in the office.'

The day was busy as we were beginning to receive letters from injured parties in the coach crash. Next day, Tuesday, there were more disturbing letters, including two from solicitors, all needing very careful attention.

During the afternoon I received a phone call from Jon saying there was business he wished to discuss so I invited them to the apartment with the suggestion my sister might like to prepare one of my special 'ready' meals for us. And that was what happened. We had said our hellos with the usual pleasantries and I opened a bottle of wine when I heard the click of the microwave. Within minutes Peggy was serving us with salmon and potato slices with garden peas which somehow had become smothered in a delicious lemon and rosemary sauce. It was culinary magic from a box.

Then Jon told me about the news he had received from his friends at the Nick. On Monday afternoon two police officers visited the prison and managed to persuade the doctors to tell them the exact nature of the injuries sustained by Edwards and Wilks and a report was passed to their superiors which immediately set in motion warrants for their arrest.

'In a nutshell, Nathan, they have both been made impotent and apparently they left prison in the fond belief that after a while, living back with their partners, offering the usual home comforts, everything would gradually return to normal. But Bert reckons this may not have happened and they have needed to seek further sexual excitement to try and bring about a recovery. Hence they are now under suspicion, with others, for the assaults on the two girls and Eva Sheen.'

'Have they been taken into custody?'

'Not a chance...strange as it may seem, they have both disappeared...gone to ground somewhere, which rather convinces me they must have a crony or relative at the Nick to tip them off. Which would explain how your visits for questioning were quickly advised to your Head Office.'

'Perhaps they'll stop persecuting me now?'

'Until our chaps catch them, I doubt it. They're evil and they've really got it in for you.'

It was Peggs who butted in. 'Well it looks as if the police have at last flushed out two suspects for the assaults and we'll just have to wait for them to be caught. Meanwhile I want to hear about Donna and her daughter.'

That took me by surprise...and then I realised. 'Oh, you've been talking to Julie.'

'Yes, she told me they've got two 'resident guests' at the moment who seem to have settled in very well. Julie says Ellie's a real poppet who calls her 'my new granny'. Julie's tickled pink with that and sounded happier than she's been for weeks...but tell us about you and Donna.'

So I told them our story (suitably abbreviated) finishing at the end with a big grin...'we're together again...oh, and Ellie wants me to take her out for a spin in The Dove on Saturday.'

They were pleased but I knew my sister wouldn't be entirely satisfied and when she spoke I recognised the mischief in her eyes. 'You said you were cross with Donna when she came on Friday evening but on Saturday you took her to the little village of Pollick and had a wonderful day with her. Come clean Nathan, you've left out the juicy bit in between!'

They were both grinning. 'OK, you win...she stopped the night.'

Peggy's face registered the usual satisfaction, having squeezed out details of my sex life, but she was immediately contrite. 'One confession deserves another, Nathan...we knew about Ellie before she went into Sea View. She has been to the Station once or twice with Donna, and Jon soon learned about her. She's a popular girl there and Bert has described her as quite a card... and at the bank, Molly put me in the picture.'

'Why the hell didn't you save me heart-ache and tell me before?'

'Because we decided not to interfere, believing if you loved each other one of you, probably Donna, would find a way...and apparently she did! Molly will be pleased ...I know she's been feeling guilty about something...probably your monkey business at the Highwayman's. She thought Donna had left you for good and I believe she's been coming onto you to make Nigel jealous.'

'I wondered about that.'

'But Donna told her after you'd met Ellie she couldn't bear the thought of losing you and would have to go and see you...which seems to have solved their problems...and I can tell you enjoyed the visit!'

'How women can be so devious and wonderful,' I said, although I do have problems understanding them.'

'I've given up,' Jon added, quickly dodging out of my sister's reach.

Obviously they were both delighted with the outcome and Jon thought it was a good excuse for a celebration, so the remainder of the evening passed very happily.

On Wednesday my name was on the list to play in a home fixture match against a team from Farmstable, so I made an early start on signing the letters for the day's post to try and make sure I was able to leave the office promptly at five o'clock and stroll up to the Green. But, of course, at ten minutes to five my Area Manager decided to ring me and I finished up running rather than strolling. The visitors' coach had already arrived and I was only able to greet some of their team as they filed out to walk towards our Pavilion. It was some weeks since we had played Farmstable, but I found all their players very friendly, which provided a stark contrast to the disposition of members of my own Club. I had Arthur and Rosemary in my team as usual but Alice had not turned up, probably because her friend Harry Wilks was absent.

Jack High

It was Tony's job to bring on the substitutes. A young guy called Rory replaced Harry and then Ruth would be brought in to replace Alice, but there the trouble began. Tony said she had refused to join me to play on my rink. He could have told me discreetly, but in a typically Tony manner, made the announcement so that half the Green could hear. Arthur and Rosemary were loyal friends who would ignore such petty behaviour, but in general it was an embarrassment, especially when the visitors became withdrawn as though I might have leprosy.

Tony put Ruth on his rink and sent the dour Miranda across to mine. She played a good game but as she never spoke, my enjoyment was soured and for me the happiest moment was when we reached the end of the match.

It was me who suggested the walk on the Prom, but we both knew it was going to be different. Rosemary made it easy for me when she asked: 'are you going to tell me you and Donna are back together again?'

'How did you know?'

'Well a lot of strange things happened this evening, starting with the story I heard that our old foreman Harry Wilks had gone into hiding. His friend Alice didn't turn up and his brother-in-law Arthur, who normally has a cheerful word or joke for all of us, hardly spoke a word. Miranda brooded in silence and you, I realised, kept looking at me as if you had a guilty secret...as if you were frightened it was going to hurt me. So quite simply I guessed...good news for you, bad news for me.'

We walked down to Rosemary's car and when she turned for our good-night kiss it had lost its earlier hints of passion. But I just hoped we had the beginning of a lasting friendship. Of course, I had no way of anticipating the horrible black clouds gathering that would ensnare the two of us.

Thursday was a happier day, at least it started that way, because in the middle of the morning's routine business, Donna and Ellie called in to the office. Paula made them welcome with coffee and biscuits and a juice especially for Ellie, then whisked her away 'to meet everyone'. Donna told me that Edwards and Wilks were still missing despite an extensive search and then asked if there were any plans for the weekend as Ellie was still eager for her trip in The Dove: 'but she's insisting she goes alone with you Nathan...I suspect it'll make her feel more grown up.'

'Well, Jon and Peggs are keen to meet you both, so if it's OK with you, bring Ellie over on Saturday morning and I'll take her up to the cottage in The Dove, while you motor up. I actually bought a life-jacket for her at the weekend...just in case!'

'That was a nice thought, and it's a lovely idea. Ellie will be delighted.'

'Why will I be delighted?' she wanted to know as she walked back into my office.

'That's a surprise,' Donna answered, 'and now it's time we did some more shopping.'

When Ellie appealed to me for an answer I satisfied her with a wink and a grin. They left me in high spirits.

We had two or three claims building up following the coach crash and as I needed to catch up on some legal advice received from Head Office I took the files back to the apartment to study after my evening meal. I had just settled down comfortably with a wee glass of port when the phone rang and I was horrified to discover I was speaking to Billy Edwards. Startled as I was, I still remembered to switch my machine on to 'RECORD'.

'I 'ope this'll be a nasty surprise for you Nathan Squires. I know you'll 'ave 'eard 'arry and me 'ave gone into 'iding, but we wanted to make bloody sure you know we've not forgotten you. I told you in court I'd get you, and things 'ave gone alright.'

'Which means you and Harry must be responsible for the assaults on the girls and Eva Sheen?'

'I'm not sayin' nothin' about them...half the fuzz think you done 'em.' I heard a distinct chuckle. 'You jus' listen and don't try to get smart. We've not finished with you... far from it...we spent a lot of time in 'ospital beds thinkin' about you and we ain't goin' to waste that. There's lots more to come 'til we finish you. We 'ear you're 'avin' it off with one of the bitches in the fuzz, a pretty one I'm told. 'Arry and me will 'ave lots of fun with 'er when we've taken all her copper's kit off. 'Arry says she's got a tasty little daughter too. Sleep well Squires and don't be a clever git and try to trace this, 'cos it's on a stolen mobile that's goin' straight into the Woody. 'Bye.'

Obviously his intention was to frighten me, and he succeeded. Not for my own sake but for the threats to Donna and Ellie. In his wishes for me to sleep well he clearly intended the opposite and again he managed it. Sleep evaded me for hours and when it came the dreams were so bad I think I just willed myself to wake up in a cold sweat.

Once I had surfaced and drunk my morning coffee, my impulse was to phone the Inspector, but then realised such information could compromise Donna's job, her position in The Force. So I rang on her mobile and gave her the details of my conversation with 'friend' Billy.

Donna was pleased to receive my surprise call, but for herself, didn't seem too upset about the threats. She believed I was the one really in danger and she and Ellie had been mentioned just to frighten me. For the latter part of it, I hoped she was right...

Billy's boast of what he and Harry might do to the girls had turned my insides over. But I did extract a promise from Donna to be more watchful. Then I agreed to have words with Jon.

So I was late getting to work and it was nearly lunchtime before I had the opportunity to phone Jon and tell him about my call from Billy Edwards. We talked about my plan for Donna and Ellie to come to the cottage on Saturday morning and he said they'd be delighted to see us but I had to bring the tape. He thought it should be handed over to the Inspector, but only after he and Donna had listened to it.

For the rest of the day I tried talking myself into believing the fugitives would be so busy avoiding capture they wouldn't have a chance to harm us...that Billy Edwards was just making idle threats. At bedtime I wasn't convinced, but I had quite a good night's sleep and enjoyed my dreams.

CHAPTER 17

DRUGGED WINE?

• • •

Saturday was perfect...the sun was shining and I was going to see Donna and Ellie and they arrived just as I finished washing up my breakfast things.

'How do we look?' Donna asked in such familiar fashion, standing holding her daughter's hand with their arms outstretched. 'Dressed for adventure!'

I saw two beautiful girls in eye-catching shorts with matching T- shirts and my heart missed a beat. 'Absolutely gorgeous and I want to kiss both of you,' and that was how the day began.

I had been out to The Dove bright and early to remove and stow away her waterproof covers and give her a good wipe over, so when Ellie and I paddled out in the inflatable the boat was looking really shipshape. Ellie was thrilled to be clambering aboard...so much so she almost fell back into the harbour, but I managed to save her from that humiliation.

She knew we were going up river and she had heard, with some protests, that there were speed restrictions. So as a surprise (with Donna's earlier consent) we donned oilskins with our life-jackets and, after cruising out of the harbour, I gave The Dove full throttle on the open seas. I saw how Ellie held her breath as we twisted and turned and the salt water sprayed into her face. When we returned to the harbour she was too excited to speak and we were halfway up the river before she managed to say, almost breathlessly: 'that was lovely, Nathan.'

Donna had waved us off from the harbour beach and when we berthed at the little jetty of the Fisherman's Cottage she was there, waiting with Peggy and Jon. Ellie was first out and, without waiting for any sort of introduction, was eagerly telling them all about the surprise, with a spray by spray account of her fast trip out on the sea, finishing with the words: 'we got ever so wet, but it was wonderful!'

The three standing on the jetty listened in silent appreciation of the exciting story and I realised that Ellie had immediately made herself one of the family and it was a happy quintet that walked, or skipped, up the garden to the table where refreshments had been prepared.

I had given the tape to Donna to bring, so when we had finished our snack lunch, Peggs challenged Ellie to a game of Swing-ball on the lawn while the three of us went into Jon's study/office to listen to Billy Edwards' threats. Donna's and Jon's reactions surprised me. Whilst my worries had been for the girls Jon thought, and Donna agreed, those menaces could more likely be idle ones designed specifically to frighten me.

'I think the one really in danger,' Jon said, 'is you. If they can avoid capture then I feel sure they will continue with their plan to destroy you, personally.' And when I looked into Donna's eyes I could see her fears were the same.

'So what do you think I should do about handing the tape over to the Inspector?'

'You should,' Donna answered, 'otherwise you could be withholding evidence. But if you do, he will stop me being involved...stop me helping you...and I don't want that. Do you sometimes forget to do things?'

Without further discussion we joined Peggs and Ellie on the lawn and Jon organised a putting competition. Then he suggested getting their boat out and soon Ellie was interested in helping as the sails were carried to the jetty and the boat was rigged. When she was ready for sailing he announced his plan to Ellie. 'As the tide's well in, Peggy and I will take you for a sail across the river to that café there'...and he was pointing to the house we could see across the water which had been built out into the river. 'We'll all have tea there, but we can sail first and leave Nathan and your mummy to follow us in The Dove. How's that?'

Ellie was delighted at the prospect of another adventure, this time in a sailing boat, and when Jon left to fetch Peggs, Ellie had me fasten on her life-jacket to make sure she would be ready for when he returned. When eventually they cast off, Donna and I waved them away and I knew that with Jon at the helm Ellie would be surprised with some new thrills.

When I looked at Donna I yearned to take her in my arms and we dallied before starting. So when we tied up at the Woodycombe jetty the others were already sitting at a table in the garden and they all joined in the cry of: 'we thought you had a speed boat, what took you so long?' There was no answer we could give to that and we all laughed.

We ordered their speciality, the cockles, a delicacy for me, but for Donna and Ellie a new taste experience. But Ellie soon tucked into hers and was ready to clear any her mother left. Then we were served locally produced raspberries and clotted cream, while Ellie had a large ice cream added. Peggs was telling us that while some people are cautious of eating shellfish, the teas were popular because if there should be any tummy troubles this would be neutralised by the cream...acting as a kind of antidote.

We were discussing whether that was fact or propaganda when I suddenly stood up to get a better look at a man I had seen walking towards a vehicle in the café car park. Immediately our conversation had stopped with the words: 'what's up?' I watched as he got into the car and then I told them.

'I have just seen Billy Edwards get into a car with a fair-haired woman and drive up the lane which would lead to Upper Woody or Rydemouth. Do you think he could have been spying on us?'

'I doubt it,' Jon answered, 'he lives in Upper Woody.'

Then Donna butted in. 'His house is being watched so he probably arranged to meet his wife or partner here. I can't pass on the information because I don't even know the man '

'But I do,' Jon said 'and if Nathan reckons he saw him, that's good enough for me.' Then he dashed off into the house.

He returned within a few minutes. 'I got straight through to the Upper Woody Nick and they're sending a patrol car after him. But there's nothing further we can do, so I'm going to finish off these delicious raspberries and cream.'

When it was time to leave, the tide had turned but the river was still full with no sign of the sandbanks. Ellie wanted us to have a race so we set off together. Donna and I were in The Dove and even when obeying the speed restrictions we managed to keep her bow in front until we were almost across. Then I allowed the tide to carry us slightly off course and with shrieks of delight from Ellie and Peggs, the sailing boat nosed ahead to reach the little jetty first.

When it was time to go home Ellie had enjoyed herself so much that all inhibitions had gone and she was offering goodbye kisses freely. When she came to me she spoke softly: 'if I give you an extra big kiss, Nathan, would you let me steer The Dove...for just a little way?' It was almost a whisper but the others heard and I saw Donna and Peggs exchange a glance with a grin and Donna murmured something about: 'he'll soon be twisted around her little finger...I did warn him!'

We returned with the arrangements as before, but in reverse...and of course Ellie enjoyed taking the wheel for part of the way. Once back in the apartment, however, she wanted to run 'home' and tell her 'new Gran' all about the exciting day. Donna did nothing to stop her and perhaps unsurprisingly we were soon embracing on my bed. I've been enraptured by exquisite variations from Mozart or Haydn but I was finding them nothing compared to what Donna's lips and mouth could do to me.

But every overture has an ending and she said she would have to go. 'I don't want to leave you darling, but I will have a daughter waiting...so if you give me my panties back, I'll tidy up and go and join her for our evening meal.'

Sunday was true to its name...lovely and warm with the sun shining, which was fortunate because we had all arranged to meet at Sea View and then have a day on the beach.

I walked into the forecourt just as Jon's car pulled in and we went into the lounge to find Donna talking to Julie, and immediately enquired about her health. She looked very pale and told us she now had an appointment date to attend the hospital for tests. Not a happy prospect, but at least progress was being made. Otherwise she was very cheerful and it was quite obvious she was happy to have Donna and her daughter staying with them.

'Where's Ellie?' I asked.

'Oh, she's helping James lay the tables for dinner tonight,' Julie advised.

'She insists that's one of her jobs. She helps Mrs.T with the beds in the morning and when wanted, shells peas for Cook. She's a little treasure. Although...' she added with a chuckle, 'Hannah reckons she eats more peas than go into the basin!'

Ellie had come into the room and immediately asked: 'are you telling stories about me, Gran?' Then, when she sat on the settee between Donna and Julie, I realised from Julie's smile of greeting just how much she was regarding her as the grand-daughter she might have had.

But it was Peggs who picked on Ellie's question and spoke to her in a conspiratorial tone. 'You were asking about a story, well I must tell you one because you are sleeping in the bedroom that I had when I was just your age...and my brother there used to keep tame white mice in a big cage in the shed at the back of the hotel. But one day he brought one up to his bedroom in a cardboard box.'

Ellie had been listening intently, but she had to interrupt: 'is that the room where Mummy sleeps?'

'That's right, and during the night the mouse bit a hole in the box and disappeared under the furniture.'

Ellie was enthralled: 'and did Nathan find it?'

'No, but I did...on my bed!'

'What did you do?'

'I screamed, and Nathan came and caught it.'

'Oh dear, I hope I won't find a mouse on my bed.'

There Julie butted in. 'With Whisky prowling around I'm quite sure we don't have mice, and Mrs. T told me she's found her asleep on your bed more than once so if there was a mouse about it'd be too frightened to go into your room knowing Whisky might be there. So there's no need for you to worry.'

'Oh, no...that's right,' Ellie agreed rather sheepishly.

We said cheerio to James and Julie, walked via the Promenade to our beach hut, and soon had the loungers out on the sands. Until they were put out there was no room to move around and get the kettle on for tea or coffee.

It was warm enough to change into swimming gear and we were soon in the sea enjoying ourselves. Then we had lunch and lounged about until Ellie suggested: 'wouldn't it be nice if we could build a sand boat like

The Dove' and that, of course, was a challenge that Jon and I couldn't resist. The sand near the hut was too dry and powdery, so armed with buckets and spades we moved down towards the sea to work where the sand was more malleable. While we toiled Ellie collected shells so that when our masterpiece had been created it was adorned with its name.

Ellie was delighted and when she sat in 'the cabin' she said: 'I shall be alright when I make it go fast because I've got my costume on.' So we left her in her little world of make-belief.

When we got back to the girls they were laughing.

'What's tickling you two?'

'Nothing really,' my sister answered, 'Donna was just telling me a joke about little fingers.'

That was beyond us, so it wasn't pursued. But on a serious note, Jon said he had heard from his friend Bert that in the early hours of the morning, police had raided The Highwayman's Retreat looking for Edwards and Wilks, without any success.

'I'm not surprised,' Peggs said, 'we know Nathan saw Billy Edwards at Woodycombe.'

'But it's a likely hideout,' Jon answered, 'we don't know where he sleeps at night and there is a family connection with the landlord. There'll be some truth in the pub's name...maybe there's a sort of 'priest hole' the highwayman used to retreat to and hide away.'

Suddenly Donna jumped to her feet. 'Who's that?' she shouted pointing to a young man talking to Ellie and immediately we both ran down the beach. The young man turned, saw us coming and started to walk away. Donna went to Ellie and I followed the guy and shouted for him to stop. He turned to face me and I was quite surprised to recognise the handsome young barman from The Highwayman's and he asked me quite politely, 'what's the problem?'

'What were you doing with that young girl?'

'I only stopped to be friendly and congratulate her on building a fine sand boat.'

So I let him walk away and returned to the girls, to find Donna reassuring and comforting her daughter.

'Whatever's the matter?'

'Ellie says that young man held her by the hand and wanted her to go with him for what he said would be a lovely ride in a real boat.'

When I scanned the beach there was no sign of him...he had mingled and disappeared into the holiday crowd, but when I looked further down to the sea, I saw a speed boat, bigger than The Dove, with two young men aboard moving off from the shore. It turned, throttled up and went off in the direction of Dead Smuggler's Cove. I couldn't make a positive identification, but I had my suspicions as to who those two young men were.

After the scare Donna wouldn't allow her daughter to be left on her own, so Ellie agreed to go back with us to the hut, but not before she had 'given' The Dove to a young boy about her own age who had been struggling to build a replica. She explained that the lever at the side was the throttle to make it go faster and we left him sitting aboard looking very pleased.

When Peggs challenged Ellie to a game of volleyball we held our Court of Enquiry and when Jon learned who the young man was he told Donna she should bring her Inspector into the frightening picture. There were daunting conflicts of interest, but she agreed that decision would be left to her.

We all had a final swim, then we said cheerio to Jon and Peggs and walked back to Sea View. I left the girls as we all wanted to freshen up and then I rejoined them at the hotel for an evening meal.

As before, when Ellie went upstairs to put her girls to bed, we took a stroll on the Prom and kissed goodnight, at the same spot, to the sound of the waves gently lapping on the shore.

But it all felt so very different. I knew Donna would be on a second week of 'lates' and we would see little of each other, but I had a horrible feeling like a premonition, that it could be for an eternity.

The next day was a complete contrast to the weekend, looking dull and cloudy and although I found plenty of work to do, as evening approached, I could have described it as mundane...mainly I supposed because I was going to a bowls meeting. Not something I was looking forward to, as I was planning to hand over my duties as Treasurer to Rosemary, having reached the point where I wasn't enjoying my membership any more. To say the least, too many of the members had become anti-social.

I was delayed at the office by a business call and when I arrived at the Pavilion I found Hubert already 'in the chair' trying to prepare the minutes and call the meeting to order, without success. I was dismayed to learn Rosemary had fallen over a hosepipe left carelessly in front of the Pavilion door and then to be told she had twisted her ankle badly. She was sitting on one of the benches with skirt raised well above her knees to allow Muriel to lift her leg and apply a cold compress to the injured ankle. Rosemary's legs have often attracted a male eye, so for the Club Captain, Duncan and the Team Captain, Tony, this was an ideal opportunity to watch and express their sympathies. Naturally I joined them and this left Hubert to huff and puff on his own, with one of his favourite moans, that our President James Gosling was absent, although he had sent apologies that he would be unable to attend.

But it was the ladies who really took charge of the meeting. Muriel said Rosemary ought not to stay and suggested she took her home in Rosemary's car as she was quite unfit to drive herself. Then despite her husband's niggles, recommended he close the meeting down and follow in their car. Rosemary was in painful agreement and suggested to me, if it was convenient, I should call on her on Wednesday evening to discuss the Treasurer's job over a meal. I said I would be very happy to comply and then, between Muriel and me, she hobbled out to her car. She was driven off with my good wishes and my promise to see her again in about forty-eight hours. So the meeting broke up and Hubert followed the ladies in his car. I went with Duncan and Tony for a couple of drinks and then we all went home.

The next two days were, for me, quite uneventful, although on Wednesday afternoon Jon phoned to tell me he'd had a business lunch at the Highwayman's. 'I just wanted to 'nosey about' a bit and noticed the young barman wasn't on duty. I enquired from the landlord and learned he and his friend had just 'buggered off in a big hurry'. When I asked if he had a forwarding address he just laughed and said they would probably be looking for barmen's jobs in Andalucia or the Costa Brava. I don't know how true that might be, but after Ellie's experience on Sunday, I believed the lads at the Nick were looking for them.

Wednesday night, of course, was rather special as I had an invitation to call on Rosemary. I had phoned and learned the injured ankle had received a doctor's examination and had been put into the usual elasticated sock with orders for it to be rested. So when I drove down the lane to the gates, to go through the usual procedure, I was surprised that she had hobbled to the door to let me in and after our friendly kiss of greeting I asked: 'where's your housekeeper?'

'Come into the lounge and I'll tell you.'

She led the way and despite the injury was looking as attractive as ever.

Her living room had the comforts of luxury and when she had settled into an easy chair with my help to get her ankle onto cushions, I presented the two bottles I had brought...a sherry and a red wine, which I knew were favourite tipples.

'Thanks, Nathan, you've kept the sherry nice and cool so shall we start with a glass of that? Olga's already opened a bottle of red on the trolley, there, so just put yours with it.' Then she added with a teasing grin, 'if I hadn't known about Donna coming back I might have asked you to open it to make sure you stopped the night!'

We both laughed and I thought how enjoyable that might have been. 'But tell me, how have you been since Muriel broke up the Club meeting?'

'Well, I've got the usual pain-killers to take and Olga's been fussing over me, and for the last two days Hubert and Muriel have practically lived here. Muriel said I couldn't get to the office so they'd bring it to me, and they've put an experienced temp in at the Quarry. They came this morning, we had lunch together and spent the afternoon in the dining room working on business matters. I managed to secure some of the contract for the development project at Padquay so we have to get that completed before next summer begins.'

'But where's your housekeeper now?'

'Ah, every Wednesday she goes to spend the night with a friend. She has a standing arrangement with a taxi firm to take her each way, but this afternoon Hubert said they would drive her to her friend's and he phoned the taxi firm to make sure she'd be picked up as usual in the morning.'

Then Rosemary added with mock coyness, 'so you see the evening is all ours.'

'And I thought I was here to talk you into taking over as Club Treasurer.'

'Pour the sherry and I'll tell you what I think of that idea.'

She did, without mincing words, telling me how she thought the whole notion was wrong, how Hubert and Tony had been so keen for me to take over the job in the first place and then after I had fallen victim to some sinister attacks and spiteful innuendoes, had quickly become turncoats, trying to move me out of the Club.

'You've done a good job, Nathan, taking over after poor old Will. Ignore the stupid tittle-tattle and tell those two puffed-up morons you're going to stay put!'

'On a question of principle, I know you're right,' I acknowledged, deciding not to mention those were also Donna's sentiments.

So the evening didn't work out as planned, but was spent in friendly debate or argument as to whether I should ignore and oppose Hubert and Tony by staying on as Treasurer, or abandon it on the basis that it just wasn't worth the hassle.

Perhaps influenced by the sherry I hadn't reached a decision by the time Rosemary suggested I pull the trolley over to see what delights her housekeeper had left us. I discovered cocktail sticks piercing thin strips of smoked salmon with an appetising scent of lemon juice, which I shared out for starters. Then I poured our drinks and put them on the little table between us with a plate each of roast turkey slices wrapped around tasty sausage meat. That was delicious with the red wine and Rosemary continued to argue I should think again about giving up the Treasurer's job. So I topped up our glasses and we drank a toast to putting two fingers up to Hubert and Tony.

Then when I inspected the other tasty snacks and nibbles I noticed Rosemary seemed to be dozing off. Quickly I reached over to rescue what was not quite an empty glass in her hand. I managed with difficulty to put it on the table. Quite suddenly I was finding it hard to focus and gratefully slumped back into the chair where I was thankful to drift away into oblivion.

I was in a deep sleep but had a strange dream; I could hear people whispering about 'him' and 'her'. Then I was being dragged somewhere, followed by more whispering when I felt as though they were trying to undress me. I was annoyed...I wasn't ill...didn't need their help...quite capable of undressing myself. The movements and whisperings continued for some time and then it all went quiet. I was aware of a subtle fragrance which seemed familiar and I was happy to rediscover sleep.

When I opened my eyes I was lying on my back looking at an unfamiliar ceiling and I didn't know whether I was awake or still dreaming. There was a chandelier glittering above me, as there were heavy velvet curtains at the windows, yet there was light at the sides and the bottoms. So if I was awake I could have slept through the night and that must be daylight shining in. Normally when I wake up I'm fairly quick to react, but my brain was befuddled. I was struggling to figure out where I was and then surprised to find I was just wearing a shirt and socks, without trousers, pants and shoes.

Some of the fog in my mind began to clear and with a sense of panic I realised a woman was lying beside me. With rising feelings of dismay I took in the scene. Her dress had been pushed up to her waist and in obedience to inherent male instincts my eyes wandered over her beautiful torso and legs. I had never seen Rosemary in less than a bikini, but I knew that naked body must belong to her, a realisation which pushed some more of the fog away.

I was starting to remember; we had spent the evening together, but what the hell were we doing lying on the carpet, half undressed? Only one explanation...we must have had sex...but I couldn't remember anything about it. Surely with a young woman like Rosemary, would I be able to forget? I must have had a drink too many. How could I betray Donna? This would be something to regret for the rest of my life. Then hope crept into my thoughts. Perhaps we never did. Rosemary was obviously still fast asleep...I must wake her...and very discreetly find out.

When I managed to get myself into a sitting position I was better able to look around and examine the room. It seemed familiar. There were two comfortable chairs which I thought we had used, and a trolley that had provided us with tasty snacks. I couldn't see any food from my sitting position, but I noticed two wine bottles. What appalled me was the sight of clothes scattered about as if they had been thrown there in a moment of impatient passion. Shoes were all over the place, my trousers and pants in a heap on the carpet, and a pair of flimsy panties on the arm of one of the chairs. I had forgotten about my tie, but I was about to find it.

I got to my knees and was bending over to wake Rosemary when I saw my tie and realised with horror that it was fastened around her neck. In a frenzy, with both hands I loosened it and cried out to her, but there was no response. She looked quite serene and lovely, but the paleness of her face frightened me and her skin felt so cold and clammy as I held her nose and pressed my mouth onto hers with three or four sharp breaths. I had only vague procedural knowledge of how to apply the kiss of life and in my anxiety, as I lifted my head, I wasn't sure if I had seen her chest rise and fall. In sheer desperation I went back to the task and continued...on and on...trying to establish a regular breathing rate, but to no avail. Poor Rosemary seemed so cold and unable to breathe properly.

Panic-stricken, still kneeling over her, I decided I must try chest compressions and put the heel of my hand on her breastbone. Then with both hands I pressed downwards. Again I had little understanding of what I was doing or why, only that I had seen it performed in countless T.V. programmes. I thought I must do it, despite being frightened I might cause injury, and as I pressed down with weight I said a little prayer that I wouldn't break her breastbone and that my efforts would restore normal breathing.

Vaguely I heard the sound of a door closing and thought, 'thank God, there is someone coming who can help me.' Then I felt a terrible bang on the head and everything went black.

Once again my mind was muddled by a throbbing pain in the head. I heard voices a long way away....coming closer...and then they were right above me. When I managed to open my eyes, I saw a uniformed police officer through a kind of haze. I realised I was on the floor and he told me to stay there as a doctor would come and examine me. Then moments later a man was kneeling over me and exploring my head and looking into my eyes with an optical torch. Then I heard him say, 'he's got a nasty bump, but the skin isn't broken, so you can take him into the other room now.'

I was helped to my feet and escorted towards the dining room, but on the way I almost collided with a police woman and the housekeeper who I hardly recognised as her hair was dishevelled and she looked as though she had been crying. Unfortunately she recognised me, even without my trousers, and I was shocked when she shouted: 'take that beastly man out of my way!' I was quickly pushed forward.

For some moments I stood with the police officer at the open doorway of the dining room looking across the room through French windows to a garden and lawn, a landing stage and the river. Apparently the view was not to his liking and he spoke very politely: 'I'm sorry sir, but I will have to move you from here,' and I was immediately guided into a much smaller room, without the view, which I was sure my grandparents would have referred to as the breakfast room. Funny I should recall them talking about a thing like that when I was having such difficulty understanding what was happening to me at that precise moment and remembering anything about the evening or the night I had spent in this house. I realised it was Rosemary's house and I could recollect I had been with her, but that was just about all.

There was a small table in the room with two dining chairs. I was asked to use one and the Constable used the other after moving it closer to the door. It dawned on me his concern was not just to stop me running about the house without my trousers. I asked him about those and again very politely he said they would need to examine my clothes. Then as if on cue another officer arrived with a white boiler type suit and I was asked to undress and change into that.

Some memories were coming back and I was starting to worry about Rosemary, but when I asked the Constable he assured me the Inspector would be talking to me about her. The door was partly open and there seemed to be a lot of people coming and going through the hall into the living room.

I could remember seeing Rosemary looking pale and poorly so asked: 'have they taken Mrs. Fletcher to hospital?'

He answered me in the same polite tone: 'there is a doctor with her, sir.'

Then once more, as if it had been a theatre prompt, a man appeared in the doorway and asked me: 'are you Nathan Squires?'

'Yes, I am.'

'Well, I'm a doctor and I need to ask you a few questions. You've had a bang on your head...how are you feeling?'

From then on there was a number of routine questions which gave me the impression he was not particularly interested in my general health, but was merely wanting to establish that I had all my marbles. I still felt there were quite a few missing, but he was satisfied enough to call the Inspector.

When the officer arrived with the Sergeant, no introductions were necessary. For seconds we stood facing one another and then he spoke.

'Nathan Squires, I am arresting you for the murder of Rosemary Fletcher. You do not have to say anything, but what you do say...'

He carried on to complete the caution, but I felt as though I had been hit on the head again and I just heard things in a state of shock. It wasn't the arrest that shattered me because I felt fairly sure I must be innocent, but the knowledge that my dear friend Rosemary was dead. The idea that I could have killed her was totally abhorrent, but with my arrest it became clear, even to my disordered mind, that someone must have murdered her. Sorrow was building up inside me bringing tears to my eyes and for the next few hours, like a zombie I just obeyed instructions.

Handcuffs were put on and taken off. I was driven to the Police Station where I was 'signed in' with the surrender of valuables. Then I was escorted to a cell... not for the first time of course...but when I heard the door slam shut, on that occasion it was terrifying.

I was fed and taken for a medical examination with blood samples being taken. The doctor was aware I had been hit over the head and asked if I had any aches. When I said it was throbbing I was given tablets to be taken with water and told they would ease the pain but make me very sleepy. Once more I asked who hit me and why, but again I was told the Inspector would provide me with details in due course.

Back in my cell I stretched out on the bunk, distressed by fear and sorrow and as the afternoon wore on, I fell into a troubled sleep. I had a horrible nightmare that I was holding something around Rosemary's neck and I saw Billy Edwards quite clearly. He was laughing and shouting at me: 'Ha, ha...Nathan Squires...we've gotcha!'

CHAPTER 18

ANOTHER MURDER?

• • •

Rupert woke me after the clang of the bolt and the squeak of the cell door, and I remembered he was my solicitor. I was a new person, starting a new life, as my friend Rosemary was dead...a fact I found so difficult to believe...or perhaps I just didn't want to, because it hurt so much. There was a dreadful realisation, I had been arrested for her murder. This poky little room, this cell, was my new home and to prove it, I had seen them write my name on a blackboard outside the door, before it was slammed shut.

Rupert told me I was going to be questioned and he wanted to know all about my evening with Rosemary – everything we had done together – but I could recall so little to tell him. I could remember finding us both half naked and my astonishment that we must have made love. I recalled the horror of discovering my tie around her neck and my efforts to restore her breathing to normal...then a shocking pain in my head...and blackness.

He explained that the housekeeper, to quote her own words, 'had returned to find me kneeling over her mistress, murdering her'. Whereupon she picked up one of the wine bottles and hit me over the head, which explained her bitter outcry when we met at the house.

The interview room and my interrogators were so familiar, but there was a grim, frightening difference. Before there had been quite a friendly atmosphere, making me feel I had been helping them with their enquiries, but all that had changed. I was a murder suspect. A very attractive young woman had been brutally choked to death, and the police believed I had done it. I didn't think I had it in my character to do such a thing, but they did and I just couldn't remember exactly what happened.

As I sat down with Rupert facing the Inspector and his Sergeant and listened to my name being detailed with the others 'for the benefit of the tape' I imagined I could hear Billy Edwards again shouting: 'hah...hah... now you know what it feels like!'

I waived the privilege of silence, feeling as I did that such action must appear as an admission of guilt, so when the Inspector asked me to tell him about the evening I had spent with Rosemary I was quite prepared to provide him with all the details...as far as I could remember...to the second glass of red wine.

'We have been making enquiries and understand you have seen quite a lot of Mrs Fletcher since your return to Woodymouth when you took over the job of Bowls Club Treasurer.'

'She played quite often in the same bowls team, although she was absent for some weeks after her car accident.'

'Yes, and the housekeeper advises us that during that period you made visits to her house, sometimes quite late at night.'

'I called as a friend concerned about her injuries, and I think it was late at night on one occasion.'

'Did you stop the night?'

'No.'

'We have had discussions with certain members of your Bowls Club and understand that at the beginning of the season you were keen to develop more than just a friendly relationship with Mrs Fletcher, but someone else captured her attentions and frustrated you.'

I knew it would be useless asking who his informants might be, but could well imagine Hubert or Tony delighting in passing on such knowledge. I stared at my attacker and fought back.

'Yes, I was interested in developing our association, but would deny any feelings of frustration. I was settling in happily in a new job in my hometown, meeting up with my sister and her partner, an old schoolgirl chum, and developing friendships with some of the young ladies in the Club. So I had no reason to be upset when Mrs Fletcher formed an attachment to someone else.'

'We can accept some of that, but wonder if any of your so-called friendships actually developed into anything. In fact, we are advised that your popularity rating with the ladies in the Club could only be described, recently, as hitting rock bottom.'

He waved aside Rupert's protests and continued. 'We have formed the opinion that you have suffered considerable frustration since you returned to Woodymouth and you went to that young woman's house, ostensibly to discuss Bowls Club business, but in reality, determined to have sex with her. You say the wine was drugged. Tests may prove you correct, but we believe you were responsible for that. You went prepared...if she was unwilling you would drug her wine. There were two bottles on the trolley and when the housekeeper hit you over the head with one, wine was splashed over your shirt and the floor, but there was still enough left in each bottle for tests to be made. Forensics are of the opinion that only one was drugged, suggesting you have been stupid or forgetful enough to pour yourself a drink from the wrong bottle – when things could then have gone wrong. Your fingerprints were on both bottles.'

'No! The suggestion is outrageous. I have never possessed any such drugs and I can remember finding the wine bottle already opened. I think Rosemary said her housekeeper had insisted on uncorking it to allow the wine to breathe. She would then have had an ideal opportunity to slip in a drug.'

'But why would she want to do that? We have reason to believe she was very fond of her mistress.'

I was clutching at straws. 'Maybe she wasn't... maybe she knows there's a healthy legacy waiting for her in Rosemary's will...and decided to speed things up, with plans to frame me for the murder.'

'It was your tie we found around the deceased's neck, and after the housekeeper was delivered, first to the gates and then to the door by taxi, it was you she found bending over the body.'

'But when we were both drugged she could have come during the night and strangled her mistress with my tie and then returned later to preserve appearances.'

'Very plausible, but we are perfectly satisfied she spent the whole evening with her friend, and you appear to ignore the fact that both you and Mrs Fletcher were partly undressed, suggesting you were intent on having sex.'

'I stared back at the Inspector in disbelief. 'My memory is still very hazy, but I feel certain that was never my intention.'

'In that case perhaps you can explain these, which we have found in the pocket of your trousers.'

I looked in horror at a cellophane bag containing a packet of pills, partly empty, which he had passed across the table.

'What are they?' I asked, half knowing the answer.

'I'm sure you know...they are similar to the "date rape" drug, Rohypnol.'

At which point Rupert insisted on a break and I was escorted back to my cell. He was a friend and did his best to reassure me all would be OK, but I could see red lights flashing and I knew when he went back to the comforts of his wife and home I would remain locked up with the minimum of good cheer.

Rupert came the next morning for a discussion, but it was not until late afternoon that we met the Inspector again. There were questions we needed to ask and he was prepared to listen and provide answers. I felt fairly sure I hadn't set out to have sex with Rosemary and said so, but of course was immediately reminded that when found we were both half naked.

'I still believe someone came when we were drugged. I've suggested the housekeeper, but you seem satisfied she spent the whole evening with her friend.'

'Yes, and we don't believe she would do anything to harm her mistress.'

'But there could have been another person or persons. You know how I have been questioned in connection with the assault cases – framed, I am sure, by Billy Edwards and Harry Wilks. Well, they threatened to "get me" and this murder could be their work, to do just that. There's a landing stage at the back of the house and they have a boat.'

'Again that's plausible but the property has the most sophisticated alarm system in Woodymouth... you will be familiar with the gates at the front which would have closed automatically after you drove in. The housekeeper used her electronic card to open them when she returned in the morning.'

He leaned forward before continuing. 'The whole of the landing stage area is covered by an electro-magnetic beam. I checked yesterday morning that it was switched on to be operational. So if anyone had made an illegal entry either to front or back, alarms would have sounded and we at the Station would have been alerted. We cannot see how anyone else could have entered the property. So the fact remains, the young woman died from asphyxiation and it was your tie we found around her neck.'

I had to protest, but was finding it difficult to stay calm. 'When I roused from the drug, I loosened the tie and tried to resuscitate her.'

'But the housekeeper states she found you bending over her mistress with both your hands on the base of her throat, intent on strangling her.'

'Well, she's got it all wrong, just as you have when you don't believe my conviction that Edwards and Wilks could be trying to frame me for Rosemary's murder.'

'I know how persistent you have been concerning those two gentlemen, with claims they were involved in sex attacks on young girls. I must, however, remind you that for both assaults you were called in for questioning, and again for the sex attack on Mrs Sheen. Photographs were taken and I do recall, when we visited your apartment, you had a small collection of pictures of a young lady in a beach-hut minus her clothes. I must advise you we found Mrs Fletcher's camera beside her body. It is with Forensics at the moment, but I am told it has your fingerprints on it and photos of an extremely intimate nature have been taken. I can only advise you, if you persist in bringing Edwards and Wilks into your defence, it may well work to your disadvantage.'

Once more Rupert insisted on a break and a recess and we returned to my cell for further contemplation.

As one day followed another, Rupert and I deliberated, mulled over the facts, planned, studied and pondered, but at each session of questioning with the Inspector and a side-kick, while we tried to find and probe into what we considered a weakness, it seemed they remained firmly resolved in their case against me.

Time dragged and I was not too pleased to learn that the magistrate had been quite happy to extend the period of my detention. Apart from Rupert I was denied visitors. I had hoped to see Jon and Peggs, but because he was an ex-member of the Force, for some obscure reason they were both denied contact. I longed to see Donna, but I never even heard a mention of her name.

I began to lose track of the days and dates and suggested to the Orderly who came to clean and tidy up my cell that I should write up a calendar on the wall.

He was a very young constable who took me much too seriously and began mentioning disciplinary procedures that would be taken against such an act!

Then suddenly I began to worry about my immediate fate. On remand, to what prison would I be sent? Presumably, apart from the suspicion of murder, I would be classed as a sex offender and I had heard stories about them being received in a very unwelcome manner by fellow inmates. Thoughts flashed through my mind of the treatment Billy Edwards and Harry Wilks had received. I had hopes, perhaps very forlorn, of one day continuing a happy love life with Donna.

Rupert, of course, would apply for bail, but warned me as the crime was murder, and evidence may be given of my possible involvement in sex attacks on young girls, then most certainly it would be refused. He did, however, hold out a glimmer of hope that sometimes the law may be influenced by circumstance. He was of the opinion that prisons were, generally, full to capacity and criminal elements amongst the illegal immigrants had added to the burden.

I was amazed. 'Are you suggesting,' I asked, 'that I could be granted bail, simply because there is no room at the prison?'

'Hopefully, yes. It is not a circumstance that will in any way affect the verdict at your trial, but as far as bail is concerned, until then it just might!'

The next few days were filled with hope and fear until the case appeared before the Magistrate at the Crown Court. It was the same 'Beak' who had been happy to extend my incarceration in my little cell, so I had little optimism, especially when Rupert informed me he played golf with my Area Manager. I didn't bite my nails, but was sorely tempted.

When the application was made we were surprised the Police didn't oppose or object and then when bail was granted I felt as if Rupert, my team Striker, had just scored the winning goal in the first round of the tournament!

But I knew it was only the first round. There were grim problems ahead, with a horrible steep mountain to climb.

It was a joyful feeling to be back home, free from the confines of my cell, but I soon realised I was not a 'free' man. I was still that new person: suspect for the murder of my friend Rosemary Fletcher. I had been warned the locals might be hostile and while I didn't actually expect anyone would throw stones through my conservatory windows, I was aware of some very icy stares when I went to the supermarket to restock my fridge and kitchen cupboards. It made me realise I had only swapped my cell for a more comfortable prison. The newshounds had seen my name on the Board at the Crown Court.

There was a message on my answer-phone advising me the Area Manager wished me to call him at the Office. When I did I was told to stay at home and he would visit me there. When we met there was still a friendly greeting, but I was soon to learn The Royal Eagle had wasted no time in installing a 'temporary' replacement for me.

'Let me guess,' I said, 'the GM's grandson straight from University.'

Deryck Coleman

I could feel my boss's embarrassment as he nodded, making conciliatory remarks about how the firm would look after me, keeping me on full salary. I knew what he meant...I was suspended...pending results of the trial. If I was exonerated I would be recalled to Head Office to await their decision as to my future, with a move, no doubt, to Scotland, Wales or Northern Ireland. If found guilty I would be sacked.

Neither of us wanted to prolong the interview, so I escorted him to his car, to witness further awkwardness. He removed a suitcase from the boot and put it on the ground away from his vehicle. 'I'm sorry Nathan, but with a new manager coming in, we had to clear your desk of all your personal things. It's an old case so you needn't bother to return it.'

I was choked...didn't thank him...just kept silent. Then when we shook hands, I knew it would be for the last time and when he drove off I was certain my career with The Royal Eagle Insurance Group had just ended.

My next visitor was Jon, still limping but looking much fitter. He told me Peggs was helping out at Sea View, but would be along shortly. We had a long chat about my circumstances, although I was aware Rupert had been to the cottage and brought them both up to speed.

'Apart from this horrible tragedy of Rosemary's murder, what news have you that might interest me?' I asked.

'Well, I keep in touch with Bert at the Nick and I've just learned they have found a metal box in the disused well at The Highwayman's Retreat...It contained photographs of the two girls assaulted at the beach-hut and the caravan, obviously taken when they had been undressed.'

'In a weird way that's good news, isn't it, having the photos out of circulation. And as Wilks is a relative of the landlord that seems to tie him into both crimes with his half brother Billy Edwards.'

'That's possible, but anyone could have hidden them there and the lads are more interested in the fact that there were no photographs of the assault on Eva Sheen. The poor young woman said there were a lot taken and there was plenty of room for them in the box. That, of course, is being examined.'

'Do they think with Eva it could have been a copycat crime carried out by someone else?'

I was denied the answer to my question as Peggs arrived from Sea View. The greeting was typical of my sister. 'My god, you look terrible,' and then she hugged me. 'We'll have to feed you up a bit and get you out into some fresh air and sunshine.'

'Well, the company has very kindly cleared my desk so I shall be able to spend all day on the Bowling Green.'

'Ah...' and I recognised distress. 'That pompous ass Sinclair has been into the bank asking if I could get the Club's account books as his wife Muriel is taking over the job of Treasurer. I should think again about going there because I have my suspicions he and that slimy toad Fairclough may have arranged for your membership to be cancelled.

'I should have guessed...I'll let you have the books to take for them.'

Realisation dawned, I would have been unwelcome there anyway.

'And how is Julie?'

'Very poorly, getting ready to go into hospital for her operation. Donna and I have been helping out as much as possible in our spare time, but Donna is planning to take some holiday so she can help full time. Julie has been coaching her for Reception duties and office work. She told me she will be much happier knowing there is someone looking after that side of the business, and Donna apparently loves it. It is a very serious operation. Let's pray it will be successful, but even so it will be months before Julie is able to go back to work.'

'I will keep in touch with the hospital and James will make sure I can visit. Nice to know you two are being so useful. But I haven't heard a word from Donna, how is she?'

'Oh...' and again I recognised confusion. 'Outwardly she is as lovely as ever, but inwardly she is seething with anger and distress.'

'Why angry? Surely she doesn't think I killed Rosemary? I thought she loved me enough to think me incapable of such a thing.'

'That may be, but apart from being worried she is very, very angry with you. If we can forget poor Rosemary's murder for the moment...just think of the circumstances. You went to the house of a very attractive young widow, to spend the evening with her completely alone, and then in the morning you were found with your trousers down...off...or whatever. Donna you will know is an emotional fireball...how do you expect her to feel towards you? She has forbidden her daughter to even mention your name and vows if you ever set foot in Sea View *you* will be the victim of a murder! Your relationship there looks doomed, but there is some consolation: Ellie spoke to me 'in secret' and she thinks the police are daft to believe you could have killed anyone and she said she was missing you.'

That little girl's words had put a patch of blue into an otherwise grey sky.

I was a 'free' man, but soon found out how restricted that freedom could be. I was well known in the town and a murder suspect on bail. Peggs took over all my shopping and Jon visited. I saw more of them than ever before. Rupert came to the apartment bringing our Barrister, and as the weather was good we drove up to the moors and discussed 'my case' while taking in the bracing air. There were many aspects to explore and Clive, the 'Brief', passed on some details from the autopsy report.

It stated Rosemary died at about 3.30 a m, which devastated me because it meant I had been trying to resuscitate a corpse. Her breastbone had been cracked, substantiating my story of trying to revive her, but Clive dashed my hopes by saying the Prosecution would be claiming I had drugged myself by mistake...that I had used the tie to subdue her, realised some time later in a confused state that I had gone too far...then tried to reverse things.

Neither Rupert nor Clive gave me any comfort and when I said I didn't think I had opened my bottle of wine they thought it would be dismissed as unsubstantiated evidence. Things looked black for me, but we enjoyed the fresh moorland air before going back to Woodymouth.

Julie was admitted to hospital and there were harassing moments waiting for her recovery. But after the operation I was with James at the hospital when a doctor came and gave us the good news that it had been successful. She was in the Special Care Unit for three or four days, then transferred to a general ward. At the end of the week James was informed she could be moved into home care provided it was not at Sea View. The doctors were aware she helped to run the hotel and were very concerned she would be tempted to get back to work too soon. They warned such an effort could be fatal as she needed months of rest.

So at Julie's bedside we held what might be termed an emergency meeting and it was decided, mainly at my suggestion, we should exchange accommodation, allowing Julie and James to take over my apartment. A part-time nurse was available, hotel meals would be provided and while James continued to manage Sea View, he could walk over to see his wife whenever he wanted and return to her in the evenings.

It was an idea fraught with problems, but at least suggested a practical remedy. Julie held my hand weakly. 'Thank you Nathan. I'm so sorry to cause all this upheaval but when you move into Sea View I can foresee it could be the beginning of a solution for everything.'

'Yes,' I agreed, although I couldn't follow the reasoning. In a few months I could be banged up in prison and in a few days I would be facing a young woman threatening to kill me. Then I remembered I was a criminal on bail and would have to seek permission to change my address.

The day arrived for Julie's discharge from hospital. Mrs T came to make up the bed and brought dressing gowns and things for her immediate needs, while I loaded my clothes and personal belongings into a hired van and drove the short distance to Sea View. I wasn't bothered by reporters. I had been happy to hear a local Councillor had run off with his young secretary and taken a large portion of the Council Tax with him. Hopefully, with a new interest, the press would leave me in peace.

It had been agreed I would not sign in, but I was involuntarily drawn to the Reception desk to gaze into the adorable brown eyes of the receptionist, noting how they glinted with green lights. I knew exactly what they stood for.

'Welcome to Sea View,' she said in an icy voice. 'That is our normal greeting for our guests, but I'm only speaking the words to you because Mr Gosling has explained what you are doing for Julie. We will try to make you comfortable, but I wish you to know my daughter and I will not speak to you unless it is absolutely necessary, and while you have previous knowledge of the hotel the top floor will be strictly off limits.'

'Thank you for your welcome. As you will be aware, future plans and thus my length of stay are a little uncertain, but while I am here I will at all times take note of your wishes and regard the top floor as a potential war zone.'

I looked for the hint of a smile, but there was no trace and I realised I would need more than words to change her attitude towards me. She was such a pretty girl, but as I looked into those lovely eyes, a shiver passed through me. She was a mother with a young daughter to protect and she could be seeing me not only as a man who had set out to seduce a charming bowling colleague, but also as the one awaiting trial for her murder. With those thoughts I felt steel shutters had slammed down between us.

By arrangement with James I was taking over their room which had once been my parents' retreat at the back of the hotel. It was another of Father's achievements, creating a comfortable bedroom and sitting room by converting an outbuilding. I had always liked it because it was spacious enough to take easy chairs as well as a desk and a dining table. I knew the double bed was going to be a constant disappointment, but at the end of the room I liked the little conservatory, similar to mine at the apartment, with steps leading down to the harbour beach. Although it was on the ground floor next to the office it was very suitable, because I could hide away in comfort from any unwelcome visitors and I was able to arrive or depart unnoticed using the back steps.

I spent the rest of the day 'moving in' and helping James to 'move out', then I returned the van to the hirer. I enjoyed my first dinner with James and Lucy the young waitress, after all the guests had left. At the other end of the dining room sat Donna and Ellie. Neither of them spoke to me, but whenever possible Ellie and I would exchange a wink and a smile. Afterwards I had a brisk walk along the Prom and went to bed with a book. I told myself I must ignore the fact that Donna and her daughter were living under the same roof.

I needed to get out and apart from 'checking in' at the Police Station I made regular calls to see Julie and to stay and talk with her. Then whenever Jon was at home I would drive up to The Fisherman's Cottage and, if he could spare the time, we would sit in the garden and chat. He kept in close touch with his contacts at the Nick and I was always eager to know about their efforts to track down Billy Edwards and Harry Wilks. Remembering the remarks of the landlord of the Highwayman's that his young barman and friend had probably skipped off to the Continent, I was always afraid my two villains might have done the same. But evidence kept popping up to suggest otherwise, for which I was grateful, because I felt when the Police ended their freedom, it might be the beginning of mine.

Jon was working to help me and had been making enquiries about Rosemary's housekeeper. He told me her trips on Wednesday evenings were to see a lady friend at her home, being well established events when they would be joined by two other ladies.

'I've learned they play cards, often for quite high stakes, but I don't know yet whether she's got debts big enough to lure her into crime. When the two ladies leave, the housekeeper goes to bed with her friend... they sleep together...which seems to substantiate the Inspector's belief that she did not return to the house during the night. Sorry if that destroys one of your theories.'

Leaving Jon I returned to the hotel to find James alone at the reception desk. Smiling, he told me Ellie was at the apartment comforting and chatting with her 'Gran'. Then Donna came in having just finished a shift.

She spoke to James, to ask after Julie and check on her daughter, but ignored me completely.

'I'll freshen up and then come down to relieve you. I'm pleased to announce I'm starting two weeks leave, so if you fancy a lie-in in the morning I'll be with Lucy to take care of the breakfasts.' Still ignoring me she skipped towards the lift.

With our eyes we followed her. 'She's marvellous,' James said. 'Such a wonderful help, a quick learner and seems to enjoy it all so much.'

'I know she's marvellous...we used to be lovers... remember? But I just don't exist in her life any more.'

'Maybe when your problems have blown over...'

'Don't you mean *if* they blow over?'

Two days later I received a call from Jon asking me to drive up to Fisherman's Cottage. He said it was important and had arranged for Rupert to join us. There was not much sun, but it was warm enough for us to sit in the garden. The tide was flowing swiftly towards the harbour mouth and, while our host poured some refreshment, we were busy watching a teenage lad struggling to row against it. Then Jon grabbed our attention:

'Harry Wilks is dead. His body was found by a party of nude bathers on the beach at Dead Smuggler's Cove.

'Hell's bells!' I said, all sorts of thoughts flashing through my mind.

'I wanted you both here because I thought this might affect your case, Nathan.'

'How did he die?' I asked, wondering whether he'd had a fall-out with his half brother Billy.

'Well, it appears to be a drowning. They found a broken up dinghy on the beach and rocks, and signs he may have been hiding away and sleeping there.'

'Any evidence of foul play?'

'The lads are a bit suspicious. Wilks was a local man, a good swimmer and sailor who would know all about the dangers of those rocks. But they think he could have been drinking heavily, capsized his boat coming back in the dark, and banged his head on a rock as he was thrown into the sea. I expect this'll make them intensify their search for Edwards.'

Rupert looked puzzled. 'That's shocking news, but I can't see how it can possibly help Nathan's defence.'

'Nothing concrete,' Jon agreed, 'but I've been working on one of his theories. The case against him is based on the belief that he went to Rosemary's house intent on having sex with her. That there were two bottles of wine on the trolley and he drugged one to be used for his companion, leaving the other one for himself. Then, it is suggested, when pouring the second glass he mixed the bottles up, became dazed, and as she was still resisting put his tie around her neck to subdue her. Strangulation may or may not have been intended.'

'That's vaguely it, but what's the theory you've been working on?' Rupert wanted to know.

'Nathan states the drugs in his pocket were planted and claims there was only one bottle opened and that had been drugged. They both drank from it and he believes someone came during the night, murdered Rosemary, and set the scene to incriminate him. He has suggested the housekeeper, or possibly Wilks and Edwards, but the

Inspector seems certain the housekeeper never left her friend during the night, and the house was well secured by a sophisticated alarm system to keep intruders out.'

Thinking or talking about Rosemary's death was painful for me, but I knew I had to face the fact and start worrying about my own life and fate. 'I agree with that. Where are you leading us?'

'Not exactly up the garden path, but to the garden and jetty behind the house. The alarm system for the front is activated by the input of a code in numbers, but I have discovered the beam which covers the rear garden and the jetty is controlled by a simple 'on' and 'off' switch. So following your theory, I believe the housekeeper could have switched off before leaving, allowing your 'friends', Wilks and Edwards, to arrive by boat, using the jetty without raising the alarm. It was a warm evening and a french window had been left ajar providing easy access for them to carry out their evil deeds. When the housekeeper returned she just whacked you over the head and switched the alarm beams back on.'

'Yes, I like it.'

But Rupert had to butt in. 'How could this tie in to Wilks' drowning?'

'Well, if the lads at the Nick are right about it being a suspicious death I think it feasible the two villains could have quarrelled because it turned out to be a murder, and then came to blows.'

Again Rupert butted in, this time to spoil everything. 'These are plausible theories, but it's all conjecture. Have you a scrap of evidence to implicate the housekeeper or the other two?'

'I'm afraid not...but I'm working on it. To me there's more sense in this explanation than the case against Nathan.'

'Maybe, but our Brief won't base Nathan's defence on a theory, however much we like it.'

'Keep working on it, Jon,' I said, 'it sounds good to me. It represents a glimmer of hope through Rupert's words of doom.'

CHAPTER 19

THE DROPPED GLOVE

• • •

The next morning Donna was in the dining room, organising the breakfasts with Lucy, so I kept out of her way and had mine in the kitchen with Cook and Hannah. Then I spent the first half of the day giving The Dove a clean up and overhaul and after lunch cruised up to the Fisherman's Cottage jetty to find Jon busy with his laptop in the garden.

'Hi, Nathan, glad you've come,' was his greeting, ''cos I've just had an interesting item of news from Bert. He tells me there was a burglary last night at Harry Wilks' place. Naturally after his body was found the lads made a routine examination of his flat, but as far as I know, found nothing of any great interest. Last night, however, someone literally tore the place apart, even ripping up the floorboards, obviously looking for something of value.'

'What do they reckon...smuggled narcotics? Surely he wouldn't be hiding duty free booze and fags under the floorboards?'

'Wilks was often a crew member when the Sinclair cruiser went to Amsterdam and Bert thinks it might have been diamonds the burglar was looking for.'

'Jeepers...that's making me wonder...I've heard both the Sinclair gardens are full of tulips and I know they always bring bulbs over with their 'duty frees'...what a perfect disguise!'

'Now, now, Rupert would dismiss that as pure conjecture, without a shred of evidence!'

'Fine, but it seems quite feasible to me.'

Peggs was late getting home because she had called in to check on Julie. So naturally, after the usual greeting, we wanted to know what she thought of her recovery.

'She is still very poorly, but told me she's quite relaxed about Sea View, knowing Donna is there full time, at least for the present.'

'I'm pleased for her. I only wish I could feel the same, but it's grim being so close to Donna and being treated like a stranger.'

'Sorry, but I can't help you there.' That was all the compassion I got and for the rest of my stay I got the impression my sister's sympathies were more for Donna than me.

The next morning I learned James was organising the breakfasts with Lucy, so I waited until the last guests had left the dining room and then went to join them. I assumed Donna had taken Ellie to school and was late returning: 'Donna not back yet?'

'Yes, she's in the office.' It was Lucy who answered. 'She's very upset...we've been talking with her but she says she just needs to be alone to think things over...I took her a coffee and some buttered toast.'

'What's the problem?' I was concerned, and thwarted by the knowledge that any attention from me would be unwelcome.

It was James who replied. 'A WPC colleague called in early this morning with some bad news. The school has received more telephone calls from the sick character who bothered them last term...he says he likes the look of the new girls and is longing to see more of them at the swimming baths. Frightening information for the young mothers.'

Then Lucy looked across the table at me: 'there was something else that upset her. Her friend broke the news that Donna's been posted to Rydemouth.'

'Well, that's dreadful news...what was her reaction?'

'She was shattered,' James said, 'and very angry that her Super should do such a thing when she and Ellie have settled in so happily in Woodymouth, but she believes it's because you two are sharing the same address.'

'Can she protest or appeal against it?'

'Apparently not and, of course, we must remember she would be rejoining family in Rydemouth.'

'Also,' Lucy chipped in, 'after receiving frightening news this morning, she must be thinking she'd be better off taking Ellie away from the local school pervert. So she's been given plenty to think about.'

'Yes.' It was appalling news for me, giving me plenty to think about too.

My future was in turmoil and it seemed I had created a similar situation for poor Donna. There was no chance of her letting me near to talk about it, especially if I was the cause of her having to move and take Ellie back to Rydemouth.

When I left the dining room she was at the Reception Desk, writing. I passed within a few yards to go to my room, but my presence was ignored completely. I felt those steel shutters between us and wondered if I would ever be able to lift them.

My relationship with her daughter was different. Donna had told her they were not speaking to me, but Ellie enjoyed organising 'secret' meetings and conversations. When she was not at school she spent a lot of time with her 'new Gran' and while she left by the front door of the hotel, telling her mother where she was going, I left to walk along the harbour sands to meet up with both 'in secret'. Julie had been made to promise not to tell Donna!

Naturally at such trysts there was an exchange of confidences and I was informed: 'Mummy is still very cross with you and now she's angry because she's being made to move.'

My trial had been fixed for five months away so I was hardly in a position to say how heart-broken I would be if they went away. I merely spoke of the possible consolations for them.

'You would be going back to live with your real Gran and Grandad...that would be nice wouldn't it?'

She pondered over that a little before answering: 'of course we love Nanna and Granpop a lot and enjoy going to see them often, but I don't think Mummy and me want to go back to live there. We like living here and I've made friends at my new school.' Then she added rather sheepishly: 'if we go back to Nanna's, Mummy and me will have to share a little bedroom.'

Julie heard that and managed a laugh.

It was after breakfast, two days later, that I had a call from Jon saying he had more news for me. So I invited him to a picnic lunch in The Dove. Cook prepared sandwiches and fruit for us and I added a bottle of wine.

It was a nice warm day and Jon was waiting for me at his jetty. The tide was well in and I thought we would enjoy just cruising up river while he told me his news.

He delivered it with a punch. 'They have got Billy Edwards in custody...found him hiding away in a secret room at The Highwayman's Retreat.'

'You always thought there might be such a room, didn't you?'

'Yes, that's how the pub originally got its name. Records show that in bygone days a highwayman was found hiding there in a concealed room. He was taken away and hanged, but I don't expect Edwards will suffer quite the same fate!'

I manoeuvred The Dove around a flotilla of two white swans and four brownish cygnets and then asked whether Billy had revealed anything about Harry's drowning.

'Actually they put him under a lot of pressure about the assaults on the two girls and Eva Sheen. Then they suggested he fell out with his half brother and was involved in the drowning. Finally they accused him of taking part, with Wilks, in the murder of Rosemary Fletcher; the Inspector followed up on your statement that someone else came to her house and carried out the dreadful deed.'

'But with what result?'

'Not a lot of help to you, I'm afraid. He's made a full confession for the assault on the two girls. He says both he and Wilks were involved, using the handsome young barmen to entice the girls into the beach hut and the caravan. When the drug began to take effect, the lads left and then he and Wilks undressed their victim. He claims Harry organised the first assault, but he owns up to planning the attack in the caravan on Tracey Lamb.'

'The exposé of a pervert.'

'Yes, which gave the Inspector a chance to close 'the peeping Tom case'…you know, where some guy has been showing an unhealthy interest in young girls. The school reported having received obscene remarks, spoken they thought through a handkerchief, by a rough inarticulate voice. David has always considered the pervert to be a more educated man using a change of voice as a disguise. But he's now convinced he has the genuine article…the real culprit…in custody.'

'When news gets around it'll be a great relief to all parents, but no confession for the murder of Rosemary?'

'No, afraid not. He'll go down for the two assaults because their prints were all over the stack of photos recovered from the well at The Highwayman's, but he denies any involvement in murder.'

'What about the attack on Eva Sheen…similar but nastier…did he put his hand up for that?'

On our trip up river we had passed the jetty and lane leading to the Quarry and I turned The Dove's nose to cross the river before cruising down towards the harbour, waiting for Jon to continue.

'Again, I'm told, he denies any participation, but... and this I find surprising...he says he's not sure about Harry. You'll recall there were two people in the attack, one supposedly called Nathan. Billy thinks that could have been Harry pretending to be you.'

'Very interesting. If he's telling the truth and it was Wilks, who was the other one?'

'I'm going to leave the lads at the Nick to tell us that 'cos Bert says they're very busy looking into Harry Wilks' life-style. He seems to have had a 'private income' which they think smells of blackmail, and naturally if he was squeezing money from someone then his drowning could look to be suspicious.'

For some time we just cruised around the harbour, finding plenty to talk about while we finished off our picnic. I was relieved Edwards had been discovered in his hideaway and not surprised he had been forced into a confession for the assaults on the two girls. I was still convinced he and Harry had been the ones to frame me for poor Rosemary's murder and it seemed my fate rested with the police, with the Inspector following up on my contention there was someone else involved. But how keen would he be to follow it up? He already had me waiting to stand trial for the crime and if he believed I was guilty, would he bother to pursue his investigations any further? We discussed and pondered over the questions but found no answer before it was time to cruise back up river to Jon's jetty where I dropped him off.

I returned to the harbour, moored The Dove, paddled the inflatable back to the beach and dragged and lifted it up the steps to my conservatory. Then I saw a pretty young girl sitting on the top step looking glum and very concerned.

'Hi, Nathan, I wonder if I will ever be allowed to have fun again in The Dove?' she grumbled in a forlorn voice.

'I wish I could tell you Ellie, but why are you waiting for me, looking so unhappy?'

Often I had seen mischief dancing in her eyes, so much like her mother, but sadly all that had disappeared and it was a very serious young lady who answered.

'It's Mummy...she's cross and unhappy and I'm worried about her.'

'Well, I know she's angry with me, but I don't know what I can do about it.'

'Mummy and me don't want to move and she has been to the Station to talk to her 'Guv' about it...he says she's got to go when she gets back from her leave...and I found her crying...and I cried too.'

I left the inflatable outside to dry off and then went with Ellie through the conservatory into my room: 'I can't bear to see either of you unhappy, Ellie. And I will try to talk to your mother, but I know it won't be easy.'

'Yes, please, Nathan, you must help her...I know she's being silly and doesn't really want to be cross with you.'

The appeal in her eyes was something I couldn't ignore and her words gave me a ray of hope. I could sense it wasn't only her mother she was worried about.

After earlier 'secret' meetings I had always checked first that 'the coast was clear' before letting Ellie sneak out into the hall. She enjoyed the furtiveness, but on that occasion I was determined to meet and talk with her mother. Unfortunately I had no conceived plan and as we stepped out of my room, Donna was there to confront us both with anger and cross words aimed at her daughter.

Immediately I went to her defence: 'I invited Ellie into my room, so you can direct your grievances towards me,' which remark only flared her temper to divert it towards me. I felt aggrieved, and fed up with being treated like a Trappist monk whenever we met, so the peace and serenity of the hotel hall was noisily shattered by our outraged voices. While the disturbance allowed Ellie to slip quietly away, it brought a greatly disturbed James from the dining room.

He spoke in a raised and distressed tone neither of us had heard before, instantly taking the heat out of our argument and shaming us into silence.

'I don't employ either of you and therefore cannot tell you to grow up and behave in a manner befitting the hotel atmosphere. I know we are all under stress at the moment, so I must just appeal to you. If you can't be lovers any more, then for Pete's sake end this vow of muteness. Talk to each other and try to be friends...as you have been to me...for the sake of my sanity!'

We were aghast at the irate words delivered by one normally so quiet and calm and as James went back to the dining room, I think we felt like two naughty children who had just been scolded by a parent.

'It was Donna who spoke first: 'I'll go to him. I haven't forgiven you, but meanwhile we must try to act like friends.'

'What haven't you forgiven? Surely you don't think I murdered Rosemary?'

'No...I know you couldn't do that, but everyone says you went there to have sex with her and I'll not forgive you for that.'

'Well, what everyone says is wrong.'

'I wish I could believe that,' and with a cold stare she turned and followed James into the dining room, I felt sure to try to calm troubled waters.

It had been revealed to us, the strain he was under...a sick wife...two helpers not speaking to one another...and one a murder suspect, a constant threat to the reputation of the hotel.

I had been taking over Office duties more and more (and enjoying them) but maintaining a low profile. Cook, Hannah, Mrs T and Lucy were all loyal members of his team but, he would be painfully aware, a careless word from them or a scene from us would jeopardise the hotel's good name.

Donna and I must resolve to work together more harmoniously...if that could be possible!

With James' blessing I was helping him to sort out certain bank and VAT charges for the Sea View account and decided to make one of my infrequent trips into town when Jon phoned: 'I just want to bring you up to date: Bert tells me they have been pressurising Edwards over the drowning of his half brother and he's been singing a bit. Billy confirms Harry has had 'a small, steady income' dating back over the years. Billy never found out where it came from and he says Harry once told him he had written a letter 'for protection' but apparently never trusted Billy enough to tell him where it was lodged. The smell of blackmail grows stronger, throwing further suspicions on the drowning, although it seems to have taken some of the heat off Billy. C.I.D. are now making further searches at the flat in the belief that the burglar may have been looking for the letter.'

I thanked Jon for the news update on the two men who had sworn to wreak vengeance upon me, and continued my mission into town. All queries on the hotel account were sorted and then I chose a small café for a snack lunch. I sought to avoid people although I was aware the cafeteria was sometimes used by office staff from the Royal Eagle. I had only just selected a table, tucked away in a corner, when I spotted Paula. I called out to her and she came to join me.

It was a friendly greeting and she was soon eager to give me all the office gossip and the low-down on her new young boss Mr Hyde-Smythe.

'I don't think he will be a success with the local farmers and trades-people. He is much too cocky for the country and rural folk.'

'Do you mean I fitted in more as a country bumpkin?'

Paula laughed: 'certainly no bumpkin, but as a local man you always knew how to handle them and you had their respect...I don't think this chap will ever earn it.'

In sober mood I told her my employment with the Royal Eagle had virtually ended, but she wasn't prepared to accept that and tried to change my disposition.

'Whatever it is you're accused of, you'll surely be cleared and then we'll be expecting you back with us.'

'Thank you for your loyalty, but there's a trial coming up and whatever the result, I face either a move or the sack and I don't want to leave Woodymouth.'

'Oh...well I've heard Jack Martyn of Martyn's Insurance Brokers will be retiring and selling his business in a few months time.'

I was reflecting on that interesting snippet of news as we finished our lunch and Paula was preparing to return to the office. She thanked me for my insistence on paying her bill and then added a parting shot.

'If you ever do get around to buying Martyn's business, don't forget me...I'll be very happy to run the little office for you.'

'Thank you again for your faith in me. I think I will drop in at the Broker's Office this afternoon.' My spirits had been lifted by some rays of hope for the future and about an hour later my good friend Jack Martyn added to them.

I had walked into town so decided to return along the Promenade. As I passed the Bowling Green I noticed a number of the rinks were occupied, but to preserve my good humour I kept walking.

In the hotel hall I saw James at the Reception Desk busy signing in a middle-aged couple for a two night stay, wanting to break their journey to Lands End. I knew he would be happy to accept their short booking as we were now out of the peak season. Then as I entered the Office I was surprised and delighted to have Donna talking to me.

'How did you get on at the bank?' she asked.

'Oh, it's all sorted,' and I told her about my lunch and conversation with Paula.

'I've had a visitor, too...Phoebe came to see me with some startling news about your friends the Sinclairs.'

'Oh, let me hear it.' I knew the messenger to be her W.P.C. colleague.

'Well. It all began with someone called Alice delivering a letter to the Nick. She said it had been written by the man found drowned and he had given it to her for safe keeping with instructions to hand it over to the police if he should ever come to any harm.'

'That'd be the Alice who used to be lead in my bowls team, a friend of Harry Wilks.'

'Well, in the letter Wilks declares he saw Muriel Sinclair push the husband of your friend Rosemary Fletcher over the edge of the Quarry to cause his death.'

I decided to ignore her obvious resentment of my friendship with the ill-fated Rosemary. 'Wilks, of course, was foreman at the Quarry at the time poor old Will died. It would now appear he's been blackmailing Muriel ever since.'

'Of course, that letter alone will never stand up in a court of law, but it has opened the proverbial can and the Inspector is eager to have words with the Sinclairs. Phoebe says they called at their house and found it locked up, so they went to the Quarry to learn they were both on holiday in Austria walking the Tyrol.'

'Presumably your chums will be waiting at the airport when they return?'

'Yes...although I don't see them all as my chums any more...but your bowling friend Alice has been talking and alerted Customs and Excise to make a mid-Channel raid on brother Sinclair's cabin cruiser. Apart from an excess of cigarettes, in their search for drugs they found some very valuable diamonds hidden away in large bulbs.'

'Blimey! It's Ray Sinclair's boat but I believe Hubert, and probably Muriel, have a financial interest.'

'Well, the boat's been impounded and Sinclair and a crew member taken into custody.'

With Donna talking to me, I hoped it was the reason she looked happier and I questioned her. For seconds we just stared at each other and then she answered.

'You needn't look at me like that, I can read your thoughts. This is still just a truce to be friends, but you are right, I do feel happier. For weeks everything has been going down and down, but at last I think we've hit the bottom. I know you've got a trial to face, but I've stopped worrying for you because I think things are going to work out OK.'

'But you are still angry with me?'

'Aaah...well, yes...but Phoebe's straightened me out on a few of the facts. Because I was so angry with you for going to see your friend I misunderstood what had actually happened.' She was blushing as she continued.'Let's just make the most of being friends again, eh?'

'OK. Did you manage to soothe James down?'

'Yes and no! At first he was cheerful, and brightened me up by telling me if I was being forced to leave Woodymouth and didn't want to go, there would always be a job for me at Sea View. Then he went a bit gloomy and told me he had been wondering if he should sell up and take Julie on a long cruise!'

'Really? It would be the lease he would sell, as they don't actually own the property.' It certainly got my grey cells working.

As each day brought the trial nearer, the thoughts that went with being tried for murder could never be described as uplifting. With a solicitor calling to discuss various aspects of my defence and a Brief sometimes coaching me to prepare myself for the possible anguish of defeat, I found it more and more of an effort to keep cheerful. With the passing of the days the clouds hanging over me grew darker and darker. Fortunately I was able to console myself by getting involved in the running of Sea View and found enjoyment in the re-established friendship with Donna. We worked together and whenever I felt down-in-the-dumps, she was a great comfort to bring me back up.

There was a morning I shall remember for two reasons. Firstly, with fewer guests to cater for, Cook had ventured to bake banana bread which James, Donna and I were enjoying at the breakfast table as buttered toast. Then Jon arrived to join us and I was pleased but curious.

'This is a pleasant surprise. I trust you're going to tell us why we're being honoured and why you're looking so pleased with yourself.'

'That coffee smells marvellous. If you pour me a cup and give me a slice of that toast I'll tell you.'

Naturally we obliged and Jon continued, to provide the second reason.

'I've been working...perhaps a little unofficially... with the lads at the Nick. I learned that in a routine search of the gardens of the Fletcher house, after the murder, a glove was found near the gates behind one of the rhododendron bushes. Thought to be a significant find it was immediately referred to the Housekeeper who unfortunately identified it as belonging to Rosemary, dropped presumably after a gardening session. So it was discarded as evidence, but it prompted me, with David's permission, to make a further search. I've been working on a theory, yours actually Nathan, that two people could have committed the murder, arriving by boat and using the jetty.'

'But it needs someone to switch the alarm beam, which covers the jetty, off and on before and after the crime, and your friend the Inspector refuses to believe the housekeeper was in any way involved.'

'Exactly...so I put Hubert and Muriel Sinclair in the frame. They were in the house on the day of the murder, just before you arrived, and could have drugged the wine and switched off the beam before leaving. Then during the night they returned by boat, committed the crime and set you up for murder. Hubert could leave by boat while Muriel would switch the alarm for the jetty back on. Then she would hide behind the evergreen bush until the housekeeper opened the gates and drove through in the taxi. The driver would naturally be looking ahead and so would she, surprised to see your car still parked outside the front door. Then Muriel would slip through the gates before they closed, and hurry away down the lane, unnoticed and certainly unaware she had left any clues behind.'

I had to butt in. 'I like it, but isn't it too much theory, without any solid evidence?'

'Not all theory...I examined the area where the glove was found and noticed some tiny fibres on the rhododendron bush. David called back the Forensics and with their findings, he now has a photograph of a garment of identical colour and material which was found hanging in Murial Sinclair's wardrobe.'

It was Donna who spoke. 'No need to ask who took that photo...sounds like some very unofficial police work!'

Jon laughed. 'Let's just hope the Sinclairs have a safe journey back from Austria!'

We only had a few days for their holiday to end but the waiting was painful...I checked with Jon...Did the Inspector get in touch with the police in Austria? He said no, but police officers had been sent to their house and to the Quarry. What if word reached the Sinclairs there was a serious problem at home? Would they return or just disappear?

After what seemed like an eternity they arrived back in the UK and we learned they had been arrested at the Airport...but the waiting began all over again. I drifted around like a castaway wondering whether charges could be brought against them.

Then came some devastating news from Jon. Murial was a suspect, but on the evening before Rosemary's murder Hubert had motored to Padquay to visit his sick sister and had stopped for two days and nights.

Jon's scenario of framing them for the crime had, he admitted, crumbled.

But then came further news that following police investigations, suspicion was directed towards Tony Fairclough as Muriel's accomplice. Jon told me that following his enquiries, they had interviewed the young woman called Jessica. She had convinced them the real predator of the young girls employed at the Quarry had, in fact, been Tony Fairclough. I waited to hear of his arrest, but word had reached him first and I learned he had disappeared. Rumour spread he had been seen in Amsterdam. So I still went to sleep with nightmares of my murder trial.

When Rupert came I was in the dining room with Donna and James, just finishing lunch. Apart from 'hello' he said nothing as he handed me a letter which I realised was from the Crown Prosecution Service. I was struck dumb, fearing the worst, but he brought me away from my fears with the most wonderful words.

'All charges against you have been dropped...you're a free man!'

For seconds we were all silent and then, with the others, I leapt up from the table with cries for celebration. We created such a racket that our shouts brought Cook and Hannah from the kitchen and Mrs T from upstairs to join us. James produced a bottle of champagne, or was it two? There were handshakes all around with a quick kiss from Donna and then we all drank a toast to my freedom, with a text message being sent to Julie. Then when Rupert and I were alone he told me about Hubert and Muriel. After being taken into custody they had been questioned over the smuggling of diamonds from Holland, about the murder of Will Fletcher, the assault on Eva Sheen, and the murder of Rosemary Fletcher. Rupert said questioning continued particularly with regard to Hubert's knowledge of the crimes. But when Fairclough was found and arrested, he and Muriel would be formally charged on the last two counts. I felt as though I was floating on air, realising, however, that James and Donna were still troubled.

When Ellie returned from school to learn the news she took it very quietly. She gave me a big hug and just said: 'I knew the police were daft to think you could kill somebody.'

The next day was Saturday and at breakfast James confided in me that Donna was still unhappy and had asked to have the morning off. Then a few minutes later Ellie came to see me in my room and I asked her about her mum. She was wearing her serious mood.

'She's had very angry words with her 'Guv' and I think she's been 'suspendered'.'

I managed to hide a smile, allowing her to continue.

'Mummy told me she's still a bit cross with you and I think it's real daft because I know she loves you...and now she's unhappy about work. I think she's gone to see her friend at the church. You've got to go and talk to her, Nathan. I lost my real dad before I was big enough to remember him proper...I've been hoping you could be my 'new daddy'.'

After those words, I promised to do something. I checked with James to put him in the picture and then drove out to the little village of Merton. Inside the church there was silent serenity with a ray of sunlight piercing through a stained glass window to create a splodge of colour on the white cloth of the altar. A little way behind sat the lone figure of a young woman, bent I imagined in prayer. I knew it was Donna because my heart always gave a funny little jump at sight of her.

I said a prayer of thanks and then walked quietly down the aisle to push into the pew beside her, making her sit up and turn tear-filled eyes towards me. 'Why are you here?'

For seconds I looked into that lovely young face, watching a tear run down her cheek, and then I spoke softly.

'Because I am now free to ask you to marry me!'

With blessed relief I saw mischief break through the tears.

'Why should I want to do that?'

I thought if it was going to be a teasing game, two could play. 'Because I'm sure it would please Ellie.'

'Huh...I need a better reason than that.'

'I am thinking if James wants to leave Sea View, I will take over the management, but I need you to help me.' I saw the news made her wipe away the tears, but noticed the mischief still there.

'Are there any other reasons?'

'There could be.'

'Then, until you tell me I'll just have to think about it.'

We left the church quietly and as we had arrived separately, we went home the same way. To say I was happy would be an understatement. Once more I was a new man, but so different from the other one, because I had been given back my future. For so long I had yearned to take Donna in my arms and tell her I loved her. Thank God, I was free to do so, and what made the feeling more delightful was believing Donna wanted the same.

It was a very happy weekend. We managed to persuade James to go back to Julie and take time off, while Donna and I settled down to the normal duties commensurate with the running of Sea View. We were kept busy with guests leaving and two couples checking in for short stays.

On the Sunday evening we had invited Peggs and Jon to join us for a late dinner to celebrate my freedom. Ellie was given a special dispensation to stay up late, so she made sure her girls were put to bed early. Cook provided a festive menu and as I had made a raid on the wine cellar, our spirits soon ran high for a very enjoyable evening. Strangely, perhaps, no mention was made of my suggestion of marriage, but Donna and Ellie were full of mischief the whole day. Then when the visitors had arrived and the girls retired to the 'powder room' for the usual gossip, they returned giggling with their own playful thoughts. I hoped it was all part of a big tease with Donna having fun, keeping me guessing, on tenterhooks.

At bedtime she yielded warmly in my embrace for a goodnight kiss, but she didn't linger and there was still no mention of my proposal. But when she left me to go to the lift, I saw once more, mischief dancing in those lovely brown eyes and I knew I would enjoy happy dreams.

On the Monday morning it was the usual rush for Ellie to get ready for school and to grab some breakfast...

more of a grab than usual because the coach was early. Two of her class mates were already sitting in the back. After the usual kisses Ellie jumped in, waved and we saw them driven away.

We were surprised and curious about ten minutes later, when another coach arrived, but after a few words with the driver, panic set in. There were frantic calls to the Nick…then Phoebe arrived…this time in uniform, with the Inspector and immediately they began asking questions.

Slowly our fears grew until Donna was almost hysterical. She was a police officer, trained to deal with horrors and the unexpected, but not when it involved her own daughter. Her colleague Phoebe knew that and was there to pacify and reassure her. She explained if a bogus driver had abducted three young girls, then a coach was not something that could be easily hidden and they were convinced it would soon be found.

After a long anxious wait for us and for two other young mothers and their families, we learned it had been found on the moors…but unfortunately, empty. When the Inspector left us, Phoebe remained, keeping in constant touch with the Nick to advise us of developments and hopefully to provide comfort to the distraught Donna. It was a terribly frightening day with fragments of information reaching us in between long painful periods of inactivity. It was actually much later when we were able to put together all the pieces and appreciate the whole story…the full horror of the girls' experiences.

It was a local constable who found the coach and after viewing some evidence reported his views that any occupants had been taken away in another vehicle. In fact, they had. The driver had produced a large knife and terrified the girls with the words: 'if you don't do what you're told I'll cut you where it will hurt.' After that they were more controllable and he was able to search each one to make sure they weren't hiding any mobiles. The girls didn't like that, but we learned he seemed to enjoy it and soon had them locked away in the back of a van.

It was, of course, much later when we were told the stories of Joseph and Lizzie the twins who travelled from their farm each morning to school. At least Lizzie did, but that morning her brother decided to play truant and his favourite haunt was Robbers Wood. As usual their driver stopped at the garage to talk for a while with the girl who took the money in the shop and Joseph slipped off the coach. It was quite a long walk through the forest, but he had plenty of time and a packed lunch to sustain him. Clearly the twins were very different in character, Lizzie enjoying school, but Joseph wanting to escape to his fantasy world.

We understood once he was deep into the forest he would be akin to all the wild creatures and would become a robber or highwayman in hiding, or sometimes Robin Hood. He climbed trees like a squirrel and that morning went to his favourite one where he could relax in the fork of its branches and look down on the little pond of fresh, clear water. From his hideaway he could study the wildlife, although sometimes people would come and in his story he mentioned that one afternoon he saw a man and a woman doing very strange things –

reminding him of the day Old Farmer Langton brought his bull over to be with Dad's heifers.

Despite the differences between the twins there was always a strong bond and whenever they were apart, they kept in touch. Up in his favourite tree, Joseph was free to send his sister messages and while she was not always able to read them, he liked to 'talk' to her, telling her of everything that was going on around him. Usually she kept quiet about it. She wouldn't tell anyone because she knew it might get him into trouble.

On that morning, however, she said she was worried when he became excited, saying there was a robber coming through the woods pushing three young ladies in front of him. Joseph thought they would soon be robbed of all their pearls and rings. Then as they got nearer he told her they were only young girls and he didn't think they would have any jewels.

When they passed under his tree we were told he heard them arguing. The girls said they hadn't any costumes and the robber said they could 'skinny-dip'. Then one of the girls said she wouldn't go in the pond because it had frogs, tadpoles and creepy things in it, but the robber gave her a push and told her to shut up.

The pond was just a few feet from Joseph's tree and he told Lizzie he saw them stop at the water's edge and start to argue again. He told her the man was not an ordinary robber, because he had seen him at the farm talking to their Dad. He said the girls sat down on the grass and took off their shoes and socks but started a bitter argument about taking their clothes off. The man said he would help them.

We learned from Lizzie that in the classroom she was frightened. She had her mobile on silent but kept feeling the vibrations as her brother went on with his messages. She didn't know what to do and she was worried about her best friend Ellie who hadn't come to school. Her teacher had said there were three girls missing and she wondered if they could be the girls Joseph kept 'talking' about. She was bothered because she knew if she told her teacher about the messages she would get him into a lot of trouble with their Dad.

At Sea View Donna was becoming more distraught by the minute, asking Phoebe time and time again what progress was being made, only to learn there was little which made her dread the worst.

Up in the forest tree Joseph was eating his lunch and telling Lizzie how the girls had been made to bathe in the pond. Then when they came out there was more squabbling because they said their panties were wet and the water had been cold. So the man was telling them to take off their wet clothes while he gave them each a big towel from his holdall and began pouring them a hot drink.

When the girls had been rebellious, shouting and waving their arms at the man, Joseph hoped they would get really angry and push him in the pond, but he was disappointed. After having the drink he said they seemed to become quieter and one of them was actually allowing the man to dry her with the towel, while another was sitting down in a grassy clearing looking as if she wanted to have a sleep.

Joseph told his sister he noticed the third girl had been watching the man and suddenly she decided to run for freedom and the man jumped up to give chase. It was an uneven race because without shoes or clothes the girl soon fell victim to thorns and brambles. Joseph said he was sorry to see her being dragged back without her towel as that had been left snared on a bramble. She was made to sit down with the other two girls while the man began fussing over them, allowing Joseph to relax again in the fork of his tree.

Some miles away there were three mums and their families far from relaxed. Just as the young girls had cried and cried out, so they were doing the same. While Phoebe was trying to comfort Donna, I was restless with frustration, unable to sit still, thinking I should be out somewhere, searching. But where? I must have walked miles up and down the hall, in and out of the dining room and the lounge. I had been told to stay in the hotel as I would be informed of developments. As time dragged, remembering how Ellie had said she was hoping I would be her 'new Dad' brought tears to my eyes.

Jon and my sister came to Sea View. He got the news from his usual source and immediately contacted Peggs who wangled time off from the bank. She was a great comfort to Donna to raise her spirits, while Jon inadvertently did nothing to lift mine.

'There's some bad news,' he said, 'Peggs knows but she won't tell Donna. The lads at the Nick are pretty certain the guy who stole the coach this morning is the pervert who's been phoning the school over the past two or three terms and David is furious. He was quite convinced he had him locked up, but now he believes it's Tony Fairclough on the loose.'

Back in the forest Joseph said he thought it was dreary just watching the man paying so much attention to the girls. Only one of them kept struggling with him while the other two sat clutching their towels, whimpering. Then suddenly things changed, making Joseph sit bolt upright and drop a biscuit. He said he was cross about that because it was his last one, but he admitted, within seconds he was more thrilled than he'd ever been with any of his Play Stations. In a wide circle there were men moving quietly and stealthily through the forest, closing in as they got nearer to the pond. As before he said he kept perfectly still and silent, almost forgetting to send further messages to his sister.

At first he thought he had called 'The Merry Men' but then saw they weren't dressed in the proper green and there were no bows and arrows. They were in ordinary suits, plain clothes, while others were in police uniforms and some, to add to his excitement, were carrying guns.

From his viewpoint Joseph said he watched the circle of figures slowly moving in closer and, while the man still kept looking at the girls, they weren't arguing with him any more and didn't seem bothered about all the attention he was giving them.

The girls didn't need to be frightened by the knife, so he had dropped it on the grass, just a few feet behind where he knelt down. Joseph remembered holding his breath, watching, as one of the men crawled slowly towards it. He had almost reached it when there was a slight snapping sound which told them all he had put his weight on a small dead branch. The lad saw each of the moving figures stand still, no doubt breathless, but he thought the figure kneeling over the girls was oblivious to the sound, being so preoccupied. After a wait the crawler continued to move forward.

Joseph said he was still holding his breath when the hand closed around the handle of the knife and all the police officers broke cover. Orders were shouted to the man to get up slowly and walk towards them with his hands up. The order was repeated and to Joseph's amazement the man shouted back defiance: 'back off, go away or I'll strangle this girl.' There was a long pause, but when his hands stretched out towards her throat a single shot rang out and much later in the day Joseph told the Inspector he thought he heard the man say: 'I was only joking' before he slumped to the ground.

We learned how an officer holding a gun came to look at the crumpled body and when he shook his head they all knew the man was dead. Then there was a surge of people all moving towards the pond. Joseph said he wanted to stay, but he couldn't wait. His legs were stiff and he knew he would have to hurry to get to the garage in time to catch the coach. He didn't want his Dad to find out he'd been playing truant again.

I think I shall always remember that day because we suffered through so many of the emotions...alarm when we learned what could have happened to the girls... distress when we knew it had...then afterwards we lived with apprehension for such a long time. When Phoebe told us they had been found alive and well in Robbers Wood there were feelings of relief and elation, but those soon turned to anxiety on learning the girls were in hospital.

Immediately, of course, Donna wanted to go and see Ellie and I was pleased when she asked me to take her. Peggs said they would stay and help James with the serving up or the clearing up of the evening meal.

We drove to the hospital in complete silence as I knew Donna was trying to come to terms with the fear from uncertainty. When we found the right ward there were long, agonising moments of waiting until we were allowed to see the girls...and then there was relief.

All three girls were in adjoining beds and I had to remark: 'three pretty girls all in a row!' The mums and dads of the other two were arriving and while their girls seemed half asleep, Ellie was drowsy but sitting up and taking notice. There were hugs and kisses and then the inevitable question: 'when can I go home?' Donna gave the inevitable answer: 'you'll have to wait, darling, until we've had a word with the doctor.'

The matronly consultant had been a comfort to the girls and she was to us. In answer to our questions she spoke directly to Ellie: 'the other two young ladies are going to stay with us overnight, but if you want to go home I can see no reason why you shouldn't.'

Ellie beamed back her thanks.

Then, turning to us, the doctor continued. 'There has been no physical harm or damage, apart from slight lacerations or scratches on her arms, legs and on her bottom. We have dealt with those...she tells me she fell into some thorns and a bramble.'

So it was agreed, and when a nurse came to prepare Ellie for the journey home, we had a quiet word with the doctor. Donna was anxious to know about the

Deryck Coleman

possibility of any lasting emotional damage and we received a guarded answer.

'As a doctor I cannot say, but as a woman I wouldn't think so. Only parts of this bitter experience will remain in her memory and Ellie is a very strong-willed young lady.'

As she had paused I couldn't resist getting in the remark: 'I wonder where she gets that from?'

With a grin the doctor continued. 'With her character I can imagine her learning to put the memories away and get on with her life.'

'But what do I need to do?' Donna was asking.

'Just give her love,' and then she added with a smile, 'spoil her a bit!'

With normal hospital procedure Ellie was being wheeled out to the car park and just at that moment she arrived within hearing distance. With a grin, she was quick to speak. 'Thank you, doctor, I'll remember that!'

It was a quiet home coming for Ellie. Normally she had plenty to say, but we didn't want to appear to be just making conversation. The advice had been: 'if she wants to talk about it, do so, but if she wants to forget, let her.' We had a meal and then after chatting to James, Jon and Peggs she said she was sleepy.

I waited for Donna to put her to bed and then went up to the top floor...hitherto a restricted area...but no longer a war zone. We went into Ellie's room and looked down at her tucked up in bed with her girls at the foot. It was a sight that brought joy to our hearts. There were more hugs and kisses, and when I said goodnight I asked if there was anything she needed. Obviously we were worried about her experiences of the day, yet when she answered, 'no thank you, Nathan,' I thought for a moment I could see the old glints of mischief back in her eyes...but then she closed them.

I left Donna sitting on Ellie's bed, suggesting she stayed with her, but I told her, if there was anything she needed, to phone the Desk and I would come up. Just as she was comforting Ellie with a bedtime story, I knew she too was in need of support. I thought when Ellie was asleep she would call me.

Downstairs I found James grappling with an office problem. I persuaded him to go home to Julie, promising I would sort it. It proved more of a challenge than anticipated and it was well into the early hours when I decided to lock up and go to bed. It had been more of a problem because of my lack of concentration while waiting, listening for the phone. I'd felt so sure Donna would ring. I knew for days she had to decide between the Police Force in Rydemouth and me at Sea View. It looked as if the uniform of WPC had won, so I went to bed.

I was just dropping off to sleep when I heard a tapping on my door. I glanced at the clock then let Donna in, afraid there was trouble with Ellie. 'How is she?'

'She's quite alright. I know it's very late, but I fell asleep on her bed.'

I had put the light on and for moments we stood staring at each other. Me, dishevelled, trying to gather my wits, Donna looking a little wan maybe after such a harrowing day, but still gorgeous in a bathrobe. She must have woken up and taken a shower. I knew she wanted to say something and my heart sank as I imagined her words: 'we'll always be friends but I'm choosing to stay in the Force.'

I spoke first: 'you're going to tell me something.'

'Yes. Do you remember the doctor's final advice about Ellie?'

'What, about loving and spoiling her?'

'Well, before she went to sleep the crafty little monkey reminded me of those words and made me make a promise.'

Suddenly my thoughts shot out of a pit of dread into sunshine, brightening when I realised Donna would be wearing nothing but talc beneath that robe. The adrenalin (or something) began to flow.

'What was the promise?'

'It was very specific...I should go down to you tonight and, if that really was a proposal of marriage, I should say...yes.'

'That's tantamount to blackmail...hardly the basis for a happy marriage...have you any feelings about it?'

'Yes!...I certainly have!'

In the morning I noticed the robe on the floor.

Printed in the United Kingdom
by Lightning Source UK Ltd.
119625UK00001BA/4-12